Backfire . . .

By two o'clock the street was as silent as a tomb. Nearly all the lights were out and those that weren't were too far down the street to have prying eyes. He opened the door of the car and closed it gently behind him. Then he pulled the cotton gloves from his pocket and put them on. Satisfied that he was alone, he crossed the street with quick, confident strides. When he was alongside the Chevy, he looked around cautiously.

There was nobody in sight. He smiled and set to work— surely, deftly, turning the car into a murder machine . . .

Backfire

Never Kill a Cop!
& Other True Crime Stories

by

Charles L. Burgess

Introduction by Jeff Vorzimmer

Stark House Press • Eureka California

BACKFIRE / NEVER KILL A COP! & OTHER TRUE CRIME STORIES

Published by Black Gat Books
A division of Stark House Press
1315 H Street
Eureka, CA 95501, USA
griffinskye3@sbcglobal.net
www.starkhousepress.com

BACKFIRE
Originally published in paperback by Phantom Books, North Sydney, 1959.

"I'd Die for You" (*Manhunt*, Oct 1958)

"Never Kill a Cop!" (*Complete Detective Cases*, Jan 1947)
"Exit—The Perfect Crime" *Confidential Detective*, March 1945
"Wedded to Death on Fatal Friday" (*News Flash Detective Cases*, April 1946)
"Give Me Liberty or I Give You Death!" (*Revealing Detective*, June 1949)
"Your Job for Two Hours—or Die!" (*Official Detective Stories*, May 1951)
"From the Bottles on Buzzard's Island" (*Official Detective Stories*, Sept 1951)
"A Killer with Women" (*Underworld Detective*, Dec 1951)
"Four Graves for Patricia Ann" (*Official Detective Stories*, Sept 1955)
"It's the Laughing Stranger from Dalton, Georgia" (*Official Detective Stories*, Feb 1956)
"Fat Man Blues" (*True Crime*, May 1956)
"Sheriff King's Last Day in Office" (*Official Detective Stories,* April 1960)
"Secret of the Granite Quarry" (*Official Detective Stories*, August 1961)
"Hell-Raiser, Girl-Hunter and Dazzling Escape Artist" (*Men*, August 1962)

ISBN: 979-8-88601-131-9

Text design by Mark Shepard, shepgraphics.com
Cover design by Jeff Vorzimmer, ¡caliente!design, Austin, Texas
Proofreading by Bill Kelly
Cover art by Victor Prezio

First Stark House Press/Black Gat Edition: March 2025

BACKFIRE: A LOST NOVEL BY A LOST AUTHOR

Charles Leo Burgess was born in Detroit on April 2, 1907, the youngest of three children. During the Depression he moved with his family to New York City, residing at times in both the Bronx and on Staten Island. It was in New York City that Burgess met and married Elizabeth Bushardt, who had moved, herself, to New York City from South Carolina. In June of 1943 they were married in Greenwich Village.

Burgess did quite a bit of traveling in his youth, prior to moving to Florida, where he settled down to a quiet life in a small bungalow in Lakeland where he died in April of 1967, having just turned sixty.

Although Burgess only had an eighth grade education, he began selling stories to true crime magazines as early as the mid-1940s. By 1950 he and his wife had moved to Lakeland, Florida, where they would spend the rest of their lives. He was by then making a living as a professional writer, on staff at *Official Detective Stories* as a "Special Investigator."

Burgess' beat for the *Official Detective Stories* was the South, with most of his stories coming from Georgia and his adopted state of Florida, where he covered high profile cases past and present. Most notably he wrote about the notorious Florida gang leader of the roaring '20s, Big John Ashley, in an article titled, "Hell-Raiser, Girl Hunter, Dazzling Escape Artist" (include in this book), which appeared in the August 1962 issue of *Men: True Adventure Magazine*.

Burgess had a knack for recreating the real-life dialogue among the law-enforcement officials featured in his stories and had an excellent knowledge of police procedures. Through extensive interviews he was able to recreate the thought process of the detectives involved in these cases, thereby adding another dimension to what would otherwise be a retelling of otherwise routine investigations and a restating of the facts of the cases.

His career as a writer parallels that of another writer whose name most fans of hard-boiled fiction and true crime stories would recognize, D. L. (D'arcy Lyndon) Champion (1902–1968). As was the case with Champion, Burgess was better known as a writer of true crime stories than as a novelist. Like the more prolific Champion, who had a long career in the pulps, but only one novel to his credit, Burgess' fiction output amounted to only two novels, *Backfire* and *The Other Woman* (previously published by Stark House as Black Gat #60) and one *Manhunt* story (included in this book).

It's interesting to note that *Backfire* doesn't seem to have been published in the U.S. at all, at least not under that title and as by

Charles Burgess, and hitherto in English only in a now, nearly-impossible-to-find, Australian edition. There was a German edition titled *Bumerang aus Gold (Golden Boomerang)* published in 1967 and a Portuguese edition as *O Anjo Branco (The White Angel)* in 1973. *Backfire* wasn't even picked up for the French *Série Noire* imprint, which rarely misses a good noir title from any country, no matter how obscure.

Editions of *Backfire* in English are so rare that, as of this writing, not a single copy is available for sale anywhere on the internet, in any form. The Australian edition, from which the text in this book was taken, only appeared in an omnibus edition as *Giant Phantom Book*, No. 11 and didn't even list the titles contained therein on the cover (see the illustration below).

Giant Phantom Book, No. 11

The two other titles included in *Giant Phantom Book*, No. 11 are *Run to Death* by Robert H. Kelston, which was published in the U.S. as an Ace Double, *Kill One, Kill Two*, back-to-back with Peter Rabe's *The Cut of the Whip* and *A Chance on Murder* by Samm Sinclair Baker, published in the U.S. as *Murder—Very Dry*, published by Graphic Books. It would follow then that *Backfire* might have also been published at one time in the United States, most likely by Graphic Books, which published two books by Baker and one by Kelston or by Ace, but neither publisher had a catalog entry with a description that matches the plot of *Backfire*.

Is *Backfire* worth the trouble it took to track down? Ultimately you the reader will be the judge of that, but we at Stark House Press think it is a lost gem that reads like the best of novels by authors such as Charles Williams, Harry Whittington and Gil Brewer.

We think you'll agree that *Backfire* is one of those books that would have otherwise been lost to history, much like some of the titles published through the Stark House imprint, *Staccato Crime*, such as *Room Service* by Alan Williams and *Men, Women, and Rattlesnakes* by Franklin P. Collier or the Stark House Mystery Classic, *The Amazing Judgment* by E. Phillips Oppenheim, all of which there are only a handful of extant copies in the world in their original editions.

Like the typical Gil Brewer novel, the protagonist in *Backfire* is an everyman sucked into a dangerous vortex not of his own making, or even, as in the best of Brewer, as a result of his own bad decisions. Someone is trying to kill Martin Powers, an ordinary guy with no money, no prospects, no enemies, no family nor even an insurance policy. What would anyone gain by his death?

It's so crazy that Powers begins to question himself and who he is and even who his new bride is. As an adopted child he knows nothing about his past, but thinks that it might hold the key as to why somebody would want him dead.

In addition to *Backfire* we have included the best of his true crime writing. We've also included his one and only short story from *Manhunt*, which, along with the publication by Stark House of *The Other Woman*, brings the entirety of Charles L. Burgess' fiction back in print.

Please feel free to let us know what you think about this recent discovery.

Jeff Vorzimmer
Associate Editor
December 10, 2024

Backfire

CHAPTER ONE

The man with the pock-marked face sat motionless behind the wheel of the darkened convertible. His small body leaned against the cushions indolently, yet in an attitude of watchful waiting. It was late, and the tree-lined street was empty of sound. Here and there a light blinked behind a curtained window, but each time he looked around, the lights were fewer. Now and then, when a car went slowly by, he would slink cautiously down in his seat until he was out of sight. He was watching the house across the street, a white frame bungalow set well back from the street. There were no lights in any of the windows, except one in the rear. Probably the kitchen, he thought. He knew all about the people who lived there, and he was impatient for them to turn out the light so that he could get on with what he had to do. He glanced at the luminous dial of his wristwatch. It was one A.M.

Every once in a while he would reach into his pockets to make sure that he had everything he needed, the small hammer, the pliers and the pair of black cotton gloves. He was a thin, ascetic-looking man of less than average height, with large inquisitive eyes and delicate, almost effeminate features. When he smiled, which was seldom, he displayed perfect teeth. He was smiling now as he thought about the man who lived in the little white bungalow, and wondered what thoughts he was thinking, on this, his last night on earth. He laughed without sound. What difference did it make what he was thinking? He was just another guy who would lose a name and become a statistic sometime tomorrow morning. We all become statistics sooner or later, he thought, priding himself on his sagacity.

Nor did the thought of killing a man bother him. It had at first, but with each new assignment the people he had to liquidate became just so many names in the obituary column. Actually, they weren't people at all, just numbers in a rapidly growing list. He patted the well-filled wallet in his breast-pocket affectionately. It was a great racket, and he was only sorry that he hadn't gone into it sooner.

A car with a revolving red light on the roof came slowly down the street, and he quickly slid out of sight. For a wild, crazy moment he thought that someone had spotted him and notified the police. Despite the coolness of the night, sweat beaded his forehead. But the car whispered by on rubber shoes, the sound of its two-way radio growing fainter as it vanished into the darkness. He took a long, deep breath. It had been close.

Suddenly the light in the bungalow blinked out. He nodded with satisfaction and shifted his attention to the 1957 Chevy that was parked in the driveway. It was the statistic's car, and the work he had to do on it would take him only a few minutes, five at the most. He glanced around at the other homes and saw that more lights had gone out since his last roving inspection. He figured that another hour would do it. By that time the entire neighborhood would be tucked in bed, and he could accomplish his mission without fear of interruption. He knew from previous vigils that the police car wouldn't be around again for two hours, so there was no danger there.

He was glad that the houses were spaced well apart. The neatly-trimmed hedges on both sides of the bungalow helped also. It was a perfect setup for what he had come to do.

He liked the method he was using tonight. It was clean and neat and just as effective as a bullet in the head. And much safer because accidents happen all the time. It wouldn't be the first car that had gone out of control and careened off the highway. There would be an investigation, sure, but who could prove anything?

The tap-tap of spike-heeled shoes stiffened him into attention. He followed their sound until he saw a young woman hurrying on the other side of the street. He hoped that she wouldn't enter one of the houses close to the bungalow, and he grinned when she continued down the street and turned the corner. Everything was going just fine.

The hour passed slowly, with leaden feet. By two o'clock the street was as silent as a tomb. Nearly all the lights were out and those that weren't were too far down the street to have prying eyes. He opened the door of the car and closed it gently behind him. Then he pulled the cotton gloves from his pocket and put them on. Satisfied that he was alone, he crossed the street with quick, confident strides. When he was alongside the Chevy, he looked around cautiously.

There was nobody in sight. He smiled and set to work—surely, deftly, turning the car into a murder machine . . .

CHAPTER TWO

The odor of boiling coffee awakened Martin Powers. It was a pleasant, tangy smell, made more so by the crisp sharpness of the October morning. Turning over on his back, he could hear Angela humming a tune as she puttered around in the kitchen preparing breakfast. Even as a child he had always liked the early-morning sounds that came from a kitchen. A sense of well-being came over him. It was a wonderful feeling, this having a home and a wife of his own. The bed was warm and he closed his eyes and smiled. He sure was a lucky guy to have a wife like Angie . . .

"Wake up, you lazy pants!"

Angela was standing in the doorway, arms akimbo, and glaring at him with mock severity.

"Be right there, honey," he grinned, tossing aside the covers. He jumped out of bed and hurried to the bathroom.

He quickly shaved and showered and returned to the bedroom. Slipping into his clothes, he looked into the dresser-mirror while he straightened his tie. He was a tall man, with a lean, wiry body, serious grey eyes and a homely, but pleasant face. His light-brown hair was parted on the side, and although he was only thirty-two, patches of grey were already appearing at the temples. He whistled a pop tune as he shrugged into a jacket.

Angela had everything ready when he walked into the kitchen. She was a tall, willowy girl, with glossy black hair that fell to her shoulders, trim legs and a slim, supple body. Her ebony-colored eyes had an oriental cast to them, giving her cameo-like features a bold, sultry look. Although she was pushing thirty, to Martin she looked more like a precocious teenager in her turtle-neck sweater, blue jeans and sneakers.

"Where are you going today?" she asked as she filled his cup with hot coffee.

"Stonehaven."

"Oh, yeah. I forgot it's Tuesday."

They sat there, sharing their breakfast and laughing with each other as they had every morning of their idyllic three-months-old marriage. Only today was going to be a very special day in Martin Powers' life, for although he didn't know it yet, somebody was trying to kill him. But even if he had been forewarned, it is doubtful if Martin would have believed it. He would have laughed instead, for he was the kind of a guy who made it a point to never bother anyone or step on anyone's toes. He had found his comfortable niche in life as a route salesman for the Delta Cosmetics Company, and with Angela by his side, he was secure in a dream world all his own.

Even if you insisted that he be careful, he would tell you that he had no shady characters for friends and that his only vices were an occasional glass of beer and a Saturday night game of penny-ante in the back room of Max Zimmer's cigar store. There was barely enough insurance to bury him, and he had somewhere between eight- and nine-hundred dollars in the bank. So no matter how you looked at it, he was just an ordinary guy who worked for a living and wanted to be left alone. That's why he wouldn't believe that anyone was trying to kill him. Nobody had anything to gain, except maybe the undertaker.

As he was leaving, Angela threw her arms around him and kissed him long and hard.

"Whew!" he exclaimed, feigning exhaustion. "I'm pooped before I even start. Maybe I'd better stay home."

Angela pointed an imperious finger at the car in the driveway. "On your way, Lover-Boy," she said, laughing.

A few minutes later Martin was headed east on Highway 92, the main thoroughfare between Keystone City and Stonehaven. He made the trip to Stonehaven on Tuesdays and Thursdays because of the large clientele his company had there. Most of the twenty-mile stretch between the two towns ran around a couple of Arizona mountains, and careful driving was a must, even in good weather.

He was only two miles out of Keystone City when he noticed that something was wrong with the car. It began swerving because the wheel wouldn't behave as it should. He was about to pull to the side when the car careened wildly across the highway. He swung the wheel frantically and pushed the brake pedal to the floor. There was a sickening scream of tires as he rammed into the side of the mountain.

Fortunately the contact wasn't too severe, but even so, Martin sat there for several minutes, too stunned to move. It had been a close call. If the car had gone the other way, he would have dropped nearly a thousand feet into the gorge. His hand shook as he wiped his forehead with a handkerchief.

He was still behind the wheel, waiting for the tenseness to leave him, when a Highway Patrol car eased alongside.

"You okay, Buddy?" asked a square-jawed cop.

Martin's grin was weak. "I think so," he said. "Something must have gone wrong with the steering mechanism. The wheel wouldn't work."

The cop got out and walked around the car, inspecting it carefully. "You have a busted fender and a smashed headlight, but outside of that you're okay," he said. "Want me to call a garage?"

"If you don't mind."

"No trouble."

The cop returned to his car and reached in and picked up the hand microphone. He spoke into it briefly and came back to Martin's car.

"There'll be a mechanic and a tow-truck along shortly," he said. He studied Martin's face. "You from Keystone City?"

Martin nodded, showed him his license. The cop studied it and gave it back. "You're a lucky guy," he said. "The car could have gone either way."

Martin took a deep breath. "I know," he said softly.

The mechanic, a pot-bellied little man named Lou Limmer, arrived about ten minutes later. After appraising the damage, he crawled underneath the car for a preliminary examination before hooking it onto the tow-truck.

Back on his feet, Limmer's beetle-colored face was grave. "I don't want to alarm you, Mr. Powers," he said. "But it looks like your car was tampered with."

Martin frowned. "I don't get it."

Limmer shrugged. "The knuckle on your tie-rod end was worked on. Somebody loosened the casing around the ball joint until it was nearly off. When it fell off you couldn't control your steering."

On the drive back to town in Limmer's tow-truck, Martin attached no sinister motive to the defective mechanism. He had no enemies and nobody hated him enough to want him dead. It was an accident, nothing more. He smiled at the serious little man sitting alongside him. What imagination some people have, he thought wryly.

As Martin expected, Angela was upset when he told her the news.

"Maybe Mr. Limmer is right, Marty," she said, her face whitening with worry. "Maybe somebody is trying to kill you!"

Martin laughed. "Don't be silly," he said. "Who'd want to kill me? I'm a nobody. You have to have a reason for killing someone."

"How about talking to the police?" Angela pleaded. "It won't do any harm."

Martin vetoed the idea. "What could I tell them? There's no proof that the car was tampered with." He put his arms around her waist affectionately. "Besides, the first thing they'll ask is why anyone would want me dead, and what can I tell them? What would you tell them?"

Angela groped for an answer. "I don't know," she admitted, shaking her head helplessly.

It took some time, but Martin convinced her that it could have been an accident, and that Mr. Limmer could have been mistaken.

Martin's car was repaired and he resumed his twice-weekly trips to Stonehaven without further interruption. As the days slipped by, the unpleasantness on Highway 92 became dimmer in his mind until nothing remained but a nebulous memory. Even Angela was finally reassured by his easy, carefree manner. Being in love, it was only natural that Martin and Angela should soon forget the unhappy incident.

Then, one night about a week later, it happened again.

They were preparing for bed when he noticed that Angela had been unusually quiet.

"What's wrong?" he asked.

Angela rubbed a hand across her forehead. "I've a splitting headache," she said. "It came on all of a sudden."

"We'll fix it," said Martin, hurrying to the bathroom. He checked the medicine cabinet, but found no aspirins. He returned to the bedroom and began dressing.

Angela sat up in bed. "Where do you think you're going?" she asked.

"We're out of aspirins. I'm going to get some."

"It won't be necessary," she protested. "I'll be okay by morning."

Martin shrugged into his coat. "Be back in a jiffy," he said, waving.

The drugstore was on Main Street, several blocks from their bungalow. The night air was brisk and invigorating, and he straightened his shoulders and breathed deeply. He thought of Angela and his face softened. Subconsciously, he began comparing her dark beauty to Lorna. Lorna, of the fair skin and shimmering blond hair. Lorna, with whom he thought he was in love until Angela came along and showed him how wrong he was.

He was so busy with his thoughts that he did not notice the car that was following him.

He was crossing the street before he realized, or sensed, his danger. He had cut between a couple of parked cars and had gone only a few steps when he was startled by the sudden roar of an automobile engine. It happened so quickly that he barely had time to fling himself violently backward. The oncoming car raced by, nicking his pants leg ever so slightly, and was gone.

The street was deserted, which meant there were no witnesses. This was not unusual, since it was after midnight, and most of the townsfolk were either in bed or watching the late late show on their television sets.

Martin leaned against one of the parked cars while he caught his breath. It was the second close call he'd had in less than two weeks. But this time there was a difference. This time he had seen his would-be assassin. True, it was only a fleeting glimpse, etched in a moment of panic, but he had noticed that the car was a black convertible.

And the driver was a man.

A man with a pock-marked face.

Martin bought the aspirins and started home, this time at a more subdued pace and infinitely more wary. The car, he was certain, had accelerated the moment he emerged from between the parked cars. He sensed rather than knew this. And he couldn't help wondering why the man with the pock-marked face wanted him dead. Death, in itself, did not frighten him; he had faced it many times in Korea. It was the *why* that puzzled him.

He knew too, that he would have to tell Angela. It would be only fair, and besides, they had solemnly promised each other during their courting days that there were to be no secrets between them, no matter what. Because of her headache, however, he decided to postpone telling her until morning.

That night he dreamed that he was walking through a long dark alley with high walls on both sides. It was late at night and there wasn't a star in the sky or a sound anywhere. It was almost as if he was the only living creature on earth. He was halfway through the alley when the walls suddenly began closing in on him. He tried to scream for help, but no sound came from his throat. He tried to run, but his legs wouldn't function properly. Numb with terror, he found himself being slowly crushed to death. The breath was leaving his body when he heard maniacal laughter somewhere in the distance. He looked up and saw the man with the pock-marked face standing on one of the ledges looking down at him. When he awoke, his heart was pounding and he was soaked with perspiration.

Angela was beside herself with worry when he told her about the close call he'd had the night before.

"You've got to go to the police, Marty," she insisted. "They'll look into it, and maybe they'll even assign someone to watch you."

Martin tried the same persuasive tactics that had worked before, but this time Angela was adamant. When he left for work, he had promised, albeit half-heartedly, to drop in and see the police. Not that he expected very much to come of it.

But Martin did not go near the police that day. Instead, he threw himself into his work with a zeal calculated to banish the tension that was building up slowly inside him. As the day wore on he found himself constantly looking for a black convertible with a pock-marked driver.

Driving home that evening, he knew there was only one word to describe the way he felt.

Afraid.

CHAPTER THREE

That night, Angela met him at the door with her usual kiss. But this time there was no accompanying embrace, no loving endearments. Instead, she pulled back, a penitent look in her coal-black eyes.

"There's someone waiting to see you, Marty," she said, taking his hand.

Martin walked into the living-room where a huge man in a blue pin-stripe sat on the sofa. The man rose to his feet when he saw Martin. He was the biggest man Martin had ever seen, tremendous shoulders, big hands, enormous body and coarse features. He had sandy hair and there was a dead cigar stuck between his thick, sensuous lips. His small eyes were like cubes of ice as he shook Martin's hand.

"You're a cop," Martin said.

The man laughed. He flipped open a wallet, revealing a silver badge. "Detective-Sergeant Sam Bannerman," he said. "Your Missus called me. She says you're in trouble."

Martin looked at Angela, mild reproof in his eyes. She avoided, his gaze and waved them to chairs. "Martin will tell you all about it," she said.

When everyone was comfortable, Martin told him all about it. He told it factually, chronologically, and without any embellishments. Bannerman chewed silently on his cigar while he talked. Angela's eyes were uneasy and she kept biting her lip. Only at the finish, when he mentioned the pock-marked man, did either of them speak.

"You didn't tell me you saw the driver," she said petulantly.

Martin took a pack of Kools from his pocket and offered them around. When the others refused, he shook one loose and lit it. "I'm not sure I saw him even now," he said, exhaling slowly. "It happened so fast. I could be wrong."

Bannerman leaned forward. "Your wife says you have no idea who is trying to kill you?"

"That's right."

"The pock-marked guy interests me. Any idea who he could be?"

Martin had given it considerable thought. He knew plenty of people, both inside the business world and out, but none them had a pock-marked face. He shook his head.

"How about insurance?"

"I have a thousand-dollar policy," Martin said.

"Property, a bank account?"

"No property and approximately eight-hundred and twenty-nine dollars in the bank."

Bannerman frowned. "Where do you keep your car at night?"

"In the driveway alongside the house."

"You have no garage?"

"Yes," nodded Martin, "but the landlord has furniture stored in it. It's only a temporary condition."

Bannerman got to his feet and went to the window, his brows knitted with concentration. Despite his bulk, Martin noticed that he walked lightly, like a well-trained fighter. He marveled that such a big man could move so effortlessly. The detective was rough and competent, and it was easy to visualize him in the back room of some precinct station beating the truth from a stubborn prisoner. Martin was sure it wouldn't be pretty.

Bannerman turned away from the window. "It don't add up, Mr.

Powers," he said, shaking his massive head. "Aside from your wife, you ain't worth anything to anyone, dead or alive." He raised his hand apologetically when he saw resentment flare in Martin's eyes. "I don't mean anything personal, believe me. But let's face it, I can't see why this guy, or any guy, would want to kill you."

"Does there have to be a reason?" asked Angela.

Bannerman jerked the cigar from his mouth and waved it. "I'm afraid so, Ma'am," he said. "I've been a cop for nearly twenty years, fifteen of them in the detective division, and except in a few isolated cases, like maybe a crackpot or something, there's always a reason why somebody kills somebody else. Money, a guy's wife . . ." He stopped short and looked at Mrs. Powers speculatively.

Martin knew what he was thinking. "Forget it," he said.

The detective held up his hand again. "Well, now. Maybe and maybe not. Tell me, Ma'am. Did you go with anyone steady before you met Mr. Powers?"

Angela smiled. "Of course. Do I look repulsive?"

Bannerman grinned sheepishly. "Far from it, Ma'am, believe me. But let's suppose you went with some guy who resented getting the brush-off. The files are full of characters who took their hate out on the new guy. In this case your husband."

"I came to Keystone City about eight months ago from New York," she said, placing her hands in her lap and studying them. "None of the fellows I went with thought seriously about marriage and neither did I. And if it will make you feel any better, none of them had pock-marks."

Suddenly, Bannerman looked tired. "In that case, there isn't much I can do," he said, picking his Stetson off the sofa.

"How about having someone guard my husband?" asked Angela.

"I'm sorry, but the captain wouldn't go for it," Bannerman said flatly. "In the first place I'd have a hard time convincing him that Mr. Powers is really in danger, and in the second place, he can't spare the men."

Angela stomped her foot impatiently. "Which means my husband has to take care of himself the best way he can," she demanded angrily.

Bannerman nodded. "That's about it, Ma'am. I'm sorry." He turned to Martin. "I can help you get a gun permit, if it'll make you feel any better."

Martin squashed his cigarette in the tray. "It wouldn't help a bit," he said. "If someone is trying to kill me, he'll make darn sure I won't have a chance to use it."

Angela was disconsolate after the detective had left. "How can they be so stupid?" she exclaimed. "A man's life is in danger and they won't do anything about it."

Martin slipped his arms around her waist and held her tight. "The sergeant is right, darling," he said. "It would be foolish to guard me twenty-four hours a day. Pock-Marks would simply wait until they removed the guard. He's got all the time in the world."

Angela looked so frightened that he was immediately contrite. "Maybe what happened were only a couple of coincidences," he said hastily. "People have near accidents every day and they don't go running to the police."

But he could see by her troubled face that she wasn't satisfied. She was unusually quiet during dinner and it worried him. Martin wished there was something he could say or do to reassure her of his safety. But there was nothing. He was trapped by circumstances and the man with the pock-marked face.

Later, they were looking at television when she suddenly switched off the picture. "Let's get out of Keystone City," she said, her face tight with anxiety.

"It's no use," said Martin patiently. "Running away won't help. Besides, we haven't the money to keep going from place to place."

"You just can't stay here!" she cried. "Marty, you're a sitting duck. You don't have a chance!"

Martin took her hands and pulled her onto his lap. She was shaking. "Easy, Baby, easy," he said. "Pock-Marks has his troubles, too. He'll have to pick the exact time and place, and if I'm careful that won't be easy."

He stroked her hair. He liked being with her, she smelled good and clean, like a freshly mowed lawn after heavy rain. He liked the way her eyes lighted up when he came home from work and the way she hummed while she was preparing his breakfast. But most of all, he liked the way she worried over him. She was both wife and mother to him, and he felt humbly grateful.

"What about Lorna?" she asked suddenly.

"What about her?"

"She was in love with you once."

"So?"

"So maybe she decides to get even and hires someone to kill you," she said. "It's happened before. Bannerman says so."

Martin thought about it. He had been thinking a lot of things ever since the near hit-and-miss the night before. Lorna was quick-tempered and impetuous. She could be a wildcat when she was riled. But murder, especially the cold, calculated kind, was foreign to her nature. Still, you could never tell about a woman. Lorna was deep. You never actually knew what she was thinking. But like most impetuous people, she could not hide her feelings, and Martin knew that his sudden marriage to Angela had shaken her badly.

Martin remembered the first time he had ever met Lorna. He'd been working for Delta Cosmetics a couple of years when he walked into the office one morning and saw a new blond behind the receptionist's desk. It was Lorna Craig. They had hit it off right from the beginning, and it wasn't long before he was taking her to dinner and dances. Later, she took him to see her folks out in the valley, near Boxvale. The Craigs were a nice, homey couple, the kind of folks he'd have chosen for in-laws.

He was sure he was in love with Lorna and she with him, but he kept putting off the one big question she wanted to hear. For one thing he wanted to be absolutely sure. He also wanted a raise in salary and more money in the bank before he took the big step. Then Angela arrived in Keystone City and made him forget Lorna. Angela Koonan had been a photographer's model in New York before coming to Keystone City. Her parents were dead and she had been raised by an aunt. When an automobile accident scarred her beautiful body, she had decided to try and forget somewhere else. She had chosen Keystone City because an uncle had once lived there.

As the days passed he saw less and less of Lorna and more and more of Angela. If Lorna saw the handwriting on the wall, she didn't say anything. Then, before he realized what was happening, he and Angela were married. It was a simple, quiet wedding after which they'd spent two glorious weeks traipsing around the country in Martin's car.

And so he wondered if Angela was right about Lorna hating him.

Martin could not sleep that night. He kept thinking about the man with the pock-marked face. Why did he want to kill him? There had to be a reason, Bannerman had said so and he should know. Pursuing the thought further, he clasped his hands behind his head and stared at the ceiling. There must be an answer somewheres. He had long since eliminated any logical reason for Pock-Marks wanting him dead. The answer, therefore, had to be an illogical one. Someone with a wild, crazy obsession he didn't know or couldn't even guess. He thought of all the people he knew, and he could find no one with the remotest reason for hating him. Most of his friends were in the cosmetics business like himself. Of course there was the gang who hung out in Max Zimmer's cigar store, and his neighbors on Woodland Street, but he'd never had any trouble with any of them.

Angela squirmed restlessly in her sleep.

Martin eased his lanky frame out of bed and reached for the pack of cigarettes on the night table. He lit one and padded softly to the partly open window. The floor felt cool and damp beneath his bare feet. There was a bright moon and a hint of frost in the brisk night air. October in Arizona was the time of year he liked best, the time when the earth grew hard and the leaves turned a golden hue and red-faced youngsters frolicked on the streets with a football. It was the time of year when it felt good to be alive.

He returned to bed and slid under the warm covers without waking Angela. Closing his eyes, he tried to concentrate on finding one sensible reason for someone wanting him dead. He thought of several, but they were too fantastic to even consider. Then, without knowing why, his mind eased gently back to his childhood. He had been an adopted child. The Powers, Tim and Sarah, had told him when he was eight years old. At first he had felt hurt and unwanted, but as he grew older the wound had healed and he thought less and less about it. Right till the end he had always called them Ma and Pa, and he doubted if he could have loved his real parents with greater fervor.

He had asked them several times about his folks, but they said they knew nothing, and he believed them. Even if they did know, Pa Powers had confided in him much later, it would be better left unsaid. What was done was done, was the old man's credo. After that, Martin hadn't bothered to ask anymore. When he was old enough to be philosophical about it, he put it down as a quirk of fate. But it did not stop him from wondering who his real parents were and why they had put him out for adoption. Maybe they were killed in an automobile accident, or maybe they were so poor that they just couldn't afford to keep him. He had wondered about it many times. Not that it mattered very much. The Powers were wonderful and kind, and they had loved and cared for him as if he had been their own son.

Martin tried to remember some of the small incidents in his life before the Powers had come into it. Most of what he could recall was jumbled and did not make much sense. His clearest recollection was being in a cemetery. He was about three years old, he thought. It was a dark, dreary day, and a tall, gaunt-looking woman was holding onto his hand as they stood before an open grave. It was misting rain and all of the people who stood around the grave had sad looks and they wore black clothes. Some of them were holding umbrellas over their heads. He had often wondered if the woman holding his hand was his mother, and if the box that was put into the ground contained the body of his father. Somehow, he could not remember anything about his father, and it bothered him. The tall woman must have loved the man in the box because he remembered seeing tears running down her face as they prepared to lower it into the ground.

There was something else he remembered. It was the Angel on the tombstone next to his father's (if it was his father's) grave. The Angel was a girl and she was made of white stone. She had a harp in her hand and she looked as if she was flying. He had thought it was very pretty, and even when they were lowering the big box into the grave he kept looking at it. Then a neat little man in a turned-around collar stepped forward and said some prayers out loud while everyone stood with their hands clasped and their heads bowed in the rain.

After that some men began shoveling dirt into the hole. Each of the others picked up a handful of dirt and threw it into the hole too. All except the lady who held onto his hand. She just stood there, sad and motionless, saying nothing. Then everyone turned and walked slowly away, leaving him and the lady and the men with the shovels. He remembered that they stayed there until the hole was filled, and that nobody spoke during all that time. As the lady started to walk away a strange thing happened; the rain stopped and the sun came out, filling the dreary cemetery with a warming, cheerful light. It seemed like an omen of some kind, because the tall lady looked down at him and smiled even though she was still crying.

His next recollection was of a clapboard house. He could not remember who lived in it, although he had a feeling he did. He tried to place the sad-faced woman in, or around it, but could not. He recalled making mud pies in the backyard, and hearing the shrill whistle of the railroad engine as it went by close to the clapboard house. From all this he had a feeling that his parents were very poor. Then his memory jumped to a big white house on a hill where there were a lot of other little boys and girls like himself. The house had tall, white columns and there was a lot of ground with green grass all around it.

He didn't even remember the Powers taking him away from the big white house on the hill. The earliest recollection he had of his new home in Corona was when Pa and Ma Powers showed him his own room. It was a very pretty room, with lace curtains and a soft bed and lots of toys scattered around. He could not recall ever having any toys when he lived in the clapboard house.

His life with the Powers, first as a child and then as a growing boy and finally as a young man, had been tranquil. Ma Powers had died when he was sixteen and he missed her so much that he had cried himself to sleep for weeks afterwards. She had told him once that she couldn't have any little boys or girls of her own, and that was why she had asked God for him. And He had answered her prayers by sending him. After Ma was laid away, Pa looked after him. But Pa Powers was never the same after Ma died. He began to shrivel up, like something inside him had died, too. He was nearly twenty when the old man went to join Ma, and two years later he decided to move to Keystone City.

So there was nothing in his life with the Powers that might account for Pock-Marks wanting him dead. Which meant that he had to go further back, to the time before he was adopted. It seemed implausible, but he could not help feeling that Pock-Marks knew something about him that he didn't know. Where he was born, even his name, perhaps. A surge of anger against his unknown enemy swept over him. Angela was right, he just couldn't sit around without fighting back. He had to find out what was behind the attempts on his life, and the only place he could start was Corona. Perhaps he could pick up the thread there.

Before dropping off to sleep, Martin decided not to tell Angela of his plans. It would only worry her, and she was upset enough as it was. He would tell her the company was sending him off on another tour to drum up business. He had made several such trips since he'd known her, so she would have no reason to doubt him.

CHAPTER FOUR

Lorna Craig was alone in the reception room when he reported for work the next morning. She was an exceptionally pretty girl in her late twenties. She was small and neatly put together, with short blonde hair that swirled coquettishly around a delicately-boned face. Her cobalt-blue eyes regarded him gravely as he sailed his hat onto a nearby couch.

"Morning, Lorna," he said. "The boss in yet?"

She shook her head. "Not yet," she said, her face strangely taut. Her voice was low and husky, and he remembered when it wasn't so very long ago when just hearing it made him tingle all over. He didn't know why, but the thought disturbed him.

"I heard what happened the other night," she said.

Martin's eyes narrowed. "How did you find out?"

"Lester Cowan told me a few minutes ago." She straightened out some papers on the desk. "He said he was driving home from the bowling alley when he saw that car almost hit you."

Martin nodded, satisfied. Cowan worked for Delta Cosmetics and was a route salesman like himself. He eased into an armchair. "Those things happen," he said.

"But that's twice, Marty," she said. "Suppose what happened the other night and that incident out on Highway 92 weren't just accidents?"

Martin fished in his pockets for cigarettes, found he'd forgotten to buy a pack and shrugged.

"How well do you know Angela?" asked Lorna suddenly.

Martin flushed. "Now wait a minute—"

"Oh, I know she's your wife and all that," she snapped. "But how well do you really know her? Who is she? Who were her friends before she came to Keystone City? Can you answer those questions?"

"Lay off," retorted Martin. "Angela's a good kid. Besides, she's got no reason for wanting me dead. I'm not Daddy Warbucks."

Lorna's nostrils flared angrily. "Maybe not, but you've got to admit that none of these things happened before you met her," she cried. "As for a reason, there may be one you don't even know about."

Martin studied the picture of George Washington on the wall. Funny Lorna should say that. He had been thinking the same things last night. And what did he really know about Angela? He shook his head in disgust. It was only last night that Angela had tried to pin suspicion on Lorna. The female of the species. He had a feeling he was whirling helplessly in a vortex.

"Let me help, Marty," she said. "We'll go to the police together."

Martin smiled. "Angela has already taken care of that. I talked to a detective last night. They can't do anything either."

Lorna looked stricken. "What are you going to do? You can't go on fighting shadows."

The intercom on Lorna's desk buzzed. She turned and went to the desk and snapped the lever. A rush of jumbled words reached Martin.

Lorna snapped down the lever. "The boss'll see you now," she said.

Martin got his week's leave of absence without any trouble. As he left the office he could feel Lorna's eyes following him. She's a good kid, he thought as he pushed the elevator button. Angela and Lorna. They're both good kids. And all because of him they hated each other's guts.

Bannerman was leaning against his car when he got to the parking lot. There were tired lines in the burly detective's face, and his rumpled suit looked as if it hadn't been pressed in months.

"Followed you this morning, just in case," Bannerman said. "Anything new, Mr. Powers?"

Martin hesitated. He debated whether to tell him about his plans, and decided against it. It was a million-to-one shot that his life before the Powers adopted him had anything to do with the attempts to kill him.

"Nothing new," he said, unlocking the car. He slid behind the wheel. "The company is sending me on a tour to drum up business. I'll be gone a week."

Bannerman threw away his old cigar, took the wrapping off a fresh one, bit off the end and then lit it. "Has the trip anything to do with what's happened lately?" he asked.

Martin squirmed. "I told you it was business."

The detective stared at the lighted end of his cigar for several moments. "It sure beats me why anyone would want to bump you off," he said.

"You said that before."

"You got anything to tell me?"

"Like what?"

Bannerman shrugged and exhaled a cloud of smoke. "When we had that little chit-chat last night, the Missus was listening," he said, his face impassive. "I thought maybe you were holding out so she wouldn't get worried."

"I'm not. I told you everything."

Bannerman nodded. "Okay, Mr. Powers. Just thought I'd ask. Remember, it's your life, not mine."

Martin watched the burly detective as he walked to a nearby squad car and drove off. Despite his brusque manner, he rather liked Bannerman. He was gruff and hard-boiled, but in his business he had to be tough. Martin started the motor and eased out into traffic. He was glad that he had Sam Bannerman on his side.

Martin drove to the bank, where he withdrew two hundred dollars from his account. He was glad that Angela had left the financial affairs of the Powers family up to him. Explaining the withdrawal might be embarrassing since the company always furnished expenses for the trips.

Angela pouted when she heard that he was going away for a week, but he was able to convince her that it had nothing to do with the attempts on his life. When he pulled out of the driveway shortly after one o'clock, he looked into the rearview mirror half expecting to see a black convertible. There was none.

CHAPTER FIVE

Angela paced the hotel room nervously. It was a cheap room, with a bed, a scarred bureau, a couple of straight-backed chairs and a night-table next to the bed. The light from the floor lamp cast a pale glow, leaving the corners of the room in shadows. Traffic sounds and the wild, discordant notes of a rock and roll tune crashed through the partially open window. Now and then she would pause and tilt her head as if listening for something or someone.

She was wearing a black velvet suit that did little to hide the softly rounded hips, the ample bosom and the incredibly small waist. Gleaming patent-leather pumps with ridiculously high heels added to her slimness. A suede bag and a black caracul coat lay on the bed.

Angela strode to the window, pushed aside the flowered curtain and looked down on the darkened, people-filled street with brooding eyes. She was angry and impatient, and every move she made showed it; the smoldering alertness in her eyes, the incessant tapping of a foot, the quick, nervous movements of her gloved hands. Why doesn't he show up, she asked herself angrily. She wondered if he was getting cold feet, but almost as she thought it, she dismissed the idea. Not Sam Bannerman. Nothing fazed him, not even murder. A soft autumnal moon hovered overhead and she looked up at it and smiled. A coldness crept into her eyes as she contemplated what lay ahead. Everything had worked out fine so far. Well, almost everything. If it wasn't for that fool, Vico . . .

A knock on the door snapped her to attention. She hurried to the door and listened for several seconds. "Who is it?" she asked softly.

A man chuckled. "Clark Gable."

Angela grimaced, pushed back the bolt with a kid-gloved finger and opened the door. Sam Bannerman stepped quickly inside.

"You're late," she snapped. "What kept you?"

Bannerman took the dead cigar from his mouth and looked at the shredded end distastefully. "Take it easy," he said softly.

Angela bolted the door and strode across the room, wringing her hands. "If I could get my hands on that Vico . . ."

Bannerman watched her with appreciative eyes. Then he turned one of the chairs around, sat on it and placed his arms across the backrest. He smiled. "Calm yourself, kitten," he said. "So Vico blew it again. Maybe the next time."

Angela turned and stared at him. "Martin's left town," she said.

"I know. I spoke to him this morning."

"I wonder . . ."

"Quit wondering," he said brusquely. "He suspects something." He caught her frightened look and shook his head. "No, he doesn't suspect us. Not yet, anyway. But he's been doing a lot of thinking, and I've a hunch that this trip has something to do with what's been happening to him lately."

Angela frowned, gnawed on a gloved finger. "How much do you think he knows?"

Bannerman looked at his cigar again. "You can answer that better than me," he said, watching her closely. "He's following up some lead, that's a cinch."

Her eyes grew hot. "How do you know what he's thinking?" she snapped.

Bannerman shrugged, said nothing.

Angela sat on the edge of the bed and crossed a slim, nyloned leg. "He told me the company was sending him on a business trip," she said.

The detective studied her legs. "You've underestimated him, baby," he said without raising his eyes. "Martin Powers has been lucky so far, but he's no dope. Sooner or later he's going to come up with some answers, and when he does there's going to be trouble."

"Where's Vico?" she demanded.

"Right behind Powers, wherever he is."

"You're sure?" She sounded skeptical.

Bannerman didn't say anything, just nodded.

Angela slammed her open palm against the bedspread. "What's the matter with Vico, anyway?" she stormed. "How many chances does he need?"

Bannerman shrugged. "You picked him, not me," he said, still looking at her legs.

Bannerman finally raised his eyes. "How much did you say was involved?" he asked.

"I've already told you."

"Tell me again."

"Approximately a half-million dollars."

Bannerman rolled the figure over his tongue and smiled. "Good," he said. "Very good. And we split it two ways."

Angela's eyes narrowed. "Three ways," she corrected. "Don't forget Vico."

The detective smiled. "I won't," he promised.

The implication sent a chill through Angela. "What do we do now?"

"We sit and wait until we hear from Vico." He studied her several moments, then shook his head and laughed.

She glowered at him. "What's so funny?"

"I was just thinking what a pair of optimists your folks were when they named you after an angel." His eyes twinkled his amusement.

"You're a ball," she retorted sarcastically. She rose and shrugged into her coat. "Keep in touch."

Bannerman threw the cigar over his shoulder, and moving like a huge cat, crossed the room and put his arms around her waist. His eyes asked the eternal question, but his lips said nothing.

Angela's eyes frosted. "Take your hands off me," she said.

"Come on, baby," he said, smiling affably. "Be nice to Daddy."

"Take your filthy paws off me," she said again.

Bannerman threw back his head and laughed.

Angela stared at him, her eyes cold and uncompromising. The silence in the room deepened. He stopped smiling suddenly, and returned her stare, neither giving ground for several long moments.

Finally, the detective flushed, dropped his eyes. He removed his hands from her waist. "What the hell," he growled. "I thought you were a woman."

Angela smiled. "Someday you may have the pleasure of finding out," she said. "Right now you've got a job to do. See that you do it."

She walked to the door trailing perfume, and without a backward glance, opened it and walked out, closing it softly behind her.

Bannerman watched her go, a baffled look on his florid face.

CHAPTER SIX

It was mid-afternoon when Martin saw the water tower of Corona on the skyline. The first step in the long road back. He wondered where it would take him.

He found parking space in front of a little diner on Main Street and got out. He put a nickel in the meter and looked around. It hadn't changed much in ten years. A few new chain stores, perhaps, but that was all. Although the population was less than six thousand, Corona was the county seat. The streets were wide and clean, and like most small towns, the redbrick courthouse stood in the center of the square. A narrow expanse of neatly mowed grass surrounded it on four sides. Pigeons strutted around aimlessly, looking for morsels. The faded green benches were fairly well filled with aged, tobacco-chewing farmers. An aura of decay and lassitude hung over the town like a pall.

Martin went into the diner and ordered the blue-plate special. He studied the few customers, but recognized no one. Ten years was a long time. People died and those that didn't got married and moved away. Others, like himself, sought greener pastures. Not that he blamed them. There wasn't much to look forward to in Corona. That's why he had gone to Keystone City. Still, his memories were here, the happy ones anyway, and a feeling of nostalgia swept over him as he looked out on the almost deserted street. He had spent the best years of his life in this town, and if he had a genie lamp he would wish Ma and Pa Powers back to life and be a kid again. He pushed his half-eaten meal away and went outside.

Back in the car, he wondered where he should start. The Powers had lived on Maple Street, so he might as well begin there. He drove across town to a quiet, residential street and parked a few doors from his old home. It still looked the same, nothing had changed. The same white houses were set well back from the same cracked sidewalks and separated from each other by the same small hedgerows. He wondered if any of the neighbors could help him, providing he could find any. Ma and Pa Powers had been kindly people, but they didn't believe in talking about their personal affairs.

As he suspected, most of the people he had known had died or moved away. The Bettancourts still lived in the little bungalow down the street, but they could tell him nothing. Neither could the Warrens or the Mangrums. Later, he spent a pleasant hour chewing the rag and having coffee with old Joe Cleary, once the town constable, now retired. Joe had buried his wife only a month before and was still in a state of shock. He remembered how close Joe and Elsa had been, and he felt sorry for the lonesome old man.

"You know, Martin," said Cleary, "you're the second person who seems to be interested in where you come from."

"Tell me about him," asked Martin.

"It was a woman. She came here one afternoon about a year ago. In early September, I think it was. Anyway, I didn't talk to her. Elsa did."

"What did she want to know?"

The old man tapped some fresh tobacco into his pipe and shrugged. "When the Powers had died and what they looked like and from what home or organization they'd adopted you. Stuff like that."

"Did Mrs. Cleary describe her?"

The old man took several moments fumbling with his pipe. "Yeah. She said the woman was in her late twenties or early thirties, and wore horn-rimmed glasses and had auburn hair."

Martin frowned. The description did not fit anyone he knew. Angela and Lorna, the only two women in his life that had really mattered, had neither red hair or wore glasses, even for reading. He couldn't help wondering who she was and why she was so interested in him.

"Another cup of coffee?" asked Cleary.

Martin checked his watch. It was after five o'clock and sense of urgency possessed him. He had a lot of ground to cover and only a week to do it in.

"Afraid not, Mr. Cleary," he said, rising. "I've got a lot of people to talk to."

He shook hands with the old man and left. But Cleary called him back. "You won't get very far pumping the neighbors, son," he said, sucking on his pipe thoughtfully. "None of 'em have the slightest idea where Tim and Sarah fetched you. All everyone hereabouts knows is that they went away one day and you were with 'em when they came back. But Uncle Willie should be able to tell you." The old man chuckled. "If anybody knows anything, he does. Uncle Willie knows everything that goes on in Corona."

Martin was dubious. "I don't see—"

"He knows," predicted Joe Cleary sagely. "Uncle Willie might not know exactly where you came from, but he'll remember where Tim and Sarah bought tickets for that time, and that should narrow it down some."

The suggestion excited him. A thought came to him. "Do you remember if Elsa sent the redhead to see Uncle Willie?"

"I'm afraid so, son."

"It doesn't matter," Martin said. But he wasn't so sure. He thanked the old man and hurried to his car. He remembered Uncle Willie as a tall, seedy-looking character who had worked in the railroad depot for more than forty years. His real name was William Michael Feeney, but nobody ever called him anything but Uncle Willie.

Uncle Willie was dozing behind his wire cage when Martin walked into the musty little combination office and waiting room. The years rolled back and Martin grinned. He couldn't count the times when he had found the old man asleep on the job.

He slapped the counter hard. "Wake up, Uncle Willie," he shouted.

The old man yawned, opened a reluctant eye and studied Martin. "When did you get back?" he asked in a whiny voice.

"You remember me?" asked Martin, surprised.

Uncle Willie yawned again, stretched his bony arms and got slowly to his feet. "Remember you?" he grunted. "How could I forget you, you young whippersnapper! You was always abothering me!"

"I need your help, old-timer," said Martin earnestly. "I'm trying to find out where Tim and Sarah got me."

The old man blinked at him. He scratched his bald head with a gnarled finger. "It's been a long time, Martin," he wheezed. "Nearly thirty years, I reckon."

"I know."

Uncle Willie peered into his face hesitantly. "I promised Tim and Sarah I wouldn't tell," he said.

"That was a long time ago," Martin said. "It didn't matter then. They're both dead now, and things have changed." He took a deep breath. "Something has happened, and I've got to know. It could mean my life, Uncle Willie."

The old man nodded. "Then I reckon it's mighty important that you know. 'Course, I never did know which Home or Institution they got you from. Tim and Sarah never told me. But they did buy tickets for Vianna, up Colorado way."

Martin repeated the name Vianna several times hoping it might ring a bell. It didn't. But at least it was another thread in the skein.

He had to ask Uncle Willie one more question.

"About a year ago," he said, "a woman with red hair and wearing horn-rimmed glasses showed up in Corona asking about me. She spoke to Elsa Cleary and she sent her to you. Does she know about Vianna, too?"

The old man flushed and dropped his eyes.

"Oh, swell!"

Five minutes later Martin was headed northeast on Highway 65. He tried to piece together what he had learned from Joe Cleary and Uncle Willie. In addition to the pock-marked man, he now had a redhead to contend with. Who was she and how was she connected with Pock-Marks? By what common denominator had they bound themselves together in a plot to kill him?

He lit a cigarette and glanced in the rearview mirror. It was almost dusk, and while he couldn't be certain, he thought one of the cars behind him was a black convertible.

CHAPTER SEVEN

It was three o'clock in the morning when Martin swung the Chevy into the graveled driveway of the Cactus Motel on the outskirts of Vianna. He was bone-weary as he crawled from behind the wheel and rang the night-button outside the manager's office. It had been a long, steady pull from Corona, interrupted only once for sandwiches and coffee. He had seen, or thought he had seen, the black convertible only once. Still, there were probably thousands of black convertibles, and it could have been a figment of his imagination. He rubbed a tired hand over his face. He'd been thinking about the car and its pock-marked driver so much lately that he was seeing them everywhere. He pressed the button again. A light snapped on inside and a pair of slippered feet approached the door. A thin-faced, stoop-shouldered old man with sleep-laden eyes peered out at him.

"You want a room?" he asked crossly.

"If you don't mind."

The man took a key from a table next to the door and gave it to Martin. "Number fifteen," he said. "That'll be five dollars. You can fill out the card in the morning." Cabin Fifteen was at the far end of the u-shaped court. Like all the others, it was painted pink and had orange shutters. Martin took the bag from the car, locked it, and went inside. It was a typical motel room, no better or worse than most. But it was clean and the bed looked inviting and Martin was satisfied. He shed his clothes quickly and took an invigorating shower. He felt much better when he slipped into bed, and in a few minutes he was asleep.

Sunlight was streaming through the venetian blinds when he awoke. For a few moments he couldn't remember where he was, and then it came to him. He shook his head groggily and looked at his wristwatch. It was after eleven.

After he had washed and shaved, he studied himself in the mirror. The cat-and-mouse game with Pock-Marks was beginning to show in his eyes. They had that haunted look. He patted some after-shave lotion on his face. Slipping into a sports shirt and a jacket, he went outside.

The old man was watering a small flower bed nearby. He looked up as Martin approached.

"Feeling better, eh?" he said pleasantly. "You sure looked beat last night."

"I was," Martin admitted. He looked around. A number of motels and cheap dining places with gaudy neon signs lined both sides of the busy highway. The raucous sound of dance music came from a nearby jukebox. He studied the cars still parked in the other motels but could find no black convertibles among them. Maybe it had been his imagination after all.

The old man dropped the hose and turned off the spigot. "You can fill out that card now if you like," he said.

Martin nodded and followed him into the little office. He filled out the white card the manager gave him. He opened his wallet and dropped five dollars on the desk.

"If it's okay with you, I'll stay another night," he said.

"It's okay with me. You a salesman or something?"

"A salesman." Martin took a pack of cigarettes from his pocket and lit one. "How many cemeteries are there hereabouts?"

"Two," replied the manager, slipping the money into his pocket. "There's St. Agnes and Greenlawn. St. Agnes is the Catholic cemetery. They're not so particular at Greenlawn, long's as you're dead." He chuckled.

The old man pointed to the stream of northward bound traffic. "Stay on this highway until you get to the other end of town," he said. "They're side-by-side. You can't miss 'em."

Martin thanked him, got in his car and headed towards town. Traffic was fairly heavy and he was surprised to see that Vianna was a good-sized town. Almost as large as Keystone City. The highway ran through the center of the shopping district and the street was filled with lunch-bound office workers and package-laden shoppers. Bells chimed in a nearby church. Twelve o'clock. Hearing the bells reminded him of the little church he and Angela went to every Sunday. Suddenly he was lonesome for her. He made a note to send her a wire telling her he would be home soon.

When he reached the cemeteries, Martin parked on a dirt road across the street and got out. St. Agnes' was the nearest and he went there first. It was a small cemetery and beautifully cared for. He began walking along the narrow sidewalks that separated the parallel rows of graves. Since he'd never known his real name, he had nothing to go on, really. Only a white angel on a tombstone. His heart sank. The whole thing seemed like a waste of time. But he walked on, examining each tombstone carefully, hopefully.

There was no white angel in St. Agnes Cemetery.

He returned to his car and wondered if he should eat before tackling Greenlawn. He decided to finish the job as long as he was here. Besides, he wasn't very hungry. Walking through the arched entrance, he saw that Greenlawn was a much larger cemetery. He took his time, working each row systematically to make sure he wouldn't miss the tombstone with the white angel, if it was here. Many of the tombstones seemed fairly new, and he guessed that he was in the more recently opened section.

And then he saw it.

It was in a far corner of the cemetery, near a high wire fence. He approached it timidly, his stomach churning. The white angel was there, just as he remembered it. She was still smiling, and she still had the harp clutched to her bosom and she appeared to be flying somewhere. To Heaven, probably There was no grave on one side of it, so the one on the other side must be the one containing the bodies of his father and mother. His face was somber as he looked at the small tombstone. The inscription read:

JOSEPH KASKO
Born: April 6, 1888
Died: March 8, 1928

LENA KASKO
Born: Sept. 14, 1890
Died: August 7, 1928

So his name was Kasko. It sounded Polish. If Lena was his mother, she had lived less than six months after his father. No wonder he had ended up in a Home. Many things kill many people, but he had a feeling that his mother had died of a broken heart. A lump of sadness welled up inside him. Although he did not remember his father and his mother hardly at all, he felt a strange affinity here that he hadn't felt when Ma and Pa Powers passed away. He couldn't define it.

Despite the years, the grave looked neat and trim and he was glad. At least they hadn't been neglected. And there wasn't much he could do for them, even now that he knew. Somehow he felt that they were happy, now that he had returned to them.

Martin took a small notebook from his pocket and wrote down the dates on the tombstone. His father was only forty when he died. Forty was much too young to die unless something had happened to cut him down. Had he been in an accident? Was he murdered? The local paper might answer his questions, he thought, sticking the book in his pocket.

He returned to the car and drove back to town. The *Daily Chronicle* was on a narrow side street about two blocks from the town hall. It was an old-fashioned two-story building. The year 1902 was chiseled into the dirty gray cornerstone. A blond girl was chewing gum furiously behind a high wooden counter when he walked in.

"Do you keep old copies?" Martin asked.

The girl kept on chewing. "How old?"

"March, nineteen-twenty-eight."

She thought a moment, then nodded and walked to a wall of shelves containing large leather-bound books with dates imprinted on them in gold letters and numerals. She found the one he wanted and carried it back to the counter.

Martin thanked her and began thumbing through the yellowed pages. Bits of dry paper crackled and fell away as he turned the pages to the tenth. Bold headlines across the front page caught his eye. HEATWAVE HITS SOUTHWEST. Below it another said: MINER TRAPPED IN CAVE FOUND DEAD. His eyes ran down the page. There was a picture of a pretty bob-haired woman. Beneath her smiling face was the caption: WIFE SLAYS HUSBAND IN JEALOUS RAGE. In a lower corner was a two-inch item about a judges' convention in Denver.

Martin turned the page. The obituary column was on the second page and he ran his finger down the list of names until he found Kasko. He read:

Kasko, Joseph. A lifelong resident of Vianna, Joseph Kasko, 40, was buried in Greenlawn Cemetery this morning. Kasko, who was employed by the Stacey Milling Company for the past twenty years, was struck down by an unidentified car early Monday morning. A veteran of World War I, he was a member of the Methodist Church as well as the V.F.W. Survivors include his wife, Lena, and one child, Albert, aged three.

Martin lit a cigarette with a shaking hand. His full name was Albert Kasko. He tried to remember hearing his mother calling him Albert or Al, but he could not. The name was completely alien to him. He studied the notice again. His father had been a millhand. Why would anyone want to kill the son of a millhand? A feeling of frustration came over him. The whole idea was beginning to look like a waste of time.

But was it? Thanks to an old man's memory and some of his own recollections he had at least found out who he was. That was something. But he was now Martin Powers and he had no intention of becoming Albert Kasko again. What purpose would it serve? Albert Kasko was dead to those who mattered most. No, he was wrong. There was one person who cared enough about Albert Kasko to make sure he was really dead. Pock-Marks. And possibly the redhead.

He turned the page to March eighth, and he found what he wanted on page one:

MILLHAND KILLED BY
HIT-AND-RUN DRIVER

Joseph Kasko, forty-year-old millhand, was run down and killed early this morning by a hit-and-run driver as he crossed Highway 52, on the outskirts of town. The dead man, who lived at 2301 Assembly Street with his wife and son, was on his way to work when he was struck down. It was around 7:20 when the incident occurred, and few people were on the street. Eye-witnesses said a heavy morning fog obscured their vision so that they could not give an accurate description of the car or its occupants. One man, Julius Guthman, who lived near the slain man on Assembly Street, said he was about one hundred feet away when Kasko was hit. Questioned closely by the police, Guthman thought that the car was a blue 1928 Buick. The only other clues at the scene were some bits of headlight glass, indicating that the hit-and-run car had suffered some damage. Chief of Police Horace Quimby is conducting a thorough investigation and promises an early arrest in the case . . .

Martin began thumbing through all the issues following the eighth, but except for an occasional item about the case still being unsolved, there was very little. He shook his head. Why should the cops break their backs because of a millhand, he thought bitterly. Who was Joseph Kasko? What had he ever done for anybody except bring a kid into the world and sweat bullets for a living?

Martin closed the book, thanked the girl again for her help and went outside. There was a restaurant a few doors from the newspaper building, and he had a late lunch. Finishing his meal, he dawdled over his coffee. He had learned much since he arrived in Vianna. He knew his real name and where he was born and how his father had died. Everything but why Pock-Marks was trying to kill him. He wondered if it had anything to do with his father's death. He tried to find a connection, but if there was any, it eluded him.

He thought about his mother. How had she died? Had she met with an accident like his father? It might be a good idea to find out.

He paid his check and went back to the newspaper office. Remembering the date of his mother's death, he secured the book and read the obituary notice. It stated briefly that Mrs. Kasko, aged thirty-eight, had passed away after a long illness. It did not say what she had died of or anything about a son named Albert. There were no relatives listed, so Martin assumed that his parents were the last of their line.

Back in his car, Martin contemplated his next move. He still had no idea why Pock-Marks was trying to kill him. He wondered if the people on Assembly Street could help him. Probably not; thirty years was a long time. Still, you never could tell. He pulled out of the parking space and headed back towards Main Street. From an officer in a parked squad car he was told how to get to Assembly Street. He drove around the ivy-covered courthouse to Fillmore Street and then east across the railroad tracks to the street where he was born.

The clapboard house he remembered vaguely as a child was gone, and in its place was a fairly new two-story frame building. He locked the car and began asking questions. Nobody remembered the Kaskos or the Guthmans. One woman thought that the Guthmans had moved away the year before she had moved in, but she wasn't sure. Dusk was beginning to fall when he knocked on the door of a rundown bungalow near the end of the street. An old lady with snow-white hair peered out at him with bird-like eyes.

"Yes?"

Martin introduced himself. "Could you tell me how long you've lived on Assembly Street?" he asked.

The woman studied him warily. "Been over forty years," she said. "Why, you lookin' for somebody?"

"Did you know the Kasko family? They used to live down the street."

The woman's eyes opened with surprise. She opened the door wide. "Come in, come in," she said, waving a bony arm. "I'm Mrs. Julia Newdecker."

Martin walked into a clean but decaying room. The blinds were down and the light from a table lamp cast a tired glow over the yellowing curtains, the worn carpet and the ageing mohair furniture. He waited while Mrs. Newdecker sat down.

"Sit down, young man," she said in a whiny voice. "Did know the Kaskos?"

"I'm Albert Kasko," Martin said.

"But I thought—"

"Powers is my adopted name."

"Oh." The woman pondered the information for several moments and then nodded slowly. "I think I understand now," she said. She went on excitedly, "I remember your father was killed by a hit-and-run driver one mornin' as he was goin' to work. Your mother, poor thing, was heart-broken. She was always sick, you see. When she died, the authorities placed you in a Home. Apparently," she shrugged, "there were no relatives."

"Do you remember where they placed me?"

"Yes, yes, I think so." She frowned thoughtfully. "It was the Mosswood Home For Boys over in Westgrove. It's gone now, burned down." She regarded him, wonderment lighting up her tired old eyes. "Albert Kasko. Well, well, well after. After all these years, imagine!"

"How well did you know my parents?"

"Quite well. Quite well. They were good people, Albert. Very religious. Your father was a hardworking man, but he didn't make much at the mill. It was hard goin', with your Mom always sickly."

Martin held up a pack of cigarettes. "May I?" he asked. When she nodded, he asked, "How did my mother manage after Dad died?"

The old woman leaned back and closed her eyes, as if by so doing she could better recall the past. "It was a strange thing, Albert," she said, finally. "Your Mom got along fine. Like I said, she was sick and couldn't work, yet she paid her bills when they became due. It didn't make sense and some of the neighbors got to wonderin' about it. Me included." She chuckled and shook her head. "So one day I made it my business to drop in and see her just as the mailman came along. It was the first of the month and he gave her a long white envelope. She excused herself and hurried into the next room."

Martin found his pulses racing. "Could you see what was in it?" he asked.

"Not at first," said Mrs. Newdecker. "I couldn't see into the bedroom from where I sat, but there was a large mirror over the mantelpiece, and by stretching a little, I could see Lena opening the envelope and take something out."

"What was in it?"

"Money."

"Money?"

The old woman nodded, a satisfied smirk on her wrinkled face. "Somebody was mailing it to her every month," she said. "I know, because old Peterson, he's the mailman, told me."

"But why?" asked Martin. "Who would mail my mother money?"

"The man who killed your father!"

Martin stared at her stupidly. It did not seem possible that his father's killer, a man who had ruthlessly left him on the highway to die, could have had any qualms of conscience. Yet Mrs. Newdecker's theory was plausible, even possible.

He took a long drag on his cigarette and exhaled deeply. "Do you think my mother knew who was sending her the money?" he asked.

Mrs. Newdecker thought a moment before shaking her head. "No, I don't think so," she said. Suddenly, she seemed very tired. "In fact, I'm sure of it."

"Why?"

"Because after she died, I went through her things trying to find the address of a relative who could take care of you. I found the envelopes that had contained the money, all six of them. There was no return address."

"Do you remember where they were postmarked?"

"I sure do. Keystone City, Arizona."

Martin's mouth felt stiff and dry. The room had become hot and oppressive. "Did they ever catch the man who killed my father?" he asked.

"No." She rubbed her hand over her wrinkled face. "You know, it sure is strange."

"What is?"

"About a year ago, a young woman showed up around here asking questions about the Kaskos. She seemed especially interested in you, Albert. I told her about the Mosswood Home and she thanked me and left. A week later it was burned to the ground."

Martin stared at his cigarette. The redhead had traced him to his hometown. He wondered if her presence in Vianna and the gutting of the Home was a coincidence. The room was very quiet. Mrs. Newdecker sat very still, her eyes closed. Only the ticking of a clock somewhere in the old house disturbed the silence. He squashed out his cigarette in an ashtray and got to his feet. The old woman's mouth had become slack and she was snoring softly.

Martin took a ten-dollar bill from his pocket and laid it on the table next to his chair. He walked carefully to the door, closing it quietly behind him. Back in his car he lit one cigarette after another while he digested what Mrs. Newdecker had told him. The facts were there for him to consider, some of them anyway. Somebody had run down and killed his father. Item one. Item two: the hit-and-run driver was never apprehended. Item three: soon after his father's death, his mother began receiving money from an unknown source. Item four: Since neither side of his family had any relatives, the money could have come from only one person, the man who killed his father. And the most incredible part was that he lived, or had lived, in Keystone

City.

Was Pock-Marks the man who killed his father? It seemed unlikely, but even if he was, why should he want to kill him now? That part did not make sense. Was it because he was afraid that someday he would find out who was responsible for his father's death and exact a long-delayed vengeance? It was only one of many possibilities, and Martin considered a number of them without much enthusiasm or conviction. He felt certain of only one thing, that his father's death and the attempts on his life were somehow entwined.

A thought struck him that Pock-Marks could have mistaken him for someone else. Maybe he looked like somebody who had aroused Pock-Mark's ire. Only a few months before he had read where a man in San Francisco had been stabbed to death by a woman who had mistaken him for someone else. It was all so confusing that he did not know what to think.

It was dark when he finally drove to the little telegraph office he had noticed earlier. He sent a wire to Angela, promising to leave for home early in the morning. Home. It had a nice sound. Then he walked three blocks to Main Street and had a leisurely dinner at a small restaurant.

Back on the street once again, he started to walk back to his car when he noticed a short, swarthy-complexioned man standing near the corner.

The man, he saw, was watching him.

Martin froze.

It was the man with the pock-marked face.

CHAPTER EIGHT

Martin stared at the little man, too stunned to move.

Pock-Marks stared back with venomous eyes.

Martin finally pulled his eyes away. He had looked at death and the experience was terrifying. Shoving his hands in his pocket, he fought down the panic that was rising within him. There was no doubt about it, he was the same man he'd seen in the black convertible. He resisted an overwhelming impulse to run. I've got to relax and think, he warned himself. A mistake now could be fatal. A reflex action made him turn and walk slowly down the street, away from the man who was out to kill him. He walked carefully, not wishing to attract attention to himself. It was still early, only eight o'clock, and he was glad that Main Street was fairly crowded with late shoppers and theatre-goers.

Glancing in the store windows, he wondered what would happen if he went right up to Pock-Marks and asked him what it was all about. Nothing, most likely. Even if he was out to kill him, he could hardly expect the man to admit it. There was also a chance that he could be wrong, that the man in the black convertible and the man behind him were not the same. But in his heart he knew different.

He had to find a way out, and it had to be fast, for time was running out. A flock of ideas raced through his head. He could find a policeman and tell him that Pock-Marks was trying to kill him. The policeman would be skeptical, ever incredulous perhaps, but because it was his duty, he would investigate. But then what? Suppose Pock-Marks didn't even have a gun on him? And if he did, wouldn't he be clever enough to have a logical reason for carrying it? Men in Pock-Marks' profession had to be smart. No, the idea wouldn't work. He was strictly on his own.

Martin halted before a gaily decorated window. Pretending to study the display, he observed Pock-Marks from the corner of his eye. He was less than a hundred feet away now, and looking nonchalantly in a store window.

Martin turned and resumed his slow pace. He tried to consider his position rationally. He felt reasonably safe as long as he stayed on Main Street. Pock-Marks wouldn't be foolish enough to try and gun him down before hundreds of witnesses, one of who might even be an off-duty cop. No, he wouldn't make any foolish moves out here in the open. He would simply follow him and wait for him to make the wrong move.

He debated his chances of darting into a side street and losing his pursuer in the dark, but something warned him that it would be too risky; that Pock-Marks would anticipate such a move and be ready. Besides, no matter how fast you run, you can't outrun a bullet. So Martin walked along leisurely, feeling fairly safe for the moment, but keeping tensely alert and watchful.

From what little he had seen of Main Street, it consisted of five blocks of assorted stores, most of which were still open for business. Martin considered each one as he passed by, weighing them for an idea or a possible means of eluding the man who so silently stalked him. At the corner he joined several other people waiting for the light to change. That's when he noticed the five-and-dime store across the street. When the light changed, he crossed the street and entered the store by one of the Main Street entrances. He walked down one of the long aisles, studying the conglomeration of cheaply-priced merchandise. When he reached the middle of the store he turned and looked back.

Pock-Marks was nowhere in sight.

Swerving quickly on his heel, he headed for the side-street

entrance he had noticed before entering the store. It was an old trick, but if Pock-Marks was waiting on Main Street for him, there was a chance he could give him the slip.

Pushing aside the door, he stepped into the street. There was no one in sight and his spirits rose. The ruse had worked! Pock-Marks wouldn't be fooled for long, though, and there was no time to lose. He started down the street, away from Main Street. He had gone only a few steps when he caught the glow of a cigarette in an alley across the street. He stopped short, his heart sinking. He could make out a shadowy figure behind the tiny light, and he knew without seeing the face clearly that his stratagem had failed.

Reversing himself, he walked back to Main Street. Midway in the block he again stopped to look at the contents of a store window. Pock-Marks was less than fifty feet from him now, and the feeling of panic returned. Would the little gunman take a chance out here on a crowded street? The possibility alarmed him and he looked around desperately for a means of escape.

There was a squad car parked near the corner, and a wild, crazy idea came to him. It just might work. Hell, it had to work!

He walked to the car and looked in the window. A gray-haired cop with a sun-blackened face was sitting behind the wheel, smoking a cigarette. He turned and looked at Martin. "Anything I can do for you, Mister?" he asked.

Martin grinned sheepishly. "My name is Martin Powers," he said. "I'm a stranger in Vianna. About an hour ago I parked my car while I had something to eat. Now I can't find it. I've forgotten where I parked it."

"You sure it's not stolen?"

Martin shrugged. "It's seven years old, but I guess anything is possible."

The cop smiled and flipped his cigarette out the window. "Okay, hop in," he said. "We'll drive around until we find it."

Martin thanked him, opened the door and eased his long frame into the car. As the car pulled away from the curb, Martin glanced back over his shoulder.

Pock-Marks had disappeared.

Driving slowly, the cop circled the block. When they were back on Main Street, Martin probed the now-thinning crowd for any sign of his stalker, but Pock-Marks was nowhere in sight.

"Where're you from?" asked the cop.

"Keystone City," said Martin. "I'm a salesman for the Delta Cosmetics Company."

"Sounds kinda cushy."

"It's not bad."

They found the Chevy where Martin knew they would, on a narrow side street about three blocks from Main Street. The cop double-parked while Martin got out.

"Where're you staying?" asked the cop.

"The Cactus Motel," said Martin. He added wryly: "If I can find it."

The cop grinned good-naturedly. "It's at the south end of town. Follow me, I'll take you there."

Which was exactly what Martin hoped he'd say. His plan had worked perfectly. Once inside the motel room, he'd be reasonably safe.

Five minutes later he braked to a halt behind the police car in front of his cabin. He got out and walked to the police car.

"Thanks, officer," he said.

The cop put his car in gear and waved his hand. "Glad to do it," he said, driving away.

Inside the room, Martin locked and bolted the door. He did not turn on the lights as he went to the window and peeked through the drawn blinds. Traffic was still fairly heavy on the highway, but he did not see Pock-Marks or the black convertible.

When he had made certain that the windows were securely locked, he removed his jacket and hung it in the closet. He fell on the bed and laced his hands behind his head. He had been very lucky. He had outwitted Pock-Marks, but he wasn't congratulating himself. Not yet. The little killer was still out there somewhere, watching and waiting.

CHAPTER NINE

Martin's trip back to Keystone City was tedious and uneventful. He had kept a sharp lookout all the way, but at no time did he see Pock-Marks or his black convertible. The little assassin was probably waiting for a more propitious moment, he thought dourly. He realized that sooner or later they would come face to face, and the prospect wasn't heartening.

It was early in the afternoon when he swung into his driveway on Woodland Street. Angela ran out to meet him, her arms extended joyously.

"Darling, you're back safe!" she exclaimed, throwing herself into his arms.

Martin whirled her around happily before setting her down. "Why shouldn't I get home safe?" he asked jocularly.

"I kept thinking about that awful man with the pock-marked face," she confessed. "I'm glad you didn't see him."

"But I did," said Martin, taking his suitcase from the car.

Angela's eyes widened with fright. "What happened?"

Martin grinned. "I'll tell you all about it over a cup of coffee," he promised, taking her arm.

While they had their coffee, Martin told her of his duel of wits with Pock-Marks on the streets of Vianna. For some reason he didn't quite know himself, he had decided not to mention the real purpose of his trip and what he had learned about himself and his parents. Apparently satisfied that his trip was strictly a business jaunt for the Delta Cosmetic Company, Angela plied him with questions about Pock-Marks and the close call he'd had in the Colorado city.

"You certainly thought fast," she said proudly, when she had finished. "But you should have gone to the police, Marty. They would have put that horrid man in jail."

Martin lit cigarettes for both of them and shook his head. "It wouldn't have done any good," he said. "If he didn't have a gun on him I would have looked foolish. After all, I can't stop people from walking on the street."

She took a long drag on her cigarette and exhaled deeply. "What are you going to do, Marty?" she asked. "It can't go on like this, and you know it."

Martin nodded, his face sober with thought. "I've thought about it all the way back," he said. "But there isn't anything we can actually do. The police have to have a reason for anyone wanting me dead, and so far we don't have any."

Angela suddenly looked pensive, and Martin noticed the change.

"What's wrong?" he asked.

When she looked at him he could see the naked fright in her eyes. "Somebody has been calling me since you left," she said. "Whoever it is, says the most terrible things."

"A man or a woman?"

Angela frowned. "It's hard to say. Whoever it is, they're doing a good job of disguising their voice. I'm worried, Marty!"

"What did they say?"

Angela looked at her cigarette. "All kinds of things. How they're going to get you if it takes a hundred years." She raised her eyes. "Marty, I don't understand all this! Why is somebody trying to kill you?"

Martin ran his hand through his hair. "I wish I knew. If I did, maybe I could do something about it. How many times have they called?"

"Three."

It couldn't have been Pock-Marks, reasoned Martin. The little gunman was much too busy following him around the country. Besides, a long-distance call would be easily recognizable since the operator always acts as intermediary before a call is completed. Then who was it? He thought about the redhead with the horn-rimmed glasses. She might do it in hopes of frightening Angela into getting him to make a wrong move.

"Did you tell Bannerman about the calls?" he asked.

Angela shook her dark tresses. She traced a lacquered fingernail across the tablecloth and shrugged. "Besides, it probably wouldn't have done any good."

"You're . . ."

The telephone rang, its shrillness echoing through the rooms. They looked at each other, the silence heavy between them. It was ringing for the fifth time when Martin jumped to his feet and hurried to the living room and picked it up.

"Yes?" he said.

There was no answer, but Martin could hear a quick intake of breath on the other end.

"Who is this?" he asked harshly.

There was a tiny click. The line was dead.

Martin waited for several moments before replacing the receiver on its cradle. He turned and saw Angela in the doorway. Her face was pale. Neither spoke for several long seconds.

"No one answered?" she asked finally.

"No, but there was someone on the other end," he said. "I could hear him breathing." He smacked his palms together angrily. "Maybe it's somebody's idea of a joke."

Angela shook her head. "Stop kidding yourself, Marty. It's someone who knows about those attempts on your life." Her eyes widened and her hand flew to her mouth. "Maybe it was Pock-Marks!"

"I don't think so. Pock-Marks isn't the subtle type. A thirty-eight is more his style."

Martin turned his back on Angela, picked up the receiver and dialed Police Headquarters. The connection made, he asked for Sergeant Bannerman, but the switchboard operator said he was out on a case and didn't know when he would be back. Martin thanked her and hung up.

"He's out on a case," he said.

"Marty, I'm scared!"

He went to her and took her in his arms. "Don't worry," he said, stroking her hair. "We'll find an out somehow. In the meantime, don't answer the phone. No matter what."

Martin held her possessively, and for the first time in his life he knew how it felt to personally want to kill a man.

CHAPTER TEN

Sam Bannerman tossed restlessly in his sleep. Except for a suit coat, he was fully dressed, even to his shoes. A three-day stubble darkened his sweat-stained face, and there were tired lines under his eyes from seventy-two continuous hours on an unsolved case. The telephone on the night-table next to his bed rang, sending a shudder through his huge body. As it continued to ring, a nerve began twitching in his left cheek.

Bannerman raised himself slowly to his elbows and swore softly. He swung his legs to the floor and turned on the lamp. He looked at his wristwatch and yawned. It was eleven P.M.

He picked up the receiver. "Bannerman," he said gruffly, running his free hand through his rumpled hair.

"Angela. Martin came back this afternoon."

"So?"

"I've got to see you right away. It's important."

Bannerman shook his head despairingly. "I'm beat," he protested. "Can't it wait until tomorrow?"

"No."

Bannerman heaved a sigh. "Okay, I'll unlock the hall door. And remember, don't park in front of the house." There was silence for several long seconds. She had never been to his apartment and he sensed her hesitation. "Look, if you want to see me so damn bad, it'll have to be here! I'm not going anywheres until I get some sleep."

"I'll be there in fifteen minutes."

The detective stared at the receiver angrily for several moments before dropping it on its cradle. Angela Powers. He shook his head as he walked to the door and unlocked it. He went to the bathroom and began shaving. He had met all kinds of women in his job, from dowagers to prostitutes, but none of them were in Angela's league. She was an enigma, a mystery. Gazing into her dark, fathomless eyes was like staring into the pits of hell. Suddenly he felt sorry for Martin Powers. The sucker didn't have a chance. Sooner or later, Angela and that creep, Vico, would get him. It was inevitable.

He finished his toilet and returned to the bedroom. Changing into a fresh suit, he wondered about the strange affinity between the sawed-off little gunman and the tall, beauteous Angela. He was old enough to be her father, and yet he obeyed her implicitly. They had obviously worked together before, but doing what and under what circumstances? Slipping on his tie, he recalled the first time he had ever met Angela. It was three A.M., and he was leaving Mark Judson's gambling casino out on the Fairwell Highway when he found her standing alongside his car. It was a warm, humid August night, yet she looked exquisitely cool in a white linen dress and white, high-heel pumps. Dark and sultry, he immediately pegged her as the most beautiful woman he had ever seen.

Walking around her and unlocking the door, he asked, "Waiting for someone?"

"Sam Bannerman?"

Her voice was soft and low.

"That's right."

"I've got something that might interest you."

He looked her over, slow and deliberate. "That goes without saying," he said, smirking.

They got in the car and drove to an all-night diner at the edge of Keystone City. Selecting a booth in the rear, they ordered coffee.

"My name is Powers," she said after the waitress had left the coffee. "Mrs. Angela Powers." When he didn't answer, she asked, "How would you like to make one-hundred-and-seventy thousand dollars?"

He took a sip of coffee and said, "That's a nice, tidy figure, Who do I have to kill?"

"Nobody," she said, staring at him woodenly. "Someone else will handle that part of it. All you have to do is see that nothing goes wrong."

Bannerman squinted at her. "You know who I am?"

Angela Powers nodded. "Of course. You're a Detective Sergeant, attached to the Homicide Division of the Keystone City Police Department."

"And yet you've got the gall to hand me a proposition like that?"

She smiled confidently. "Why not?" she said. "Even if you don't agree to come in with me, what can you prove? You need another witness to our conversation before you can book me."

Bannerman nodded, pulled his lower lip. "And I thought all beautiful women were dumb."

She studied him for several moments. "Well, how about it?"

The detective held up his hand. "Just a moment. First, some questions. Why pick on me?"

"I did some checking, naturally," she said. "And one of the things I learned is that you're such a lousy card player that you're in hock to Mark Judson for nearly ten grand. Does that answer your question?"

Bannerman's eyes glinted dangerously. "Did Judson send you?"

She shook her head. "No. Nobody knows about this deal except you and me . . . and the man who'll do the job."

The detective put a match to his unlit cigar. "Who's the patsy?"

"My husband."

"That figures," nodded Bannerman, exhaling deeply. "And when he goes on the big trip, you inherit. That it?"

"Something like that."

"Tell me about the guy who's doing the job."

"That won't be necessary," she said. "We can call him Vico for the time being. He knows his business, I assure you."

"You're not from Keystone City," he said.

"No."

"What else do I have to know about the deal?"

She finished her coffee and leaned against the leather cushion. "It's quite simple," she said. "Vico's job is to take care of my husband. But if he should fail, which isn't likely, I'll naturally have to coax him into contacting the police. That's where you come in. With you on the inside, the cops, in this case your superiors, won't know a thing. It begins and ends with you. Period. Like it?"

Bannerman thought it over for several moments. It looked foolproof. "Sounds good," he admitted reluctantly. "But if it's an insurance deal you can count me out. Those insurance dicks never give up."

"It's not insurance."

"How much is involved altogether?"

"Approximately a half-million dollars."

Bannerman whistled. "Not bad," he said, pursing his lips. "And we split three ways?"

She nodded, watching his face. "That's it. How about it?"

"I'm in."

That was almost two months ago.

He was slipping into his coat when he heard the impatient tap of high heels in the foyer. Taking a final look in the mirror, he went into the neatly furnished living room. Angel was pacing back and forth.

"Well, what's it this time?" he asked.

Angela turned and faced him, her features tight with anger. "Martin came face-to-face with Vico," she said.

Bannerman frowned. "And Vico let him get away?"

"Vico's a fool!"

Bannerman fell tiredly into a chair. "Tell me about it."

Walking nervously back and forth, Angela told him everything that Martin had told her when he returned from Vianna a few hours before. Bannerman listened, his eyes lidded with concentration.

"What are you going to do now?" he asked when she had finished.

"I'm sending Vico back to New York," she said testily. "You and I can do the job ourselves."

He crossed his legs and smiled thinly. "No dice, baby."

She stopped pacing and glared at him. "Why not?" she demanded. "You scared or something?"

Bannerman looked around for a cigar, saw none and shrugged. "Sure, I'm scared," he admitted. "Only fools aren't scared, and Sam Bannerman is nobody's fool." He leaned forward, placing his elbows on his knees. "Oh, I've killed a couple of guys in my time, but every time I had the badge behind me, backing me up all the way. If I knock off your husband, it'll have to be without the badge, and that I don't like."

Angela's lips curled. "You like to play it safe, is that it?" she sneered.

"That's it," said Bannerman easily. "That's why I've been around as long as I have."

"Then do it!"

"Don't be silly. You couldn't get away with it."

"Why not?"

"Because a wife is always the Number One suspect when a husband is murdered," he explained patiently. "The minute they find Martin's body, they'll start digging into your past, and not for the past five or ten years, baby, but all the way from the time you were wearing diapers. They'll keep on digging, too, until they find out about that half a million dollars. What'll you tell them when they find out?"

Angela's face sobered as she listened and she sat heavily in one of the armchairs. "But we've got to do something," she said desperately. "God, I can almost taste that money!"

"Then say nothing to Vico when he contacts you," Bannerman said. "Tell him you want the job done, no matter how many times he fluffs it." He shook his head. "I haven't any confidence in that little runt, somehow. He'll spill all he knows if he's caught. I'll bet on it."

"Vico won't talk."

"What makes you so damn sure?" asked Bannerman angrily. "I've seen some pretty tough cookies fall apart when the pressure is on."

Angela smiled. "Vico won't talk," she said again.

Bannerman stared at her, unconvinced. "What was Martin doing in Vianna?" he asked.

"Company business," she lied.

Bannerman's eyes narrowed. "Do you believe him?"

"Why not?" She examined the tip of her gloved finger. Then she looked at the burly detective. "There's something else. Somebody's been calling me on the phone."

Bannerman shook his massive head. "It's always something," he said disgustedly. "What did he want?"

Angela shrugged. "I couldn't tell whether it was a man or a

woman. Whoever it is says he is going to kill Martin."

"It sounds like Vico. You're sure it isn't him?"

"I'm positive."

Bannerman frowned. "How many people are in this deal, for Crissakes?"

"Only three," she said, pouting. "What should I do?"

"Does Martin know about these calls?"

Angela nodded. "One came today while he was there," she said. "There was somebody on the other end, but they hung up without saying anything."

"What did he tell you to do?" asked Bannerman.

"He said not to answer the phone any more. To let it ring."

Bannerman nodded. "Good idea. Do like he says."

Angela rose, straightened her coat around her. "I've got to get back. He thinks I've gone to a movie. I'll get in touch the moment Vico contacts me."

Bannerman watched her leave. He slammed his fist against the armrest angrily. Someday, he promised himself.

CHAPTER ELEVEN

With two days left of his week's leave of absence, Martin decided to spend them tracking down the car that had killed his father. Because of the time element, he held out little hope of success. Angela was washing the breakfast dishes when he drove downtown to the City Hall. Parking his car in front of the ivy-covered building, he took the elevator to the third-floor room where the files and outdated city directories were kept.

The record room smelled old and musty. He found the directory for 1928 and took it to one of the scarred tables and sat down. Thumbing through the yellowed pages, he found what he was looking for under automobile repair shops. Running his finger down the page, he found that there were six shops in Keystone City thirty years ago. Most of the owners were undoubtedly out of business now, others were probably dead. But he had to start somewhere, and they seemed like his best bet.

He copied the names and addresses on a piece of paper and replaced the directory on the shelf. Back in his car, he studied the list and decided to check the nearest one first. It was only seven blocks away, on Frontier Street, and he drove there. It was a dirty, redbrick building, sandwiched between a four-story warehouse with a condemned notice tacked on the door and a rundown bungalow. Martin parked his car and walked inside. A tall, powerfully-built man in greasy overalls had his head under the hood of a late model car.

The mechanic heard Martin's footsteps and cocked his head, "Yeah, what can I do for you?" he asked.

Martin's grin was apologetic. "This may sound a little crazy, but I was wondering if you could tell me who owned this shop about thirty years ago?"

The man jerked his head from beneath the hood and blinked. "Thirty years ago!" he exclaimed. "I was only a six-year-old."

"I guess," said Martin lamely.

The man pulled a dirty rag from his hip-pocket and wiped his hands. "That's going back to 1928," he mused, shaking his head. "Joe Walz had the shop a long time before I took over, and his father, Pete, had it before him. I guess Pete Walz had it then."

"Could I speak to him?"

"Not unless you're psychic. He died ten, eleven years ago."

"How about Joe?" persisted Martin.

The man shook his head. "Joe's buried in Korea somewheres. That's how I latched onto this shop. His widow sold it to me."

"How about records?" asked Martin. "Old statements telling what was done on each job, and the date. Stuff like that."

The mechanic chuckled. "After thirty years? Brother, you're sure an optimistic guy. There was nothing like that around here when I took over."

Martin thanked him and went back to his car. He sat there a few minutes, smoking a cigarette and weighing his chances. It looked hopeless. It was a million-to-one shot that he would find the mechanic who repaired the hit-and-run driver's car of thirty years ago.

The second shop was on Roundtop Avenue, but nothing was there when Martin got there. Just an empty, weed-filled lot. He asked some questions about the man who once owned the shop and learned that he had died in 1931, and that his wife and two children had long since returned to Germany. The third, fourth and fifth stops were equally unproductive. In every instance the 1928 owners had passed on, and any job records had long since been destroyed.

Driving to the final one on Blanding Street, Martin wondered about Pock-Marks. He hadn't seen the little assassin or his black convertible since the night in Vianna when he had eluded him. But he wasn't kidding himself. He knew that Pock-Marks was around somewhere, biding his time. When conditions were to his liking he would act, and fast.

He wondered, too, about the redhaired woman who had traced his past all the way to Vianna. Like Pock-Marks, he had no doubt that she was also around somewhere. She was the one who pulled the strings, probably. He was glad that he hadn't told Angela about the redhead or what he had found out about himself in Vianna. She knew and loved him as Martin Powers. Albert Kasko was dead to the whole world except two people. And they wanted him dead, too.

The shop on Blanding Street was an oblong-shaped, corrugated building. Next to it was a small parking lot where a number of battered cars were awaiting face-lifting. Martin parked at the curb and got out. An overalled mechanic was sitting on a wooden box near the entrance, eating a sandwich. A lunchbox lay on the ground beside him. It was Lou Limmer, his pudgy benefactor on Highway 92.

Limmer looked up and grinned. "Hello, Mr. Powers," he said. "The car on the bum again?"

Martin shook his head. "No, everything's fine," he said He squatted on his haunches. "I'm trying to find out about something that happened thirty years ago, and I'm hoping you can help me."

Limmer took a bite of his sandwich and nodded. "Fire away."

"How old are you, Mr. Limmer?" Martin asked.

"Forty-seven."

"How long have you had this shop?"

Limmer swallowed, smacked his lips and frowned. "Let's see. I took over in 1935. That would make it twenty-three years."

"And who had it before you?"

"My old man."

"He wouldn't be still alive, would he?" asked Martin.

Limmer's eyes twinkled. "Nothing can kill my old man," he said. "You think he can help you?"

"There's a chance he can. Do you know if he's got his old records stashed away anywheres?"

"What kind of records?"

"Repair bills," said Martin. "How much was done on each job and the date?"

Limmer shook his head. "No, I'm sure he threw them out many years ago." He paused to take another bite of his sandwich. "But if you have a specific job in mind, I'll bet he'll remember it. He's nearly eighty, but his mind is as sharp as a tack."

"Could I speak to him?"

"Sure thing." Limmer got to his feet and pointed down the street. "See that two-story stucco?" he asked. When Martin nodded, he said, "Well, that's where the Limmer clan hangs out. Tell the old man exactly what you're looking for, and if he did the job, he'll remember it." He shook his head and chuckled. "And he'll tell you exactly how much he got for it, too."

Martin drove to the stucco house and rang the front doorbell. A short, pleasant-faced woman in her early forties, opened the door.

"Could I speak to Mr. Limmer, please?" asked Martin. "His son said it would be all right."

The woman nodded and stepped aside. Martin walked into a neatly furnished living room where an elderly white-haired man sat sprawled in a chair, reading. He looked at Martin over his glasses.

"The gentleman would like to talk with you, Grandpa," said the woman. She waved Martin to a chair and left the room.

The old man laid aside the book and waited.

Martin leaned forward. "Thirty years ago," he said, "a man was involved in an accident with his car. It was a 1928 Buick, painted blue. The accident was up north aways, in Colorado. There's a chance that he had the car fixed up that way somewhere, but I'm hoping he waited until he returned here to Keystone City. I'm also hoping that he went to your shop to have the work done."

"What year was that again?" Limmer had a surprisingly strong voice.

"1928."

The old man pursed his lips thoughtfully. "That's goin' a way back," he mused. "That was the year I opened the shop on Horry Street at the south end of town. Three years later I moved to Blanding Street, where it is now. The town was small then, and there weren't many folks who could afford a new car, much less a Buick. How badly was she damaged?"

"I'm only guessing," admitted Martin, "but I figure he had a busted headlight and a damaged fender."

Limmer swung his glasses in a little circle. "I don't remember the job," he said slowly, thinking hard. "I ain't sayin' I didn't do it, mind you, but I just don't recollect it."

Martin leaned back, disappointed. "It was a long shot anyway," he said. "It would have been a miracle if you had remembered."

Limmer frowned, picked up the book on his lap, looked at it absently and put it down. "What'd the fellow do, hit somebody?" he asked.

"My father," Martin said. "He was killed instantly while he was on his way to work. He never had a chance."

The old man squirmed in his chair. "Tough," he said. "I don't know if it'd help any, but I seem to remember that Marvin Rickles and old Judge Chandler owned Buicks around that time. Whether they were blue, I couldn't say."

"Any idea who did their work?"

"Pete Walz, but he's been gone a long time. So's his son, Joe."

Another dead end. His search seemed filled with dead ends. Martin thanked the old man and left.

Outside, he walked slowly to his car and got in. For some reason the name Chandler gnawed at him, although he didn't know why.

There was a lead there somewhere, and he couldn't put his finger on it. He knew all about Judge Amos Rutherford Chandler. Everyone in Keystone County did. The old man had been one of its illustrious citizens until his death about a year ago. He'd been a lawyer, a judge and a congressman. Everyone had loved and respected the old man. They even had his statue in Macaram Park.

Martin felt hungry and he glanced at his watch. It was nearly two o'clock. He started the car headed for Dorry's. He did not see the black convertible following him.

CHAPTER TWELVE

Dorry's was a popular eating spot in the downtown section, about a block from the office building where Martin worked. Despite the hour, it was still fairly crowded and Martin was surprised to find most of the tables occupied. He was looking around for an empty spot when somebody called his name. He turned and saw Lorna sitting alone in one of the booths.

Walking across the room, he couldn't help thinking how exceptionally chic she looked in a shawl-collared blue suit of spotted wool, and the smile she gave him made him forget his troubles for the moment.

"Aren't you dining a little late?" he asked, worming into the booth.

Lorna took a sip of coffee and nodded. "Those bi-weekly reports held me up," she said, grimacing. She put the cup down and studied him for a moment. "How did you make out?"

Before he could answer, the waitress appeared with a menu. Martin studied it and ordered a chicken salad sandwich and coffee. When the girl went away, he asked guardedly: "What do you mean?"

She smiled vaguely. "The gang at the office knows you didn't go on a business trip," she said. "Scuttlebutt has it that someone is trying to kill you. So it wasn't difficult to put two and two together."

"And that means?"

"That you're trying to find out who's behind the shenanigans." Lorna finished her coffee and pushed a cigarette from a pack alongside her plate. Martin lit it for her. Then he lit one for himself.

He shrugged. "I guess it's no secret then," he said, smiling wryly. "I drove up to Corona where I lived with my adopted parents. It was the only place I could start. A nice old guy up there who works for the railroad remembered my foster parents buying a couple of round-trip tickets to Vianna, Colorado. When they came back, I was with them. So I went up there, looked around, and found out who I really am."

Lorna moistened her lips. "And who are you, Marty?"

The waitress came with the food and went away. "My real name is Albert Lasko," he said. "My father was a millworker. He was killed in a hit-and-run accident when I was only three years old. Mother died less than six months later. There were no relatives, so the authorities put me in a Home."

He wondered why he was telling her all this when he hadn't even told Angela, but the words seemed to come from someone else. Between mouthfuls of food he told her about Pock-Marks and the close call he'd had with the little gunman in Vianna. He also brought her up-to-date on his efforts to find the Buick that killed his father.

"And that's it," he said, finishing his sandwich and pushing his plate aside. "I'm no better off than when I started."

"I don't agree," Lorna said firmly. She squashed out her cigarette. "You know who you are, and you know that this pock-marked man, whoever he is, had something to do with your father's death."

"It's only a guess, and you know it."

Lorna placed her elbows on the table. "What does Angela have to say about all this?" she asked.

"I haven't told her."

Her eyebrows arched in surprise. "Why not, for Heaven's sake?"

Martin studied his cigarette. "Poor kid, she's scared enough as it is, It would only make things worse."

"And that's the only reason?"

Martin caught the implication. "I told you once to lay off," he said brusquely. "Angela has no reason for wanting me dead."

"None that you know of, you mean?"

Martin took a long drag on his cigarette and exhaled deeply. He said nothing.

"What about the police?" persisted Lorna. "Can't they do anything?"

Martin shook his head. A thought hit him. "Somebody has been calling Angela on the phone," he said, watching her closely. "Whoever it is, it's upsetting her terribly. You wouldn't know who it is, would you?"

Lorna stared at him, her face suddenly white. "Why . . ."

"It was you, wasn't it?"

Lorna bit her lip. She dropped her eyes and nodded.

"But why, for God's sake?" asked Martin hoarsely. "What did you hope to gain?"

She shrugged. "I wanted to help, and it seemed like a good idea. I thought if I could frighten her, she would do something to give herself away."

"You think she's behind all my trouble, don't you?" he asked incredulously. His eyes were cold.

Lorna nodded, her eyes down.

Martin shook his head. "I know I should be angry with you, but I'm not." He hesitated, and said, "I'm sorry you feel that way, Lorna."

Lorna's lips trembled. She was close to tears. "I couldn't help it, Marty," she said. "Your life was in danger, and I wanted to do something, anything, to help you. It won't happen again."

She wrinkled her nose at him and tried to smile. "I'd better get out of here before I'm a mess," she said. She reached for her bag and gloves and eased out of the booth.

Martin helped her on with her coat. She turned and their eyes met.

"You're a good guy, Marty," she said, her voice an emotional whisper. "If you ever need a crutch, don't forget Lorna. Promise?"

Martin nodded, embarrassed by the sincerity in her eyes "I promise," he said gently.

Martin felt strangely uneasy after Lorna left. He couldn't help thinking what a good sport she'd been after the shabby way he had treated her. The restaurant was emptying out, and the sounds of voices and dishware were muted now. He ordered more coffee because he wanted more time to think. Think of what? Think of the mess he had made of Lorna Craig's life or the knife or bullet he would get some dark night when he least expected it?

The waitress brought the coffee and he sipped it absently. The name Chandler eased back into his chain of thoughts and he wondered why. He had never even spoken to the old man, although he remembered seeing him once during one of the local Fourth of July parades. He seemed like a nice old man, tall, white-haired, dignified. His reputation had been impeccable. You didn't get your statue in Macaram Park unless it was.

He finished his coffee and walked slowly back to his car. It was minutes after three, and he didn't want to go home just yet. The sun was warm on his back as he thought about the two names old man Limmer had given him. Maybe there would be something about them in the newspaper morgue that would give him a lead. He got in his car and drove to the Gazette Building on Market Street.

Leaving his car in the parking lot behind the building, he went inside and was directed to a room on the second floor. The Librarian, a Mrs. Hesta Beems, made him sign two request slips before giving him two large manila envelopes. He sat at a large cigarette-scarred table and opened the file on Judge Amos R. Chandler. There were hundreds of clippings, beginning with his sensational debut as a fullback on the local high school football team and ending with his death in Miami the previous year at seventy-eight. It was weighty and voluminous, and Martin shook his head as he pored over the countless clippings.

Glancing through them, he could find nothing which would link the dead lawmaker to his own predicament. As far as he could see, Amos Rutherford Chandler had led a most exemplary life. If he could believe all the nice things said about the man, he certainly would not have been the type to leave a broken body lying in the road to die.

Martin pushed the clippings back into the envelope and tackled the one on Marvin Rickles. While there weren't nearly as many clippings as the judge's, Rickles had been a well-known and respected figure. Owner of Keystone City's first department store, he had been one of the leading philanthropists in the Southwest for many years. He had passed away two years before Judge Chandler, and there was nothing among his clippings that would connect him with an obscure millworker named Joseph Kasko thirty years before.

Martin lit a cigarette and stared at the envelopes. He had drawn a blank. But the feeling that he was close to the answer still persisted, and he could not understand why. He tried to remember everything about his past, hoping to find a connection, but he could not.

He returned the envelopes to the librarian, thanked her, and left. Night had fallen, bringing with it a cool breeze from the valley. He walked to his car behind the building, his thoughts filled with frustration. The lot was almost empty now, most of the *Gazette's* employees having long since gone home.

Martin was unlocking his car when he heard a stealthy footstep behind him. Alarmed, he whirled, but too late. Something hard was pushed against his back.

"Okay, Buddy, raise 'em up, nice and easy."

The voice was low and tinged with an Italian accent.

Martin's breath quickened as he slowly raised his hands. The man behind him frisked him quickly and expertly.

"Okay, Buddy, you can turn around now. But no tricks."

Martin turned, his body sick with fear. It was dark, but he didn't need a floodlight to see that the man was Pock-Marks.

CHAPTER THIRTEEN

Pock-Marks grinned up at him. It was an evil grin, a grin of anticipation. He stood just far enough away to discourage any attempt to jump him.

"Get in," Pock-Marks said, waving the gun.

Martin wet his lips. His stomach was churning, and he tried not to let his fear show. "You've got the wrong guy," he said evenly.

Pock-Marks shook his head. "I don't think so."

"You must have."

"You're Martin Powers?"

Martin nodded. His throat felt tight and dry.

"And you live at Two-eleven Woodland Street?"

Again Martin nodded, reluctantly.

Pock-Marks grinned, shrugged his scrawny shoulders. "So?" he said. "I make no mistakes, Buddy. I never make a mistake."

Martin studied the little gunman. Close up, he looked weak, almost puny. But his gun made him as big as Carnera, and he knew it.

"Why?" asked Martin.

Pock-Marks squinted at him, his beady eyes alert. "Why what?"

"Why are you going to kill me?"

Pock-Marks shrugged. "What's the difference?" he asked. "Either way you are dead. The reason don't matter."

"It does to me."

The little gunman chuckled. "I see your point, Buddy. But we're wasting time. Get in, and do it nice and easy like. You understand?"

Martin lowered his hands and eased into the car until he was behind the wheel. He kept his hands in sight where Pock-Marks could see them. With a gun only inches from his head, he wasn't taking any chances.

Pock-Marks waited until Martin was settled before slipping into the back seat and closing the door. He caught the frustrated look on Martin's face and grinned.

"Thought I'd sit up front with you, eh?" he chuckled. "This way is much safer." He paused, looked around the darkened parking lot carefully. "Okay, start it up, Buddy. Remember, the first wrong move and you begin making like a dead man."

Martin believed him. The little gunman was an old pro at this business. He switched on the ignition and started the car.

"Now back up and drive down Market Street," said Pock-Marks.

Martin groaned inwardly. Market Street was a dark, residential street that ran parallel with Main Street. He couldn't try anything there. He put the car in gear and made a right turn into Market Street.

The gunman was obviously taking him south into open country. Out where the land was flat and dry and covered with mesquite and cactus and sagebrush. He could lay out there for days, even months, without being found. Except by the buzzards. The prospect was frightening, and Martin could feel a wave of desperation sweeping over him. He would have to do something before they got to this barren, desolate land.

Pock-Marks' chuckle startled him.

"I know what's goin' through your mind," he said. "You're thinkin', how can I jump this guy and take that gun away from him. Ain't that right, Buddy?"

Martin said nothing.

"Sure, that's right, and I don't blame you," Pock-Marks went on. "If I was in your shoes, I'd be doin' the same thing. Only it's no use. I've been doin' this a long time, and I don't make mistakes."

A red light loomed ahead and Martin's pulse quickened with hope.

"You made a couple," he said.

"You mean those other two times?" Pock-Marks shook his head. "Those weren't my ideas. This way is my idea, Buddy. You like it?"

"Who's paying you to do this?"

"Who says anybody's payin' me?"

"Nuts!"

Pock-Marks chuckled again. "Maybe you're right, Buddy. Maybe somebody is payin' me." He pressed the gun against Martin's neck. "In case you don't know it, Buddy, you just passed a red light." His voice was as cold as death. "Don't try it again, I'm warnin' you!"

It was the only red light on Market Street, and Martin could feel his chances slipping away with each passing second. He thought about ramming into another car, or hitting a telephone pole, but he discarded the ideas. Pock-Marks would kill him anyway.

The houses were becoming fewer now, and spaced further apart. In a few minutes they would be in open country.

"What's your name?" asked Martin.

"Why?"

Martin shrugged. "Since you're obviously going to kill me, I thought I'd tell St. Peter who's responsible."

Pock-Marks chuckled. "You're a funnyman," he said. "Why not? You can call me Vico."

"Vico what?"

"Just Vico, Buddy. Whatcha want, my life story?"

Martin kept his eyes on the road. They were passing fewer cars now, and a mantle of silence seemed to have settled over the land. What a way to die, he thought bitterly. Fifteen months in Korea, eight of them in the thick of it without a scratch. Inchon. Pork Chop Hill. Knocked off by a scrawny little punk he could break in two if he didn't have that gun. But he had a gun, and that was the difference between living and dying.

He thought of Angela and a knot gathered in his stomach. They had been married less than four months, and for the first time in his life he had really had something. He wondered what she would do now. Go back to some form of modeling, most likely. He wished, in his passing, that he could have left her something more than just heartaches, but that was the way the ball bounced sometimes. He wondered, too, about Lorna. She'd miss him, the look in her eyes this afternoon told him that. He knew he was getting maudlin, but he didn't care. The dead can't cry.

Vico's guttural voice snapped him back to reality. "Still thinkin', eh?" he said. "Don't blame you none. Helps to pass the time."

"How much am I worth to you dead?" asked Martin.

"Who says you're worth anything?"

"Then you're doing it because it gives you a kick," said Martin sarcastically. He didn't know why, but something told him to keep the little gunman talking. Maybe, somehow, he'll drop his guard just long enough . . .

Vico laughed. "Sure, I'm gettin' paid. Gettin' paid real good, too. Lotsa dough." He poked the gun in Martin's neck. "But I getta big kick outta it, too. Makes me kinda feel big. You know what I mean, Buddy?"

"No."

Vico laughed again.

The last house had disappeared now, and there was nothing ahead but flat, barren land. Here and there a gas station interrupted the monotony, but they were dark and silent, like the land. Just like he would be in a little while.

"There's a dirt road a short ways ahead," Vico said. "It's on the left. Turn into it."

"Suppose I refuse?"

"It don't make any difference," said Vico. "I can put a slug in you out here and dump you."

It was getting colder now. Martin could feel the cold air seeping into the car even though the windows were up. The side road loomed in his headlights, and he turned left into a narrow dirt road. He gripped the steering wheel hard. It wouldn't be long now.

They had only gone a short way when Vico nudged him with the gun.

"Okay, Buddy. This is far enough."

Martin brought the car to a slow stop and switched off the ignition. He sat motionless while Vico eased himself out of the car.

"Okay, come on out. And take it easy."

Martin worked himself from under the wheel until he stood facing the little gunman. He judged the distance between them as about five, six feet. Still too far to take a chance.

"All right, start walkin'," ordered Vico.

Martin didn't move. "Can't we make a deal?" he asked.

Vico grinned. "You're wastin' your breath, Buddy."

"Look, if somebody is paying you, I'll double it!" Martin clenched his fists desperately.

Vico shook his head. He was enjoying himself. "Somebody's payin' me, all right," he said. "But a lot more than you got."

"How do you know? I've got lots of money in the bank."

Vico laughed. "I know exactly what you've got in the bank, Buddy. I know the amount right down to every last stinkin' penny!"

Martin shook his head. The little gunman didn't make sense. How could he possibly know such things? He lifted himself slowly on the balls of his feet. Now, he thought. It was now or never. He started to turn away. Then, with a lightning-like movement, he flung himself down and sideways at the little gunman, grabbing his legs and reaching for his gun hand in the same motion. He heard Vico grunt with surprise as a bullet whined harmlessly over his head.

They threshed around on the ground violently, Martin holding Vico's gun hand with desperate tenacity. Vico grunted and squirmed and tried to wriggle free as they rolled over and over on the sandy ground. Martin was frantic now as he tried to work his left hand closer to the gun without losing his precious grip on Vico's arm. The little gunman was puny looking, but he had the strength of two men as they kicked, bit and gouged each other for an advantage.

Martin worked his right hand free and slugged Vico in the face. It was a hard blow, but it landed a little too high to be effective. Still, he knew that he had hurt Vico. He started to swing again, but Vico's knee came up with lightning speed and caught him in the stomach. He gasped with pain. He had to get that gun. Without it he was a dead man.

Vico writhed like an eel as Martin slowly eased his left hand up towards the gun. But this time the little gunman's arm slipped from his grasp, and Martin cried out in alarm.

Vico chuckled insanely as he rolled away and came up facing Martin, his gun poised. Martin scrambled after him, but even as he started to dive towards the little gunman, he knew it was going to be too late. A hot flash exploded in his face and he could feel a numbing shock in his left shoulder. But his momentum carried him into the half-crouched Vico, sending him sprawling.

Martin climbed swiftly to one knee as another shot rang out. He swayed dizzily to his feet. There was no longer any pain, no sense of feeling. He staggered away from the little gunman and fell headlong over a mesquite bush. For a long, agonizing moment he saw everything with unbelievable clarity. The stars shone with a brilliance he never imagined, and the sounds seemed to multiply until they hurt his ears with their roaring. Then he could feel himself falling, falling, into an abysmal blackness from which he was sure there would be no return.

CHAPTER FOURTEEN

Martin opened his eyes and stared into a well of blackness. He could see nothing and for the moment, he could feel nothing. His body was numb with cold, and he lay there for a long time unable to comprehend where he was or what had happened. Then, as his mind slowly cleared, the pain came with it. A small rock lay near his face and he reached out and touched it with frost-nipped fingers.

It did not seem possible, but he was alive!

He raised his head slowly and looked up at the sky with incredulous eyes. Despite the gnawing pain in his shoulder, he twisted his body and looked around. His car was gone and so was his tormentor, Vico. He turned over on his back and touched his injured shoulder with his right hand. It came away sticky with blood.

In the distance he could hear the occasional whine of a car on the highway. He remembered now that it wasn't far away, that Vico had made him stop soon after he had turned into the narrow dirt road. The cold was more biting now, and he realized that he had to move about to keep from freezing. With a grimace of pain he pulled himself, first to one knee and then the other, and finally, slowly, carefully, to his feet. His head swam, and he swayed uncertainly for several moments. When he was sure of his footing, he looked around until he found the dirt road, and taking a deep breath, staggered forward.

Once or twice his knees began to wobble beneath him, and he paused until the spell of weakness went away. He stopped, occasionally, to get his bearings. He had to stay on the road; to wander off it in his condition would be fatal. Once he stepped into a rut and fell headlong, and it seemed an eternity before he could regain his feet.

If I can only make it to the highway, he thought. Somebody will come along and find me. He slipped to one knee and a wave of nausea came over him. He almost blacked out, but he fought it off until his mind cleared.

A car went by, its headlights probing the darkness like avenging eyes. His mind was dazed with shock and cold, and he knew that he was on the brink of passing out. But he continued to stagger forward, his jaw set determinedly.

He had no idea how long it took him to reach the highway, but the first twinges of dawn were showing when he reached it. His strength finally gone, he fell to his knees and then slid forward slowly on his stomach. He knew he was laying in the road; that a passing car might not see him in time. But he was too cold and tired to care. Suddenly, nothing seemed important anymore.

From somewhere in the distance he heard a car come to a screeching halt. Then a couple of doors slammed and he could hear footsteps hurrying towards him. There were excited voices, from somewhere a siren, and then nothing.

When Martin came to, he was in a bed in a spotlessly clean room. A sharp-featured woman in a nurse's uniform was taking his pulse. When his eyes opened, she looked up at him and smiled.

"So you've come around," she said pleasantly. "How you feel?"

There was no pain, no headache even. "I feel okay," Martin said. "Where am I?"

"You're in the City Hospital."

"How long have I been here?"

"Two men brought you in early yesterday morning," the nurse said. "They found you out on the Fairwell Highway."

The door opened and a tall, dignified looking man in white jacket walked in. "I'm Doctor Prentis," he said. "How's it going?"

"Pretty good," Martin said.

Dr. Prentis adjusted his glasses and studied the chart at the foot of the bed. "I guess you know you're a lucky fellow," he said.

"I know." Martin looked from one to the other. "Does my wife know I'm here?"

"She was here all day yesterday," said Dr. Prentis. "So were the police. If you feel up to it, one of them is waiting outside now."

Martin nodded. Dr. Prentis signaled to the nurse with his eyes and the two of them left the room. Martin wasn't surprised when Sergeant Bannerman walked in a few moments later.

The burly detective pushed a chair close to the bed and sat down. He looked naked without his cigar. "I see that you and the pock-marked guy finally met," he said.

Martin's grin was weak. "That we did, Sergeant."

"Tell me about it."

Martin felt his forehead and was surprised to feel bandages. "How many times did he get me?" he asked.

"Twice. In the left shoulder and head. But he was a lousy shot, both wounds aren't serious."

Martin closed his eyes, and it was several moments before he opened them and said, "He surprised me as I was getting into my car . . ."

"Where?"

"The parking lot behind the Gazette Building." When Bannerman didn't say anything, he went on: "He made me drive south, out on the Fairwell Highway. I looked for a chance to jump him, but he was a smart little devil. Finally, he made me turn into this dirt road. A few minutes after we got out of the car, I jumped him. I tried to get his gun, but he was as slippery as an eel. His first shot got me in the shoulder. The next one knocked me flat." He paused and shook his head in wonderment. "I thought sure I was a goner."

Bannerman took a notebook from his pocket. "Describe him," he said.

"He's short, about five-feet-five, and scrawny looking," Martin said. "Dark complexioned. Talked with an Italian accent. His name is Vico."

The detective looked up from his notes in surprise. "He told you his name?"

"Why not?" asked Martin. "As far as he was concerned, it was a one-way ride. What did he have to lose?"

"Did he say anything else that would help us get a line on him?"

"I don't think so. It's still a little hazy. But he did say he was getting paid plenty for the job."

Bannerman scowled. "Anything else?"

"No." Martin remembered his car and he asked about it.

"We found it on Market Street, about a block from the Gazette parking lot. I had it towed to the police garage where the lab boys went over it for prints. They found nothing. Your wife has it now."

The door opened and Angela walked in. Her eyes brimming with tears, she hurried to the bed and fell across Martin with a sob. They kissed and Martin could taste tears. After several moments, she straightened and took his hand and pressed it to her cheek fervently.

"Thank God, Martin," she said brokenly. "Thank God you're safe!"

Martin smiled, drinking in her presence gratefully. "Everything is going to be all right now, honey," he said. "Sergeant Bannerman knows who we're looking for now."

Angela wiped her eyes with a handkerchief and looked at the detective with questioning eyes.

Bannerman cleared his throat. "Your husband says the gunman told him his name was Vico," he said. "We'll put out an all-points bulletin on him right away. If he's got a record, we'll find him." He paused to look at his notes. "By the way, Mrs. Powers, do you know anyone named Vico?"

Angela shook her head "I never heard the name before."

The detective recited the description Martin had given him. "Does it ring a bell?" he asked.

"No."

Bannerman frowned, closed the notebook and put it in his pocket. "He sounds like a cheap gunsel to me," he said bitingly.

When nobody said anything, Bannerman got to his feet and pushed back the chair. "I'll be going," he said. "If you should recall anything else, Doctor Prentis will contact me at once."

After the detective left, Angela kissed Martin again and fondled his face. "I thought I'd go out of my mind when you didn't come home the other night," she said. "I called Bannerman around three o'clock in the morning. He told me to wait a few more hours, and if you didn't show up by then, he'd spread the alarm. The hospital called me at six. Sam was here when I got here."

Martin squeezed her hand. "I'm glad it's over," he said. "Vico won't get far."

"I hope not," she said, shuddering. "It must have been awful for you."

They were talking about thirty minutes when Angela leaned down and kissed him. "I'll go now, so you can rest," she said. "I'll be back tonight."

She was putting on her gloves when the door opened and Lorna Craig walked in. The two women stared at each other for several moments, neither speaking. He could feel the tension building up and it made him uneasy. He hoped that Angela would not make a scene.

"Honey, this is Lorna Craig, the girl I told you about," Martin said.

"I know," Angela said frostily. "See you later, Marty."

Lorna's face was white as Angela Powers walked out. When the door closed quietly behind her, she turned and looked at Martin. She was near tears.

"You're going to be all right," she said. She sat on the edge of the bed and took his hand. "What happened, Marty?"

Martin told her everything, from the moment Vico surprised him in the parking lot until he lost consciousness on the highway. Lorna listened avidly.

"The police are going to pick up this . . . Vico?" she asked when he had finished.

"Yes. Bannerman's putting out the alarm right now."

Her eyes still misty, Lorna said, "I heard about it this morning on the eight o'clock news. I came as fast as I could."

"I'm glad," Martin said.

"Are you, Marty?"

"Of course!"

She rose, walked to the window and looked out. Her back was to Martin as he studied her. Lorna was a beautiful woman. And kind.

"What's the matter, Lorna?" he asked.

She turned and faced him, her eyes pleading. "Run, Marty, run!" she cried, waving her arms. "Run so fast they won't catch up with you!"

"I won't have to run," he said impatiently. "They'll catch Vico."

She shook her head in despair. "But that won't be enough, and you know it. There's more than one of them. There's got to be."

Her words startled him. She was right! He stirred uneasily. Putting Vico behind bars would not end his nightmare. There were others, like she said. Vico had admitted as much before he shot him.

"I can't run, Lorna," he said, suddenly tired. "But you're right. Whoever is behind Vico won't stop now. If Vico can't do the job, he'll get someone who can."

Dr. Prentis came in. He looked from Martin to Lorna and smiled. "I'm sorry, but Mr. Powers should rest now," he said.

Lorna sighed, patted Martin's hand and left.

"How long will I be cooped up here, Doc?" asked Martin.

"Three or four days should do it," said Dr. Prentis. "Neither wound is serious. You suffered more from shock and loss of blood."

Dr. Prentis gave him a sleeping pill and left. The room was warm and quiet. Martin closed his eyes and a face appeared from the dark recesses of his mind. It was a swarthy face. An evil face. It was the face of the man who tried to kill him, and Martin's sleep was troubled.

CHAPTER FIFTEEN

Martin spent four days in the hospital. The oblong-shaped scar on his forehead where the bullet had creased him, resembled a table-furrow left by a forgotten cigarette. His shoulder ached somewhat and his left arm was a little stiff, but otherwise he felt wonderful. He didn't even have to have his arm in a sling. Walking with Angela towards their car, he knew he had been miraculously lucky, but he also knew it couldn't last. The percentages were heavily against him now.

The weather had turned cold and the wind whipped against the car in angry bursts as they drove home. The car was like an ice-box and he was glad that Angela had brought along his overcoat. He watched her finely molded face as she tooled the car expertly through the early morning traffic. Hair drawn back in a pony tail and wearing a black wool dress and a high-neck cardigan, she looked much younger than her twenty-nine years. She was so ecstatically happy about his coming home that it gave him a warm, pleasant glow.

They were turning into Woodland Street when he thought of Lorna. He had not seen her since that uncomfortable encounter with Angela. It wasn't that she did not want to see him, he was sure of that. It was because she was wise enough to avoid a scene.

Angela swung into the driveway and into the open garage. She switched off the ignition and turned to face him. "Surprised?" she asked, her eyes crinkling.

"When did Mr. Grayson remove the furniture?"

"Yesterday afternoon," she said, sliding out of the car. "Come on, I'll make some fresh coffee."

They were sitting in the breakfast nook when Angela's mood suddenly changed. "It can't go on like this, Marty," she said.

Martin didn't answer right away. He stared out the window at the rust-colored grass, the eucalyptus tree that was shedding its pods.

"I know," he said finally.

"We could go away. Nobody would find us."

"Vico would find me." Martin shook his head wearily. "Vico has a pipeline into my mind. He knows exactly what I'm going to do and when I'm going to do it." He sipped his coffee and put the cup down. "Take that time I went to Stonehaven. Vico had my routine down so pat that knew when to fix the car. And that night I got you the aspirins. He was waiting for me then, too. He was also Johnny-on-the-spot on the trip to Vianna and when I came out of the Gazette Building last week." He shook his head.

"It can't go on like this," Angela said again.

A plane droned overhead on its way to Claybank Airport. Outside, a white-and-green city bus went by with an asthmatic roar.

"I know," he said. "I've got to do something."

"But what?"

"I've been asking myself that same question over and over for the past four days," he said. He looked straight ahead, beyond her. "I get all kinds of answers, but only one that makes any sense. Find Vico."

She chewed her underlip anxiously. "What can you do that the cops can't?" she asked.

"I don't know. It's only a hunch, but I've a feeling that Vico and I are going to meet again."

Angela clasped her arms with both hands and shook her head. She was close to tears. "You're a fool, Martin Powers," she said. "Vico will kill you next time."

"Maybe, but that's the way it'll be."

Angela got to her feet and took their cups to the sink, her spike-heels clicking on the vinyl floor. Her back to him, she said stiffly: "If you go through with it, Marty, I'll leave you, so help me!"

Martin turned and stared at her. "You don't mean that."

"I do, I do, I do!" she cried, pounding her hands against the sink in a frenzy of emotion.

He went to her quickly and put his arms around her. Her body was rigid. "You don't understand," he said gently. "This isn't only something for the police. It's gone too far for that. It's become a personal matter between Vico and me, and I've got to find him and bring him in. Dead or alive."

She turned and buried her face in his chest. "It's no good, Marty," she sobbed. "It's no good."

He whispered in her ear. "Don't worry, honey. Chances are I'll never come even close to finding him. But I've got to try. I've got to!"

"But Vico is clever," she mumbled. "You said so yourself."

"Yes, he's clever. But he's already failed three times."

He tilted her head back and kissed her lightly on her tear-streaked face. "And I've got a feeling that his luck has run out."

Gradually, he was able to convince her, and in the end she responded by laughing and crying and kissing him all at the same time. That's what I like about her, he thought, stroking her hair. The way she can change from one mood to another. It was like shutting a faucet off and on. But he wouldn't want her any different for all the money in the world. She was his, for now and always, and he promised himself that nothing, not even Vico, was going to interfere with this part of his dream.

Martin hung around the house for two days. He looked at TV, and listened to the police calls on the radio, but there was nothing new on Vico. They were looking everywhere, but the little gunman had vanished. On the afternoon of the second day, Martin drove downtown and talked his boss into giving him an indefinite leave of absence. He did not want a time clock hanging over his head when he started looking for Vico.

He had coffee with Lorna in a little shop around the corner from the office, but it was a strange and different Lorna from the one he had known. He could not put his finger on it exactly, but she seemed more subdued.

Not that he blamed her. She had nothing to gain by worrying about him. He was happily married, and so she was out of his life forever. But her aloofness made him a little sad. He didn't know why, but he had hoped to keep things the way they were before he had married Angela. It was ridiculous, of course. He had rejected her for another woman.

He had made a choice and he must abide by it. But it did not lessen the hurt.

Bannerman dropped in Friday night to report that he had turned the city inside out for Vico without any luck. The burly detective hesitated at the door to warn him to be extra careful.

"It wouldn't surprise me if that little punk came to the house," he said. He turned to Angela. "Take good care of him, Mrs. Powers."

Angela smiled. "I will, Sergeant."

By Saturday afternoon, Martin was getting restless. He had to find Vico, but where could he start? An idea had come to him during the night, and he was anxious for six o'clock to come when Angela would leave for an appointment at the beauty parlor. It wasn't much of a plan, but it was better than sitting on his hands.

After dinner, he helped Angela with the dishes. When they were dried and put way, Angela hurriedly changed into a wool beige suit. Standing in the doorway, Martin watched her dress.

"I'll have to hurry," she said, glancing at her watch. "I had a six-thirty appointment and it's almost that now. Mrs. Bixby will have a fit if I'm late."

"Want me to drive you?"

"That won't be necessary," she said, shrugging into her coat. "I don't want you outside the house, especially at night."

Martin grinned. "If anybody knocks, I'll crawl under the bed."

Angela gave him a peck on the cheek. "I'm serious, Marty," she said. "Promise you'll be careful?"

Martin nodded, patted her backside affectionately.

After she had left, Martin picked up the telephone directory and turned to the yellow pages. Turning to the tourist courts, he saw that there were approximately sixteen outside the city limits. Vico wouldn't be crazy enough to stay at a local hotel, but a tourist court, especially if it was some distance outside the city, might appeal to him.

He was about to dial the first number when he thought: What did I actually know about Vico? It might not even be his name, or if it was, it was possible that he had registered under another name. Names meant little to a killer. The way it looked, he would have to depend on someone recognizing Vico by his description. Not many people were as horribly pock-marked as the little gunman.

Suddenly, the phone rang, startling him. He picked up receiver.

"Martin Powers?" asked a muffled voice.

"Yes. Who is this?"

"My name doesn't matter." There was a short pause, then, "Would you like to know where Vico is?"

Martin's hands were damp. "Of course," he said. Judging by its timbre, the voice could be either male or female.

"Then listen carefully, I'll only tell you this once. There is a small, orange-colored bungalow exactly one mile south of the La Fiesta Motel. You'll find him there."

The voice still baffled him. He had to keep his anonymous caller on the phone. "Why don't you notify the police . . . ?"

The line clicked dead.

Martin held the receiver in his hand for several thoughtful moments before replacing it on its cradle. Was it a trap? The voice hadn't been Vico's, he was sure of that. Then whose was it? Could it have been the redhead who knew about his past? The voice could have been a woman's.

He picked up the receiver and dialed police headquarters. When the connection was made, he asked for Sergeant Bannerman. The operator told him that Bannerman was out on a case and she didn't know when he'd be back. Martin thanked her and hung up.

Martin wandered through the rooms aimlessly. He was trying to make up his mind about seeking out Vico. He tried to convince himself that his caller was someone who had spotted Vico going in or out of the bungalow. Analyzing the call from every angle, he doubted that it had come from anyone connected with the little hoodlum. Certainly, they wouldn't be foolish enough to tell him where Vico was. It did not make sense. Unless there was a reason he did not know . . .

He checked his watch. It was seven o'clock. Making up his mind, he secured a double-edged paring knife from the kitchen and put it in his pocket. It wouldn't be much good against Vico's gun, but at least it was something. Besides, he had learned to use a knife pretty well in Korea.

He got in his car and headed south, on Highway 61. The La Fiesta Motel was an elaborate horseshoe-shaped affair about five miles from town. It was one of the newer ones that had been built during the recent boom, and he had no trouble finding it. He drove past it until he came to the orange-colored bungalow. It was about two hundred feet off the highway, and Martin studied it closely as he drove by. It was dark and looked deserted. He found a dirt road a few hundred yards further down the highway, turned into it and doused his lights.

Before starting back through the woods, he took a pencil flashlight from the glove compartment. The air was raw and he pulled his coat collar around his throat. There was a full moon overhead and he had no trouble finding his way. The woods were empty of sound and the feeling of danger which had possessed him when he left home, had seemingly evaporated in the crisp night air. He was taking a foolish chance, and he realized that Vico might accomplish tonight what he had failed to do on three previous occasions. But he felt strangely sure of himself, somehow. Perhaps it was because, for the first time since it all started, he was doing the stalking instead of being stalked. The hunted had become the hunter.

The bungalow was still dark as he emerged from the woods. He hesitated a moment, then cut sharply to his left, behind the house. That's when he saw the black convertible, hidden in a clump of cottonwoods. He advanced slowly, warily, towards the back door and tried the knob. It was locked. So were the two rear windows.

Martin paused. There was something fishy about the whole thing, and for a fleeting moment he felt like returning to town. Sam

Bannerman and his men were paid to handle situations like these, so why should he stick his neck out? As he started to walk away, he noticed one of the side windows.

It was open a few inches from the bottom.

There was a cold feeling at the base of his neck as he lifted the window noiselessly and climbed across the sill. Inside, the darkness and the quiet were terrifying, and he crouched expectantly. Nothing happened. He took the pencil flashlight from his pocket and played it around the room, extending his hand away from his body in case somebody took a shot at him. He was in a bedroom. The furniture was cheap and despite the rumpled bed, there was a musty, unlived-in air about it.

Without making a sound he took off his coat, folded it neatly and placed in on the floor beside him. He then took the paring knife from his pocket and tiptoed quietly to the door. He found himself in a narrow hall, and his flash ferreted out three more doors. The first was a small toilet, the second a kitchen. He walked stealthily to the third door, and flattening himself against the wall, peered cautiously inside the room. It was a fairly large living room, with a couch, two faded armchairs, a couple of end tables and a threadbare rug.

And a man's body.

Martin stiffened as his light fell on the sprawled figure of a man. He waited several moments, then throwing caution aside, he eased into the room until he stood over the body.

There was a bone-handled knife sticking out of the man's chest.

It was Vico, and he was dead.

Martin let out his breath slowly, and with it went the hate that he'd had for this man. He had seen death in many forms, but until now it had always been an impersonal thing. Still, he felt no sense of loss for the little hoodlum. Vico had died as he had lived, by the sword.

He dropped to one knee and felt the dead man's hand. It was still warm. Vico had died recently, perhaps in the last half-hour or so. Martin flicked off his flashlight, and when his eyes had become accustomed to the darkness, his eyes probed the room searchingly. The silence hung like a shroud and he began to feel uneasy. His brain kept warning him that it was a trap: to get out of there immediately. He intended to, but first his probing fingers went swiftly through Vico's pockets until he found a wallet. It was crammed with money. Blood money for Martin's blood.

He flicked on the flashlight and examined the wallet more closely. There was nothing in it except money, and he was about to put it back in the dead man's pocket when he felt something crinkle in the compartment reserved for cards. He removed a faded snapshot.

Focusing his light on it, he saw a young man in his late teens holding a baby in his arms. The man was thin and pale-looking even then, and his mouth had the same cruel smile.

It was Vico.

Martin turned the card over and read the ink-stamped words: "Al Morris' Photo Shop, 3500 Grand Avenue, St. Louis, Mo." Below it was the cryptic notation, A-1052.

Martin slipped the picture in his pocket. He was putting the wallet in Vico's coat when he heard a scraping sound. It seemed to come from somewhere outside the house and he quickly doused his flash. He was starting to turn when a gun barked with frightening suddenness and a bullet whistled by his face. He threw himself face down on the floor and held his breath. He lay very still and waited, the smell of cordite strong in the room. A few moments later something thudded onto the floor near the window.

Then silence.

Martin did not know how long he lay there, motionless, waiting. The shot had come from the north side of the house, near one of the windows. He pointed his flash in that direction and saw that a window was open a few inches. There was something on the floor directly below the window. It was a gun, and he recognized it as the one Vico had used on him.

He got to his feet slowly, and then it hit him. The reason for the anonymous call and for Vico's murder. The little gunman had failed to accomplish his mission, and was therefore expendable to his employers. But they weren't through with him, even after sticking a knife in his chest. He, or she, had dangled his dead body as bait to lure him to the bungalow. Then, while he was busy looking at the body, a shot would snuff out his own life. When the police came it would took like two men had engaged in mortal combat, each killing the other. There would be no questions asked, because it was all there in black and white for all to see.

Clever.

Martin knew now that he had to get out of there fast, before the police came. He hurried to the bedroom and picked up his coat. Before slipping out the window, he wiped his fingerprints from the woodwork with his handkerchief. There was no sound in the woods as he trotted back to his car.

He was almost at the city limits when he heard the mournful wail of a siren. Vico's killer hadn't wasted any time. A few moments later a black and white police car roared by, its revolving red light blinking furiously.

Martin watched the disappearing car in his rearview mirror, and for the first time in weeks he felt like smiling. The trap had been baited, but the pigeon had flown.

CHAPTER SIXTEEN

Martin looked out the plane window at the sprawling metropolis that was St. Louis. Nearly a mile below him, the murky waters of the Mississippi wound tortuously like a coiled snake. A steady stream of traffic moved across its many streets like so many ants. A huge Ferris Wheel, its metal gleaming in the early morning sun, caught his roving gaze. He counted three bridges spanning the mighty river, and he guessed there were more.

As the plane began its bumpy descent, a buzzer sounded somewhere and a light flashed on over the cockpit door, revealing the words, "Fasten your belts, please."

Martin secured his safety belt around him. The plane was circling over the airport when he thought of the night before when he had stood over the body of a man who had been hired to kill him. A man whose picture he hoped would put an end to his nightmare. He had driven straight to the Claybank Airport after leaving Vico's bungalow. He hadn't even left a note for Angela. She would be furious and she would worry, too, but she would understand. The news of Vico's murder would bring an inquisitive Bannerman hurrying to his house. The burly detective might even suspect him of killing Vico. He took the picture from his pocket and studied it carefully. Even in death, the little hoodlum seemed to be mocking him.

The plane landed at the Lambert-St. Louis Municipal Airport without incident, and Martin found an Airway Cab outside the Administration Building. He gave the driver the address on Grand Avenue and settled back on the seat.

He tore his mind away from his troubles and concentrated on enjoying the sights. It was an old city, a historic city, St. Louis, but there was a freshness about it that belied its turbulent past. It was a long drive across town, and he passed cemeteries, a golf course, the fabulous Forest Park, Washington University and street after street of neatly-kept homes and lawns. It was a beautiful city, and Martin was enthralled.

"Okay, Mister, here we are."

The cabbie's words broke his reverie, and he got out and paid his fare. Thirty-Five Hundred Grand Avenue was an old two-story stucco building. Gold lettering on the upstairs windows said that the photography shop was on the second floor. He climbed a flight of worn wooden steps to a frosted glass door and went inside. It was a small room containing two leather armchairs, a few file cabinets and a fairly new desk.

A tall, sparely-built man with a smooth pate and protruding eyes was behind the desk. He looked up from racing form and smiled.

"Anything I can do for you?" he asked.

Martin went to the desk, took the picture from his pocket and dropped it on the green blotter. "Can you tell me anything about this man?" he asked.

The photographer studied the picture. "It was taken a long time ago," he said. "The face isn't familiar."

"Look on the other side."

The man turned the snapshot over and read the wording. "Al Morris has been dead about twenty years," he said. "The guy who bought the shop from him is dead, too. My name's Kresky. Joe Kresky."

"Glad to know you," said Martin. "I'm Martin Powers. Can you help me?"

Kresky pulled at his lower lip. "I dunno," he said. He looked at Martin quizzically. "You a cop?"

Martin shook his head.

Kresky waited for more, but when it wasn't coming, shrugged. "There's a number on the back," he said. "That might help."

"The man's name is Vico, I think," Martin said.

"Then what do you want from me?"

"If his name is really Vico, and where he lives."

Kresky went to the battered row of file cabinets and pulled out one of the drawers. "Vico, eh?"

"I think so."

The photographer thumbed through a row of oblong-shaped folders until he found the one he wanted. He took it back to the desk and shook it. A single negative and a small piece of paper fluttered out.

"His name is Vico, all right," said Kresky, studying the paper. "His full name is Anthony Vico. The picture was taken in 1930. It doesn't give the baby's name."

"Do you have an address on him?" asked Martin.

"Yeah, it's Forty-Two Seventeen Lodi Street. That's over in The Hill."

"Where's that?"

"The Italian section. Yogi Berra and Joe Garagiola were raised in that neighborhood. You a baseball fan?"

Martin nodded, smiled. "Yogi catches for the Yanks. Garagiola is a sports broadcaster here in St. Louis."

"Yeah, you got it. You a stranger around here?"

Martin nodded again. "How do I get to Lodi Street? I haven't a car."

"Take a northbound streetcar on Grand Avenue," Kresky said. "You can get one a block down, on Shenandoah. Get out at Shaw Boulevard and transfer to a westbound Lafayette Street car. Ride to the end of the line at Daggett and Marconi. Lodi Street is two blocks west."

Martin thanked him and walked to the corner where he boarded a streetcar. Twenty minutes later he alighted at the corner of Daggett and Marconi Avenues. He walked west to Lodi and started checking the numbers. There was a tightness in his stomach now that he couldn't explain. He had a feeling that his search was nearly over, that in a very few minutes the curtain would be lifted and the person behind Vico would stand revealed.

Lodi Street was located in a typical middle-class neighborhood, with the well-kept and the rundown houses leaning tiredly against each other. There was litter in the streets and a garbage can in front of almost every house. The people on Lodi Street were poor, and they toiled hard for what little comforts they had. Their kids would be tough and wily, and while most of them would grow up to be hard-working citizens like their fathers, it was inevitable that here and there a Vico would be spawned.

Forty-Two Seventeen was one of the tired houses. It was badly in need of paint and several of the windows were boarded. A pimply-faced youth in a black leather jacket lolled indolently against the wooden railing, a cigarette dangling from his lips.

"Does the Vico family live here?" asked Martin.

The youth stared at him with insolent eyes. "Never heard of them," he said.

Martin wondered if this would-be tough was one of those misunderstood juveniles he had read so much about. An embryo Vico, he thought wryly, as he started to climb the rickety stairs.

The youth quickly sidled in front of him. "Get lost," he said.

Martin returned the boy's stare. "Step aside, little man, before I step on you," he said evenly.

The boy's lips came together in a snarl. But he moved to one side.

Martin smiled, walked up the stairs and went into a small vestibule. He could feel the boy's eyes glowering on his back. There were letterboxes on one wall and he studied them. They were Italian names, but none was named Vico. He decided to ask questions anyway. Maybe one of the present tenants would remember Vico. The little hoodlum wasn't the kind people forgot in a hurry.

Martin went into a narrow hallway and knocked on the first door he came to. It was opened almost immediately by a thickset, swarthy complexioned man with snow-white hair. The man said nothing, just blinked his eyes at him quizzically.

"My name is Martin Powers," Martin said. "I'm looking for a family named Vico. Can you help me?"

The man opened the door wider. "Come in, come in," he said, waving a hairy arm. "The name is Enrico Ricci."

Martin walked into a spotlessly clean kitchen that smelled strongly of spicy foods. He could hear a man and a woman arguing in another part of the building. His host gestured to a chair beside an oilcloth-covered table and he sat down. Ricci studied him narrowly. "Vico, you say?"

Martin nodded, waited.

"Why you want to know?"

"It's a personal matter," explained Martin. "I'm no cop, if that's what is bothering you."

"Goddamn right, that's what is bothering me," Ricci said harshly. "You gotta personal reasons, eh?"

"Yes."

Ricci sat at the table, leaned forward and folded his hands in front of him. "Yeah, I usta know a man named Vico," he said. His breath smelled of vino. "Heesa no good, that Tony Vico. *Madre mia*, he makea lot of trouble for everybody!"

"I know," Martin said. "He made some for me."

Ricci's eyes brightened hopefully. "Ah, you wanta kill him, no?"

"No. Tony Vico is already dead."

Ricci looked disappointed. "Then what you wanta know about him for? Heesa dead, so it don't makea sense."

"I want to know about his people, who they are and where they are now," explained Martin.

Ricci mulled over what Martin said and nodded. "Hokey, that makea sense," he said, shrugging. "It don't makea any difference, Vico got nobody. His mother and father died a longa time ago, when he was about twenty, twenty-one years old. He hadda one sister, but she died a longa time ago too."

"How about his sister's husband?"

"Heesa dead, too. In 1939, I think." He shook his head. "All a the old-timers a dead. All but Enrico Ricci."

"How about cousins?" asked Martin.

Ricci's head bobbed up and down. "Cousins? Yeah, got them, I guess. But I don't know who they are, believe me."

Martin took the picture from his pocket and pushed across the table. "Recognize him?" he asked.

Ricci squinted at the picture and nodded. "Yeah, sure. That's a Vico when he was a younga man." He shook his head. "He was a *persona cottiza*, even then."

"The baby in the picture?" asked Martin. "Do you know its name?"

His host studied the picture more closely. "The picture was taken a longa time ago," he said, frowning. "Lemme see, it was taken around a nineteen-a-thirty, somewheres around there. Vico was about twenty-year-old then, and already he'd a been in prison. But the bambino, I don't know."

Martin shook his head in disappointment. The trip to St. Louis was a blank. He was still on the merry-go-round.

Suddenly, Ricci slapped his hand on the table. "The bambino!" he cried. "I know who it is. Shesa his niece. His sister had a one child, and shesa her!"

A knot twisted in Martin's stomach. Here it comes, he thought. But either way, he had to know.

"Do you remember the niece's name?" he asked.

"Sure theeng! I remember her name. It was Angela. Angela Moretti."

CHAPTER SEVENTEEN

There was a police car in front of the house when Angela returned from the beauty parlor. She was almost abreast of it when Sam Bannerman opened the door and stepped out and grabbed her arm. The detective was breathing heavily and there was an angry scowl on his face.

"Where's Powers?" he asked brusquely.

Angela wrenched her arm free. "How should I know?" she snapped. "I've been at the beauty shop all evening."

"Let's go inside and talk."

Angela led the way inside the house and snapped on the lights. Bannerman made a swift inspection of the four-room bungalow and returned to the living room where he found Angela on the divan, waiting, her dark eyes wary.

"What's wrong?" she asked.

Bannerman halted in front of her, his legs spread wide. "Vico is dead," he said.

Angela's eyes widened with surprise. "That can't be," she said. "Nobody knew where he was but you and I."

She showed no sign of grief as Bannerman took a fresh cigar from his pocket, bit off one end and lit it. He kept his eyes on her all the time.

"Are you trying to say that Powers killed him?"

Angela tucked her legs beneath her and smiled. "Have you any better ideas?" she asked.

The detective shook his head. "He couldn't have killed Vico. You said yourself he didn't know where the little punk was hiding out." He fell into an armchair and closed his eyes tiredly. "It's nearly eleven. Where is he?"

"I told you I don't know. How did Vico die?"

"He was stabbed," Bannerman said, opening his eyes. He watched her with lidded eyes. "Why should anyone want to kill him?"

Angela threw back her head and laughed. "How naive can you get?" she cried. "Why shouldn't anybody kill him? Vico's been a very bad boy for a very long time. He's killed before, many times. What makes you think somebody don't want to kill him?"

Bannerman studied the end of his cigar. "It was strange," he said. "Somebody telephoned headquarters and told the dispatcher there was a dead man in that bungalow. I wonder who it could've been?"

The room was quiet, only the occasional hum of traffic invaded the room. Angela got to her feet and looked down at him. "You suspect Martin, don't you?" she asked.

Bannerman hesitated, frowned. "He had a motive."

"And since he's not here, he also had the opportunity. Are you going to arrest him?"

"It's not quite that bad," he said. "Let's say we want to talk to him. However, if the lab boys find his prints in that bungalow, he'll have some explaining to do." He took a drag on his cigar and exhaled. "But picking him up for murder isn't what we want, is it?"

"No, it isn't," she said. Her eyes grew cold. "He'll still get the money even if he goes to jail for murder. But there are other ways . . ."

Bannerman shook his head. "Do you remember the first time we met?" he asked. "You said my job was to see to it that my superiors didn't get wind of our little deal. I kept my part of the bargain. Nobody at headquarters knew that somebody was trying to kill your husband until Vico blew the whole thing wide open when he bungled that job out in the country. That brought the top brass in and fast. You got a break when I was assigned to the case, only now it isn't hush-hush any more. It's out in the open where everybody can see what's going on . . ."

Angela started to interrupt, but Bannerman raised his hand.

"Let me finish," he said harshly. "If I pick him up for questioning, I'll have to give him every chance to tell his story. That means the boys at headquarters will listen real hard, too, especially if he identifies Vico as the man who tried to kill him. So it looks like your little scheme has blown up in your face, baby."

Angela crossed the room in two fast strides and gave the detective a stinging slap across the face. "Don't ever say that again, do you hear!" she screamed.

Bannerman looked at her, his face mottled with rage. "Do that again," he hissed, "and I'll kill you!"

Angela pushed her face close to his, her eyes glowing with fire. "There is another way out, if you want to listen," she said.

Bannerman composed himself with an effort. "Okay, talk."

"Right now, Martin is a fugitive. Right?"

"More or less."

Angela straightened, brushed a dark tendril from her eyes with an impatient gesture. "What could they say if you had to shoot him for resisting arrest?" she asked quietly. "It would be perfectly legal, because you'd have that precious badge backing you all the way."

Bannerman concealed his admiration from showing. "You think of everything, don't you?" He leaned forward, his hands on his knees. "Did you kill Vico?"

Angela's eyes mocked him. "I'm no killer," she said.

It was the detective's turn to laugh. "You'd kill your own mother if you thought you could get away with it," he said. He got to his feet and walked to the door. He was opening it when Angela's voice stopped him.

"Well?" she snapped.

He turned. "Well, what?"

"Are you going to take care of Martin?"

Bannerman took a snub-nosed revolver from his holster and examined it carefully. "It's a two-way split now, isn't it?" he asked.

Angela licked her lips and nodded.

"Then I'll take care of it," he said, putting the gun back in its holster.

CHAPTER EIGHTEEN

It was late the following afternoon when Martin alighted from the plane at Claybank Airport. He had felt and acted like an automaton ever since he had left Enrico Ricci's apartment on Lodi Street. His talk with the amiable Italian had shattered his dream-world into tiny pieces, and along with them had gone his reasons for living. He still did not know why Angela had wanted him dead, and at the moment he could not have cared less.

The wind had a biting edge as he walked to his car in the parking lot near the Administration Building. He walked listlessly, with his head down, and he did not notice the woman standing alongside his car until he had almost reached it.

It was Lorna Craig.

She threw herself into his arms with a strangled sob. "Thank God,

Marty, you're safe," she cried, clinging to him desperately. "I've looked everywhere for you."

He wanted to ask her why, but the words stuck in his throat.

Lorna pulled herself free and looked at him searchingly.

"Do you know that Vico is dead?" she asked.

"Yes, I know."

Her lips trembled as she fought back the tears. "The police haven't said so openly, but they think you had something to do with it."

"I didn't kill him."

Lorna shook her head violently from side to side with relief. "Thank God," she murmured over and over.

Martin unlocked the car and they got in. He started the motor, then waited while it warmed up. "How did you know where to find me?" he asked.

Lorna brushed away a tear and smiled. "I've been doing a lot of detective work on my own," she said proudly. "When the papers said you were being sought for questioning in Vico's murder, I knew you couldn't be home, so I looked everywhere for your car. I checked the bus stations, the railroad depot and all the garages. I finally thought of the airport and there it was.

"I know one of the girls in the ticket department and she told me that a man answering your description had bought a round-trip ticket to St. Louis the night before last," she went on. "About an hour ago she called me at the office and said you were coming in on the 4:40 flight. I took a taxi and here I am."

Martin squeezed her hand reassuringly, but said nothing.

"What now?" she asked.

Martin shook his head. He didn't know what to do or what to say. His mind was still numb with disbelief.

"Drive to my place," urged Lorna. "A drink will pick you up. Besides, I've got news for you."

He drove to a modern five-story brick building on Keystone City's west side. It was Moorish in design, with an imposing entrance of white stucco and grille work. He found a parking spot near the building and they got out and went to her apartment on the third floor.

Martin took off his coat and hat while Lorna fixed the drinks. He fell wearily onto the divan and looked around the familiar room. It was a warm, comfortable room, and he and Lorna had spent many wonderful evenings here. They had held hands and looked at television and talked and dreamed about the future. Their future. But it all seemed so long ago, and he shook his head sadly.

Lorna returned with two glasses of burgundy and they sipped their drinks in silence for several moments.

"I've been to St. Louis," he said finally.

"And you've come up with something?" she asked gently.

"I'm afraid so," he said, finishing his drink and putting the glass on the coffee table. "You've been right all along."

"So Angela has been behind those attempts on your life."

There was neither bitterness or triumph in her voice, and Martin felt a new respect for this woman who had every reason to be both bitter and triumphant.

"Yes," he said.

Then he told her everything, beginning with the anonymous phone call he had received while Angela was at the beauty shop, and ending with Enrico Ricci's fatal words in the cold-water flat on Lodi Street.

When he was finished, Lorna joined him on the divan, compassion in her face and in her voice. "How you must have suffered, Marty," she said, placing her hand over his.

Martin offered her a cigarette, and when she shook her head, lit one for himself. "It hit me pretty hard," he admitted, exhaling deeply. "The signs were there for me to see, but I guess I just didn't want to believe them. For the first time in my life I'd really had something. A wife, a home and maybe, someday, a couple of kids."

He paused, shook his head. "Forgive me, Lorna. I've no right to be crying on your shoulder like this."

"Don't start feeling sorry for yourself, Martin Powers," she said, her nostrils distending angrily. "I've had a selfish reason for every moment I've worried about you. I love you. I guess I always will." She shrugged and her laugh was hollow. "It's just one of those things we can't help."

Until a moment ago he had never felt so alone. Now, suddenly, he felt better. "You said you had something to tell me."

Lorna leaned forward, her eyes shining. "Remember that day in Dorry's when you told me about your trip to Vianna, and how you were checking on the Buick that ran down your father?" When Martin nodded, she continued: "You mentioned two names, Marvin Rickles and Judge Amos Chandler, so I did some checking. I concentrated on the month of March, 1928, the month your father was killed. Marvin Rickles vacationed in Miami Beach that year, so I knew he couldn't have had anything to do with your father's death. But when I checked on Judge Chandler, it was different." She paused to catch her breath. "The judge attended some kind of a convention in Denver that month . . ."

Martin jerked upright with sudden thought. "Why, sure! I remember reading an item in the Vianna *Daily Chronicle* about a judges' convention being held there."

"That's right," nodded Lorna quickly. "So I did some fast checking at the courthouse, and found out that Judge Chandler attended that convention."

Martin's exuberance suddenly faded. "But that doesn't prove it was his car that hit my father," he said.

"No, it doesn't," admitted Lorna, "but several people who knew the old judge for many years, swear that he owned a blue Buick that year."

"That'll help, but even if he did run down my father, how does that tie in with Angela's attempts to kill me?"

"I'm coming to that." Lorna's face radiated excitement. "Once I had made absolutely sure that Judge Chandler could have been the man who killed your father, I contacted some people in Miami. They gave me the name of a local attorney who handled his affairs after he died, so I got in touch with him. He said that the judge had no living relatives when he passed on, so he left his entire estate of a half-million dollars to you!"

Martin stared at her in shocked silence. "A half-million dollars?" he cried. "Are you sure?"

Lorna nodded vigorously. "He said that if you could prove you were the son of Joseph and Lena Kaska, the money was yours."

"But I can't prove it," said Martin helplessly. "The Westgrove Home for Boys has burned down."

"How about that old lady you talked to? That Mrs. . . . ."

"Julia Newdecker?"

Lorna nodded eagerly. "That's the one! She'll help you, Marty. And I'm sure there must be others who were employed by the Home who will remember you." She paused, then, "After all, Angela had to have some way of finding you."

Martin squashed out his cigarette in an ashtray and lit another. "Ever since I learned how my father died, I tried to put myself in the killer's shoes," he said slowly. "What went through his mind as he drove away from the scene on that foggy morning? How did he live with himself afterwards, knowing that he had killed another human being?" He shook his head. "Now, I think I know. The poor guy probably suffered more than anyone knew. He had to make restitution somehow but he had to do it without revealing himself. That's why he sent that money to my mother anonymously every month until she died. And that's why he remembered me when he died."

Lorna nodded, her face solemn. "I've been putting a few pieces together, too," she admitted. "He had nothing to gain by going to the police and admitting his guilt. He was a judge, a person of standing in the state. What good would it have done if he went to prison? He couldn't help your mother in jail. So he did the next best thing, he took care of her as long as she lived, and now he's taken care of you."

Martin nodded. "Angela must have learned about the inheritance somehow," he said. "Once forewarned, she set out to find me before the lawyers did. When she found me, the only thing left was to become Mrs. Martin Powers." He smiled wryly. "I wonder what she'd have done if I'd been married?"

"Vico would have handled it."

It was fantastic, but Martin knew she had spoken the truth. Angela wanted the money, nothing else mattered. Not even murder would stop her.

The word murder made him think of Vico.

"Do you think she killed him?" asked Lorna, reading his thoughts.

"I think so," Martin said. "She has the capacity to kill. But I've got to make certain."

"How?"

Martin went to the telephone-table and checked the directory for Mrs. Bixby's Beauty Shoppe. When he found it, he dialed the number. A pleasant-voiced woman answered.

"Mrs. Bixby?" asked Martin.

"Yes."

"This is Martin Powers, Angela's husband. I understand my wife had an appointment with you the night before last."

"Yes, Mr. Powers, she did."

"Could you tell me what time it was for?"

"'Just moment while I check my appointment book," said Mrs. Bixby. "Ah, here it is. The appointment was for eight o'clock."

Martin thanked her and hung up. Angela was a murderess. He told Lorna what he had found out. "She could have called me after she left the house," he said, pacing the floor nervously. "Then went out and killed Vico before I got there. Later, after she thought she had killed me with that shot through the window, she called the police."

"How could she be sure you'd go out there alone?"

"She couldn't, that was the chance she had to take," Martin said. "But it wasn't much of a gamble, since I told her I intended to find Vico, cops or no cops."

The telephone rang, sharp and shrill. They looked at each other for several moments, indecision on their faces. Lorna finally went to the phone and picked it up. "Yes?" Martin watched her eyes widen with fright. She looked at him and her lips wordlessly framed the name, "Angela."

Martin shook his head.

"I haven't the slightest idea where your husband is, Mrs. Powers," she said stiffly.

She listened for a few moments, her body rigid, then slammed the receiver down. "She says I'll go to jail if the police find you here," she said.

"She's right, Lorna. I'd better be going."

Lorna suppressed a shudder. "Be careful, Marty. She'll kill you if she gets a chance."

Martin took her hands in his. "I don't think so," he said thoughtfully. "I'm convinced that she wouldn't do anything that would lose her that money. But now that Vico is dead, she'll think of another way."

"What are you going to do?"

"I'm going to tell Sam Bannerman everything," he said, "and let him take it from there. He'll know what to do."

He shrugged into his coat and picked up his hat. He went to the door, hesitated a moment, and turned.

"Wish me luck," he said.

She crossed two fingers and held them up for him to see. "Call me when it's all over," she said. "I'll stay near the phone."

He nodded and went out.

CHAPTER NINETEEN

Martin did not go to Police Headquarters after leaving Lorna's apartment. Instead, he drove around for a while, trying to collect his thoughts before he tackled Sergeant Bannerman. He stopped at a roadside diner and ordered coffee and a hamburger, but he had to push the sandwich away. He had no appetite for food after what had happened. It was nearly seven o'clock when he finally braked in front of the squat, red brick building that served as Keystone City's Police Department.

Bannerman was studying a sheaf of typewritten reports when he walked into his office. The burly detective put a scowl on his face when he looked up and saw Martin.

"It's about time you showed up," he said, jerking his cigar from his mouth. "Where've you been?"

Martin pushed a chair next to the desk and sat down. "I've been out of town," he said.

"Just like that. Did you know that Vico has been murdered?"

"I know," nodded Martin wearily. "I was there."

Bannerman straightened. "Are you confessing?"

"Don't be silly. Vico was already dead when I got there."

Bannerman pushed the papers to one side. "Suppose you start at the beginning," he said.

Martin lit a cigarette, took several deep drags and began. He told the detective about the anonymous phone call he had gotten a few minutes after Angela left for the beauty shop; how he had gone out to the orange-colored bungalow and found Vico dead on the floor with a knife in his chest, and how somebody had taken a shot at him while he was bending over the body.

"Did you see who it was?"

"It was too dark. Anyway, I know who it was . . . now."

The detective studied him warily. "Who?"

"Angela Powers, my wife."

"That's pretty strong talk," Bannerman said, leaning back in his chair. "Are you prepared to back it up?"

Martin reached into his pocket and dropped the snapshot he had taken from Vico's body on the desk.

Bannerman picked it up and studied it for several moments. "What's this supposed to mean?" he asked.

"Recognize the man?"

The detective pursed his lips. "Vico?"

"That's right," Martin said. "That was the little bum when he was twenty years old. Know who the baby is?"

"I can guess . . . Mrs. Powers?"

"Right again. Only her name then was Angela Morretti."

"Where did you get this picture?" asked Bannerman.

"I found it in Vico's wallet just before Angela took a shot at me," Martin said. "There's a photographer's name on the other side. I went there and he told me everything I needed to know."

Bannerman's eyebrows went up. "You went to St. Louis?"

"Yes. I traced Vico to a house on Lodi Street, in the heart of the Italian section. An old man named Enrico Ricci spelled it out for me and it wasn't pretty. He said that Vico's full name is Anthony Vico and he was Angela's uncle. Also, he's been in trouble with the cops since he was able to crawl."

Bannerman tapped the picture against his fingertips thoughtfully. "Then the way you got it figured, Angela hired Vico to kill you," he said.

"Don't you?"

The detective shrugged. "It doesn't matter what I think. It's what a jury thinks that counts." He leaned forward, his eyes boring into Martin's. "Since you seem to have all the answers, why did she want to kill you?"

Martin had to smile. "That's always bothered you, hasn't it?" he grinned. "Well, it so happens that I'm about to inherit a half-million dollars."

Bannerman looked skeptical.

"I don't blame you," Martin said. "I thought it was crazy when I heard it, too. But I've been busy, and I've done a lot of checking. Do you remember when I went on that trip?" When Bannerman nodded, he went on: "My investigation took me to a little town in Colorado called Vianna. I was born there. I found out that back in 1928 my father was killed by a hit-and-run driver. The man was never apprehended. My mother died a few months later, and since I had no living relatives, they put me in a Home for adoption. A nice couple named Powers took me and brought me to Corona to live."

Martin paused to light another cigarette. Bannerman waited, saying nothing, his face a mask.

"After they died, I came to Keystone City to live," Martin went on. "Then I married Angela, and you know the rest."

"Not quite. You still haven't said why she wants to kill you."

"The man who killed my father was Amos Rutherford Chandler."

The big detective's eyes blinked with surprise. "The big shot judge who died about a year ago?"

"The same," Martin said.

Bannerman relit his dead cigar and frowned. "That's quite a story," he said. "And this Judge Chandler is the one who is leaving you all that dough. Why?"

"Who knows?" Martin shrugged. "Call it conscience or retribution, or anything you like. I like to think that he tried to square things the only way he knew how."

The two men were silent for several moments, each busy with his own thoughts. A detective walked in, saw that Bannerman was busy, and went out.

Bannerman finally asked, "And you figure I should arrest Mrs. Powers, is that it?"

"Why not? She had a reason for wanting me dead, and the man she hired was her uncle. What more do you want?"

"Proof. All we've got so far is a theory, and your theory at that. A judge and jury won't go for it, and a smart lawyer will fill it full of holes."

Martin bristled. "What do you want, a signed confession?" he asked sarcastically.

"It would help," nodded Bannerman, looking at his cigar placidly. "I know how you feel and I don't blame you, but look at it this way. What proof do we have that Tony Vico is your wife's uncle?" Martin started to protest, but the detective waved him silent. "Hear me out first. The chances are we'd have a lot of scrounging around to do before we find someone who could prove they were related. But suppose we can't? Then we have no case against your wife for the simple reason we can't prove collusion. She can laugh in our faces and we can't do a thing."

"You mean she goes free?" asked Martin incredulously.

"Something like that. I'm just trying to show you what we're up against. If I went to the D.A., with what we've got, he'd throw me out." Bannerman paused, flicked some ashes off his cigar. "And here's another thing. Let's say that we can prove Vico was Mrs. Powers' uncle. What proof do we actually have that he tampered with your car, or tried to run you down or took you for a ride out in the country? It's just your word against a dead man's, and in the law books, it won't be enough."

Martin got to his feet, his face flushed with anger. He started for the door, but the detective's sharp command stopped him.

"Where do you think you're going?" he snapped.

"If you can't do anything, then I'll handle it my way," said Martin, opening and closing his hands angrily. "I'll make her confess if I have to strangle it out of her."

Bannerman shook his head impatiently. "Sit down and cool off, Mr. Powers," he said. "That won't get you anywhere, and you might get into a lot of trouble."

Martin returned to his chair reluctantly. "So we just sit here and do nothing?" he asked belligerently.

Bannerman pointed his cigar at Martin. "Look, Mr. Powers. I've been a detective a long time. There are laws, and evidence has to be tied together according to those laws." He waved his cigar. "Now I'm not saying that your wife isn't guilty. I think she is. In fact, I've had a feeling all along that she was behind those attempts on your life, but without proof what could I do?"

"Everybody suspected her but me," said Martin bitterly.

The detective nodded. "The husband is always the last to find out, only in your case it isn't too late," he said. "If we want to get evidence against your wife, we have to outsmart her. Get her to talk."

Martin shook his head. "That she won't do. Angela is no dope. She's shrewd and she's hard."

"She can be fooled," Bannerman said. "If you'll help."

"I'll do anything I can."

"Good. Then here's how we'll work it. We'll go to your home together, only I'll let myself in the back way while you're talking to her. Get her to talk, to confess, rather. Naturally, she'll deny everything at first, but keep pounding away at her. Bear down hard. Show her the picture you found in Vico's pocket. Tell her about the old guy you spoke to on Lodi Street. It should work if you make it strong enough. When she blows her top, I'll be in the next room listening to everything." He leaned back and smiled. "Then we'll have her as tight as a drum."

The idea sounded good to Martin. He realized that the detective was right about getting sufficient evidence against Angela. The loopholes had to be closed so that Angela couldn't slip free.

"Okay, I'll do what you say," Martin said. "But suppose she won't crack, what then?"

Bannerman got to his feet. "Then we'll have to go along with what we've got. It isn't much, but maybe we'll get lucky."

The detective squashed out his cigar, shrugged into his overcoat and the two men left the office. They were crossing the police parking lot when Bannerman suddenly snapped his fingers.

"I forgot to tell the Dispatcher where I'll be," he said. "Get in the car and wait. I'll only be a few minutes."

Martin got in the car and stared morosely out the window. It was a cold, starless night. And it would be a long night, the longest and loneliest of his life.

CHAPTER TWENTY

The two men were silent on the drive across town. It was past the dinner hour, and the traffic was heavy with fun-seekers and theatre-goers. Smoking quietly, Martin envied them with their light-hearted camaraderie. Not too long ago he had felt as they did, but too much had happened in too short a time and he felt old and disillusioned. In a few minutes he would confront the woman he loved and, accuse her of being a murderess. The thought sickened him and he forced it from his mind.

Bannerman parked several houses from his bungalow and doused the lights. He chewed his dead cigar and looked at Martin.

"Feel up to it?" he asked.

Martin nodded. "Why did she do it?" he asked in a strained voice. "Why? Why?"

"She had half-a-million reasons."

Martin started at the detective, through him. "Money? What's money compared to what we had?"

"It's a little late for philosophizing," Bannerman said curtly. He tossed his cigar out the window. "You got a key to the back door?"

Martin removed a key from his keyring and gave it to the detective. "The back door leads into the kitchen," he explained. "Make sure she doesn't hear you."

Bannerman and Martin got out of the car.

"You go first," said the detective. "I'll wait until you're inside before I circle around back." He put his hand on Martin's arm. "Remember, she's got to spill the lot or it's no go."

Martin nodded and started for his house, his stomach churning. He wondered what Angela would say when he accused her of trying to kill him; of sticking a knife into her uncle's chest. Would she admit her guilt or would she deny it? Somehow, he didn't care. What they'd once had was as dead as Vico.

There was a light in the living room as he walked up the porch steps and inserted his key in the front door. Angela was waiting for him in the living room, lines of worry etched on her beautiful face.

"Where have you been?" she exclaimed, wringing her hands. "I've been half out of my mind worrying about you."

Martin stopped and looked at her. "I've been on a trip," he said.

She hurried towards him and threw her arms around his neck. She kissed him several times before she was aware of his unresponsiveness. She pulled her face away and looked at him searchingly.

"Is there something wrong, Martin?" she asked.

"You'd better sit down. The next few minutes might be a little rough."

She stepped back, still regarding him curiously. "You seem different, somehow," she said. She sat on the couch and crossed a slim, nyloned leg. "Why didn't you tell me you were leaving town?"

"There wasn't time. There was a lot to do."

Angela smiled, reached for the humidor on the coffee table, took a cigarette from it and lit it. "You make it sound so mysterious," she said, exhaling. "Suppose you tell me about it."

She's such a beautiful woman, he thought, looking at her. The most beautiful woman I've ever known. It was hard to believe that she has the face of an angel and the heart of a viper.

"Well?" she asked impatiently.

"I received an anonymous phone call shortly after you left for the beauty parlor that night," Martin said. He stood next to the telephone-table; he had not moved since he came into the room.

Angela made a wry gesture. "If it was another one of those calls," she asked, "why should it disturb you so?"

"This call was different." He was stalling for time until Bannerman could slip into the house. "Whoever it was, told me to go to an orange-colored house on Highway 61. They said I would find Vico there."

Angela quickly uncrossed her legs. "You didn't go!"

Martin nodded. "I went."

"But you might have been killed!" she exclaimed.

"I almost was. Vico was there, just as the caller said. Only he was dead. There was a knife sticking out of his chest."

She closed her eyes and shuddered. "How awful."

"Yes, it was pretty bad," Martin said. "And while I was there, somebody took a shot at me through a window."

Angela started to rise, changed her mind and fell back on the couch. "But who would do such a thing?" she cried, her face white. "Vico was dead. Whoever killed him was on your side."

"Not quite. You see, Vico's employer hoped that by killing me the police would think that Vico and I had killed each other."

Angela wet her lips. "Vico's employer?"

"That's right. Vico was just a hireling. A paid gunsel, I think he'd be called in the underworld."

"How fantastic!"

"Yes, wasn't it?" He paused, looking at her hungrily from her dark hair to her small, slippered feet. "But Vico's boss made one mistake. She should have examined his wallet more carefully after she killed him. There was a snapshot in it, and it was that snapshot that finally tripped her up."

Angela composed herself with an effort. She sat straight, her body tense. "She? You mean a woman actually hired Vico to kill you?"

"Yes."

She didn't say anything, just stared at him, her eyes holding his like a snake's. Tension was heavy in the silent room. "It was you, Angela." He tried to make the accusation sound harsh, damning, but the words came out soft and gentle.

Angela's laugh was hollow. "You must be joking, Martin," she said.

"I wish I was," Martin said, his face sad. "How I wish to God I really was!"

"But I went to the beauty parlor—"

"Your appointment wasn't until eight o'clock," the words rushed out. "I know, I checked with Mrs. Bixby. You left here before six-thirty, plenty of time to get out to the bungalow, kill Vico and then call me."

Angela shook her head in disbelief. "I can't believe what I'm hearing," she said. "My own husband accusing me of murder . . ."

"Save it," he growled. "You're good, sweetheart. Very, very, good. You could have made a great actress without even half trying. You had it all planned, down to the littlest detail, only Vico fouled it up for you, didn't he? In fact, he botched it three times, and three strikes are out in your league, aren't they?"

"Martin, you're talking crazy . . ."

"Am I, Angela?" He shook his head. "I'm stupid, but not crazy. Not yet, anyway. Take that night you had the headache and I went to get you the aspirins. Vico was waiting for me that night, snug as a bug in his little black car. How did he know I'd be going out that night? That should have tipped me off, but I was in love, and a man in love is a blind man . . ."

"Martin . . ."

"And that night when Vico took me on the one-way ride out in the country," he went on relentlessly, "he said something that I didn't get at first. When I tried to bribe him to let me go, he only laughed. He said he knew exactly how much money I had in the bank, down to the last lousy cent. Now how would he know that unless you told him?"

Angela sat very still, staring up at him with fascinated eyes. "But why should I want you killed?" she asked desperately. "I had nothing to gain by your death."

"Not much you didn't!" scoffed Martin. "Only a half-million dollars that old Judge Chandler left me when he died."

Angela's mouth tightened, and she squashed out her cigarette with a shaking hand. "I never even heard . . ."

"Save it," snapped Martin. "You found out about that inheritance somehow. Maybe you were the judge's secretary, I don't know. But when you found out about it, you went looking for me. Fortunately for your scheme, wills take a long time to be probated, so you had plenty of time to trace me from Vianna to Corona and then here. You covered your trail very cleverly by having your hair dyed and by wearing horn-rimmed glasses. You were pretty smart, but not quite smart enough."

"Martin, I swear . . ."

"Don't swear to anything, baby, it wouldn't be worth damn." He took the snapshot from his pocket and flung on the couch. He watched the blood drain from her face when she looked at it.

"It's you and Vico," he said. "I went to St. Louis and found out what I wanted to know. You're Vico's niece."

A change came over Angela and she looked at him, her eyes blazing, her body crouched like a panther's.

"All right, so you know!" she cried. She tossed the snapshot to the floor. "Yes, I tried to get that money, and hired Vico to do the job." She spat contemptuously. "Only the fool bungled the job."

"How did you find out about the money?"

Angela got to her feet, her eyes smoldering with hate. "I was old Judge Chandler's secretary," she said, her voice brittle. "I came across a copy of his will one day and it interested me very much. I knew if I could find you before his lawyers did, I could lay my hands on a fortune. Imagine, a half-million dollars! Once I had it, I could go anywhere and do anything I had ever dreamed. Paris, Rome, Cairo . . ."

"So you killed to get it."

Angela's face was damp with sweat. "Sure, I killed Vico. He was waiting for me that night to make other plans for disposing of you. He never suspected what I was up to until it was too late."

"And then you tried to kill me."

Angela slithered towards him, put her hands on his face and kissed him on the mouth tenderly. "Look at me," she said, "and tell me that you can't find it in your heart to forgive me."

He pushed her away violently, causing her to stumble backwards onto the couch. She braced her hands behind her on the cushions, her face a mask of fury.

"All right, you've made your choice," she screamed. "After you're dead, I'll take care of that loud-mouthed Ricci!"

The bottom suddenly dropped out of Martin's stomach. She knew about Enrico Ricci! But how? He hadn't mentioned the little Italian's name. There was only one way she could have known. Bannerman must have called her while he waited for him outside Headquarters. Martin's knees were weak as the terrible implication dawned on him. Sergeant Bannerman was in it with Angela! There could be no other answer. He felt the walls closing in around him, and his eyes searched the room wildly, seeking a means of escape.

His roving glance fell on the telephone and an idea came to him. But he would have to work fast, before the man behind the door could come out with a .38 clutched in his huge, hairy fist.

Martin turned his back on Angela and picked up the phone. He dialed two digits before Angela's voice rang out:

"Who are you calling?"

Martin ignored her, quickly dialed two more numbers.

"Sam!" screamed Angela.

The door to the kitchen opened and Sam Bannerman stood there, his gun aimed at Martin's back.

"Put that phone down," he snapped.

Martin placed the receiver carefully across the cradle and turned slowly, his back to the phone. He looked at Bannerman, his face hard.

"So you were in it with her," he said.

Bannerman nodded, his face flushed with excitement. "All the way," he said. "How did you get wise?"

"When she mentioned Ricci's name. Only you and Lorna Craig knew I had spoken to him, and I knew Lorna hadn't told her."

The detective turned to Angela, his face white with fury.

"You're as bad as Vico," he said. "If it wasn't for all that dough, I'd pull out of this deal right now."

"It's finished anyway," Martin said. "You can't kill me and still get the money."

Angela smiled. "We can sure try, can't we, Sam?"

Bannerman's anger subsided as he looked first at Martin and then at Angela. "How do you want to play it?" he asked.

Angela rose to her feet, smoothed out her dress. "It's easy. All we have to do is take him out in the country somewhere. You can say that you were questioning him about Vico when he tried to escape. You had no alternative but to shoot him. Simple?"

"Not quite," said Martin quickly. "At least three detectives saw me walk into Police Headquarters voluntarily. They saw me sit down and talk with your buddy-buddy. So why should I try to escape?"

Dubious glints came into the detective's eyes. "He's right," he said.

"That doesn't change anything," Angela said. "Just say he got panicky when you caught him in a few lies. They always take a cop's word."

"Not always." Bannerman shook his head. "I don't know. Lieutenant Rusk is no dope. He can smell a frame a mile off."

Angela's eyes moved restlessly. "Then maybe you got a better idea?"

The detective grinned. "Yeah, maybe I have. Maybe it would be better all-around if I finished you both off right now. That way it would be my word against yours, and you couldn't say anything for you'd both be dead."

"How about the money?" asked Angela, her voice rising.

Bannerman looked at her contemptuously. "The hell with the money," he said harshly. "I wish I'd never heard of you or that money . . ."

Angela's face was haggard. "Do it my way, Sam."

Bannerman shook his head. "I don't know. Powers is right, the brass would get suspicious. If he hadn't walked into Headquarters maybe we could have done it your way. But not now."

"But you just can't shoot us down like this!" cried Angela, moving towards him.

"Stay where you are!" barked the detective, turning the gun at her. "I don't trust you anymore."

Martin laughed, drawing their attention. "It's very amusing," he said. "Honor among thieves and all that."

"Okay, Buster, you get it first," Bannerman said, raising his gun.

Martin watched the detective's trigger-finger tighten with fascinated horror.

Suddenly a shot rang out.

Bannerman turned slowly, a look of incredulous disbelief on his heavy face. His arms fell to his sides and his huge body twisted convulsively. He was trying to bring his gun hand up when a second shot rang out. Martin watched as the tiny red spot on Bannerman's shirt became larger and larger . . .

Angela stood near the mantelpiece, a small revolver in her hand. Her face was coldly impassive. Only her eyes moved, and they shone with a sadistic gloating.

Bannerman stumbled forward, the gun falling from his nerveless fingers. He clutched at the backrest of an armchair, missed, and fell to his knees, the same look of disbelief on his face. Then, slowly, majestically, like a huge battleship going down for the last time, he slid quietly to the floor, twitched once or twice and was still.

Angela turned to Martin, a look of triumph on her face. "Okay, husband, get going," she said, gesturing with the gun.

"It's all over, Angela," he said. "You're finished. Kaput. You've killed a cop, and they never forgive you for that."

Angela smiled. "Correction, please. You killed Sergeant Bannerman, not me."

Martin shook his head. "You continue to amaze me," he said.

"Quit stalling," she said, her face tightening. "The car is outside. Head for it."

"The car isn't outside. We came in Bannerman's car."

Angela studied his face, saw the truth in his eyes. "Okay, then we'll use his car."

She went to where Bannerman lay face down on the floor. Keeping the gun and her eyes on Martin, she stooped and sent an exploring hand through the dead man's pockets.

When she had the car keys, she straightened and stepped over the body.

"Okay, I've got them," she said. "Now get moving."

"You won't get away with it, Angela," he said.

"I'll get away with it," she said confidently. She waved the gun menacingly. "I'll tell them that you killed Bannerman when he found out that you had stabbed Vico. Then you forced me at gunpoint to accompany you in the police car, but in trying to get away, you lost control of the car on the highway and it plunged into the gorge. Only just before it happened, I jumped to safety." She smiled, pleased with herself. "Pretty neat, eh?"

"It smells," Martin said. He pointed to the gun in her hand. "The cops will check that out and find that I've never owned a gun in my life."

Angela's laugh was tinged with hysteria. "You must take me for a fool!" she exclaimed. "Of course this gun belongs to you. Don't you remember, you purchased it about two months ago from a mail-order house in Chicago?"

Martin stared at her, speechless.

"Sure you did. I filled out the coupon in a magazine and sent a money order in your name. When it arrived, I signed for it in your name. Are you satisfied?"

"How about the handwriting?"

Angela took her coat from a chair and shrugged into it, keeping the gun pointed at Martin. "I printed your name on the coupon, on the money-order and on the receipt," she said. "Even the best handwriting experts in the country disagree on the origin of printed writing. Now get going!"

Martin turned and walked slowly to the door. He opened it and stepped onto the porch. Angela was close behind him, but not close enough to jump her.

"Don't try anything cute," she whispered. "Remember what happened to Sam Bannerman."

He went down the steps and along the cement walk to the sidewalk and then he turned right, towards where Bannerman's car was parked. The street was quiet, and there was nobody in sight. Martin's hopes faded with each step he took towards the car. His plan with the telephone hadn't worked.

As he neared the car he could hear the click of Angela's spike-heels on the sidewalk behind him. He stood irresolute at the car door, his hands at his sides.

"Okay, open it and get in," she commanded sharply. "You'll drive while I sit in the back."

Martin opened the door and slid under the wheel. Angela was opening the back door when they heard it.

The screaming wail of a police siren.

"You tipped them off, damn you!" screamed Angela, jumping into the car. She threw the keys onto his lap.

"Now get going fast, or I'll blow the top of your head off!" she said hoarsely.

Martin inserted the keys and turned the switch. He pressed his foot on the starter and it purred into life. With the gun prodding him in the back of his neck, he pulled away from the curb. The siren was getting closer.

"Okay, step on it," barked Angela. "And remember, husband dear, they can only make me sit in that hot seat once, no matter how many people I kill!"

CHAPTER TWENTY-ONE

Martin drove south on Woodland Street, his mind seeking desperately to find a way out of his predicament. Traffic was light in this residential area, and he made good time. But the siren still wailed behind him and his hopes rose. They had seen him pulling away and were giving chase.

"Okay, turn right at the next corner," ordered Angela.

Martin made the turn on two wheels. She was heading for Highway 92, that winding, twisting two-lane road that led to Stonehaven. He thought: Somewhere along that dark stretch of macadam she will make me slow down, slug me over the head with the gun butt and jump before the car plunges into the gorge. It was the same fate that Vico had planned for him in what now seemed a lifetime ago. He had been lucky that time, but Lady Luck was a fickle woman.

They were doing seventy when they went through a red light at the intersection of Coley's Corners and Highway 92. Angela pressed the gun in his neck and he increased the speed to eighty.

"We won't make some of the curves at this speed," he complained.

"Let me worry about it, eh?" retorted Angela. "Just concentrate on the driving."

Cars whizzed by them as Martin manipulated one hairpin turn after another. Once, he thought the car was going to turn over, but it managed to right itself and stay on the road and he breathed easier. But he couldn't keep it up; there were other curves ahead, some of them much more dangerous.

"That police car is still behind us!" cried Angela. "Step on it. We've got to lose them."

"It won't work," he said.

He received a stinging blow on the side of his head and for a sickening moment he thought he had lost control of the car. It swerved across the white line and he had a difficult time getting straightened out.

"Do that again and we'll both get killed," he gasped.

"Then keep your crummy ideas to yourself!" she screamed. "Next time I'll put a bullet through your head."

Sign posts and billboards flew past them as Martin pressed his foot on the accelerator. It can't last, he thought. Even if he managed to make all the turns, a blowout or some mechanical failure was inevitable. It was an old car and couldn't take the punishment he was giving it.

He could feel Angela breathing on his neck as they came to the worst curve of all.

"There's a very bad curve ahead," Martin said. "Let me slow down to sixty."

"You do, and you're dead," she cried. "Keep going!"

The tires screamed as he hit the turn and the car teetered precariously. Angela yelled in fright, but Martin swung the car to the right after it had skidded perilously close to the white guard railing on the opposite side of the road. It was some moments before Martin could catch his breath.

"One more like that and it'll be all over," he said, gritting his teeth.

"That was close." Angela's voice was shaky. "I don't hear the sirens now. Maybe we've lost them for a few minutes."

This would be her chance, Martin knew. With the police car some distance back, she would be able to accomplish her mission without fear of being seen. That could mean only one thing; if he was to live, he would have to make his move before she did.

"Start easing up on the accelerator," commanded Angela.

This was it. Driving with his right hand, he dropped his left onto his lap and then eased it towards the door handle. If he could open it and jump before she realized what was happening, he'd still have a chance. Even so, he might lose his life. But it was better than certain death at the bottom of the gorge.

A car's headlights appeared in the distance and Angela said, "Wait until this car passes."

She no longer kept the muzzle of the gun pressed against his neck, but he knew she still had it ready for instant use.

When the car went by, Angela asked, "How fast are we going?"

"Eighty."

"Slow down gradually to sixty."

When the needle showed sixty, she said, "Now ease down to fifty."

When the needle hits forty, she'll slug me and jump, he thought. It's now or never.

His left hand around the door handle, Martin tensed his body for the sudden leap from the speeding car. He would have to do it quickly, and without warning, otherwise she might have time to pump a few shots at him.

They were rounding a wide curve when Martin made up his mind. He jerked open the door with a lightning movement and then jumped free. He landed on his side with a jarring thump, and covering his head with both hands, rolled over and over until he was stopped by the guard rail. His body was numb with shock as he watched the disappearing lights of the car as it swerved wildly across the highway. There was a piercing scream and the sound of metal as the car went hurtling through the guardrail and down the steep slope of the mountain into the gorge a thousand feet below.

Lying there, he could still hear the car as it plunged downward. Then came a heavy silence, followed by a flash of fire and the crackling of flames.

Angela was gone.

Wearily, he climbed to his feet. He was dazed and shaken, but he was sure he had no broken bones.

He was leaning against the guardrail when the police car screeched to a stop at his side. A tired-looking man with a beak nose and thinning hair peered out at him.

"Your name Powers?" he asked.

"Yes."

"Where's your wife?"

Martin nodded towards the gorge. "She was going to kill me," he said. "I jumped before she realized what was happening. She was in the back. She never had a chance."

"I'm Lieutenant Michael Rusk. Where's Sergeant Bannerman?"

"He's back in my place, dead. My wife shot him."

Rusk turned to the uniformed officer in the car. "Contact City Hospital and have them send an ambulance out here on the double," he said. "And tell the Emergency Squad to get out here also."

Rusk took a crumpled pack of cigarettes from his pocket and pushed it towards Martin, who accepted one gratefully.

After the cigarettes were lit, Rusk asked, "What was Bannerman's part in this deal?"

Martin told him the whole story, beginning with the morning his tampered car almost went off the road, and ending with his jumping to safety a few minutes before. While he was talking, an emergency crew arrived and checked the smoldering wreckage in the gorge that had once been Martin's car.

And his wife.

Martin was sitting in the police car with Lieutenant Rusk when an overalled policeman stuck his head in the window. He looked at Martin and shook his head. "Sorry, feller," he said, "but she's dead." He gave Rusk a manila envelope. "We found this in the car."

Rusk opened the envelope. "It's a .25 caliber Colt automatic," he said, examining the gun without touching it.

Rusk closed the envelope. "Sam was a bad apple," he said quietly. "A good cop, but a bad apple."

He looked at Martin. "That was a cute trick you pulled with the telephone," he said. "How'd you work it?"

"My back was to Bannerman when he came out of the kitchen," Martin said. "When he ordered me to put the phone down, I saw a paper matchfolder on the table, so I put it between the receiver switch and the little uprights that hold the phone in place. That way I didn't break the connection. I knew if I talked loud enough, Miss Craig would hear me and contact the police." He shook his head. "What took you so long?"

"She couldn't use her phone because you had your receiver off," explained Rusk. "So she had to go to her next door neighbor's and call us. When I learned what was happening, I got in touch with the phone company and they made arrangements for me to listen in."

"Then you heard everything?"

"Not everything," said Rusk, "but enough. I heard the shots and I heard you tell your wife that she couldn't get away with it. I got out there as fast as I could."

"You did fine," said Martin fervently.

CHAPTER TWENTY-TWO

It was nearly one A.M., when Martin got into his car outside Police Headquarters. He'd had to tell his story to a variety of brass, including the Commissioner himself and a host of his top flunkeys. There were statements to sign and reporters to talk to and pictures to be taken, and now as he drove home, he felt incredibly tired.

Through it all, Lieutenant Rusk had been most cooperative. The tired-faced officer could have made things extremely rough for him, but because he had told his story honestly, Rusk had believed him. A number of thoughts raced through his mind as he drove through the sleeping city. He could stay at the bungalow tonight, but in the morning he would look for a furnished apartment. He couldn't stay longer than one night; there were too many memories to contend with. He would see Angela in every room, in everything he touched.

She was an evil woman, but she had made him incredibly happy during the four short months they were married. He would forget her in time, but he knew there would always be a small segment of her in his heart.

He turned into the driveway and into the garage. There was a light in the living room, but Rusk had assured him that Bannerman's body had been removed.

He closed and locked the garage doors and walked slowly into the silent, empty house. He looked around the living room and saw the stain on the carpet where a man's life had ebbed and died. He could still see the look of amazement on Sam Bannerman's face when Angela's first bullet hit him.

He took off his coat and hat and tossed them on a chair. He was bone-tired, but he wanted some coffee before he hit the sack. In the morning he would be able to think more clearly. Now he was confused and depressed.

The coffee was perking when he heard the click of a woman's high heels coming towards the kitchen, and for a long, terrible moment, he thought that it had all been a dream and that Angela was still alive.

But when the footsteps stopped, it was Lorna Craig standing in the doorway, a wistful smile on her face.

"Coffee, Lorna?" he asked.

Lorna nodded. "Are you all right, Marty?"

"I'm all right." He looked at her and smiled. "I want to thank you for what you did tonight."

She shook her head. "That's not enough."

Martin frowned. "What's not enough?"

"Thanking me like that. It isn't enough."

Martin looked into her mischievous eyes and understood. He went to her and took her in his arms and kissed her softly.

"Now that's better," she whispered. "Much better."

THE END

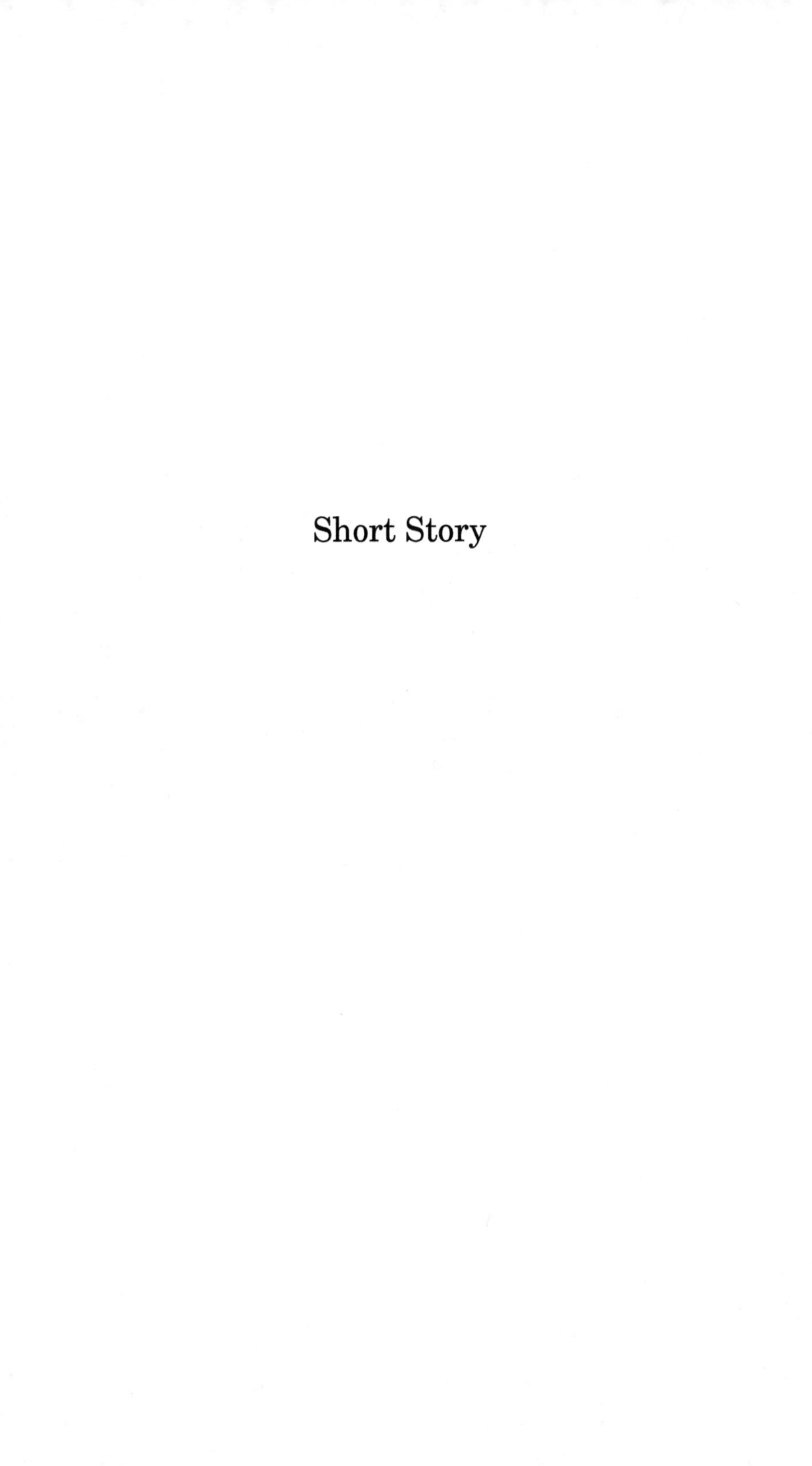

Short Story

I'D DIE FOR YOU

Manhunt, October 1958

Pineville was a tiresome twelve-hour drive from the city, most of it over bumpy back roads a million miles from nowhere. But Dawson didn't mind. Angela was there and she needed him. That was all that mattered.

It was four months since that crazy night when she eloped with Richard Emory III, but to Dawson it seemed like four years. There had been a void in his stomach ever since; a slow, gnawing emptiness that made him so sick he wanted to crawl away somewheres and die. He gripped the wheel hard and glanced at the dashboard clock. Two bells. In less than four hours they'd be together again. Just like always.

Hearing from her again was like a miracle. Only last night he was sitting in Tony's place drinking a beer and listening to the rain splashing against the dirty windows. He was alone, as usual, with his blues. And then the phone rang and he heard her voice and suddenly the rain stopped and the sun came out . . .

"Miss me, Johnny?" she whispered.

"Miss you? God, I never thought it would be this bad!"

She laughed, soft and musical. "I've missed you, too, Johnny." She paused. "How about joining me up here?"

"Pineville?" he exclaimed. "What about Emory?"

"That's what I want to talk to you about," she said. "I've just had a great big wonderful dream, and you're the only one who can make it come true, Johnny."

That's when he told her he'd come, and that's when she told him where to meet her and when. So here he was, only four hours from the rendezvous, a roadside tavern a few miles south of Pineville. Come to think of it, it wasn't a tavern at all. And Pineville wasn't a sunbaked little town in southeastern Missouri. It was a castle in Spain. It was the jackpot at the end of the rainbow.

He smiled, lit a cigarette, and let his mind roll back to the last time he saw Angela. It was at the Club Royale, and Emory was with her. Tall, sleek, smug-faced Emory, with his two-hundred dollar suits and supercilious smile. He'd had one too many, and when Emory said something he didn't like, he'd belted him on the button. The cops came and hauled him away, and the next day the judge gave him sixty days in the stockade to cool off.

The sixty days wasn't hard to take, but not having Angie around when he came out, was. At first he thought he'd go crazy. Everything he looked at reminded him of the places they'd been and the good times they'd had. Sometimes he wondered why they hadn't gotten married. He shook his head. Maybe it was because he was an angle guy, and anybody along the Main Stem will tell you that an angle guy has no business getting hitched.

Anyway, it knocked him for a loop when she went off with Emory. Not that he blamed her. Emory was loaded. He had class too, even if he was a yellow-belly. And what could he give her? A smelly room in a fifth-rate hotel. Meals cooked on a two-burner hot-stove. Three-buck shoes. No, he didn't blame her one bit. Just the same, her leaving sure blasted hell out of his insides.

Maybe she was leaving Emory, he mused hopefully. He nurtured the thought for several minutes, found it savory. Not tonight, of course, but maybe some day soon he could ask her to marry him. She'd have to get rid of Emory first, but divorce laws being what they were, it wouldn't be too difficult. He pressed harder on the accelerator. He wanted to hold her in his arms so bad it hurt.

The tavern was crowded, but he spotted her right off. She was tucked away in a corner booth, and the smile she gave him made his heart do handsprings. She was a tall, willowy brunette, with olive skin, wide-set, tilted green eyes and soft, kissable lips. He could almost taste them as he slid into the booth.

"You're right on time, Johnny," she said softly.

He grinned. "I had a good reason."

They ordered bourbons and waited until the waiter brought them and left. "It seems like years," she said.

"I know."

"You're looking good, Johnny." Dawson nodded, "How's Emory?"

"I loathe him!"

Hope flickered in his eyes. "Oh?"

She sipped her drink slowly. "I meant when I said I had a wonderful dream, Johnny," she said, their eyes locking. "You're in it all the way. But first we need money. Lots of it. And Emory's going to give it to us."

Dawson smiled indulgently. "Just like that, eh?" he said, snapping his fingers.

Angela smiled. "That's right, Johnny. Just like that." Her green eyes glowed in the dim light. He had never seen her so keyed up. "I've got it all figured out. Are you with me?"

"I'd die for you, baby," he whispered passionately. "You know that."

Angela nodded. "Yeah, I guess I do. Now listen closely and remember everything I tell you. First, remember how I can swim?"

He remembered everything about her, the touch of her hand on his; the way her hips swayed when she walked; the good, clean fragrance of her lithe body when she came out of the water. Yes, he remembered that she was an excellent swimmer. One of the best he'd ever seen.

Angela leaned forward, squeezed his hand with flame-tipped fingers. "He doesn't know how good I really am," she said. "I've never told him, and now I'm glad. We've got a cabin nearby, and several nights a week we go canoeing on the lake. We're going out tonight. After we're out a while I'll start an argument. He's easily riled, so it won't be hard. We'll scuffle and I'll fall overboard. Only I won't come up. I'll stay underwater until I'm sure he won't see me. He'll think I've drowned."

"Suppose he dives in after you?"

"Un unh. He can't swim."

Dawson frowned. "Where do I come in?"

Angela stared at him over the rim of her glass. "You were standing on the bank and saw us fighting," she said, a note of intensity creeping into her voice. "You saw him push me into the water. Later, you'll call him on the phone and tell him you saw the whole thing. You'll make it sound like murder."

"Blackmail," said Dawson tightly. "Think he'll go for it?"

"Hook, line and sinker," Angela assured him. "He's afraid of his own shadow. You know that."

"He'll recognize me."

"So what? If he gets curious, tell him you were passing through Pineville on your way to the coast, and just happened to stop off to pay us a visit."

"What happens when they don't find your body?"

Angela laughed. "Don't let it worry you, Johnny. There's a strong undercurrent that sweeps downstream into the Mississippi. Several people have drowned in that lake and their bodies have never been found."

Dawson lit a cigarette thoughtfully. It wasn't a bad idea. Not bad at all, and it just might work. Emory frightened easily, he had proof of that.

"How much do we ask for?"

"A hundred grand," said Angela. "All in cash. And don't let him put you off. He can lay his hands on that much within twenty-four hours."

"It sounds good," Dawson admitted.

"It is good. Now listen; when I surface, I'll go straight to the cabin. You wait for me there. Then you can take me to a motel on one of the back roads somewheres. Once there, I'll dye my hair and change into low-heeled shoes and horn-rimmed glasses. Nobody'll know me. When you get the dough we'll head for Mexico."

"Won't Emory go to the cabin, too?"

Angela shook her dark tresses impatiently. "Not a chance. He'll be too busy trying to get help. That'll give us plenty of time to get to a motel." She checked her wristwatch. "It's six-thirty. Come on, we've got to work fast."

Outside, Angela headed for a cream-colored Cadillac. "Hop in," she said. "First, I'll show you where our cabin is. Then we'll come back to your car."

Easing into the car, Dawson felt something hard and metallic under his legs. It was a heavy wrench.

"Throw it in back," snapped Angela. "The dumb cluck is always leaving his tools around."

Ten minutes later she braked on a lonely dirt road. Scrubby bushes and tall, gaunt-looking pines met Dawson's roving scrutiny.

"The cabin is straight ahead, about a hundred yards," said Angela, pointing.

Dawson could make out a tiny light flickering through the trees. "Any other cabins around?"

"It's the only one this side of the lake," Angela explained. "How about it? Got everything straight?"

"I think so," said Dawson. Quickly, he went over the plan she had outlined in the tavern. Angela listened carefully, nodded when he was through.

"Good," she said, wetting her lips. "How about a kiss for old times' sake?"

Dawson took her in his arms and kissed her hungrily. She was soft and purry, like a kitten. Time always seemed to stand still when they were in each other's arms. And in a few short hours she would be his forever. Thinking about it made him want to shout.

Later, when they had returned to the tavern, she said, "Be at the cabin at nine sharp." She leaned forward and kissed him on the cheek. "Good luck, Johnny."

Dawson smiled as he watched the big Caddy's taillight fade into the gathering dusk. All his life he had dreamed of the Big Caper. The Big Deal. The One Job that would put him on Easy Street for the rest of his life. Now he was getting it and Angela in a single evening. He rubbed his chin in disbelief. It seemed too good to be true . . .

It was exactly nine o'clock when he parked his Chevy alongside the cabin. He looked around cautiously before getting out. The cabin was dark, and only the night sounds of the woods disturbed the eerie silence. He went up on the porch and relaxed in a rocker. There was a full moon, and from where he sat he could see the water shimmering through the trees.

For time to time he checked the luminous hands of his watch. Nine-five. Then nine-ten. If everything went according to schedule, Angela should be in the water by now. He got up and began pacing the porch. He wished he wasn't so nervous. A premonition of disaster assailed him, but he shook it off. What could possibly go wrong? Angela had everything figured to the minutest detail. Despite the humid weather, his hands were like ice, and he cursed himself for being a fool.

He patted his pockets for his cigarette case before remembering he had given it to Angela when she asked for a cigarette. She had probably put it in her bag by mistake. And no wonder, he grinned. She had a lot on her mind. A hundred grand worth.

It was nine-fifteen when he heard a car turn into the dirt road that led to the cabin. A moment later the headlights picked him out, held him in their harsh glare. Controlling himself with an effort, Dawson suppressed a desire to flee. Something had gone wrong, he sensed it now. But what? He stuck his hands in his pockets to keep them from shaking.

Two figures emerged from the car and approached him warily. It wasn't until they were a few yards away that he saw the green and blue uniforms. State Police. His body went rigid. They were pointing guns at him!

"What are you doing here, Buddy?" one of them asked.

"I'm waiting for Mr. and Mrs. Emory," said Dawson calmly. "No law against it, is there?"

"Mebbe," said the shorter of the two officers. "What's your name?"

"Dawson. Johnny Dawson. I'm an old friend of Mrs. Emory's."

The two officers studied him a moment. "Take a look inside, Bob," said the shorter man. "I'll keep him covered."

"You're wasting your time," said Dawson irritably. "There's nobody home."

"We'll look anyway."

Dawson watched the man called Bob climb the steps and test the door. It was unlocked and the officer stepped inside, gun poised. A moment later a light snapped on. Dawson fidgeted nervously.

"Holy Cow, Jim!" exclaimed Bob hoarsely. "Get in here fast."

"Okay, Buddy," said Jim. "Walk straight ahead and no tricks."

Dawson stepped inside the cabin. The room, he saw, was a shambles. Chairs and tables lay overturned and smashed. Glassware was broken.

"Over here, Jim," said Bob. "Behind the couch."

A man lay on his back, his face bruised and battered. His blonde hair was matted with blood. It was Richard Emory III, and he was dead.

"There's the murder weapon," said Bob, pointing with his gun.

It was a heavy wrench. Dawson recognized it as the same one he had handled in the car.

The older officer, Jim, gave him a quizzical glance. "If we find your prints on it, Buddy, you're a dead duck," he said.

Dawson choked back a laugh. How stupid could you get? He had walked into it like a five-year-old kid. He had to hand it to Angela. She was a smart cookie. Sweet Angela. Even the fight he'd had with Emory would be evidence against him. And then, from somewheres in his subconscious, he remembered telling her he would die for her.

"And here's a cigarette case," said Bob, stooping. "There's some initials on it. Let's see. They're J.D. What'd you say your name was, Buddy?"

Dawson didn't answer. He couldn't. He was laughing so hard he was crying.

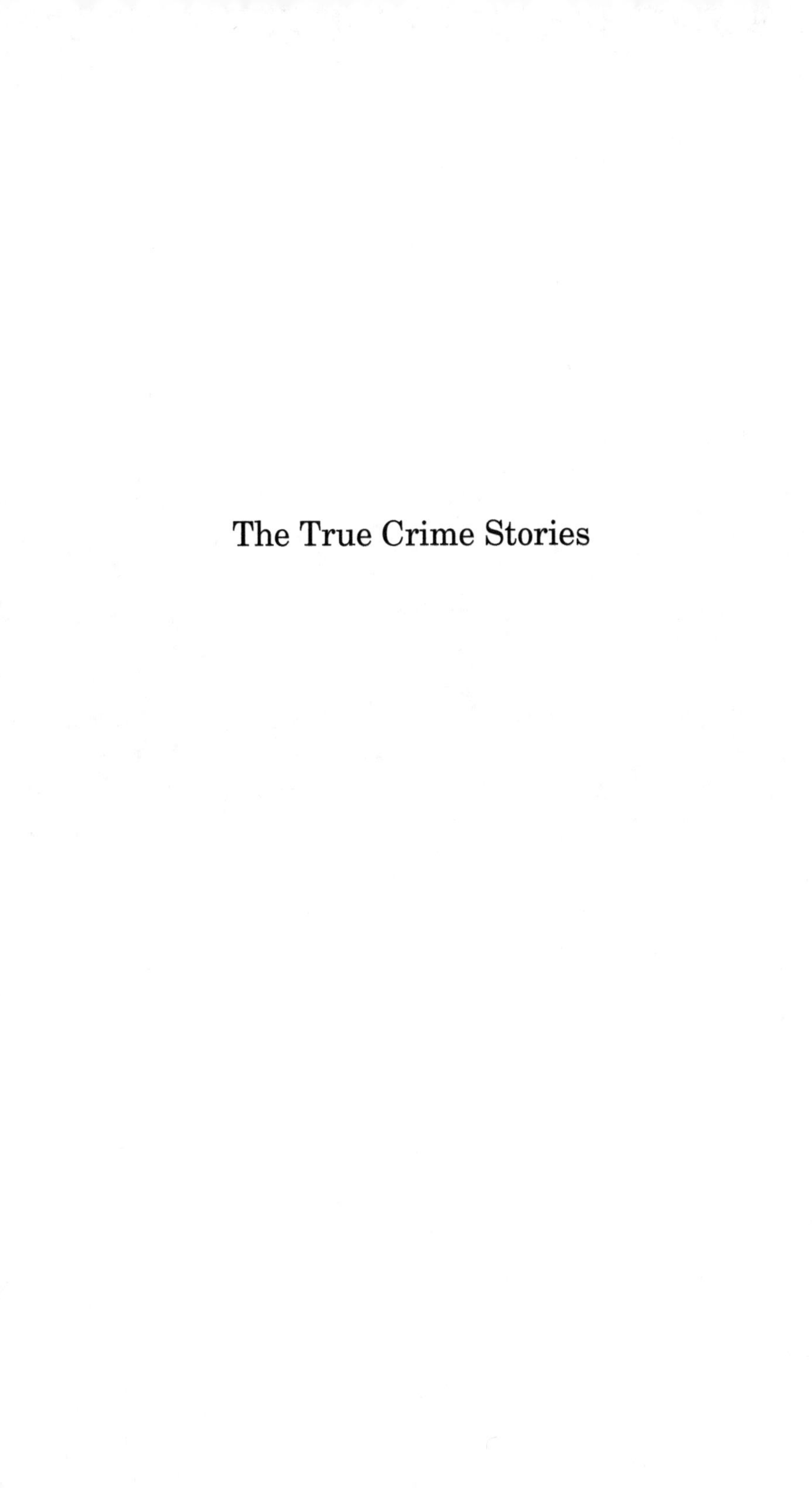

The True Crime Stories

NEVER KILL A COP!

Complete Detective Cases, January 1947

A pre-dawn haze hovered over the New Jersey countryside shortly before five o'clock on the morning of November 9. Flashes of lightning made weird patterns in the sky as sounds of thunder rolled in from the west.

Two state troopers, Warren Yenser and John Matey, piloted their squad car along the New York-Philadelphia highway a few miles from Linden.

"I'd like to lay my hands on the guy driving that car," muttered Yenser, his lean jaws hardening.

Matey nodded, but said nothing.

Through the rear view mirror, Matey, who was driving, saw a pair of headlights, pin points of light in the distance, careening wildly and coming fast. Could this be the car back again?

"Take a look, Warren, this may be 'em coming," instructed Matey.

Yenser twisted in his seat and glanced back. The steady hum of rubber on macadam reached his ears. "It may be," he whispered softly. "We'll know in a . . ."

The car shot past with a roar as the sounds of an overheated radiator cut through the still night air.

"Hear that hissing?" snapped Yenser grimly. "Let's go!"

Matey stepped on the accelerator, the squad car jumping as though propelled from a rocket. They could make but the dim tail light of the disappearing car as it bobbed and weaved along the highway a good half-mile ahead.

The two officers, their eyes glued on their speeding quarry, saw the needle of the speedometer slowly rise from 60 to 65; then to 70 and 80. Now they could see the other car coming into focus as the drama unfolded on the silent New Jersey road.

Suddenly they saw its orange and black license plate in the glow of their powerful headlights and then they were abreast of the car. Matey, his eyes glued on the road, snapped, "Give 'em the whistle, Warren."

Yenser raised the whistle to his-lips, then suddenly lurched heavily against his partner, his head falling over the wheel. Matey, confused by the strange actions of his partner, momentarily lost control, the car swerving crazily off the highway. Just in time, he checked its mad flight as it headed straight for a telegraph pole.

Pushing Yenser away with his right shoulder, Matey shouted, "What's wrong, Warren?"

In the pale glow from the dashboard Matey saw blood coursing down his partner's face. Suddenly he realized that Yenser had been shot. The roaring of the motors had deadened the report of the bullet.

Maneuvering back onto the road, Matey pushed the pedal to the floor. Precious seconds had been lost, but he could still see the dancing red tail light in the distance. Manipulating the speeding car with one hand, he loosened his holster and removed his service revolver with the other.

Again the needle rose with the rising crescendo of the motor to 80; then 85 . . . then 90. Slowly but surely, the other car came into view. Now it was less than 100 feet ahead and Matey snapped the spotlight on the car, making it stand out clearly in the bright glare.

Again the injured Yenser slumped over towards him. This time Matey pushed his partner back with his right hand. He gritted his teeth as he thought, "Is Yenser dead?"

The smashing of glass interrupted the hum of tires and motors. Someone in the other car was going to shoot through the rear window. Nothing daunted, the avenging state trooper nodded with satisfaction as his squad car kept gaining steadily every minute.

He saw a spurt of flame and then heard the metallic "ping" of a bullet as it smashed into his radiator. Grabbing the steering wheel with his right hand, Matey leaned out the window and emptied his gun at the car. But again Yenser fell sideways against him, causing the car to careen wildly for a few seconds. Fighting to keep it under control, Matey saw the car disappear around a bend in the highway.

Spying an all-night diner, Matey drove into the parking space with a screeching of brakes, jumped out and ran inside. The counterman, looked up in surprise as the disheveled trooper burst in at the door.

"Got a phone?" snapped Matey.

"Yeah," he nodded, indicating a wall phone.

"Take a look at my pal outside," said Matey, inserting a coin in the box. "He's hurt badly."

The counterman nodded and hurried outside. A few seconds later Matey was talking to the Elizabeth police.

"There's a car heading your way. I think there're two men in it. It's a brand new Chevrolet coupe, yellow wheels, Pennsylvania plates, number D-C-two-four-oh. Rear window busted. They just shot my partner. Take no chances, they're armed!"

Breathlessly, he hung up as the counterman returned. One look at his face and Matey's fears were confirmed; fears he had hated to admit when Yenser's body slumped against his.

"Nobody can do nothin' for him," said the counterman.

Matey sat on a stool and shook his head, dazedly.

Meanwhile his call to Elizabeth had roused that town's police force into early morning activity. Red lights flashed on all call boxes over the town as a radio broadcast the alarm to cruising prowl cars.

On the corner of Broad and East Jersey Streets was a call box used by policemen of two beats. Patrolman Alex Geiger was the first to receive the news. Carefully recording the details, he hung up after announcing, "Mike Morris is coming along now. I'll tell him."

Briefly, Geiger relayed the instructions to his comrade in blue. "How about getting that cabbie ready, just in case?" suggested Geiger, pointing towards a taxi and its driver.

Crossing the street, Geiger ordered the cabbie to run his motor and get ready. Suddenly a car loomed up and came tearing up East Jersey Street.

"Maybe this is it," muttered Morris, craning his neck.

As the car shot past, its radiator hissing steam, he exclaimed, "That's it! Pennsylvania plates and the rear window's busted!"

While Morris sprinted across the street to call Headquarters, Geiger jumped into the taxi and the car spurted in pursuit.

A radio officer sat hunched over a huge map of Elizabeth and its environs. With one hand he was making rapid calculations and with the other he was listening to Morris' excited report. According to the route followed by the Chevy, it was heading for Newark across the Jersey meadows. He felt, too, that the car was trying desperately to get back on the main highway leading to that metropolis and that if they stuck to East Jersey Street they could come right into it.

He grabbed the microphone and barked orders to all cruising patrol cars:

"Make for the main highway and East Jersey Street. Head off that coupe. Believe there are two occupants. Be careful, they are armed. Signing off."

The first prowl car to reach the intersection of East Jersey and the main artery leading to Newark was occupied by officers Keck and Carolin. Both men had their service revolvers ready for instant use.

The faint glow of a new dawn showed in the east as the two men waited tensely. A pair of headlights from an oncoming car flooded the darkness of East Jersey Street.

"That look like it, Leo?" asked Keck, switching off his lights.

Officer Leo Carolin strained forward trying to pierce the gloom. "Don't think so, Ernie, it looks like a big truck to me. Yes, that's what it is."

As the huge truck came abreast of the patrol car a smaller car shot out from behind its screening shield and whizzed by the startled officers.

"There it is!" shouted Keck, hoarsely.

Carolin grabbed the transmitter. All squad cars are equipped with a two-way communication system enabling the men in them to talk to Headquarters and vice versa.

"Patrolman Carolin calling," he snapped as the squad car bolted forward in a burst of speed. "That coupe just passed us goin' like a bat outta' hell! We're after it. Now they're shootin' at us and I'm firin' back!"

The staccato sounds of pistol shots reverberated over the ether as the radio officer sat in tense silence listening to the drama coming over the airways.

"Keep after 'em, Carolin," rooted the radio officer excitedly.

Carolin paid no heed to the words sputtering over the speaker. Breathlessly he relayed the events in the same manner as a fight announcer gives the blow-by-blow description of a fight.

"Whew! A bullet just went through the windshield! Right between Keck and me! We're gaining on 'em. They're turning into Schiller Street now, heading for the tracks. Their goose is cooked, it's a dead end street!"

The man at Headquarters barked instructions over the microphone to other prowl cars:

"Go to Schiller and Trumbull Streets. Fugitives heading for railroad tracks. Be careful, Keck and Carolin are right behind 'em. Signing off."

"We're on Schiller Street," barked Carolin. "They're stopping. They know they're stuck. Two men are jumping out and running towards the railroad yards. We're getting out. Signing off."

Braking to a fast stop along the dirty, cobble-stoned street, lined with vacant warehouses and adjacent to the Jersey Central Railroad yards, the officers jumped out and leveled their guns.

Running past the abandoned car, they spied the two men making for an alleyway between two warehouses which lay directly alongside the tracks.

Spurts of orange flames and the ominous sounds of bullets whizzing within inches of their heads only spurred the two bluecoats on. Returning the fire, they saw the fugitives disappear among the long line of box cars strung along the tracks.

By now countless other squad cars had arrived on the scene with officers spreading fanwise in an effort to head off the retreating killers, for now it was a known fact that Trooper Warren G. Yenser was dead.

A half hour later, Carolin, back at his squad car, called Headquarters: "Sorry, but we lost 'em. We've found a shotgun and two empty whiskey bottles in the car, along with a button. Looks like the button came off an overcoat because it's got some heavy gray material sticking to it."

"Good work, Carolin," word came back, then: "Bring in everything you can find for fingerprints."

Rain had started to fall over northern New Jersey some minutes before. Men standing before huge maps, planning the strategy in this chessboard game of death, knew that beyond the railroad yards were fields of wild weeds and that the ground would be muddy. Instructions were therefore issued for all policemen to be on the lookout for anyone with muddy shoes and burrs on their clothing and a missing button on a light gray overcoat.

Like a giant octopus, the long, sinewy arms of the law covered all railroad and bus terminals as well as highways, tubes and ferries.

The Chevrolet coupe was found to have been stolen the night before from a dentist in Philadelphia.

Meanwhile, Trooper Matey told of the circumstances leading to their first meeting with the killers in the abandoned car. Listening attentively to his story was Captain John J. Lamb, Chief of State Police detectives.

"We were giving the driver of a truck a ticket when this car suddenly appears. It swerved so close to Yenser that it barely missed him by inches. We hopped into the squad car and gave chase, but by that time it had disappeared. We had just about given up hope when it showed again. The rest you know."

While this conference was in progress, a startling event was taking place about two miles away . . .

Patrolman Alex Geiger, making his rounds after returning to his beat, stopped for a third time at the Pennsylvania Railroad Station which was on his rounds. For the third time he looked questioningly at Leroy Rhodes, the ticket agent.

"Anything new?" he asked, hopefully.

The agent nodded. "Just sold a ticket to a guy for Philly. He's upstairs now. The train doesn't leave till 7:56."

Geiger glanced at his watch . . . 7:15.

With eager steps he climbed to the train platform above the street level. He swung his eyes along the narrow station and spied a man with a cap pulled low over his forehead. Even in the dim light of a gloomy, overcast day he could see he was wearing a gray overcoat. Geiger's eyes sought the front of the coat. The bottom button was missing! What's more, the man's shoes were wet and muddy.

Geiger drew his gun and advanced warily. The man wheeled at the sound of the officer's footsteps. A look of surprise crossed his round, swarthy features. Spying the gun in the officer's hand, he threw his own hands skyward in a gesture of surrender.

"What's the idea, copper?" he snarled.

"Keep 'em up, buddy," warned Geiger, running his free hand expertly over the man's form. He was unarmed.

Ten minutes later the man sat sullenly across the desk from Captain Lamb. Seated nearby were Prosecutor Douglas M. Hicks, then prosecutor of Middlesex County, and one of his crack assistants, Detective Sergeant Walter L. Simpson.

A search through the suspect's pockets gave no hint of his identity. A large amount of silver, plus a few greenbacks and two silver dollars, were found on him.

"What's your name?" asked Lamb.

"Eddie Woods."

"Where you from?"

"Philly."

A report lay on the desk stating that two men had held up the Palm Gardens Cafe on Ridge Avenue, Philadelphia, only two hours before the murder of Trooper Yenser. Significantly enough, $80, including two silver dollars had been taken.

"Who was your partner?" asked Lamb.

"Partner?" muttered the man. "I don't know what you're talking about."

Woods steadfastly denied that he had taken part in any holdup; or had been in the Chevy when Trooper Yenser had been slain. It was evident to the officers that further questioning would be useless without something definite with which to link the suspect to the murder.

The processing of the two whiskey bottles answered this need. Several sets of prints were obtained, one of which matched Wood's prints perfectly. The shotgun and the abandoned car yielded only smudges.

Checking "Woods" fingerprints with the criminal files in the Quaker City, it was soon learned that the prisoner was really Eddie Metelski, notorious safecracker and burglar, who had a long record.

Confronted by this proof of his true identity, Metelski confessed to his real name, but clammed up, refusing to give any further information.

At a conference in Hick's office, Captain Lamb said earnestly: "This man is a professional thug. He won't crack; there's no use waiting for that. I've just contacted the police of New York and Philly and there's no record in their files matching the second set of prints found on the bottles. There's only one thing to do, and that's check up on Metelski's friends. That's the only way we'll learn who the other man was."

With this in mind, Detective Simpson was dispatched to Philadelphia. Assisted by Detective William Leinhauser, who was familiar with Metelski's past, he learned that the latter had been seen in the company of one Albert Morton, nicknamed "Whitey" by his cronies.

Playing both ends against the middle, Captain Lamb again confronted the prisoner. He mentioned the names of several of Metelski's close friends. The suspect readily admitted knowing them, but when Lamb casually mentioned the name of Whitey Morton, he acted puzzled and shook his head.

To the astute Captain Lamb, that was the tip-off. "Whitey" Morton had been his partner on that fatal ride!

Lamb received a setback, however, when it was definitely ascertained that the second set of prints on the bottles did *not* belong to Morton. Was there a third person involved in the killing, or was Morton really innocent? Keck and Carolin had seen only two men run from the car but they could easily have been deceived in the hazy light covering the fog-enshrouded city.

Things started happening fast now. Detectives, led by Sergeant Simpson, stormed "Whitey" Morton's rooming house residence on North Sixteenth Street in Philadelphia only to find their quarry had flown. His wife said she hadn't seen him in two days and had no knowledge of his whereabouts. She admitted that he knew an Eddie, but didn't know the last name. Simpson then put a 24-hour tail on the house.

A canvass of the neighbors around the Lentz Avenue house revealed the interesting news that at ten o'clock that morning a thin-faced man had left Metelski's home accompanied by a buxom girl named "Babe" Connors. The man's description tallied with that of "Whitey" Morton.

Late Saturday night, approximately seventeen hours after Yenser's murder, the telephone rang on Captain Lamb's desk. It was Detective Simpson calling from the Quaker City.

"We've just picked up the Connors girl," he said. "She came with an empty grip to take away his clothes."

"Will she talk?"

Lamb could hear Simpson's chuckle. "Not that girl. She's tighter than a drum. From what I can gather, 'Whitey' and the wife don't hit if off any too well."

"Okay," instructed Lamb, "bring her in, but don't let the newspapers know a thing about it."

Lamb's idea was eventually to smoke out Morton through the girl. Not knowing whether the girl had run out on him or had been picked up by the cops, he'd leave his hideaway and come looking, and the cops would be waiting.

The mysterious fingerprints on the bottles were explained when the movements of the murder duo were closely checked into. They had stopped at a roadside tavern following the cafe holdup and invited the customers to take a "swig" from the bottles. Some of the patrons had accepted, thereby leaving their prints.

On Monday morning came startling news in this thrill-packed case. The landlady of a rooming house on North Fifteenth Street, Philadelphia, smelled gas escaping from one of her rooms. Following the fumes, she realized they came from a room she had just rented on Saturday night to a young man and his "wife."

Notifying the police, the room was broken into and a man was found sprawled in death, a suicide by gas. Alongside him on the bed lay a newspaper clipping telling of the fate usually meted out to cop killers—death in the electric chair.

Matching his fingerprints with those on file, it was found that Albert "Whitey" Morton had taken the easy way out. Tortured by a gnawing fear of the chair and worried over the continued absence of the Connors girl, he had ended his life.

Further reconstruction of the crime convinced the authorities that they had the actual killer of Trooper Yenser under lock and key. Morton was known in the Philadelphia underworld as an expert driver, and witnesses to the Palm Gardens holdup testified it was Morton who jumped behind the wheel when the pair made their getaway.

Metelski was quickly indicted and held for trial. However, two days before the big show, on Saturday, December 14, 1935, Metelski and a young hoodlum named Pete Semenkewitz, escaped from the Middlesex County Jail!

Captain Lamb was infuriated when told the news. Metelski had homicidal tendencies and in effecting his sensational escape had almost killed another man. He and Semenkewitz had entered a garage across the street from the jail and badly beaten up a mechanic, but fled without obtaining their objective, a car. But Lamb knew they wouldn't be long without one.

Checking on recent visitors to Metelski he learned that the day before the break he had talked with his parents and a Joan Menkowitz, husky-throated nightclub singer.

Questioning the parents, Lamb was convinced they had nothing to do with their son's break, but the Menkowitz girl was another story.

Heavily rouged, with carmine lips and a voluptuous figure, she stared at her interrogators insolently.

"How did Metelski get that gun?" snapped Lamb. (The killer had flashed a gun in effecting his break.)

"How should I know?" was the sullen answer.

"Where is Eddie now?"

An insolent smile played around the corners of her mouth. "Wouldn't you like to know?" she mocked.

Lamb decided to dispense with efforts to make her talk. There was no doubt she had sneaked a gun into Eddie's cell, enabling him to overcome two guards and escape from the small jail.

Prosecutor Hicks' office became the hub around which a gigantic web was being spup in Middlesex County. Feverish activity was everywhere; teletypes clicked, calls were made to warn all law enforcement officers who, in turn, notified all cruising patrol cars to be on the alert.

At 2:30 Sunday morning stark realism was suddenly injected into the prosaic lives of a man and wife who were owners of a roadhouse, located in the heavily wooded country outside of Plainfield, New Jersey.

They had just retired when they heard the sounds of heavy footsteps coming up the hall stairs. Their bedroom door was thrown open. The lights were snapped on and two men, eyes glaring and guns leveled at them, stood in the doorway.

The man recognized Semenkewitz immediately; the young thug had formerly been employed about the place as a handyman. He also recognized Metelski from the killer's pictures in the newspapers.

"What do you want?" the tavernkeeper demanded.

"Keep your trap shut and you won't get hurt," hissed Metelski, giving Semenkewitz a signal with the gun.

Semenkewitz then strode to the closet and grabbed two suits of clothes and two overcoats, threw them over his arm and joined Metelski standing in the doorway.

"I want the keys to your car," demanded the killer.

"You'll find them in the cash register downstairs behind the bar," the man replied, while his wife, on the verge of hysteria, struggled desperately to control her emotions.

With pulses beating fast, they listened as the two men strode into the bar. Then they heard them leave and the garage door open. From a position by the window, the man saw the desperadoes drive hurriedly along the driveway, then crash sickeningly into a telegraph pole.

The two jailbreakers, miraculously unhurt, jumped from the wrecked car and disappeared into the woods bordering the wild Watchung Mountains. The tavernkeeper hastened to the telephone to give the alarm.

In less than twenty minutes the whole section was alive with police officers. Prosecutor Hicks and Captain Lamb made temporary headquarters in the roadhouse to facilitate the search.

Because most of the section was inaccessible to cars, the posses had to plunge through the thick undergrowth on foot. Torches were lit and held overhead to light the way through stygian blackness. The job was fraught with danger because the two men they were seeking probably would shoot without hesitation and in the glare of the torches the searchers made perfect targets.

When the sun rose over the Watchung Mountains the next morning, the fugitives were still at large. Overhead a plane droned back and forth, swooping low to give the police officer, equipped with special binoculars, the best possible chance to spot the criminals.

Prosecutor Hicks, back at his desk in New Brunswick, hit on a ruse. He figured that Joan Menkowitz had not only slipped the gun to Metelski, but had made arrangements to meet him at some secret hideaway.

Playing his hunch, he ordered the husky-throated nightclub singer to jail and then gave a statement to the newspapers to the effect that she had convinced the police of her innocence of any wrongdoing in the break from the Middlesex County Jail.

He next assigned Detectives Stockburger and Long of the state police to check back over the girl's activities of the past week. This they did, and learned that the girl had been seen around the West Kinney Street section of Newark, a street lined with cheap rooming houses, saloons and pool halls.

With a picture of the singer in their pocket, they started canvassing the neighborhood, hoping to find the house picked for the rendezvous.

Tuesday night saw another surprise in a case full of surprises. Detective Grauley of the Newark Police contacted Hicks at his home with the information that Metelski and Semenkewitz had held up a Plainfield barber and escaped in his car . . . They had slipped through the police cordon around the Watchung Mountain area!

The barber's car was found on Monday morning outside of Newark. The gas tank was empty. Evidently fearing a police broadcast on the car, they had decided to ditch it and make the rest of the way without it.

Hicks had just digested the news about the car when Stockburger phoned to say that on Friday, the day before the jailbreak, a girl, answering Joan Menkowitz's description had rented a room on West Kinney Street, paying a week's rent in advance.

Would Eddie Metelski and his pal head for it? Convinced that they would, police, under Captain Timothy Rowe, converged on the neighborhood, occupying hallways and alleyways, while others, dressed in nondescript attire, sauntered up and down West Kinney Street.

The entire neighborhood was thoroughly covered, but so conveniently placed were the officers that residents of the section knew nothing of what was going on.

The hours dragged by slowly. Daylight faded and the blanket of night descended gloomily over the gloomy street.

Suddenly, just before eight o'clock, two figures approached warily from Halsey Street. Breathlessly, the sleuths watched. In the darkness they couldn't be sure. The pair stopped, talked for a few minutes, then one turned and entered a diner on the corner; the other walked into an alley that ran between a garage and a rooming house.

Stockburger crossed the street and peered into the diner. He smiled with satisfaction and entered. Stopping directly behind a man seated at the end of the counter he whipped out his gun, prodded it into the man's back and snapped:

"Don't move, Semenkewitz! Just throw up your hands!"

Semenkewitz turned pale, but complied, slowly. Stockburger frisked him and found a .32-calibre gun in a back pocket.

Meanwhile, right behind Metelski came Detective Grauley, gun in hand. At the other end of the alley was the open ground of an automobile parking lot. From this end came Detective Francis Long, stalking his prey. From every conceivable hiding place men emerged, walking swiftly towards but one destination.

The unlighted alleyway was dark, sinister. Metelski, about halfway through, spotted the burly figure of Long coming towards him. A sixth sense warned the killer that Fate was catching up with him. He turned quickly and ran in the direction he had come, only to halt in confusion as Grauley and other shapes materialized out of the darkness of West Kinney Street and closed in on him.

Before Metelski could make a move, Grauley was on him, a smashing right to the jaw sending the killer staggering backwards against Long who pinioned Metelski's arms to his sides. A few seconds later, disarmed and his hands shackled, it was the end of the road for Eddie Metelski, cop killer.

This time the law wasn't taking any chances of having him escape. He wasn't entrusted to a small-town jail but, instead, was imprisoned in the imposing edifice which houses Newark's unlawful. The .38-calibre gun found on him proved to be the weapon that fired the slug into the state police squad car.

Metelski, awaiting trial, admitted that the ruse of his girl friend's release from jail had completely fooled him. He had gone to West Kinney Street to keep a previously arranged rendezvous.

As the date for the killer's trial approached. Joan Menkowitz admitted her part in the jailbreak. She had smuggled the gun to Metelski the day before, securing it from it's hiding place in his home in Newark. She pleaded guilty to aiding Metelski and received a five-year rap for her loyalty. Pete Semenkewitz also pleaded guilty and got a fifteen-to-twenty-year sentence. No charges were made against Babe Connors.

Metelski went on trial January 6, 1936. He was found guilty. On August 4th, Eddie Metelski had to be helped through the green door to pay with his life for the life he had so wantonly taken. The underworld warning, "Never kill a cop," is good advice.

Joan Menkowitz and Babe Connors are fictitious names, used to protect the identity of actual persons.

EXIT—THE PERFECT CRIME

Confidential Detective, March 1945

Ed Kettenring was going to kill. For years he had taken the kidding of the townspeople without complaint. Now even his wife was making remarks about his thin, pale face; his mousy, almost servile manners.

But all that was over now. Reassuringly he patted the ominous bulge in his back pocket. It felt good; gave him a feeling of strength. With any kind of luck, Charlie Cavanaugh hadn't long to live.

Guiding the car, he gazed at the red flames in the distance. A house in town was on fire.

As the car spun along the lonely country road the illuminated dial on his dashboard showed three A.M., on this September, 1931 morning. The cool night air gave him an exhilarating feeling of importance.

His thoughts flew backward to the humiliation he had suffered that afternoon. Alice had been driving, as usual, and had an accident, smashing the windshield and winding up in a ditch. The children had suffered minor cuts. Charlie Cavanaugh had to show up just as he was bawling her out.

"Shut up and get this car back on the road!" he had barked at him.

If it had come from anyone but Cavanaugh it wouldn't have been so bad. Just because he was the chief of police of Bernardsville, New Jersey, gave him no license to go around telling him to shut up. And in front of his wife, too.

He gritted his teeth. He'd never hear the last of that incident. Alice would throw it up to him at every chance she'd get. "Why don't you try to be like Charlie Cavanaugh? Why don't you be a man?"

His thick lips and his pale, bloodshot eyes moved spasmodically as he thought of the future torture he would have to endure.

He pressed the pedal to the floor. He must get there soon and see for himself. Through the early morning haze he could make out the faint silhouette of a barn. The Wiggins farm. He'd be there in a few minutes now.

Suddenly he saw people. They lined the sidewalks and the road. They were dressed in night clothes as the fire had struck without warning while the town lay at rest. He switched off the headlights and swung the car down West Street.

In that brief glimpse he realized that the house next to his was on fire. That meant that tin God Cavanaugh would be about, strutting his stuff.

Parking the car under a big, shady elm, he closed the door softly and walked quietly through the weeds and bushes that ran parallel with Prospect Street and the front door of the Cavanaugh house.

Stealthily he pushed the branches aside and looked. The fire was under control and the crowd was thinning out. So much the better. He reached and pulled out the gun. It felt so cool and strong lying there in the palm of his thin, bony hand.

The set-up was perfect. A feeling of power crept over his thin, wasted frame. He chuckled softly to himself as he thought how easy it would be. He had the night shift at the Veterans Hospital at Millington. He went on duty at eight P.M., and went off at eight A.M. His alibi was airtight.

While his two buddies slept, he had dressed in the dark, walked to the garage and driven to Bernardsville. He hadn't met one car on the road.

Suddenly he saw the door of the Cavanaugh home open and the familiar husky figure of the police chief step out and stand on the front steps, buttoning his raincoat. A hint of rain dampened the cool night air.

This was the chance he had been waiting for. Now, for only one brief moment perhaps, but a moment no one could take away from him, the fate of Charles Cavanaugh hung in the balance. For in this brief moment, Ed Kettenring could play God, the power of life or death was his, to do with as he saw fit. And he saw fit to kill!

Slowly he raised his arm, releasing the safety catch first, and took aim. But his hand stayed, suspended in midair.

Who was that familiar figure crossing the lawn in front of the chief's house? He peered closely through the dense undergrowth and cursed. It was Alice, his wife!

Crouched there in the darkness, the damp dew on his clothes and hatred in his heart, he could almost see the look of idolatry in his wife's eyes. He had seen it before and he knew it was there now.

He saw his wife talk for a few moments with the husky, goodlooking man on the steps, then turn and walk slowly across the neatly mowed lawn towards their home.

Quickly he raised his arm, aimed and pulled the trigger. The first shot missed, he knew it instinctively. But the second didn't. He saw Cavanaugh's body jerk backwards from the impact of the bullet. Saw him lurch off the steps and plunge forward across the grass like a football player carrying a ball through the line. A woman's piercing scream sounded terrifyingly loud on the quiet night air. It was his wife's scream!

Bent almost double, he saw Cavanaugh totter, his hands clutched to his stomach, then pitch forward on his face.

Quickly slipping the gun into a back pocket, he slid from the bushes and made for the car. He started the motor as sounds of excitement reached him from the other street. He pushed the stick into gear and gently eased it down the grade.

He smiled confidently as he piloted the car over the dismal country road.

It had been so easy.

Not until he reached a little creek about three miles out of town did he stop. Only the early morning mist and the eerie chirping of the crickets accompanied him as he walked down a small, narrow path to the water's edge.

With a feeling of regret he tossed the steel barreled gun into the water. A faint splash, a few bubbles and it was gone. It had been a good friend; the only one he had, really.

The motor purring softly, he drove into the hospital garage. By morning the motor would be cooled and no one would be the wiser. Softly he ascended the stairs and peered at his two fellow employees closely. A smile crossed his face when he saw their blank, peaceful faces. They were dead to the world.

He undressed quickly and quietly and jumped into bed. A sardonic leer swept his face when he thought of Charlie Cavanaugh lying on the ground, his face a mask of death.

With such pleasant thoughts running through his mind, Kettenring fell asleep, a smile on his lips.

The next morning he awoke, fresh and invigorated. He whistled a gay tune as he worked. At eight his wife would appear with the car and honk the horn. She would be full of news, she always was. Only one unpleasant thought rose to spoil his happiness. She'd never know. And he wanted, more than anything else in the world, to tell her how he had got the best of her swaggering hero.

The honking of the horn interrupted his thoughts. He picked up his lunch box and waved to his fellow workers. Alice had the door open for him when he reached the car. He could see by her flushed face that she was just bursting with news. He knew he must pretend to be surprised, to gaze with amazement as his wife unfolded a story he knew by heart.

"Ed," said Alice as the car spun down the graveled driveway and into the road leading to Bernardsville, "Charlie Cavanaugh's been murdered!"

Ed Kettenring had all he could do to keep from laughing, instead, he turned to his wife and said incredulously; "No! Who did it?"

Alice compressed her lips before answering. "They don't know, yet. He was shot last night as he stood on his front steps. I was talking to him just before it happened. As I walked away, I heard two shots. I turned around and saw Charlie stagger off the steps and fall right at my feet."

"So Charlie Cavanaugh's dead," said Ed, making a clucking sound and giving his voice the right amount of disbelief.

"They found a footprint of a man's left shoe in the ground behind the bushes on Prospect St.," Alice went on excitedly. "Everyone seems to think it may mean something."

Kettenring smiled inwardly. He knew even if the moulage cast matched his, it wouldn't be sufficient evidence. No one would believe that little, insignificant Ed Kettenring would commit murder.

"I suppose the town's full of cops?" he asked, trying to make his voice sound casual.

"Yes," she nodded. "They're all over the place. They seem to think the four rum-runners Charlie ran out of town last week had something to do with it."

"I always thought he went too far in making those speakeasy raids," he said, glibly. Things were going better than he expected. The police were suspecting Cavanaugh's activities in a one-man crusade he had conducted against violators of the Volstead Act as the cause of his death.

As his wife drove into the driveway of their home he saw two men enter the Cavanaugh home across the street. A momentary feeling of uneasiness possessed him when he recognized them. One was Charlie Allegar, chief of detectives of Somerset County, and his right hand man, Joe Hanlon, a shrewd detective.

He knew both men were good cops. They took nothing for granted and they usually got what they went after. He followed his wife, wondering how much they knew.

Kettenring spent the morning working on his garden in the backyard. He could hear the screeching of brakes and the sounds of activity as cars drew up before the house across the street. He heard they had taken Charlie's body to the morgue to probe for the bullet.

He smiled as he thought of their wasted energy. They'd never find the gun that fired that bullet. It was at the bottom of the creek.

Picking weeds, he ran over the events of the previous night for a possible loophole. He had read where every murderer leaves some clue that eventually trips him. But everything checked perfectly.

As the morning wore on he felt a desire to see the man he had killed. Being a fellow townsman it would be expected of him. Answering his wife's call to luncheon, he washed up, shaved, and changed into his good suit.

Alice looked at him appraisingly when he entered the kitchen. "Anybody would think you're going to a funeral the way you're dolled up," she said.

"Next thing to it, my dear," he smiled. "I'm going over to see Charlie."

Pouring the coffee, Alice said: "Mr. Allegar stopped me this morning."

Kettenring felt his body grow rigid under the table. He could feel his legs get numb and his feet cold. What would the chief of detectives possibly want with his wife?

"What did he want, dear? Did he ask you if you killed Charlie?" he jibed, hiding his anxiety.

"No, of course not," she replied seriously. "I happened to be the last person to talk with him and I was the nearest when the shots were fired. He didn't say so in as many words, but I could see they are wondering if I had any connection with it."

Kettenring could feel his body relax. Routine investigation, that's all it was. The cops had to show the taxpayers they were on the job.

"They asked me if I had a .38 calibre gun in the house," Alice went on. "I . . ."

"What did you tell them?" he snapped harshly, his jaws snapping.

"I told them no, of course," she said, looking at him with surprise. "What else could I tell them?"

Kettenring drank his coffee without answering. He must control himself. What a sap he was. Of course she couldn't tell them anything. She didn't know the gun had been hidden in his tool box for the past couple of months.

Buying that gun in a New York City hock shop had been a clever move. Signing a fictitious name for it in backhand hadn't been bad, either. They'd never trace that gun in a million years, even if they did find it. Not after he got through filing those numbers off. Oh, he heard about a chemical that brought the numbers out again, but they wouldn't bring out *those numbers.*

Late that afternoon he filed past his victim's bier. He made his face sorrowful, and even managed, by hard work, to get a tear into one eye.

People stood around, talking in hushed tones, paying silent tribute to a man who had done his job faithfully and well. Kettenring, bored, added his eulogies along with the rest. The trip wasn't wasted however, for he learned that the police were stumped; they were running around in circles.

His wife drove him to work that night in tight-lipped silence. The smooth running motor lulled his mind into peaceful thoughts. Everything was going to be fine now. Not once had Alice brought up Cavanaugh's virtues. You can't very well brag about a man who got killed, can you?

"Why so quiet?" he asked, breaking the silence.

Keeping her eyes on the road she said: "How did your clothes get so damp, Ed? I hung them up after you left for Charlie's house."

Kettenring started. He cursed himself for being so careless. He had meant to hang them up himself.

"I guess I got 'em wet when I was washing the car this morning. Why?"

"I was just thinking."

Alice's reluctance to talk bothered him. Experience with her had taught him that when she got to thinking, it would be just too bad—for him. He had to find out what she was mulling over.

"Still thinking about Charlie Cavanaugh's greatness?" he asked vindictively.

"No. But I was thinking it was possible you killed him." She said it slowly, as if weighing each word carefully.

"Me!" he exclaimed, trying to suppress his dismay. "You know me better than that," he scoffed.

She nodded absently. "That's just it, Ed, I do. I know how you hated him. Oh, not only you alone, but everyone in town who crossed him. He wasn't popular, but he got things done."

"Why pick on me? I must say though that you flatter me," he said with forced gaiety.

She took her eyes from the road and looked straight at him; through him. "I wonder?" she said musingly.

As Ed Kettenring worked that night, his troubled mind ran the gamut of wild and unreasonable thoughts. How much did Alice know? Did she really suspect him?

That night he didn't have a call out of Millington. This time of the year was always slow. He started wondering how Allegar and Hanlon were making out, if they were getting anywhere.

Alice called for him the next morning as usual. Nothing was said about Cavanaugh or the efforts of the police to bring in the killer. Just about the children and how they were doing in school.

He noticed with relief that Alice had lost her reticence of the previous evening and was her old bubbling self again. That could mean only one thing; she had eliminated him as a murder suspect.

As they turned into their driveway he caught Hanlon peering at him from behind the curtains of the Cavanaugh home. With a vague feeling of uneasiness he slammed the door and walked inside.

Over and over he tried to convince himself he had made no slipup. Only one person in the world knew the real motive for the killing. Himself. If he just kept his head, they'd never suspect him.

He eagerly awaited his wife's return from her daily shopping trip.

She always managed to get the town gossip on those forages.

At last he heard her step in the kitchen. Helping her off with her coat, he tried desperately to stem the flow of questions which trembled on his lips.

"Any news?" he asked casually.

"A little," she replied, busily preparing the noon day meal. "The police are now convinced it's a town job. That someone in Bernardsville harbored a grudge against Charlie."

Kettenring laughed hollowly. "Then they better arrest the whole town."

That afternoon he couldn't sleep. A late summer's heat wave made the room hot and sticky. The curtains of his bedroom hung limp as perspiration poured from every pore in his emaciated body.

What made them change their minds? Had Alice conveyed her suspicions of him to anyone else? He thought not. Alice wasn't that foolish.

That night he found his car laid up for repairs. As he busied himself about the garage he thought of its last trip. It hadn't been used since the night of the murder. It had done a good job that night; it deserved an overhauling.

His thoughts rambled to Allegar and Hanlon. Strange they hadn't come around to see him yet. He expected it because of the hot words he had had with Cavanaugh a few hours before the chief's death.

The next morning, as he awaited his wife's usual signal, a car drew up before the garage, its tires making a crunching sound on the gravel.

He started when he recognized them. Charlie Allegar and Joe Hanlon. He worked on unconcerned. He must be cool and indifferent. He found himself dreading the meeting which was inevitable. He felt his flesh creep when he heard their step alongside.

"Hi'ya, Ed," said Hanlon, affably. Kettenring turned and faced the detectives. He was calm.

"How are you fellows?" he answered. "Payin' me a visit?"

He thought he detected a gleam in Allegar's eyes. But it was gone as fast as it had come. "What makes you think we're coming to see you, Ed?" asked Hanlon.

Kettenring laughed, a nervous, forced laugh. "Oh, I don't know. Cops always interview everybody, so I've heard. Have to make the taxpayers think they're on the job."

"Heard you had an argument with Cavanaugh before he was killed!" Allegar said.

"Sure," nodded Kettenring, relieved. Just the usual checkup, as he expected. "My wife ran the car off the road. He hopped on me for bawling her out. Why?"

"You didn't like Charlie, did you?" asked Hanlon.

Kettenring shook his head. "I didn't hate him if that's what you mean. I was against his highhanded methods, yes."

"Tell me, Ed," asked Hanlon casually. "Were you in Bernardsville the night of the murder?"

"Of course not. My hours here are from eight at night . . ."

Allegar waved him quiet. "I know," he said tersely, "until eight in the morning. You know, Ed, that makes a beautiful alibi. Unbreakable, I'd call it."

"I wasn't thinking of it as an alibi," protested Kettenring, smirking triumphantly. "I was just stating my hours."

"Where's the foreman's office?" asked Allegar.

Kettenring jerked a thumb over his shoulder. "In the back."

"Be seeing you," said Hanlon as they moved off.

He watched covertly as the two men disappeared into the cubby hole office in the rear of the garage. Mike, the foreman, would tell them that he had slept here that night; that the car hadn't been out of the garage since the day before Charlie was killed.

He thumbed the nozzle control on the water hose confidently as he swung the flowing liquid over the concrete floor. Footsteps caused him to glance up. They were striding to a car—his car. Why were they looking his car over?

Feeling good, he swung the hissing stream of water playfully against the white washed walls. His ears, alert to every sound, heard them coming back. He shut off the water and faced the two men calmly.

"Everything okay, boys?" he asked.

"We're taking you in, Ed," said Hanlon, gravely.

He could sense, rather than see, the eyes of the others, his fellow workers, gazing at him. What had they found in his car that could possibly give him away?

"You're nuts," he managed to stammer.

Allegar shrugged his shoulders. "Perhaps, Ed. You were pretty clever, but you guys always slip up on one thing. If it wasn't for that, you'd have committed the perfect crime."

"I still don't get it," said Kettenring, a feeling of weakness possessing his body.

"All right, Ed, we'll tell you," said Hanlon wearily. "Every time your car leaves the garage your mileage gauge is checked. Am I right?"

The inkling of a terrible mistake dawned on his panic-stricken mind. "Yes," he said weakly.

"On your last trip the day before the murder your gauge showed 14,455 miles when you returned," continued Hanlon. "Your foreman's chart still shows that mileage because the car hasn't been out of the garage since. On official business, that is."

Hanlon paused to let his words sink in. "Your car, however, shows 14,465 miles. It's just about ten miles from here to Prospect St., Bernardsville. Those ten miles will send you to the chair, Ed."

Kettenring felt the earth slipping away from beneath him. He tried desperately to regain control of his befuddled mind.

"You can't arrest a man on stuff like that," he shouted.

"It'll help," snapped Allegar. "I imagine the moulage cast we made of your footprint will help a little, too."

At police headquarters in Somerville he dazedly parried the countless flow of questions thrown at him by a sea of faces surrounding his chair.

Suddenly he found himself telling of the night of horror. How he hated Charlie Cavanaugh because of his strong, superior complacency, his overbearing arrogance. When he had finished he gazed blankly at the faces staring at him. What had he said? Was he out of his mind? Where was that self-control he had always said he must have?

"Where did you hide the gun?" asked Hanlon, kindly.

"Gun? What gun?" Kettenring leered at him craftily.

"The gun you killed Cavanaugh with," snapped Allegar.

"I killed Cavanaugh? You're crazy," laughed Kettenring wildly.

Arraigned in November, 1931, Kettenring pleaded not guilty to the slaying of Bernardsville's chief of police on the grounds of insanity.

He was committed to a state mental institution. Two years later he was released as sane and held for trial on October 9th, 1933.

For five days his lawyers put up a heroic fight to save their client but the jury returned a verdict of murder in the second degree. On November 3, 1933, Supreme Court Justice Joseph L. Bodine sentenced Kettenring to a term of 15 to 20 years at the State's Prison in Trenton.

But Edward Kettenring never served his sentence. He died before his term was half finished. Alice Kettenring followed him soon after.

WEDDED TO DEATH ON FATAL FRIDAY

News Flash Detective Cases, April 1946

November 20, 1945: In the crowded courtroom, the judge's gavel raps sharply, "The prisoner will rise . . . have been found guilty of murder in the first degree . . ."

The words conclude a case that had begun more than three years before—three years of constant, intensive police work to trail down a murderer. A case replete with surprise, suspense, strange twists and turns; in short, all the trappings of fiction. So to go back to the beginning . . .

The body lay face downward in a shallow rain-filled ditch on lonely King Road. Overhead, low clouds raced across an inky sky as four police officers stood grouped about the body of a man garbed in the uniform of a U. S. Navy petty officer,

Sergeant Willard Schauers of the Lawrence Park barracks of the Pennsylvania State Police turned to the husky, bespectacled man at his elbow. "You were here first, sheriff. What's it all about?"

Sheriff Fred Lamberton of Harborcreek rubbed his chin reflectively. "I still haven't all the details clear myself, sergeant," he answered. "Arthur Ferris called me less than fifteen minutes ago and told me someone was shot. I called you and hustled right on out."

Schauers glanced at his wristwatch. "It's 3:30 A.M. now. This poor fellow must have been shot just a few minutes ago. Do you know him?"

Lamberton nodded. "He's Floyd Wilkinson. Lived in Harborcreek all his life. He was a good kid."

A short distance from the body stood a four-door sedan with both front doors open. Schauers turned to Corporal John Mehallic and Trooper David C. Hoffman.

"Check the body and everything around here," he ordered. "I'm going to the Ferris place to ask some questions."

Schauers jumped in Lamberton's car for the quarter-mile drive to the Ferris home. It was ablaze with light. Climbing the steps, they found Ferris waiting for them.

"She's in here, officers," he said nervously. "Follow me."

Lamberton glanced at Schauers and shrugged. It was the first they knew about a woman being mixed in the case. In the living room they found Ruby Eastman, a beautiful girl of about twenty, slumped in an armchair. Her eyes were swollen from weeping.

"Why, Ruby," exclaimed Lamberton, surprised. "What are you doing here?"

The sight of a friendly face caused the girl to break into a fresh paroxysm of crying. While they waited for the tears to stop, Lamberton recalled that Floyd Wilkinson, the dead man, had returned home only recently to marry pretty Ruby Eastman. With a start he realized that the marriage was to have taken place that very morning of Good Friday, April 3rd, 1942. The groom had been murdered on his wedding day!

Ruby regained her composure and faced them. "Is Floyd—dead?" she asked tremulously.

Lamberton nodded. "I'm afraid so," he replied. "Tell us what happened."

Miss Eastman explained that she and Wilkinson had attended a prenuptial party given for them the evening before. Instead of returning when it was over, they drove to King Road to make plans for the day when Floyd would be discharged from the navy. They had failed to notice a car rolling to a stop behind them. A figure emerged and slipped through the darkness.

They hadn't realized their danger until the stealthy figure had jerked open the door on the girl's side and was pointing a gun at them.

"He asked Floyd for his money," Ruby went on. "Floyd gave it to him. It was in a leather wallet. That would have ended it if the bandit hadn't grabbed me by the arm and started to pull me from the car. That made Floyd furious. He jumped from the car and grappled with the man. I took my chance and ran for help. Suddenly I heard shots. I turned and looked. The bandit was standing over Floyd and pumping bullets into him.

"I heard him call for me to stop, but I continued to run as fast as I could. When I got here I woke up Mr. Ferris and he called the police."

"This man, had you ever seen him before?" asked Schauers.

Ruby Eastman shook her head. Asked to describe him, she replied: "I didn't get a good look at him, but I did notice he was wearing a plaid shirt, riding breeches and high boots. He was young, no more than twenty-three."

"Did you notice what make car he was driving?"

"No. I was much too frightened to notice," replied Miss Eastman, shuddering.

Further questioning failed to add to the meager clues thus far obtained from the girl. To identify an unknown figure materializing in the night, committing murder and slipping away again into oblivion— that was the superhuman task confronting the law. Thanking the distraught girl, Lamberton and Schauers returned to the scene of the crime. They found that the body had been removed to a Harborcreek mortuary where an autopsy would be performed that morning.

"I found this in the bushes, near the body," said Mehallic, handing Schauers a wallet. The latter rifled it, saw it contained the slain man's papers, but no currency.

"So far robbery seems to be our motive," said Schauers. "But finding a killer dressed in a riding habit is a tall order. Those outfits are fairly common."

"Around here they are," assented Lamberton. "I've had trouble along this road for the past three weeks. Plenty of spooners getting held up."

"Yeah, I know," nodded Schauers. "But remember, this guy went further."

"I wonder if Ruby Eastman could have known the killer?" mused Lamberton. "Three in the morning is a little late even for guys who hold up parked cars to be out. One or two A.M. is their limit."

Small, well defined footprints found near the ditch suggested that the killer was not a tall man. State Police laboratory experts quickly made moulage casts of them. Wilkinson's car was towed to the barracks at Lawrence Park, to receive a thorough going-over for fingerprints. Meanwhile, a search of the vicinity disclosed several cartridge shells.

"These came from a .32 automatic," said Schauers, fingering them thoughtfully.

Within hours after the murder one of the most extensive manhunts in western Pennsylvania was under way. Police departments of eight states were provided with the killer's sketchy description. Members of the state police's mobile units prowled the countryside in and around Erie, the county seat, asking questions of farmers, but without success.

A friend of Floyd Wilkinson's was questioned but could recall no enemies of the slain man.

"Floyd was a swell guy," he stated sadly. "Everyone liked him."

Lamberton tried another angle. "Did Ruby Eastman keep company with anyone before she met Floyd?"

"She went to dances and had a good time, but that's all. She wasn't serious over anyone, if that's what you mean."

The autopsy report stated that Wilkinson had been shot three times, the death bullet being one that entered his back, pierced his heart and lodged in the chest. The absence of powder marks on the clothing indicated that the killer had stood above his helpless victim and ruthlessly fired into the sailor's prone body.

Identification men from the state police found prints on the car, but they belonged to Miss Eastman, to Floyd and to his step-father, Clifford Pahanco, from whom he had borrowed the car.

A search of the murder scene failed to turn up the ignition keys belonging to Pahanco's car. A tag, he said, bearing the name "Dutch Mill" had been attached to the key ring. Police reasoned that the killer had taken the keys to prevent any attempt to follow him in the car.

The ticket agent at the Harborcreek railroad station was questioned, but said no one answering the killer's description had purchased a ticket since the time of the murder.

"It's a cinch he didn't ditch his car and escape by train then," mused Lamberton.

"And he's not a Harborcreek man or Miss Eastman would have recognized him," said Schauers. "It's certainly peculiar where he could have gone to."

Mrs. Irma Weeks, who lived near the scene of the crime, volunteered information that corroborated part of Ruby Eastman's testimony.

"It was unusually hot last night," she said. "I heard a shot on the road some distance away. I thought at first it was an auto backfiring, but when it came several more times, I knew it was pistol shots. The time was exactly ten minutes after three. I happened to look at the clock, so I'm sure."

Mrs. Weeks stated that no car passed her house during the next ten minutes. Outside, Schauers remarked: "That means the killer was headed towards Erie. Which doesn't help us a bit."

"These cases in which the relationship between the killer and the victim is a purely accidental one are headaches," commented Sheriff Lamberton. "There's nothing in the victim's background to provide us with a clue to the killer's identity because the two met apparently only by chance."

Hoping to land the killer in a roundup of known criminals, Schauers and Lamberton questioned dozens of men brought to the Lawrence Park barracks during the morning. District Attorney, Burton R. Laub of Erie County assisted in the questioning.

During these sessions Miss Eastman stood hidden behind a glassed-in partition. She could see the men as they paraded before the police, but they couldn't see her. As each one filed past she continued to shake her head. The killer had eluded the dragnet.

Weeks passed fruitlessly. With the passing of time some of the investigators, particularly Sergeant Schauers, became openly skeptical of the young woman's story. Lamberton agreed that she might be withholding something. The county authorities posted a $500 reward for the slayer's capture and an Erie newspaper added a similar amount. This move resulted in a flood of tips, which the police investigated only to find them all false.

Then occurred a dramatic event that at first seemed unrelated.

On the night of March 16th, 1943, Mrs. Mildred Haight, a resident of Corry, a small town 35 miles southeast of Erie, was cruelly beaten on a dark side street and left for dead. Chief of Police John Flanigan waited anxiously by the woman's bedside for 24 hours before she could be questioned.

Then, asked to describe her assailant, she replied: "He was short and stocky, had dark curly hair and a pug nose. He wore a blue denim shirt, riding breeches and high boots."

The description tallied. The killer of Floyd Wilkinson had struck again!

Further questioning revealed that Mrs. Haight had clawed her assailant viciously with her fingernails. "I'm certain that I left scratches on his face," she said weakly.

Encouraged by this lead, Flanigan enlisted the aid of the state police in broadcasting an alarm for all citizens to be on the alert for a stockily built man of about 22, wearing a riding outfit and bearing tell-tale scratches on his face. And that same morning he received a telephone call from the office manager of a large corporation.

"One of my employees reported for work this morning with his face a sight," said the official. "He's Frank Bromley."

Flanigan knew Bromley well. Back in September, 1941, Bromley, in love with a girl named Dorothy Drayer of Union City, asked her to marry him. When she refused, he kidnapped her across the state line into Ohio. Apprehended and brought back, Bromley was charged with violation of the Lindbergh Law but was never prosecuted.

Later Bromley had gone skating on Lake LeBoeuf, and there met Miss Drayer with another man. Upon picking a fight, he was severely beaten by the young woman's escort. Depressed, he had gone home and shot himself, but swift action by a local doctor had saved his life.

On April 2nd, 1942, Dorothy Drayer had married Woodrow Clayton. With a start Flanigan realized that April 2nd was the day before Floyd Wilkinson had been murdered. Could there be any connection between the two events? Flanigan meant to find out!

The chief first went to the manufacturing plant and arrested Frank Bromley on suspicion of having beaten Mrs. Haight.

"You're crazy," sneered the curly haired Bromley. "I was home in bed last night when it happened."

At Bromley's home, a thorough search failed to unearth the riding clothes Mrs. Haight said that the man wore. Disappointed, Chief Flanigan contacted Bromley's friends and learned that Bromley had been fond of a girl named Ruth Carnes.

At the girl's house he learned some interesting facts. Questioning the father, he discovered that Ruth had been forbidden to see Bromley, an order which had made Bromley furious. Armed with a gun, Frank had stormed into the Carnes house only to be disarmed by Mr. Carnes.

"When did this happen?" asked Flanigan, interested.

"The night before last, on March 15th," replied Carnes. "I took the shells from the gun and gave it back to him."

"Have you the shells now?"

Carnes nodded and left the room. He returned and dropped six cartridges into the sheriff's hand. They were .22's. Flanigan was disappointed. Floyd Wilkinson had been killed by a .32 caliber bullet.

Returning to his office, he put through a call to Sheriff Lamberton in Harborcreek. An hour later Lamberton walked into his office with Sergeant Willard Schauers. Briefly Flanigan told them of his suspicions concerning Frank Bromley.

"You believe he killed Wilkinson?" asked Lamberton. "Why?"

"Don't you get it?" exclaimed Flanigan. "The night after Miss Drayer's marriage to Clayton, Wilkinson gets murdered. On another occasion, Bromley is thrown out of Ruth Carnes' house. The next day Mrs. Haight is beaten and almost killed."

"Meaning?" asked Lamberton.

"Meaning that Bromley must be our man! He apparently goes berserk when he receives a big disappointment in a love affair. Then he takes his revenge on somebody else. Anyway, it's a theory."

"Mmm, you may have something there," nodded Schauers. "But how are we going to prove Bromley killed Wilkinson?"

Flanigan grinned sheepishly. "I was afraid you'd ask that. But I'm going to start working on it."

Frank Bromley was brought to Mrs. Haight's bedside at the hospital. She positively identified him as the man who had beaten her. Bromley only shrugged.

"Yeah, I did it, all right," he announced calmly. "But don't ask me why, 'cause I don't know."

Later that week Bromley was arraigned on the beating charge, tried and given a sentence of 16 to 25 years in Western Penitentiary. After he was taken away to begin serving his long sentence, Flanigan phoned Schauers at the Lawrence Park barracks.

"I'm convinced Bromley killed Floyd Wilkinson," he said tersely. "And I'm going to try to prove it."

"If you need any help, call on either Lamberton or myself," said Schauers. "And good luck."

Flanigan's first task now was to probe into the youth's background. He learned that Bromley was one of 12 children. The family, left destitute when Frank's father abandoned them, had lived on relief. As a boy Frank spent nine years in grammar school without progressing more than seven classes. Checking on his school behavior, the officer learned that Bromley had been regarded as a bully with an uncontrollable temper.

This data only strengthened the chief's belief that Bromley was a murderer at heart. Checking on the members of Bromley's friends, Flanigan learned more interesting facts. One was that Steve Wesson, a mill hand, had acted very queerly immediately after the murder of Wilkinson. He had been seen by his neighbors heading for the woods on the outskirts of town on numerous occasions; Each time he carried a small bundle under his arm. What was in that bundle and what was it for?

Flanigan knew that Wesson and his wife Martha were highly respectable citizens of Corry. For this reason he knew he must go slow and have positive proof before making any accusations.

As yet Bromley had no inkling of the suspicions against him on the Wilkinson killing. Delving into the suspect's private life, he learned that his two closest friends were Walter Hunt and Sam Werner, both of Corry.

Flanigan also learned that Bromley had owned a Ford coupe at the time of the Wilkinson murder, but had disposed of the car shortly after—a highly suspicious circumstance. Flanigan recalled Lamberton mentioning a gang of hoodlums holding up spooning couples in parked cars along King Road shortly before the murder, yet mysteriously enough, immediately after Wilkinson was slain, these nightly depredations had ceased. Why? Was the killer a member of this gang who was now lying low?

Flanigan located young Hunt first. The youth was brought to the local headquarters and questioned. The wily police official tried an old trick on his young suspect.

"Bromley tells me you two used to stick up couples in parked cars over Harborcreek way," he said matter-of-factly.

Hunt paled. The policeman's calm assurance convinced him the jig was up. The ruse worked! "Yeah, me and Frank pulled a few last year," he admitted reluctantly.

Flanigan hid his elation. "Suppose you tell me about it," he urged.

"Frank owned a Ford coupe then," explained Hunt. "We used to drive around the outskirts of Erie and Harborcreek and spot cars. If any of 'em looked like a cinch, we'd stick 'em up. Frank held the gun on 'em while I did the searching. We got away with about eight or nine of 'em on the roads east of Wesleyville."

Flanigan knew King Road lay in that general direction. Things were getting warm. Furthermore, the method of operation was identical with the method used by the killer on the night of Floyd Wilkinson's murder, except that the killer had worked alone that night.

"Did you ever see Bromley wearing riding breeches, high boots and a cap?" asked Flanigan.

Hunt shook his head. "Never while I was with him," he answered.

"What caliber gun did Bromley own?"

"A .22," was the prompt response. Flanigan saw his hopes of slapping a murder rap on Bromley evaporating. The murder gun had been a .32.

Flanigan decided to hold Hunt as a material witness pending further investigation of the case. He next turned his attention to Sam Werner. The latter lived in the same house as Bromley and had always been close to the suspect. That night, accompanied by two deputies, he corralled Werner in a Main Street pool room.

At headquarters the swarthy-faced youth denied participating in any hold-ups with Bromley.

"I knew he used to operate with Wally Hunt," admitted Werner, "but I never went along with 'em."

No amount of questioning by the police could get him to change his story. He substantiated Hunt's testimony by admitting that Bromley frequently carried a .22 caliber revolver. He denied, however, that he ever saw him garbed in a riding outfit. Flanigan finally released the youth with a curt warning not to leave town. The Corry police chief next questioned Steve Wesson about his disappearing act in the woods.

"Somebody's been giving you pipe dreams," grinned Wesson humorously. "What would I be doing in the woods?"

"That's what I'm trying to find out," snapped Flanigan, grimly. "You and Bromley were pretty close, weren't you?"

"Yeah, we got along," nodded Wesson. "Listen, chief, unless you charge me with somethin', make it snappy. My time's worth money."

Stymied on all sides so far, Flanigan decided to have a talk with the former Dorothy Drayer, now Mrs. Clayton. The comely 21-year-old brunette was surprised to see him when he called.

"Mrs. Clayton, I want you to tell me what you know about Frank Bromley," urged the police officer. "You went with him for some time, I gather?"

"Yes, I did," Mrs. Clayton acknowledged. "I liked Frank at first. I liked him a lot. But he had an ungovernable temper. He caused me embarrassment on many occasions before my friends. I couldn't stand it any longer, so I broke off with him."

"I see. Did you ever see him wearing a riding outfit? You know, breeches, high boots and all?"

"No, I never did, but he did mention that he liked to go horseback riding."

"Did he say where he took this exercise?"

"He may have, but I don't recall it now."

Flanigan took a list of names from his pocket. He read them slowly. "Do the names Walter Hunt, Sam Werner, Steve Wesson, or Ruby Eastman mean anything to you?"

Mrs. Clayton nodded. "Sam Werner's an old friend of Frank's. Ruby is an old girl friend of mine who lives in Harborcreek."

Flanigan was dumbfounded. "You know her?"

The girl laughed. "Why, Ruby and I used to go on double dates with Frank and another young fellow named Tom Smith."

"You mean Ruby Eastman knows Frank Bromley?" exclaimed Flanigan, startled.

"Of course. When we went on these dates Tom was usually my escort. Frank was Ruby's. They're old friends."

Flanigan was elated. Thanking her, he quickly contacted Sheriff Lamberton and Sergeant Schauers by phone. Briefly he related the latest twist in the bizarre case. Both men promised to be in Corry the next morning.

When Lamberton and Schauers arrived in Flanigan's office a stockily built young man sat opposite his desk. He was Tom Smith, a resident of Wesleyville. When the introductions were completed, Flanigan turned to Smith.

"Tom, Mrs. Clayton tells me you and Frank Bromley went on double dates with her and a girl named Ruby Eastman. That right?" he asked.

Smith nodded. "Sure, it's right. We took in the hot spots around Erie many times."

The Wesleyville youth denied, however, accompanying Bromley on his holdups, although admitting he saw the other carrying a loaded .22 caliber revolver on many occasions.

"Tell me, Joe," asked Schauers, "did you ever see Bromley wearing riding breeches and high boots?"

Smith nodded. "Yeah, several times. He told me he wore that outfit to throw the cops off. You see, he only wore 'em when he pulled solo jobs. Yeah, and another thing, he also owned a .32 automatic."

The officers exchanged significant glances. After locking Smith in a cell as a material witness, they investigated his actions on the night Wilkinson was murdered. They found that he had been confined to a hospital bed and was completely in the clear.

"Your hunch about Bromley is beginning to pay off, sheriff," said Schauers thoughtfully. "He probably heard about Ruby's forthcoming marriage to Wilkinson and felt he had to get even somehow."

"Especially so as it happened right after Carnes threw him out of the house," added Lamberton. "He had to let off steam—by killing Wilkinson!"

At Schauers' suggestion, Frank Bromley was brought from Western Penitentiary and lodged in the county jail at Erie. Later he was brought face to face with Ruby Eastman.

"Isn't that the man who killed your fiancé?" Schauers asked her. Bromley's face turned pale.

Ruby Eastman shook her head. "I —don't think so," she faltered.

"Never saw the dame before in my life," laughed Bromley, regaining his composure.

The officers were startled. Miss Eastman was taken to another room and informed of Mrs. Clayton's testimony. She was asked to reconsider her statement, but she stuck adamantly to her denial of knowing Frank Bromley. Discouraged, the lawmen returned Bromley to the penitentiary that night. Again their case seemed hopeless. But they hadn't given up.

More time passed. Then in the fall of 1943 Sheriff Lamberton accompanied a convicted burglar named "Tulsa" Yates to Western Penitentiary. On the ride from Harborcreek the police officer casually suggested that Yates strike up a friendship with Bromley and endeavor to learn anything possible that might be evidence in the Wilkinson slaying.

Although the idea was good, Lamberton didn't expect many results from it. So he was agreeably surprised on the morning of April 10th, 1944, to receive word that Yates wanted to see him at the penitentiary.

Hurrying to the jail, Lamberton was soon closeted with Yates in a private room.

"What did Bromley say about the Wilkinson job?" asked the sheriff.

"Not much, at first," answered Yates. "But he did tell me that if the cops ever found out what he had hidden in a certain Corry cemetery, he'd be a dead pigeon."

Lamberton knew Bromley was referring to the missing murder gun and the ignition keys the killer had taken. "He told me he wanted some things removed from the cemetery," Yates went on, "and that he'd have me take care of them when I got out. I asked him if it was a body, but he only grinned and shook his head.

"Then two nights ago he spilled every thing. He gave me the whole set-up on the Wilkinson killing. He shot the guy because he resented his muscling in on his girl."

Lamberton nodded. The long case seemed nearing a successful

climax. He instructed Yates to continue questioning Bromley and to let him know if he learned anything more.

Accompanied by Schauers, Lamberton hurried to Corry, where they contacted Sheriff Flanigan. They explained what Yates had said.

"There are five cemeteries in this town," said Flanigan. "It could be any one of 'em that the evidence is hidden in."

"Which one is nearest his home?" asked Schauers.

"St. Elizabeth's."

"Okay," nodded the state officer. "Let's try that one first."

United States army authorities were contacted and a request made for a loan of a mine detector which could locate buried metal objects. The request was granted and two army men, experts in its use, accompanied the detectives in the tedious job of locating the missing items. Then began a strange search, day after day, through the cemeteries, passing the mine detector over grave after grave in hope of hearing it buzz to announce that the missing gun, so vitally needed, and the incriminating ignition keys were buried below.

For months the Army experts searched nearly every inch of ground in and around thousands of ghostly white memorial stones, but Bromley had hidden the evidence too well. They could not locate it.

Meanwhile, however, evidence of another kind was building up. At Western Penitentiary, Bromley suddenly refused to say anything more about the Wilkinson case to Yates, indicating that he had grown suspicious of the other convict. But on November 27th, 1944, the lawmen once more questioned Ruby Eastman as to whether she knew the curly-haired youth. And at long last she broke down, and sobbingly admitted that she did know Bromley, and that on the night of her fiancé's death she had recognized the mysterious murder figure as Bromley.

"Why didn't you tell us this before?" Lamberton asked sternly.

The girl wept. "I didn't want anyone to know I was having dates with anyone else while Floyd was overseas," she sobbed. "There wasn't anything wrong in it, but I was ashamed . . ."

Now that the truth was out, the officers deemed it unnecessary to have the incriminating murder gun to bolster their case. In late December Bromley was transferred once again to the jail at Erie. Again he was brought face to face with Ruby Eastman, and again his features turned ashen pale, although he retained his composure. But this time, the girl's story gave him no assistance.

"That's the man who shot and killed Floyd on the morning of April 3rd, 1942," she said firmly.

Frank Bromley smiled sardonically throughout the dramatic scene.

While he languished in his cell to await trial on a charge of first degree murder, the officers again questioned Steve Wesson. The latter, realizing that his buddy's case was hopeless, now readily confessed taking food to him, immediately after the slaying of Floyd Wilkinson, in the mysterious packages he had been seen carrying into the woods.

"He figured Ruby would turn him in, that's why he hid in a hunter's shack in the woods," said Wesson. "When she didn't, he thought she hadn't got a good look at him that night, and was safe."

Lamberton, Schauers and Flanigan at last had enough evidence to bring Bromley to trial, they decided. District Attorney Laub concurred. On March 5th, Corporal Mehallic went before Alderman William Heisler and swore out a warrant charging Bromley with first degree murder. It was exactly two years, eleven months and four days after the cold blooded killing of Floyd Wilkinson. And thus a dramatic hunt lasting nearly three years drew toward a close.

Just before the trial a resident of Slade Road, Harborcreek, informed Schauers that, coming home from work on the morning of the murder he had seen a Ford coupe speed past him on King Road. He positively identified the car as belonging to Frank Bromley.

"How can you be sure?" asked Schauers.

"I usta' live in Corry," replied the man. "I knew Bromley well. It was his car, all right."

On November 15th, 1945, Bromley went on trial in Erie's Superior Court for his life. His attorneys pleaded eloquently for their client. However, the authorities had too strong a case. They put Ruby Eastman, Joe Rivers, Steve Wesson and Tulsa Yates on the stand, and with their evidence the result was a foregone conclusion.

On November 20th, after a hectic five day trial, Frank Bromley was found guilty of murder in the first degree. The jury was out a bare two hours and a half. However, they recommended life imprisonment for the slayer. This sentence Judge J. Orin Waite imposed two days later.

Editor's Note: *The names Walter Hunt, Tom Smith, Sam Werner, Steve Wesson, Ruth Carnes and Tulsa Yates, used in this story, are fictitious to protect the individuals involved from possible embarrassment.*

GIVE ME LIBERTY OR I GIVE YOU DEATH

Revealing Detective Cases, June 1949

Sheriff Harry Weatherholtz was tired. All day long he had sat behind his desk directing a road block which bottled every highway in Wyandot County, for no less a personage than the fabulous John Dillinger who had broken out of the Lima, Ohio, jail early that morning.

Now it was nearing midnight and he was eager to call it quits for the day. He was shrugging into his heavy ulster and was about to say goodnight to Deputy Paul Frey when the phone rang, loud and shrill.

"Now what," he grumbled irritably as he reached for the receiver.

It was a young man's voice and he sounded excited. "Sheriff, this is Wally Combs. I've just spotted a man's body out on Highway 23, midway between Carey and Upper Sandusky. Better get out here right away, I think he's been murdered!"

Weatherholtz swore to himself. "Okay, Combs. Stay where you are and don't touch anything," he warned. "And see that nobody else does, either. We'll be right out there."

Pausing only long enough to put through a call to the coroner's office, Weatherholtz and Frey sped out the darkened highway until they spied a car parked near a large cornfield which the sheriff recognized as the old V. P. Reile place. Braking behind the machine, the two men jumped out.

Combs, a youngish looking man in his 20s, led them to a narrow ditch just off the road. He pointed. "He's in there," he said huskily.

At the sheriff's direction, Frey swung the car around so that its headlights were focused on the scene. Under the glare of the lights, Weatherholtz saw that the body was partially concealed under a muddy quilt.

Removing the quilt he saw that the victim was in his 50s and fairly husky. He lay sprawled on his back, his sightless eyes staring upward. The corpse was naked except for shorts.

Dropping to one knee beside the body, Weatherholtz stared at a number of bluish colored, odd-shaped bruises on the man's face and chest. The right eye, he observed, had been all but shot away. Around the wound the skin was scorched, indicating that the gun had been held near the eyeball when the shot was fired.

He rose and shook his head. "Whoever did this certainly didn't like the guy," he muttered.

"This looks like the work of Dillinger's mob to me," said Frey.

Their conjectures were interrupted by the arrival of Coroner O. C. Stutz of Wyandot County. The latter made a swift examination. "Shot once, through the eye," he said tersely. "I doubt if he'd been dead more than an hour. Maybe two."

"Would you say he got those bruises before or after he was shot?" asked the sheriff.

"Before. Bruises don't show once a man's been dead."

"Any idea what caused them?"

Coroner Stutz frowned. "I can't quite figure them out," he answered slowly. "Whatever it was the killer used, it broke several bones in the face and throat."

Weatherholtz questioned Wally Combs, but beyond explaining how he had come to find the body, the latter could tell him nothing of importance. After excusing the young man, Weatherholtz began a minute search of the ground for clues.

He didn't have far to look. Near the rim of the ditch he discovered the unmistakable imprint of a woman's spike-heeled shoe! Had a woman committed the grisly deed? He wondered.

A careful search of the vicinity revealed nothing further of importance, however.

After the body was removed Weatherholtz spied a small white object lying where it had been. Stooping quickly, he saw that it was a calling card which read:

> "R. V. Brown
> Collector of Indian Relics
> Powhattan Point, Ohio."

The victim, he reasoned, had to be either R. V. Brown or a business acquaintance of Brown's.

Hurrying back to his office in the Upper Sandusky town hall, Weatherholtz contacted the Powhattan Point police by telephone. They informed him that Robert V. Brown was well known there as a peaceful, law abiding citizen who made a substantial living by exhibiting and lecturing on Indian relics and customs.

According to the Powhattan Point authorities, Brown had spent the summer showing his collection at local small town carnivals. With the opening of schools he had undertaken a tour of the school circuit.

Brown, he learned, had left Powhattan Point on October 9, 1933, four days before. His itinerary was to skirt the West Virginia border to St. Mary's and continue on to northern Ohio.

The body was positively identified that afternoon as that of R. V. Brown. Mrs. Agnes N. Drennan, the slain man's aunt, made the identification at the city morgue.

"It's my nephew," she nodded tearfully.

Mrs. Drennan explained that Brown had compiled a sizable fortune from showing his exhibits. "He enjoyed traveling about the country in the large green bus he always used," she said sorrowfully.

The sheriff told her about the spike-heeled footprint. Mrs. Drennan shook her head. "I can't imagine Robert hiring a woman," she said positively. "He was a bachelor, you know, and quite scary of women."

She produced a letter from her nephew which was postmarked Marietta, Ohio, two days before. It was a short, newsy note which contained nothing of importance until the last paragraph. Sheriff Weatherholtz' interest was aroused when the slain man mentioned having an argument with a carnival owner the night before in New Lexington.

The argument, explained the note, was over receipts, and mentioned the owner's name as Sidney Beckman.

After the woman had left, Weatherholtz thought about the note. Had the argument been more violent than Brown intimated? Had Beckman trailed the relic collector to an isolated spot along Highway 23 and killed him?

It was an angle, he reflected grimly, worth looking into.

Contacting the New Lexington police officials, the sheriff learned that the traveling carny had moved on to Mt. Vernon, in Knox County. Accompanied by Deputy Frey, he sped southeast to the bustling little community. He found the carnival pitched on the outskirts of the town, but his quarry, Sidney Beckman, was gone.

"He sold me the whole shooting match last night," said Jim Halleck, a beefy, red-necked man in his early 50s. "Kind of sudden it was, too. I don't know what came over the guy."

"Any idea where we can find him?" asked the disappointed sheriff.

Halleck frowned. "He mentioned something about getting a fresh start in New York. You might try there."

Weatherholtz jotted down Beckman's description in his notebook and then asked: "Do you recall putting on an Indian relic show a few nights ago?"

Halleck nodded. "I sure do. Swell show it was, too. What do you want to know about it?"

The sheriff explained how they found Brown's body in the ditch off Highway 23. "Did he operate the show by himself or did he have an assistant?"

"Heck no, he had a woman working with him," said Halleck quickly. "She was a thin, sharp-featured woman. And a regular tartar she was, too."

"What makes you say that?"

Halleck chuckled. "I went to Brown's bus about an hour before the show opened that night. The door was open when I got there and I could see him backed against the wall with the dame backhanding him something awful.

"Brown acted like he was scared to death of her. He finally slipped to the floor, half out. Then, while he lay there, she lifts her spike-heeled foot and brings it down on the guy's face with a thud. All the time she's doing it she's laughing. I don't know how many times she stomped him, because I couldn't bear to see any more."

With the carny owner's story Weatherholtz suddenly had the answer to the odd-shaped bruises on Brown's face and chest. They were high-heel marks!

Halleck described the woman as a hard-faced redhead in her late 30s or early 40s, about five feet six in height and weighing around 120 pounds. When not garbed in Indian costumes, Halleck said she usually wore a black dress and black shoes.

Keeping on the move, Weatherholtz and Frey drove to the little town of Powhattan Point in eastern Ohio. By discreet questioning he learned that a redheaded divorcee named Eva Timmer, who answered the description of Brown's assistant, had disappeared from town about the time the collector started on his tour.

He was told the woman had once been a five-a-day performer on both the Keith and Pantages circuits during vaudeville days. Like countless others however, Eva Timmer found herself without steady employment with the advent of the talking pictures.

Mrs. Anna Devore, a neighbor of the victim, was a valuable source of information to the investigators.

"The way that woman treated Mr. Brown was a shame," she declared. "He hardly knew her more than 24 hours when she took charge of everything. Mr. Brown couldn't make a move unless she sanctioned it.

"The day before they left on the tour, October 8, I think it was, Eva got into a terrible tantrum over something poor Mr. Brown did. Or didn't do, I don't know which. Anyway, she slapped him around something awful. They were making so much noise I asked my husband to see what it was all about.

"When he got there he found Eva punching Mr. Brown in the face. He decided it was none of his business, so he came back."

The sheriff returned to Upper Sandusky with a multitude of sixty-four dollar questions plaguing him. For instance, where was the dynamic redhead now? How had Brown gotten involved with her? And why had the mild-mannered bachelor let her treat him like a common serf?

Back in his office in the Wyandot County seat, Weatherholtz began using the same dragnet that had been spread for John Dillinger to catch the mysterious green bus and its homicidal occupant.

When all the arrangements were completed, Weatherholtz breathed easier. He was confident that the fiery redhead would be in police hands within a matter of hours.

He was wrong.

As the hours slowly ticked away without any word of the green bus and its occupant, another theory rose to plague the hard-working officer. What if the redhead wasn't the killer after all? Maybe her body was lying in a ditch somewhere riddled with bullets. Was the Dillinger outfit tied in somewhere?

Weatherholtz put through a long distance call to New York asking the Big Town police to be on the lookout for Sidney Beckman. When he was assured of their cooperation he hung up.

Unable to sit idly by, Weatherholtz summoned Frey and the two men began backtracking on the green bus. Driving back to Mt. Vernon, they interviewed restaurant and gas station proprietors along the highways leading north for word on the big, cumbersome vehicle.

Most of their inquiries along Highway 23 brought only blank stares and negative shakes of the head. But here and there they learned enough to convince them they were on the right track.

"Sure, I saw it," said one gas station attendant. "It seemed strange seeing a big jalopy like that being driven by a woman. She stopped here for gas."

At a diner near Marion, Ohio, they learned that the green bus had passed by only 14 hours before. "She ate her food like the devil himself was after her," said the counterman. "She was a hard looking skirt."

The sheriff was certain he was on the right track when the counterman described the woman as a redhead, and wearing a slinky black dress and black pumps.

"That's her all right," he said grimly, as he geared the car into high. "We're getting close."

At Perrysburg, they learned that the fast moving bus was only a short distance ahead of them. Ignoring the fact that they hadn't slept in more than 24 hours, the two men pushed on, determined to overtake their quarry before someone else joined Robert Brown in Valhalla.

Then, halfway between Perrysburg and Millbury, Frey spotted a weatherbeaten green bus parked behind a darkened gasoline station.

He nudged Weatherholtz excitedly. "There it is, Sheriff," he exclaimed. "We've found her!"

Weatherholtz pulled over to the side of the road and alighted. Making as little sound as possible, the two men advanced towards the bus, their revolvers out and ready.

"She's probably asleep," whispered Frey.

"Maybe so," grunted Weatherholtz, "but don't take any chances. We're dealing with a killer who won't hesitate to do it again if she has to."

Rapping loudly on the door, the sheriff shouted: "Open up! We're police officers!"

After several moments a light flicked on inside. They could make out the symmetrical figure of a woman moving cautiously behind the drawn shades of the bus.

"Open up or we'll knock the door down!" shouted Weatherholtz angrily.

The rattle of a key in the lock was followed by a hawk-faced woman peering at them from the open doorway. Weatherholtz noted with satisfaction that she was garbed in the habitual black dress and shoes.

The woman stared at them with beady eyes, her right hand holding a flashlight and her left hand concealed behind her back. As she started down the steps she suddenly flashed the bright beam of light into the officer's faces, blinding them. As fast as she was however, Weatherholtz moved a split-second faster.

Anticipating her move, he closed in and pinioned her left arm against her body. "Grab her gun, Paul," he cried hoarsely.

Frey slid behind the struggling woman and wrested a shiny .38 calibre revolver from her grasp. "I got it, Sheriff," he snapped jubilantly, locking her wrists with his handcuffs.

While the woman glared at him balefully, Weatherholtz entered the bus. The inside was a shambles. Separating the rear of the bus from the front was a hanging curtain. Cooking utensils, a stove, dishes and other odds and ends were scattered about the interior in wild profusion.

Splattered over the walls were ominous brown spots which he had no doubt were of dried blood. On the floor near the curtain was a large oval-shaped stain. More blood.

Returned to Upper Sandusky, Eva Timmer vehemently denied that she killed Robert Brown. "He and I got into an argument one night and he just up and left," she said, shrugging. "I haven't seen him since the show we did in Mt. Vernon."

Weatherholtz tapped the .38 significantly. "There's no use lying, Eva," he said briskly. "A ballistics test of this gun will prove it was the one used to kill Brown. Now, how about it, why did you kill him?"

For several long hours the two men pounded away at the sullen faced woman, but without success. Prosecutor H. L. Mason joined in questioning her early the next morning.

Finally, after eight hours of grilling, the woman admitted killing Brown, but said she had done so in self-defense. "On the night of the shooting we retired to cur separate compartments as usual," she began. "Then, about ten o'clock, I awoke to find Brown standing over my bed, a wild gleam in his eye. I screamed, but he clamped his hand over my mouth and we struggled.

"I managed somehow to break away from him and run from the bus. I was standing outside in the cold shivering for about five minutes before he promised to behave himself.

"I believed him and went back. We were hardly inside when he started to paw me all over again. During the struggle he reached under his pillow for the gun he always kept there. I just happened to get it before he did, that's all."

"I see," smiled Weatherholtz. "Now suppose you tell us what really happened?"

Eva glared defiantly at the ring of faces around her. "I don't know what you mean," she said, her eyes narrowing. "I have told you the truth."

The sheriff shook his head. "No, you haven't, Eva. Before Brown died you beat him to a pulp. We found high-heel marks all over his face and chest where you stomped him after knocking him down. Then, while he lay helpless at your feet, you got the gun, pressed it against his eye and pulled the trigger, killing him instantly. That's what really happened, isn't it?"

The woman's eyes were two slits of hate as she glared at Weatherholtz. After several minutes she nodded. "Okay," she snapped, "so I killed him. He took in about $300 in Mt. Vernon and was trying to hold some of it out on me."

"Why did he have to give you anything?" asked Mason, puzzled. "It was his bus and his relics."

Eva grinned crookedly. "They might have been his, but I was the boss. I ran the show. I had him eating out of my hand from the very first. That's why I insisted on that arrangement before we started out."

"What arrangement?"

"That I was to boss the show. Although everything was in his name, he agreed to turn all the profits over to me and to do whatever I'd tell him."

"And when he didn't you'd beat him up, is that it?" asked Mason.

Eva nodded. "When he'd get out of line I'd slap him around. On the night of the murder he said he was fed up, that if I didn't give him his liberty, he'd give me death.

"We got into a row and we wrestled," she went on. "I was much stronger than him and I soon got him down. I then beat his head into the floor with my foot until he was out cold. I got the gun, leaned over and shot him through the eye. When we got outside of Upper Sandusky I stripped off his clothing and dragged him outside and threw him in the ditch."

Eva Timmer went on trial in the Wyandot County Courthouse on February 6, 1934, before Judge Russell H. Kear. After a trial lasting three days she was found guilty of manslaughter and sentenced to St. Mary's Reformatory for Women for 20 years. However, after serving less than a year, she was pronounced a borderline case and removed to the Lima State Hospital for the Criminally Insane.

On November 20, 1940, Eva managed to escape from the hospital in a daring, well-planned break. Today she is still at large, a constant menace to society, wherever she is.

Note: *The name Sidney Beckman is fictitious to spare possible embarrassment to an innocent person.*

YOUR JOB FOR TWO HOURS—OR DIE

Official Detective Stories, May 1951

That Sunday, February 11, 1951, was much like any other Sunday to the khaki-clad deputies of the Jefferson County Sheriff's office in Birmingham, Alabama. The usual number of irate phone calls reporting domestic squabbles, roadside drunks and highway accidents kept them on their toes all day. The dreary routine wasn't broken until shortly after eight o'clock that evening when Communications Officer T. W. Dockerty received a call from a semi-hysterical woman that brought him to sudden attention.

"Wait a minute, Lady, calm down!" he urged. "You say your daughter's boy friend just killed a man? How long ago? . . . About an hour? . . . Where? . . . What's the man's name? . . . Yeah, I got that; he's a taxi driver . . . But what's his name? . . . What's your name? . . . Say, don't hang—"

The line was dead.

Dockerty removed the earphone from his head and frowned. Tearing off the top sheet of his memo pad, he strode into the muster room. Two deputies, J. L. Boggan and Floyd West, were there.

"What's up, Dock?" asked Boggan.

Dockerty told them about the call. "She was all right until I asked her for names, then she hung up," he finished. "What do you make of it?"

"Probably another crank."

"I don't think so," replied Dockerty. "I can usually spot 'em. This dame sounded pretty excited."

"Don't worry about it," advised Boggan. "If a hackie's missing we'll know soon enough. They have to call their dispatcher after every trip."

Boggan was right. At nine o'clock, P. W. Whitman, owner of the Whitman Yellow Cab Company, informed Headquarters that his dispatcher was unable to get in touch with one of his drivers. Boggan and West drove immediately to the taxi office and went inside.

Whitman was worried. "It's not like Woods," he said anxiously. "He's one of my most reliable men. Always punctual and never touches a drop."

"What's his full name and where does he live?" inquired Boggan, pulling out his notebook.

"Clyde G. Woods, and he lives on Sixth Avenue, North," replied Whitman. "He's in his early fifties, about medium height and weight, and wears glasses. A real nice fellow."

"When did you hear from him last?"

Whitman looked at his report sheet. "At five forty-five. He phoned in from one of our call-boxes near Legion Field."

"Did he say where he was going?" asked West.

"All he said was that he had an out-of-town fare. He hung up before we could get his destination."

Further questioning revealed that Woods was 52 years old, married and the father of three children. He had worked for several other Birmingham cab companies before joining the Whitman outfit six months before. His record was spotless.

"How much dough did he have on him when he disappeared?" asked Boggan.

"Not more than a dollar or so," replied Whitman. "He only went on duty at five o'clock. Of course, he might have had some money of his own."

The deputies instructed Whitman to call them at once if he heard from Woods, and returned to Headquarters. With the possibility of dirty work growing stronger by the minute, Boggan decided to call Sheriff McDowell at his home and give him the news.

The Sheriff, a heavy-set, sharp-eyed investigator, lost no time in getting to his office. His first move was to give the local radio stations a complete description of the missing man and the cab and request that they broadcast it periodically in hopes that someone would recognize it and call his office. Next, he phoned the local offices of the Alabama State Department of Public Safety and asked for help.

"There's six interstate and two state highways leading out of Birmingham," McDowell told Boggan and West. "We can't cover all of them. That's why we need help."

Leaving Deputies Earl Cooper and C. O. Hames, Junior, behind to handle any developments that might arise, McDowell, West and Boggan drove across town to Legion Field. Parking near the Eighth Avenue entrance, the investigators began a canvass of every store and home within a two-block radius of the Whitman Company's call-box, which was located a short distance from the main gate.

Because it was Sunday night, most of the stores were closed. The proprietors of those that were open, however, were questioned closely. The officers had no luck until they talked to the elderly owner of a soft-drink stand.

"Yeah, I remember seeing a Yellow Cab parked down the street around a quarter to six," he said thoughtfully. "From here it looked like two passengers were getting into the cab, a man and a woman."

"Can you describe them?" asked McDowell.

"The man was short and slender and wore khaki pants and shirt. I wouldn't swear to it, but he looked like a kid."

"And the woman?"

"She was taller and heavier than the boy, and well-dressed. I'd take her for twenty-five or so."

"Did you see which way the cab went?"

"No, I'm afraid not," he said apologetically. "I didn't pay too much attention to it. In fact, I couldn't even tell you if those two actually got into the cab. I just saw 'em standing close to it."

Encouraged by this information, the officers resumed their canvass, concentrating on the homes nearest to the spot where the cab had been seen. After several blanks they picked up more news at the home of Mrs. Herbert Sinclair.

"I was leaving for the movies when I saw this young man hail the cab," she told them. "I usually don't notice things like that, but I couldn't help being interested when this well-dressed young woman came running up and started talking to the cabbie and the young fellow."

"Could you hear what was said?" "No, but whatever it was the woman didn't like it. She looked like she was angry."

"Did they get in the cab together?" "No, only the young man did. When the cab drove off she was still there on the corner."

She described the young man as in his late teens or early twenties and wearing khaki-colored clothes. He had a thin, sallow face and was about five feet five or six.

"I don't know the woman's name, but I think she's a waitress in the Oak Bar over on Seventh Avenue," she said.

"Did you see which way the cab went?" asked McDowell.

The woman nodded. "Yes, it made a U-turn and headed north."

McDowell was about to leave when he asked, "You said the young man wore khaki clothes. Was he in the service?"

"No, I don't think so. It didn't look like a uniform."

The officers thanked her and hurried to the Oak Bar, about two blocks away. There the proprietor recognized the description of the unknown woman as fitting one of his waitresses, a Mabel Gill, who had gone off duty at 5:30, but probably could be found at her rooming-house on Vanderbilt Road.

McDowell and his men drove to the address, which was located in the residential part of town.

The waitress, a brunet in her late twenties, readily admitted talking to a cab driver, although she had no idea if he was Woods.

"I was in a hurry to get home; I was expecting a telephone call from my mother in Los Angeles," she explained. "I saw this cab and I was going to take it but that kid beat me to it."

"Did you argue with the cabbie?" asked McDowell.

She flushed. "I guess I did get a little excited. I asked the young man to let me have the cab but he said something about a heavy date."

"Did you happen to hear where he was going?"

"I'm not sure, but when I got there he was telling the cab driver something about the place being just off Highway Seventy-eight, about ten miles from the city."

The officers returned to Headquarters, where disquieting news awaited them. Whitman, the cab owner, had heard nothing from his missing employe. He had phoned all of the city's hospitals but Woods was not in any of them.

"This is the first time I've ever looked for a body without even knowing if anybody's been killed," McDowell declared.

"It's a beaut, all right," said Boggan. "But at least we've got something to go on now. That young fellow's description, and the fact that they took Highway Seventy-eight."

McDowell's fingers drummed nervously on his desk as he contemplated his next move. "I'm afraid it doesn't help much," he said. "There's a flock of little communities along Highway Seventy-eight as far as Jasper. It looks like I'll have to ask the State Highway boys to turn the area between here and Sumiton inside out. Maybe they'll come up with something."

Meanwhile the usual number of phone calls had been coming in to Headquarters from persons who had heard about Woods' disappearance on the radio. Although these tips were run down promptly, nothing worth while developed until early the next morning.

Then a promising lead was received from an elderly man whose farm was located just off Highway No. 78, about five miles northwest of Birmingham.

He had been on his way home around 8:30 the previous evening, he said, when he saw a man and a woman standing over the prone figure of a man.

"They were only a few yards off the highway and I could see that they'd been drinkin," he explained. "I was goin' to stop, but I changed my mind when I saw the woman kickin' the poor guy in the face. I decided not to call the police until I heard the cab driver was missin'."

"Did they have a car?" asked the officer who took this call.

"Yes, but I didn't notice if it was a taxicab. I didn't wait to take a good look."

Although he was questioned at some length, the farmer was unable to give much of a description of the couple except to say that they were young and about medium height.

McDowell induced him to take them to the spot. Inspecting the area carefully, the investigators saw ample evidence of a struggle.

Scuffed earth, trampled weeds and a number of blood-splattered leaves were found within a five-foot radius. From skid and tire markings, they deduced that a car had run off the right side of the road into the underbrush. But it's gone now.

An exhaustive search uncovered no further evidence. As a result, McDowell had to be contented with taking pictures of the tire markings and salvaging a number of the blood-splattered leaves.

The Sheriff was in a thoughtful mood on the drive back to Headquarters. "If it wasn't for that anonymous phone call, I'd say the farmer saw the actual killing," he declared. "But it seems to me if this woman's daughter had a hand in the killing, the mother wouldn't notify the police. Maybe this is an entirely separate incident."

Deputy Hames rushed out to greet them as they reached Headquarters. "They just found Woods' cab stuck in the bog near Lake Purdy," he said. "There's no sign of Woods, but the cab is plenty blood-splattered."

In a few minutes Sheriff McDowell was roaring northwest in a squad car accompanied by Deputies Boggan, West, Hames and Cooper.

At the bog, the Birmingham officers found a number of people waiting for them, including the local farmer who had discovered the missing car. The taxicab was on a lonely side road about 200 yards from the lake. Both front doors were open and the keys were still in the ignition.

A careful search of the machine was made after Deputy Cooper had taken pictures of it from every conceivable angle. In the car the officers found a woman's black, humidor-shaped handbag, an empty bottle of brandy, a pair of shattered spectacles and a flashlight. The driver's compartment was splattered with blood, indicating that Woods had been injured or killed while sitting behind the wheel.

Examining the contents of the odd-shaped bag, the Sheriff found the usual feminine articles, lipstick, compact, a small change purse containing 55 cents and some tissues. He was about to close the bag when he spied several paper match folders partially concealed by a torn piece of lining.

Studying them, he was startled to find that one of them was from the Oak Bar.

He showed it to Boggan.

"Why, that's where the waitress works!" exclaimed the deputy.

McDowell nodded. "She didn't tell us all she knew, that's a cinch."

"Maybe that yarn about a long-distance call from California was the bunk," Boggan said.

McDowell studied the match folders more closely. When he was finished he held the handbag to his nose. "Whoever owns this bag doesn't smoke," he said thoughtfully. "Not one of the paper matches has been torn out and there's no tobacco odor in the handbag. What did she want the matches for?"

The broken spectacles, which McDowell learned had belonged to Woods, and the flashlight were carefully dusted for prints, but yielded none. The bottle of brandy, however, had two worthwhile clues, a clear impression of a right thumb and the name and address of the package liquor store where it had been bought.

Meanwhile a thorough search of the sparsely settled area unearthed no further clues. Nor was the body of the missing cab driver found. Leaving West and Hames behind to canvass the near-by homes for anyone who might have seen something, McDowell and Boggan drove to the liquor store.

The Sheriff laid the bottle on the counter.

"Can you tell me who bought this?" he asked.

The clerk glanced at it. "I think so," he said. "That's peach brandy, and I don't have too many calls for it. I sold the last bottle to a young man around a quarter after six Saturday night."

"Ever see him before?"

"No."

"How old was he?"

"I asked him that, too; I didn't want to get into any trouble. But he swore he was twenty-one. He got real nasty about it."

The clerk could not add anything to the description furnished by Miss Gill and the housewife, Mrs. Sinclair. McDowell and Boggan left him and hurried to the Oak Bar.

Although Mabel Gill was busy with some early morning customers, the Sheriff drew her to one side and showed her the match folder.

"Ever see this before?" he inquired.

The waitress shrugged. "Sure, the boss has 'em printed by the thousands. What's so special about that one?"

"That cab you almost took last night was located this morning out by Lake Purdy, splattered with blood," said McDowell evenly. "There was a woman's handbag in the cab, and these matches were in it."

Mabel Gill paled, despite her heavy make-up. "What's that got to do with me?"

"That cab picked you up later, didn't it?" demanded the Sheriff.

"No, I swear it! I never saw it again!"

"How did you get home?"

"I walked until I found another cab. A Red Top, I think it was."

McDowell wrote the information in his notebook. "That shouldn't be too hard to verify. What time did you get home?"

"About twenty after six. My call came through fifteen minutes later."

McDowell eyed her sharply. "That young man who wouldn't let you have his cab—you've seen him before, haven't you?"

She shrugged. "What's the use? You'll find out anyway. Yeah, I've seen him before. He's been in here several times. But I don't know anything about him. I don't even know his name."

"Ever speak to him?"

"No, he usually plays the bar. Ask Willie, the barkeep. He might be able to help you."

"Why didn't you tell us you'd seen him before?"

"I didn't see why I should get mixed up in anything. I didn't know him, so I figured I'd keep my mouth shut."

Further questioning was of little value. "Okay, that'll be all for now," said McDowell.

The bartender readily recognized the youth from McDowell's description but again did not know the name, nor had he seen the youth on the previous day. The bar had been closed on Sunday— sale of liquor on Sunday is banned in Alabama—although the restaurant part of the establishment, where Miss Gill worked, had been open.

The bartender made one observation, however, which interested the Sheriff. This youth often had visited the place without hat or coat, which could indicate that he lived somewhere in the neighborhood.

A stack of reports addressed to Sheriff Holt McDowell were waiting when he reached his office. One stated that an analysis of blood from the blood-splattered leaves revealed it to be Type O. According to his family physician, Clyde Woods had Type B.

"Which means we can forget about that incident on Highway Seventy-eight," he said, tossing the report aside.

Nor had Deputy Cooper's search for finger-prints on the taxicab uncovered anything startling. The only clear prints belonged to the missing man. A second lab report revealed that the bloodstains found in the taxicab were the same type as the missing man's.

Unquestionably, now, Woods had been killed. But where was his body? Who had slain him? Why?

Hames and West returned from their canvass of the Lake Purdy area, tired and leg-weary.

"Any luck?" asked McDowell.

"We talked to everyone living within a quarter-mile of where the car was abandoned," said Hames. "No dice. Even an old hermit who has a shack about two hundred yards from the spot didn't see a thing."

"Then you drew a blank?"

"Not entirely. One man who lives near the highway says he was almost run down last night by a Yellow Cab when it came tearing into that dirt road where we found the car. He yelled so loud that the driver got out and threatened to bust him one. This fellow says the driver was only a kid and as high as a kite, wearing khaki-colored clothes that had dark stains all over 'em."

"What time was this?"

"About ten o'clock or so. If you ask me, the kid must have dumped Woods' body into Lake Purdy."

"Did this man see anyone else in the cab?"

Hames shook his head. "Nope. Only the kid."

McDowell was mulling over the advisability of having the lake dragged when the phone rang. He recognized the excited voice of Marshall Allen, one of his deputies.

"We got the body!" Allen cried. "On Lovick Road, about ten miles out of town!"

The Sheriff instructed him to stand by and a few minutes later two squad cars filled with officers were speeding northwest on Highway No. 78. After a fast drive they swung into a deserted-looking dirt road and parked behind Allen's squad car. With Allen was his partner, Deputy B. M. Dinken, and O. C. Brooke, a Whitman Company cab driver.

Woods lay on his back, his head and face covered with ugly welts and bruises. His brownish-gray hair was matted with blood, his nose and mouth twisted cruelly out of shape.

Coroner Joe Hildebrand of Jefferson County estimated that Woods had been killed between seven and nine o'clock the night before, with a blunt weapon that might have been a hammer. And Deputy West soon found a bloodstained hammer half concealed in the weeds.

A search of the victim's pockets yielded a half-empty tin of tobacco, a briar pipe, a man's handkerchief with the initials "C.W.," and fifteen cents in change. The absence of a wallet or jewelry suggested that robbery might have been the motive.

While Cooper was setting up his camera, McDowell studied the scene. The area was heavily wooded, mostly with barren scrub oak and tall pines. The ground was a thick carpet of overgrown weeds and dry leaves There was no sign of a struggle anywhere, and except for the gore-splattered body little blood was in evidence

"He was undoubtedly killed in the cab and his body dragged here," Boggan said. "Notice his hands. Sheriff? Not a mark on 'em Which means he probably didn't get a chance to put up a fight."

McDowell agreed "Somehow, though, I can't believe he was killed for his money alone," he said. "It's too vicious for that."

Brooke, the cab driver, had found the body. He was driving toward the city on a call when he happened to glance into the woods and saw a man lying on the ground. Believing it might be his missing coworker, he stopped the cab and investigated. When he saw he had stumbled onto his friend's body, he had hurried to the highway and flagged down the first car he saw.

Returning to his squad car, Sheriff McDowell held a council-of-war with Boggan and West.

"We're getting nowhere fast," he said. "However, let's see what we've got so far. A young punk hires a taxicab, directs the driver to this forsaken place and knocks him off. We've got a fair description, and we're fairly certain he lives somewhere near the Oak Bar. As far as Woods' past is concerned, it's spotless, so it has to be robbery."

"The killer could be a screwball," suggested Boggan.

"Yeah, he could be. We've still got to find him, whoever he is. The flashlight and the broken spectacles belonged to Woods, so the only physical evidence we've got, besides the hammer, is the woman's handbag."

"And those things are a dime a dozen," remarked West.

"This one isn't," replied McDowell. "I've never seen one quite like this before."

"What've you got on your mind. Sheriff?" asked Boggan.

"Somebody ought to recognize this bag and tell us who owned it. If we can find that woman, we can possibly find the killer."

West asked, "What do we do, take the handbag to every door in Birmingham?"

"We will if we have to. But it would be a lot smarter to start right here, in the neighborhood where the body was found. I doubt if the killer picked this road at random; he probably was on his way to some specific house. If that doesn't work, we'll try the neighborhood of the Oak Bar, and then the Lake Purdy region. Let's go."

Soon McDowell, West and Boggan were knocking on farmhouse doors in the Lovick Road area.

For hours, they kept at their task. No one had seen the bag before, although one woman, who lived across the road from a church, had seen something peculiar involving a taxi-cab the previous evening.

"It stopped in front of the church," she said. "Two boys got out. However, when a young girl tried to get out, too, the cab driver pulled her back and drove away."

"Did you recognize any of them?" asked McDowell.

"No, it was too dark. But I could tell from the girl's voice that she was young and frightened."

And then, finally, Mrs. Olin Rucker identified the bag. It belonged to a sixteen-year-old neighbor girl named Peggy Gates, she said.

"You're sure it's hers?" asked McDowell.

Mrs. Rucker smiled. "My, yes. I've seen Peggy carrying it many times."

McDowell asked for directions to the Gates home. Five minutes later the officers were knocking on the door of a neat frame farmhouse. A pleasant-faced woman in her forties opened the door.

"Yes?" she asked.

"We're police officers," said McDowell. "Do you recognize this handbag, Ma'm?"

Mrs. Gates paled. She licked her lips nervously. "Yes, it belongs to my daughter, Peggy. I figured you'd be around sooner or later. Come in."

When the officers were seated in the comfortable parlor, McDowell said, "We'd like to speak with Peggy, too."

Mrs. Gates left the room and returned a few minutes later with a good-looking, blonde girl of about sixteen.

"Suppose you tell us all about this, Peggy," McDowell said to her. "How your bag got in that cab and just what happened. This is a very serious business."

Peggy sat facing them, her fingers twisting a handkerchief nervously. Slowly, gradually, she told them the following story, Sheriff McDowell claimed later:

Peggy's boy friend, a youth named Sam Peoples, had called on her Sunday evening, wearing a cab driver's cap. He told her that he'd just been given a job with a cab company. He wanted to take her for a ride, and finally he agreed to drive her and her two brothers to a church meeting.

At the church, however, he would not let Peggy get out of the cab. Instead, he turned around and drove back along Lovick Road. Frightened, the girl somehow managed to knock the car out of gear and jump out, leaving her handbag on the front seat. Peoples then drove off in the cab.

Peggy went home, where she noticed bloodstains on her dress and shoes. She and her mother decided that Sam had been lying, that he had taken the cab and somehow injured or killed the driver. Mrs. Gates then had made the anonymous telephone call to the Sheriff's office.

Peggy also admitted that the match books in her purse were hers; she did not smoke but she saved the books.

McDowell and his men drove immediately to Peoples' home, on Sixth Avenue in Birmingham. The youth's parents—Sam was only eighteen—were quite worried. He had been out all night, they said, had returned home around seven in the morning, put on his brother's Navy uniform and left the house, without saying a word to anyone.

A search of the young man's room yielded a pair of khaki trousers, a shirt and a handkerchief all stained with blood.

The Sheriff immediately put out a city-wide alarm for the youth's capture. He was described as eighteen, five feet six inches tall, 140 pounds, with dark, wavy hair and wearing a Navy uniform.

McDowell also called Chief of Detectives Charles L. Pierce of the Birmingham Police Department. He explained the latest twist in the case and requested his cooperation.

"If Peoples is anywhere in the city we'll nab him," Detective Pierce promised.

Two hours later City Patrolmen C. L. Tucker and E. J. Glass spied the slim, sallow-complexioned youth in a taxicab as it halted for a red light. Peoples surrendered meekly. Taken to the Sheriff's office, he protested his innocence.

Some time later McDowell said, he broke down and confessed when he was shown pictures of the slain cab driver.

"I killed him," he said dully, according to the Sheriff. "I wanted to impress my girl friend by pretending I had a job.

"I asked the cabbie to loan me the car for a couple of hours but he wouldn't. I told him, 'Give me your job for two hours or you'll die.' He still wouldn't. I got a hammer and hit him again and again. Then I dragged him in the woods and hit him a few more times. I went through his pockets and got thirty dollars.

"After Peggy left me, I drove around awhile. Finally the car went into a ditch and I couldn't get it out. I fell asleep behind the wheel. When I awoke it was dawn, so I went home."

Sam Peoples was arraigned in the District Court on Friday, February 16, 1951, and charged with first-degree murder. At this writing, further legal action is expected soon.

The names Mabel Gill and Peggy and Mrs. Gates, used in this story, are not real but fictitious in order to protect the identity of innocent people. The name of the Oak Bar also is fictitious.

FROM THE BOTTLES ON BUZZARD'S ISLAND

Official Detective Stories, September 1951

Darkness long since had fallen over the city of Augusta, Georgia, when a detective brought the little old lady into the office of Chief of Detectives W. M. Terry.

Terry, weary from hours of overtime work, already had his topcoat on and was ready to leave.

"What is it?" he asked.

"Chief," the man said, "you'd better hear this story. It sounds like it might be plenty serious."

Terry shrugged out of the coat and hung it up. "Sit down," he said to the woman. She was in her fifties, he judged, and had long, stringy hair and an angular face. Worry wrinkled the corners of her eyes.

"Now what's the trouble?" he asked.

She straightened her dress. "It's my granddaughter," she said. "She's lost. I'm near frantic."

Terry took out a missing-person report from his desk drawer and wrote down the date—April 21, 1951. It was almost midnight.

"She's only seven," the woman went on. "Lois—that's her name, Lois Janes. I sent her to the store at half-past nine and she didn't come back. We're near out of our minds."

The distraught woman said she was Mrs. Mamie Price, the child's maternal grandmother. She was 55 years old and lived on Broad Street.

"Like I said, I sent Lois to get some groceries at Tuten's, and that's almost next door. But she just didn't come back. By ten o'clock I was some worried so I went after her. The store was closed and I knocked on Tuten's door and they weren't home either.

"Then Cherry—that's Lois' mother—she came home at eleven and she said I should tell the police. She's out looking right now, Cherry is."

"Cherry is your daughter?"

The woman clasped and unclasped her hands nervously. "Yes. Mrs. Cherry Logan. She was married before; that's how come Lois has a different last name, just like her brother, Stephen. Poor Cherry, she don't know what she's going to do."

"Have you talked to all your friends and neighbors?" asked Terry.

"Everybody. We asked everybody. Nobody's seen her."

Terry jotted down the information. "Has she ever gone away before?"

"No. Not Lois. She wouldn't go anywhere without letting me know. She's such a sweet, obedient child. I'm worried sick."

Mrs. Price described the clothes Lois was wearing. Brown-and-white sandals, tan stockings, a pink dress and a light gray coat. She had light-brown hair parted on the side and her eyes were brown. She was a frail child, only three feet tall and weighing less than 70 pounds.

Terry tried to reassure the woman. Lois would show up shortly, safe and unharmed, he said. In the meantime, he promised her, the police would do everything they could.

When she was gone he sent for Detectives Ben Cheek and S. L. Crouch. Briefly, he told them the woman's story.

"Tell me, Chief," said Crouch, "why do kids always get lost on Saturday night?"

"It's probably the usual thing," agreed Terry, "but a lost child that age worries me. Look into it and if anything worth while develops, call me at the house."

The detectives drove to the missing girl's home, a ramshackle frame house on upper Broad Street. Stores, run-down houses and repair shops lined both sides of the street. They found the anxious mother and stepfather, Mr. and Mrs. Logan, in the parlor. Mrs. Price sat facing the door, an expectant look on her gaunt face.

"Any news yet?" inquired Cheek.

Mrs. Logan, a dark-haired woman in her late twenties, shook her head. "Nothing." She bit her lips to keep back the tears. "I'm afraid."

"Keep your chin up. Have you talked to the Tutens yet?"

"No. They went to a party on Telfair Street somewhere. They're not home."

"Hasn't anybody seen the child since she left the house?" asked Crouch.

Logan, a powerful-looking young man, answered. "Yes, two people. Clyde Deans, who lives down the block, says he was looking for his little girl, Sandra, to take her to the movies, and he found her walking along Broad Street with Lois. That was about a quarter to ten.

"Then Lena—that's Mrs. Lena Johnson, Lois' aunt who lives across the street—saw her looking at the television set in the liquor store. But that's all. No one's seen her since."

As Logan was talking, a second young couple entered the room.

"This is my brother, Elmer, and his wife, Frances," said Mrs. Logan. "They've been out looking for Lois, too."

Mrs. Logan explained that her brother and his wife had arrived from Macon about an hour before the little girl disappeared.

"Grandma wanted to fix them something, that's why she sent Lois to the store," she said.

The detectives urged them to relax, and then left. Outside, they snapped on their flashlights and poked little holes in the darkness as they searched the littered area behind the Price home. Slowly they made their way westward as far as the Charleston and Western Carolina Railroad tracks. They found nothing.

For several hours they continued the search, reaching Broad Street again at four A.M. A light was on in the Tuten apartment. Cheek knocked on the door and it was promptly opened by a stocky, middle-aged man.

The Tutens were surprised to learn of Lois' disappearance. They had not seen the child that evening, Tuten said. "We usually stay open until ten o'clock on Saturday nights," Tuten explained, "but we were invited out tonight and closed up early. We were probably closed when Lois came here."

"What time did you leave?" inquired Cheek.

"It was about ten minutes to nine when we locked up," Tuten replied. "It couldn't have been any later, because it was just nine o'clock when we got to the house on Telfair Street."

The detectives thanked the couple. Back at Police Headquarters they immediately put out a missing-person alarm on the teletype and police radio to all law-enforcement agencies in Richmond County. Hospitals were called, but no one had been admitted who resembled Lois Janes. The authorities in North Augusta, on the South Carolina side of the Savannah River, also were queried.

Lois Janes was lost.

All day Sunday she remained missing. The day passed without a break in the case.

Early Monday, Terry, Crouch and Cheek went to Chief of Police F. B. Green's office for a conference. They decided that the entire area north, east and west of the Price home should be searched tor the missing child.

"I think we can eliminate the area to the south," Green said. "It's well-populated. Offhand, I'd say the Augusta Canal is our best bet, and we'll have to face the probability that the child is dead. We may have to drain the canal."

"Better hold off awhile on that. Boss," said Terry. "It takes twelve hours to empty and another twelve to refill, which means that more than three thousand mill-hands will be thrown out of work. I think the week-end's the best time to do it."

Green agreed. "I'll ask Major Smith at Camp Gordon to send us some men to help in the search."

Later that morning 200 members of Company C, 504th MP Battalion, under Captain Philip Cohn and Lieutenant Schlesinger, gathered in the desolate bottoms north of the Price home.

Following plans laid out by Crouch and Cheek, the soldiers started out in a west northwestern direction. They walked slowly, scarcely an arm's length apart, probing into every nook and cranny. The missing girl's own father, Curtis Janes, and her stepfather, Logan, joined the khaki-clad volunteers in the search.

Every spot that possibly could conceal the body af a seven-year-old child was examined painstakingly. By the time night fell, the entire area from Broad Street to the Savannah River on the north, and as far west as Chafee Park, had been turned inside out. But still no sign of little Lois.

Chief Terry questioned the grief-stricken parents again and again, without result. He tried to be hopeful in their presence, but he realized that probably Lois would not be found alive. The child's home life was apparently happy and circumstances surrounding her disappearance indicated that she had not run away.

Newspapers and radio stations picked up the story; soon everyone in Augusta was looking for Lois. But Tuesday, Wednesday and Thursday passed with no news. A brief flurry of excitement swept through Headquarters late Thursday when a couple of hikers found a bloodstained dress on the shores of Lake Olmstead. It was rushed to the Price home, but the parents stated flatly that it was not their daughter's.

Everyone who lived on Broad Street, or near it, was questioned and still nothing was learned.

"I can't figure it out," Chief Terry said. "Somebody must have seen Lois that night. Broad Street is crowded with shoppers on Saturdays. If she was lured into a car or walked off with a stranger, it's incredible that somebody didn't notice it."

Ben Cheek, hollow-eyed from lack of sleep, shook his head. "It beats me, Chief. We've covered every inch of ground north of the Price home all the way to the river, west as far as the City Stockade and east to the city limits."

And then, shortly after six o'clock Friday morning, Terry was awakened at his home by a telephone call from Radio Patrolman L. W. Hosmer.

"A fisherman just found Lois Janes' body near the sluice gates," he reported.

"I was afraid it would end like that," said Terry. "We'll be right out."

Fifteen minutes later the narrow catwalk on the south side of the canal was crowded with police officials of every rank. First to reach the scene were Chief Terry, Detectives Crouch and Cheek and Richmond County Coroner N. F. Widener:

While Coroner Widener made a cursory examination, the officers studied the pitiful remains. Lois was fully clothed, even to the sandals and the gray coat she'd worn when she disappeared. Her skin was turning black and her pinched little face was bloated to twice its normal size.

Meanwhile, Chief Terry questioned Lovey Ivey, the man who had found the body.

Ivey, a thin, wizened old man, said he was a fisherman by occupation and lived on Walton Way in Augusta.

"I was just comin' back from settin' my minnow traps upstream a ways," he said. "I seed somethin' bobbin' up and down in the water near the sluice gates. It looked like a head, with the hair spread out. Right away I knew it was that girl everybody's been lookin' fer."

Ivey said that after he had pulled the body ashore he ran down Eve Street looking for a telephone. Instead he ran into Patrolmen Hosmer and Wayne Worthy, cruising the area in their squad car. When the officers, too, saw the body, they notified Chief Terry.

Terry took the fisherman's address and excused him with thanks.

By that time Coroner Widener had completed his hasty examination.

"Her left ear is missing and she has numerous lacerations on her face and head," Widener said. "They might have been caused by turtles. I doubt very much, however, that she's been in the water since last Saturday night."

"What makes you say that?" inquired Cheek.

"The body is too well preserved for one thing. For another, she would have come up before this if she'd been in the water that long."

"Can you tell what killed her?"

"Not a chance. You'll have to wait on the autopsy for that. It may interest you to know that she was not molested."

The autopsy, performed later that morning by Doctor E. R. Fund, pathologist at the Medical College of the University of Georgia, revealed no trace of water in the little girl's lungs. It also verified the coroner's opinion about the absence of any obvious motive. A second autopsy was performed by Coroner's Physician Doctor Marion Silver Friday evening and Doctor Silver declared that Lois Janes had been strangled to death a short time after her disappearance.

Seated in Terry's office when the report came in, Crouch said, "From what we've learned, the kid wouldn't have wandered off with a stranger. Maybe she knew the man who killed her."

"Maybe she did," Terry replied. "But still what's the motive?"

"Lets look at it this way," said Cheek. "Suppose whoever did it had a morals crime in mind but Lois got suspicious and tried to yell.

Maybe he strangled her to keep her quiet."

"It's a good theory," admitted Terry, "and I think we'll have to go along. I want everyone in our morals files picked up and questioned. Find out what they were doing between the hours of nine and eleven this past Saturday night."

Because a number of known offenders lived outside the city limits, Terry enlisted the aid of Sheriff Gary Whittle. The Sheriff immediately assigned Deputy J. S. Wilson to the case.

During the next 24 hours, a countywide roundup of all such offenders was made. They were hustled to Chief Terry's office where they were questioned carefully about their whereabouts at the time of the slaying.

Among those being sought was a man named Harold Dink, who had been picked up a score of times on suspicion. Dink was in his late fifties. He lived on Boy Scout Road, just beyond the city limits, and frequently patronized the stores in the upper Broad Street area where the victim lived.

When Deputy Wilson drove out to his shack, he was not at home.

The deputy went over the one-room dwelling carefully. He was about to leave empty-handed when he discovered a bloodstained shirt under a loose floorboard.

Before returning to Headquarters, Wilson questioned Dink's neighbors. He learned that Dink seldom worked and was an inveterate drinker. No one knew where he got the money to buy liquor.

And one neighbor told Wilson that Dink had been drinking especially heavily since the previous Sunday, the day after Lois Janes vanished.

Deputy Wilson put a stakeout at the shack and broadcast a wanted bulletin on the missing man. Wilson felt confident that he had not left the area, and he was right. Dink was picked up late Sunday evening.

He was a short, powerful-looking man with small, squinty eyes and a beak-shaped nose.

Taken to Chief Terry's office, Dink was surly and uncooperative at first.

"Why are you always houndin' me?" he asked. "I ain't done nothin'."

"Where were you last Saturday night from nine to eleven o'clock?" demanded Terry.

Dink's eyes narrowed. "Last Sat'day night?"

Terry nodded.

"I was fishin' out by the city pump station. I always go fishing on Sat'day night."

"Did anybody see you?"

"Nope. I always go alone."

Terry showed him a snapshot of Lois Janes. "Do you know this girl?" he asked, watching the man's face closely.

Dink's face paled when he saw the photo. "Yeah, that's the Janes kid, the one who was found in the canal."

"How do you know her so well?" demanded Crouch.

"I saw her pitcher in the papers."

Wilson brought out the blood-stained shirt. "I found this hidden in your shack. Where did the blood come from?"

"That's my blood." Dink's face was wet with perspiration. "I cut my arm awhile back when I was choppin wood." He rolled up his left sleeve, revealing a jagged three-inch scar.

After Dink was taken away Cheek asked: "What do you think, Chief?"

Terry lighted a cigaret and shrugged. "We may know whether he's leveling or not when we have the bloodstains analyzed. If it s the girl's blood type and not his, he'll have some tall explaining to do. In the meantime let's see if we can find someone who saw him on Broad Street the night Lois disappeared. That fishing alibi sounds phony to me."

Two detectives were assigned the job of tracing Dink's whereabouts on the fatal night.

Meanwhile, the other ex-convicts were released from custody when their alibis stood up under close scrutiny.

Monday found two new developments in the case. J. Frank Faulk, chief technician of the South Carolina Law Enforcement Division at Columbia, was brought to Augusta at Chief Terry's request to give Dink a lie-detector test. The second development came when Doctor Herman Jones, eminent Atlanta criminologist, arrived to perform still another post mortem on the body.

Crouch and Cheek went on with their hunt. Neighbors were re-questioned, but they could add little or nothing to the investigation. None of them had heard an outcry or sounds of a struggle—and once again the detectives remembered Chief Terry's theory that someone close to the slain girl might be responsible for her death.

"It's a beaut, all right," said Cheek as the two men halted for a bite to eat. "Whoever knocked off that kid, he had to be somebody who knew the layout around here. How else would she disappear so completely? Also, it had to be somebody whose presence on Broad Street didn't attract any attention. That's a close-knit neighborhood. A stranger there would have been noticed."

"If that's so," Crouch said, "the motive might not be what we're looking for. It might be something personal."

"The way I see it, the only other motives would be money or revenge. Nobody wants revenge on the kid's family as far as we know, and there's no money involved. Money would have to be insurance and the family can't afford to carry enough insurance to make it worth while."

"So," asked Crouch, "where does that leave us?"

The two men resumed their canvass of the neighborhood. Their persistence was rewarded an hour later when they learned that a middle-aged eccentric named Vinnie Karst had been seen talking to Lois Janes on numerous occasions.

Karst was picked up and questioned. He swore he had not seen Lois Janes for several days prior to her disappearance, nor had he been near Broad Street on the fatal night. An intensive investigation into his background and whereabouts on the night of the crime proved that he was above suspicion.

Meanwhile, Harold Dink passed the lie-detector tests with flying colors. When an analysis of his bloodstained shirt revealed the blood to be his type and not the child's, he was released from custody.

Doctor Jones made his report early Thursday morning. He stated that the victim's ear had not been nibbled off by turtles as previously believed but had been removed by a sharp-edged cutting instrument.

However, his finding on the length of time the body had been in the water caused the greatest surprise.

"There is ample evidence to show that the body was in the canal less than twenty-four hours," he reported. "Also, from a chemical analysis of the victim's clothing, I find strong indications that she was buried underground for some time."

The report put the investigators in a quandary. Since Lois had been missing five days, and her body in the water only one, where was she hidden the other four days? And why had her killer suddenly decided to throw her into the canal where she surely would be found within a short time?

As a result of Doctor Jones' report, the investigators went into a huddle in Terry's office. The disturbing angle raised by the Atlanta physician had them stymied.

The discussion lasted two hours and led them nowhere. Finally the officers decided to look around for some other possible motive.

Before they filed out, Terry instructed his men to question the neighbors for a third time. "Change your tactics," he advised them. "Instead of asking the obvious questions, find out who came and went in the Price household, and how well off the Prices were financially."

"You think Lois was killed for insurance?" asked Cheek.

Terry shrugged. "It's a possibility."

Crouch and Cheek, adopting a new viewpoint, again made the rounds of the neighborhood. Deputy Wilson meanwhile decided to have another talk with Lovey Ivey, the man who had found the body.

The address Ivey had given, however, turned out to be B. K. Gunter's Bait and Tackle Shop.

Gunter smiled when Wilson inquired if Ivey lived there. "No, he doesn't. I buy minnows from him, that's all."

"Do you know where I can find him?"

"He lives in a lean-to along the river somewhere."

Ivey was spotted later that day in his boat and questioned. He explained that because his home was hard to reach, he gave the tackle shop as his address. Questioned again about the circumstances surrounding his finding of the body, Ivey told substantially the same story as before.

"Did you ever see the Janes girl before that morning?" asked Wilson.

"No, Sir. Never."

"Do you know either of her parents, or Mrs. Price?"

"No, Sir."

When an hour's grilling failed to uncover anything of importance, Wilson released the fisherman.

Interviews with neighbors and investigation of the Price family was just as fruitless. Three weeks passed without a break in the case. Newspapers, magazines and broadcasters took up the cry. Who had killed little Lois Janes? Why was she slain and where had her body been hidden for four days?

The investigation of Lois' family revealed that the slain child had been insured for $2,000. Hardly enough, reasoned Terry, to warrant such a crime. Besides, with the child's mother as the sole beneficiary, insurance as a motive was far-fetched.

As the hot, humid Georgia days of May sped by, the case looked more and more hopeless.

Then, on the sun-drenched morning of May 24, a neighbor of Mrs. Price, who had been out of town during most of the investigation, returned. Deputy Wilson drove out to question this woman.

"I don't know anything about it," she said, "except what I read in the newspapers. It's a terrible thing, isn't it?"

Deputy Wilson agreed. "You knew them pretty well, didn't you?" he asked.

"Not so very well; we're just neighbors. I hear Lovey Ivey found the body in the canal."

"That's right."

"It's funny, isn't it?" the woman asked.

"Funny? Why?"

"With him and the child's grandmother being such close friends."

"Friends?" Wilson was startled. "Are you sure?"

"Of course I'm sure. Why, I've seen them standing on the corner many a time talking away for almost half an hour, the two of them. And sometimes the little girl with them."

The information puzzled Wilson and Chief Terry, too, when the deputy reported. Ivey, they knew, had denied knowing Lois Janes when she was alive, and had denied any connection with the slain girl's family.

Apparently he had lied.

But why?

And why had Mrs. Price indicated that she did not know Ivey?

"This fellow Ivey," Wilson told the chief of detectives, "is an impoverished old duck who apparently does a lot of drinking. He needs money to buy liquor with. A man like that might be capable of killing someone for fifty or a hundred bucks."

"A hired killing?" Terry asked. "Then who did the hiring?"

Wilson shrugged. "The grandmother may have needed money, too, although how she could get any out of this killing I don't see."

Terry's fingers drummed the desk top nervously. "Unfortunately, this is all a wild theory. The fact that they lied about knowing each other doesn't prove a thing in connection with the killing. We've got to establish a motive and dig up some concrete evidence."

Wilson rose, his face grim. "I'm going to ask Crouch and Cheek to help me talk to some of the businessmen near the Price home. Maybe we'll turn up something."

Returning to the Broad Street neighborhood, the investigators concentrated their fire on the tradespeople. At Tuten's they learned that Mrs. Price was several months behind on her grocery bills. At the drug and butcher stores they heard the same story. Nor was that all. Records at City Hall revealed that the elderly woman was several years in arrears on her land and water taxes.

Despite the implications raised by these disclosures, Terry still hesitated. "Everything we have so far is purely incidental," he argued. "We need something more tangible, something that will show the grandmother could profit from the killing. But it's beyond belief—the child's own grandmother!"

"Got any ideas?" asked Cheek.

"I think so. It's a cinch the child wasn't slain in the vicinity of the Price home. I think it would be a good idea to go over Ivey's shack the first thing in the morning. You may come up with something."

Lovey Ivey was nowhere in sight when Crouch, Wilson and Cheek found his shack on the banks of the Savannah early the next day. Their painstaking search of the house and grounds failed to unearth anything that would link Ivey with the crime. They were about to leave when Ivey appeared. Despite his casual manner, they sensed his wariness.

"Howdy, boys!" He smiled. "Lookin' for somethin'?"

"Just a social call," replied Cheek. "By the way, Mister Ivey, where were you the night Lois disappeared?"

Ivey rubbed his weatherbeaten face thoughtfully. "Near as I can recollect," he said slowly, "I was right here, sleepin' off a binge. I usually hang around the shack on Saturdays."

"Where do you catch your minnows?"

"Anyplace along the river. I got no particular spot."

"Ever been on Buzzard's Island?" Wilson asked.

Ivey's eyes narrowed. "I never go near the place. It's haunted."

The officers knew he was referring to an old legend which claimed that the spirits of Civil War soldiers still roam the tiny island.

They thanked him and left.

Back in their squad car, Crouch inquired: "What gives with Buzzard's Island? How does it tie in?"

"Just that if I were looking for an isolated spot, Buzzard's Island would be the spot that I'd pick."

"You may have something," Cheek said. "People around these parts usually steer clear of the island on account of that old superstition."

Following through on the thought, the officers rented a boat and rowed out to the island, which lies in the middle of the swirling Savannah River a few miles west of the city. At first they could find nothing. As they were about to leave, Cheek, poking through some debris, called the others over.

"I think I've got something," he said. "Notice these two bottles of rubbing alcohol?" The detective carefully placed a forefinger in each bottle and held them up for inspection.

"What about them?" asked Wilson.

"When we were searching Ivey's shack I noticed quite a few of these bottles around. Ivey possibly drinks this stuff instead of liquor. I know it's a long shot, but if we can find out where and when these were bought, we may be able to place Ivey on Buzzard's Island recently. Which means we've caught him in another lie."

The bottles were rushed to Headquarters where they were carefully dusted for prints. The results, however, were negative.

Undaunted, Chief Terry compiled a list of firms selling drugs or sick-room supplies throughout the city and gave it to Cheek.

"There's a good chance Ivey may have bought a considerable amount of the stuff at one particular store," he told them. "You've got Ivey's description, so hop to it and good luck."

Starting with the northwest section of the city because it was nearest to Ivey's home, the officers wound their way in and out of a score of business establishments from Brinson Street to Milledge Road. Several proprietors admitted handling that particular brand of rubbing alcohol but failed to identify Ivey as one of their customers.

However, at a drug store near Julian Smith Park the investigators got their first nibble when the owner recognized Ivey's description.

"Sure!" He chuckled. "He comes in here often. His name is Lovey Ivey."

"Does he buy any rubbing alcohol from you?" inquired Ben Cheek.

"I'll say! He claims the stuff helps his rheumatism, but I have an idea he uses it internally."

"When was the last time he bought some?"

The druggist frowned. "Let's see. It was a little while ago, I believe. On a Saturday."

The Janes child had disappeared on a Saturday.

"Can you tell us exactly?" pressed Cheek.

"Sure. He bought the last two bottles I had and I made a notation in my memo book to order some more. Wait a minute and I'll see."

The druggist thumbed through a well-worn ledger until he found the page he wanted. "Yes, here it is. I made the note on Saturday, April twenty-first."

That was the day Lois Janes had vanished.

Shown the bottles, the druggist readily identified one of them by the crayon numeral, "49", scrawled across the face of the bottle.

"It was on the shelf; that's why I marked the price on it," he explained.

The jubilant investigators picked up Ivey an hour later and rushed him to Headquarters.

Questioned by Terry and Chief of Police Green, the old man stubbornly denied having had anything to do with the Janes child, or being anywhere near Buzzard's Island on the night of the slaying.

He refused to crack until Wilson showed him some snapshots of the victim's body at the morgue. After studying the pictures for several minutes, his face impassive, he suddenly covered his face with his hands and sobbed without restraint.

When he regained his composure, the chief of detectives announced later, he said, "I did it! I did it! I didn't mean to harm the kid, please believe me."

Terry sent for a stenographer. "Suppose you get it off your chest," he urged Ivey.

Chief Terry declared that he then confessed the slaying and quoted the confession as follows:

"It was that old witch, Mrs. Price, who put me up to it.

"She offered me seventy-five dollars to do away with the kid, and like a fool I agreed. I was drunk, and didn't know what I was doin'. All I could think of was the alcohol I could buy with that kind of money.

"I was walkin' down Broad Street, mindin' my business, when I met her. She and I usually stop and chat for awhile, so it weren't nothin' unusual. That's when she asked me if I wanted to make seventy-five bucks. I said sure, who do I have to kill? I was only kiddin', of course.

"But the old lady never batted an eye and said she wanted me to kill her grandchild, Lois. I don't know what made me say yes, but I did. I figured I could make it look like an accident by pushin' her in the river and nobody'd be the wiser. Sure enough, I spotted Lois walkin' along the street that night and she was alone. We got to talkin', and I told her I had some candy for her if she would come with me. She said okay and followed me.

"We walked to the river and took the boat to Buzzard's Island. When we got there and I kept puttin' her off about the candy, she got suspicious and actin' up. She started to run, but I grabbed her around the neck and we both fell hard. I kept my hands around her throat until she stopped strugglin'."

Ivey said he hid the body in a pasteboard box on the levee bank until the following night, when he turned it over to Mrs. Price, according to Chief Terry; however, Mrs. Price returned the body to him two days later, explaining that the situation was getting too hot, and told him to get rid of it.

On the following night, Thursday, April 26, he tossed it into the canal, Terry claimed, and decided to "accidentally" discover the body the next morning so that it would get a decent burial.

"Did Mrs. Price pay you the money?"

Ivey shook his head. "No, she did not. She said I'd get it when the insurance was paid."

Mrs. Mamie Price, her dark eyes snapping defiance, was taken into custody and booked on suspicion of murder. Informed of the fisherman's confession, she mocked and laughed derisively.

"The old coot's as crazy as a bedbug!" she scoffed. "Nobody around these parts believes anything that fellow says."

With Mrs. Price behind bars, valuable information reached the police. Mrs. Price, they learned, ruled her brood with an iron hand. She had demanded that the child be insured for $4,000, not $2,000 as previously believed, and her mother installed as sole beneficiary.

Two days before Lois disappeared, Mrs. Price had made inquiries at several automobile agencies regarding the purchase of a new car.

Lovey Ivey and Mrs. Price were indicted by a Richmond County grand jury on June 4, 1951.

The stern-visaged grandmother went on trial first. The trial began on Monday, June 25, before Judge Grover C. Anderson in the Richmond County Courthouse in Augusta. After three days, during which Lovey Ivey repeated his confession from the witness stand, Mrs. Price was found guilty of murder with a recommendation of mercy. Judge Anderson promptly sentenced her to life imprisonment at the Georgia State Prison at Reidsville.

Lovey Ivey is being held in Augusta on charges of murder as this issue of OFFICIAL DETECTIVE STORIES goes to press.

Neither in his alleged confession nor in his testimony at Mrs. Price's trial did Lovey Ivey clear up two of the points raised by Doctor Jones' autopsy. He said nothing about burying the child's body underground before throwing her in the river, nor would he admit cutting off her ear. The body was completely intact when he placed it in the water, police officers quoted Ivey as saying.

The names Harold Dink and Vinnie Karst used in this story are not real but fictitious in order to protect the identities of innocent persons unwittingly involved in the investigation.

A KILLER WITH WOMEN

Underworld Detective, December 1951

Joe Balli surveyed himself in the mirror and liked what he saw. A man in his middle thirties, Balli knew that women were especially attracted to him, and that pleased him. Angelina, for instance. There was a woman!

Several rooms away he could hear the raucous voice of his wife, Mary, scolding their two-year-old son, and he frowned. Life had become a steady succession of quarrels ever since they were married in Galveston, Texas, six years before. For months now he'd been trying to think of some way to ditch Mary and the kid and marry Angelina.

Thoughtfully, he slipped into a leather jacket and pulled up the zipper. He donned his cab driver's cap and straightened his tie. There was only one way to deal with people who wouldn't listen to reason, he decided. Murder.

He was surprised and pleased to find that the idea didn't shock him any more. He would need a clear head when the time came, and now he knew the time was near. He couldn't stand his wife's infernal bickering much longer. Whatever happened to her now she had coming to her, he told himself stubbornly.

Slipping quietly out the back door, he slid behind the wheel of the cab and gunned the motor. In less than ten minutes he would be with Angelina at their rendezvous on Bourbon Street.

She was waiting for him when he entered the dimly lit restaurant in the heart of New Orleans' teeming French Quarter. Winding his way carefully between the maze of white-clothed tables, he hurried to their favorite booth. She looked up, her smile held little warmth.

"Hello baby."

"Hello Joe. You're late."

Balli nodded. "Yeah. I got tied up in traffic. Forgive me?"

"I suppose so."

Balli noticed her mood, "What's the matter, Angie? You got something on your mind?"

"Yes. I've been doing a lot of thinking about you and me, Joe. How long we been going together? It's been quite a while, hasn't it?"

Balli frowned. "Oh, I don't know. Six, seven months maybe. Why?"

Angelina leaned forward, her dark eyes probing into his. "I hate to rush into things, Joe, but where are we going? What's going to happen to us?"

"What do you mean?"

Angelina sighed. "Okay, so I'll draw you a diagram. When are you going to ask me to marry you? Or are you allergic to wedding bands?"

Balli grinned and took one of her neatly gloved hands in his. "Just a little while longer, baby. I promise."

Angelina withdrew her hand. "Why the delay? You're not married, are you?" she snapped sharply.

Balli laughed. "Married? Me? Of course not! Whatever gave you that idea?"

The girl shrugged. "Nothing, I guess." Suddenly her eyes narrowed to smoldering slits of fire. "If I thought you were lying to me, Joe, I'd stomp your eyes in!"

Balli spent the next half hour and several drinks placating and assuring her of his love and fidelity. For some reason she seemed hard to convince and it worried him. Had she been checking up? He breathed easier when he saw the fire finally fade from her eyes. She didn't know—yet. But he'd have to watch his step. Angelina was a redhead and they played rough.

Balli was convinced that he had to do something and fast. Angelina wouldn't wait forever. During the next few days, a number of ideas raced through his mind, but he quickly discarded them. No hit or miss plans for him. Then suddenly, it came to him. The perfect plan. Carefully he went over it again and again. It would work, he was sure of it. He decided to kill his wife on Monday. That would give him three days to smooth over any loose ends that might crop up. . . .

Captain Joseph Sonnenberg was about to go off duty when the phone rang. Monday, April 23, 1951, had been a busy day, and he was anxious to get home and relax. The moment he picked up the receiver, however, he knew he wasn't getting any sleep that night.

"Yeah, I got the address," he said. "Eleven thirty-nine Saint Philip Street, ground floor. Okay, we'll be right out. In the meantime don't touch anything."

Ten minutes later he was standing over the body of a woman in her early 20's. The fully clothed victim lay face up on the kitchen floor. Tied around her throat in a vicious knot was a short piece of rope. An empty ice tray lay close to her left hand.

Sonnenberg looked up as a bevy of officers entered the room. Captain Dowie, a stocky, florid-faced man, was in the lead, closely followed by two members of his homicide squad, Detectives Arthur Jordan and Allen Dupre. The quartet was studying the body when Coroner Gillespie arrived.

They waited while the medical man made a cursory examination of the dead woman. Finally, he looked up. "Dead about an hour, no more," he said tersely. "As you can see, she was strangled."

"Did she put up a fight?" asked Dowie.

Dr. Gillespie examined the dead woman's hands. "There's no indication of it." He pointed to a wet spot on the floor near the ice-cube tray. "She was probably removing the tray from the Frigidaire when her murderer came up behind her and slipped the rope over her head. She didn't have a chance."

Dowie nodded. The medical man's theory made sense. "What do you know about her, Cap?" he asked, turning to Sonnenberg.

"Not much. Her name is Mrs. Mary Balli. She's 20 years old, married and has a two-year-old son, Joseph, Junior. Her husband's name is Joseph Balli. He's a cab driver."

"Where is he?"

Sonnenberg shrugged. "According to Mrs. Lena Martinez, the dead woman's sister who lives upstairs, Balli takes his cab out every morning and doesn't get home until around six P.M."

Dowie checked his watch. "It's almost six now. Maybe he can tell us what this is all about when he gets here."

Leaving Sonnenberg to look after things, Dowie climbed a short flight of carpeted stairs to question the victim's sister, Mrs. Martinez. The latter, who bore a remarkable resemblance to the dead woman, seemed stunned by the tragedy. She said that as far as she knew, her sister had no enemies. On the contrary, she was quite popular in the neighborhood.

"How did she and Mr. Balli get along?"

Mrs. Martinez hesitated. "All right, I guess. They had their spats like other married folks, but nothing serious."

"Any arguments between them lately?"

"No, not that I know of."

Mrs. Martinez explained that her sister met Balli in Galveston shortly after his divorce from his first wife in 1945. Balli was a truck driver then, working at the Navy Air Base in Hitchcock, Texas. They had moved to New Orleans five years ago, but had only been living in the murder house a month.

"Did you find the body?" inquired Dowie.

"No, a man named Robert Williams found Mary. He lives up the street."

Mrs. Martinez revealed that her sister was employed as a machine operator in a textile mill a few blocks from the house. Because work at the plant was slack, she'd said she hadn't bothered to report for duty that morning.

"How did your sister get along with the other girls?" probed Dowie.

Mrs. Martinez frowned. "Come to think of it, she did have a fight with one of the girls a while back. The other girl was let go because of it."

"What's her name?"

"I don't know her last name. Her first name's Stella."

When Mrs. Martinez promised to check her sister's things to see if anything was missing, Dowie thanked her and left. He found Williams, a personable young man in his early twenties, on the porch. Questioning him closely, Dowie learned that he had been brought to the house by two neighborhood children.

"They stopped me on the street and said something about a lady being dead, so I followed them into the house," said Williams. "When I saw they were telling the truth, I called the police."

"Was there anyone loitering around the house before you found the body?"

"No, sir."

Dowie took Williams's name and address and excused him with thanks. He then talked to the two children. They said they were playing in the hall when they noticed that the door to the Balli apartment was open. When they investigated they found Mrs. Balli's body. Like Williams, they saw no one hanging around the house prior to their finding the body.

Dowie thanked them and rejoined Sonnenberg in the kitchen. He found the precinct captain studying the short piece of rope which was used to murder Mrs. Balli.

"Make anything out of it?" inquired Dowie.

"Not much," replied Sonnenberg glumly. "It's about three and a half feet long and has been recently cut from a longer piece. However, it's ordinary clothesline rope, which practically makes it impossible to trace."

A thorough search of the premises failed to uncover any additional clues. It wasn't until they examined the hall outside the Balli apartment that they got their second lead, an odd-shaped piece of worn leather.

"It's a lift from a woman's spike heel," said Sonnenberg quickly.

"It certainly doesn't belong to Mrs. Balli," said Dowie. "She was wearing low-heeled sandals."

Nor did a check of the slain woman's wardrobe reveal a pair of high-heel shoes. Examination of Mrs. Martinez's shoe rack also proved entirely unproductive.

"Maybe a woman killed Mrs. Balli?" suggested Sonnenberg.

"It's possible," agreed Dowie. "It doesn't take much strength once you've got the rope around your victim's neck. However, we know it's got to be someone who Mrs. Balli trusted enough to turn her back on."

"Maybe she was going with some guy and his wife got sore. I've known women to kill for less."

"It's a good angle," nodded Dowie. "Suppose we talk to a few of the neighbors? They may have seen something."

They did. A woman who lived across the street from the Ballis said that she saw a pretty redhead enter the murder house about an hour or so before the police arrived.

"How long did she stay?" pressed Dowie.

"Five, ten minutes. I can't be sure."

"Can you describe her?"

"I think so. She was about five feet eight in spike-heeled shoes. She was wearing a white linen dress and carried a large patent leather handbag. She was about twenty-three years old."

The woman added that the redhaired woman appeared somewhat agitated when she left.

Another neighbor said that she was looking out the window when a taxi stopped before the house around three o'clock and Mrs. Balli got out. After talking to the driver for a few minutes the two of them went inside. He emerged five minutes later and drove off.

"Did you notice what kind of cab it was?" asked Dowie.

"Yes, it was a Red Top."

Their informant said the cabbie was about medium height and weight, somewhere in his late twenties, and good looking.

Dowie jotted down the information and left. Outside, he said: "Suspects are popping all over the place. The redheaded woman and the cabbie had good opportunities, and we mustn't overlook the husband."

"Whoever did it knew Mrs. Balli wasn't going in to work today," said Sonnenberg thoughtfully. "Which means it could be an inside job."

Back at the murder house, Dowie sought out Mrs. Martinez.

"This Stella you mentioned," said Dowie. "Do you know what color hair she has?"

"Yes, she's a redhead."

Dowie nodded thoughtfully. The trail was getting warm, he decided grimly.

When Dowie returned downstairs he found Assistant District Attorney Peter Campagno waiting for him. The homicide sleuth quickly brought him up to date on what he had learned thus far. The men were about to leave when a tall, scholarly looking man in his late fifties, entered the apartment.

"My name is John Meeker," he said. "I'd like to speak to the officer in charge."

"That's me," said Dowie. "What's on your mind?"

After explaining that he was a friend of the Balli family, Meeker said: "I met Balli a couple of days ago on Canal Street. He seemed unusually worried and I asked what was troubling him. He said that he had caught his wife fooling around with another man, a cabbie like himself. When he ordered the man out of his house, the man got very angry and threatened him.”

“What kind of threats?” pressed Dowie.

“Joe didn’t say, but he was obviously afraid for his life. When a neighbor told me his wife had been murdered, I hurried over to tell you about it.”

“Did Balli tell you the man’s name?”

“No, he didn’t.”

“Can you tell us anything about the Ballis?” inquired Dowie.

“I liked them very much,” replied Meeker. “They seemed very much devoted to each other, and it certainly was a shock to learn that Mrs. Balli played around. Although she was an extremely good-looking woman, I somehow got the impression that she was crazy about her husband.”

After Meeker left, one of the lab men announced that a score of legible fingerprints had been uncovered in the apartment, all but two of which had been made by the victim, Mrs. Balli.

“Check those two with our files,” instructed Dowie. “It’s very likely you’ll find their mates in the license files, seeing as how Balli’s a cab driver.”

Meanwhile, Detectives Jordan and Dupre had learned that a redhaired woman, answering the description of the one seen leaving the murder house, had been observed boarding a Broad Street bus shortly after four o’clock. According to their informant, she was crying.

“Find out which bus it was and question the driver,” ordered Dowie. “If she was as agitated as our witnesses claim, the bus driver ought to remember her.”

Next, Dowie called Joe Balli’s employer, the Veteran’s Cab Company, and learned that Balli had not contacted the office since one o’clock that afternoon. Fearing the worst, Dowie instructed Detective Charles Wersling to get the police dispatcher to send out an all-points bulletin on the missing man.

Accompanied by Capt. Sonnenberg, Dowie drove to the textile mill where the comely victim was employed, and sought out the personnel manager.

“We’re looking for a redhead whose first name is Stella and who was recently discharged for fighting,” explained Dowie. “Can you help us?”

“I think so,” nodded the employee. He rifled through a pile of 3x5 index cards until he found the one he wanted. “Her full name is Stella Marshack,” he said. “She’s twenty-two years old and she lives on

Allen Street."

"What do you know about her run-in with Mrs. Balli?" asked Sonnenberg.

"According to what I heard, there's been bad blood between them for some time," replied the mill worker. "It seems Stella once attended a party at the Balli apartment and took a fancy to Mary's husband, Joe. Whether Joe gave her a play or not, I can't say, but I do know that Stella and Mary hated each other's guts after that."

As for the brawl that resulted in Stella Marshack's dismissal, it took place in an alley behind the plant.

"It's a lucky thing somebody interfered," he explained. "Stella had Mary on her back and was stomping her in the face. Witnesses say she would have killed Mary. When a checkup showed Stella had started it, she was fired."

Dowie and Sonnenberg drove to the address on Allen Street after leaving the plant. Inquiries revealed that Stella Marshack had a large hall bedroom on the second floor. Receiving no answer to their repeated knocking, Dowie induced the landlady to open the door. A careful inspection of the room, however, failed to yield anything that would connect the redhead with Mrs. Balli's murder.

"Her clothes are all here, so that's some consolation," mused Sonnenberg. "At least we know she hasn't skipped."

Questioning the landlady, they learned that the suspect left the house shortly after two o'clock, saying she wouldn't return until late.

"She seemed terribly upset over something," she said. "I tried to find out what was bothering her, but she won't confide in anybody."

After Dowie made arrangements to have the house watched, he returned to headquarters with Capt. Sonnenberg. Electrifying news awaited them.

"Better hop over to St. Philip and Bergundy streets right away," Chief of Detectives Harry Daniels told him. "Jordan and Dupre have located Joe Balli's cab, and there's blood splattered all over the front seat!"

Dowie and Sonnenberg sped to the spot, a run-down neighborhood several blocks from the murder house. The cab doors were open and the keys were in the ignition. A number of fresh bloodstains were visible on the cushions behind the driver's seat, the steering wheel and the dashboard. Balli's wallet, containing his personal papers but no money, lay on the back seat.

"It certainly looks as if Balli met the same fate as his wife," said Dowie glumly. "But what about the body? This is a well-populated neighborhood, which makes it practically impossible for anybody to remove a body unseen."

"Maybe Balli was knocked off elsewhere and the killer left the car here to throw us off?" Sonnenberg suggested.

"It's an idea. If he's really dead, it's a cinch his death is tied in somehow with his wife's."

"Meaning Stella Marshack?"

"Why not?" countered Dowie. "The dame is supposed to have a violent temper, and there's no telling how deeply she felt towards Balli. Let's ask some questions around here. We may come up with something."

A check of the homes nearest to the taxicab uncovered nothing, however. When it was apparent that they could learn nothing of importance in the area, Dowie and Sonnenberg returned to headquarters. A message on the former's desk informed him that Stella Marshack had returned to her room. Accompanied by Detective Jordan, Dowie hurried to the address.

The officers found the good-looking suspect in her room preparing a late supper. After they identified themselves, she waved them to chairs.

"What can I do for you guys?" she inquired.

"Mrs. Balli was murdered late this afternoon," said Dowie, watching the woman's face closely.

She turned, a look of amazement on her face. "Mary? Dead?" she exclaimed. "Why, that's impossible! I spoke to her a few minutes before five. She was all right then."

"Why did you go there when you were on bad terms?"

Stella fidgeted. "So you know about that? Well, I might as well tell you the truth. I went there to tear her limb from limb, but she wouldn't open the door when she found out who it was."

Dowie looked skeptical. "You went there looking for trouble and an hour later they found her dead," he said. "Pardon me if I don't believe you."

Stella crossed a nylon-clad leg nervously. "It's the truth, so help me!" she said anxiously. "If I'd gotten into her apartment I know I would have given her a good going over, but I didn't even see her. She spoke to me through the door. That's why I was so darn mad."

Dowie studied the woman closely. Her story sounded plausible enough. Finding the heel lift in the hall outside the apartment was a strong point in her favor, he admitted.

"What about you and Joe Balli?" he asked.

Stella shrugged. "It was just one of those things," she said. "I met Joe at a party a couple of months ago, and I kinda went for the guy. I knew he was married and had a kid, but he sure had a great line. He said he liked me because I was a redhead. His first wife was a redhead, too."

Dowie nodded. "Go on."

"There isn't much more to tell. His first wife had five kids by him and lives in Victoria, Texas. He met his second wife when she was only fourteen. He sure is a great ladies' man."

Dowie advised Stella Marshack not to leave town and returned to his office. He felt reasonably certain that she had nothing to do with the murder, despite the fact that she was there around the time it happened. He was studying the shortened length of rope used by the killer when Detective Dupre entered with a short, powerful-looking man in his early 30's. The man wore a cab driver's cap and was obviously nervous.

"This is Bob Benoit, chief," said Dupre. "He's the cabbie who took Mrs. Balli home this afternoon."

Dowie waved him to a chair. "How well do you know Mrs. Balli?" he inquired.

"I never laid eyes on her until this afternoon," maintained Benoit, twisting his cap nervously. "I was cruising along Canal Street when she hailed me. It was a fifty-cent trip, but when we got to her place on Saint Philip she had only forty cents in her bag. She told me to come inside with her and she'd give me the other dime. That's all there was to it, I swear it!"

"You were inside for at least five minutes," Dowie pointed out. "Did it take that long for her to get the money?"

"No, not exactly. After I got the dime she asked if I wanted a glass of beer. I said 'yes' and she got two cans out of the refrigerator. When I finished the drink I left."

"Did you notice anyone or a car in the vicinity when you left?"

The cabbie frowned. "No, I don't think so. There was another cab parked around the corner on Miro Street, but that was all."

Dowie straightened in his chair. "This other cab, can you remember what company owned it?"

"Yeah, it was a Veteran's Cab. The city is full of 'em."

Dowie thanked the cabbie and released him. Then he turned to Jordan and Dupre. "That other cab," he said. "Does it give you any ideas?"

Jordan rubbed his chin. "Balli drives a Veteran's Cab. You can't mean—"

"That's just what I do mean," said Dowie grimly. "It might have been a coincidence that Stella Marshack was around when the murder occurred, but we can't write off the cab as another one so easily. I want the two of you to turn Miro Street inside out for anyone who used a Veteran's Cab around three o'clock this afternoon. Hustle back here the moment you get anything."

After the officers left, the autopsy report came from Coroner Nicholas J. Chetta's office. It stated that Mrs. Balli met death by strangulation sometime between four and five o'clock that afternoon. The rope had fractured her larynx, indicating that the killer was a person of considerable strength. A second report, this time from the lab, stated that Balli's blood-type had been obtained from his family physician and had matched the bloodstains found in the abandoned car.

Dowie hurried to Campagno's office where he quickly briefed the young assistant district attorney on the latest developments.

"You figure Joe Balli killed his wife?" asked Campagno when he was finished.

"I'm sure of it," replied Dowie. "From what I can learn about him, he's crazy about redheads. His first wife was one, and so is Stella Marshack, and I'll bet a month's pay he's got another one on the string right now. He's planned this caper pretty well, but too many redheads tripped him up."

Jordan and Dupre were waiting for him when he returned to his office.

"No dice, chief," said Jordan. "Nobody around Miro Street hired a cab this afternoon."

"That settles it," snapped Dowie. "We're going back to the Balli apartment and turn it inside out. We've got to find out who that third redhead is!"

A thorough inspection of this missing man's room failed, however, to reveal the name of Balli's latest paramour. Questioning Mrs. Martinez a second time, Dowie learned that the suspect was extremely fond of fish food, and frequently patronized a certain restaurant on Bourbon Street.

With a snapshot of the suspect they drove to the restaurant. The manager nodded when he saw Balli's picture.

"Sure, he comes in here a lot," he said. "Angelina's his girl friend."

"Is Angelina a redhead?"

The man raised his eyes in ecstasy. "And what a redhead!"

They discovered that Angelina's last name was Prima, and that her father ran a tavern on Calumet Street, and lost little time in getting to the address. Papa Prima blanched when he learned that his daughter's lover was a married man wanted for the murder of his wife.

"But that can't be!" he exclaimed, horrified. "My girl and Joseph are going to be married someday."

"Don't bet on it," advised Dowie. "Where is your daughter now?"

Prima kept shaking his head. "She's with Joseph. They left for Rayne early this afternoon."

Dowie returned to his office where he put through a call to the

Acadia parish authorities in Rayne. He gave them complete descriptions of the wanted pair and requested that they be picked up on sight.

He felt confident that it wouldn't be long before Balli would be in custody, and he was right. At three A.M. the next morning word came from Rayne that the couple had been apprehended.

Jordan and Dupre brought them back to New Orleans later that day. The girl was stunned when she learned of her lover's duplicity. She swore she had no idea he was married.

Meanwhile, Balli, grilled incessantly for eight hours, finally broke down and admitted his guilt.

"Yes, I killed her," he sobbed. "She and the kid were in my way. I couldn't go on living with her any more. That's why I got into the house the back way, strangled her when she wasn't looking and went back to my cab. Nobody saw me. Then I cut myself on the wrist and let blood splatter on the cushions so that you'd think I had been murdered, too."

"Didn't you know it would get into the papers and that your girl friend or her parents would read about it?" asked Dowie.

Balli grinned. "You think I'm dumb, eh? Everybody thought my name was Joe Garcia, even Angelina. It was a wonderful idea, but something musta' went wrong."

Joseph Balli was indicted ten days later on first degree murder charges and will be tried sometime during the Fall term. Meanwhile he has lots of time to rue the day he began preferring redheads to blondes or brunettes.

FOUR GRAVES FOR PATRICIA ANN

Official Detective Stories, September 1955

For awhile, the detectives didn't hear about the man in the new, green pickup truck. The case of Patricia Ann Cook was ominous, serious—a vital problem. But it didn't bring with it the dread, tightening fear until they learned about the truck.

It began inauspiciously enough on the Monday evening of June 20, 1955, when Mrs. J. C. Waters of No. 618 East Nineteenth Street, Rome, Georgia, reported that her fourteen-year-old daughter, Patricia Ann Cook, was missing under peculiar circumstances. Patricia Ann, the mother said, had been sun-bathing in her back yard, and she was gone now, and the only clothes that were missing were her bathing suit and a flowered beach robe.

Detectives Oscar Williams and Bill Terhune went through the usual moves. Lakes and swimming holes were searched. The detectives questioned the missing girl's friends and relatives, they called every hospital within a 50-mile radius of Rome, they talked to employes at the railway and bus terminals.

They didn't learn a thing.

Patricia Ann still hadn't reappeared in the morning. Worried, the detectives took the problem to Chief of Police Smith Horton.

"How about the girl's background?" suggested Horton. "Maybe something in it will give us a lead."

"I went into it thoroughly," said Williams. "Her stepfather is crazy about her, and she about him. Her real father, Johnny Cook, has remarried and is living in Armuchee. Patricia Ann spends a couple of week ends every month with him and his wife, so there's no friction there. In fact, I couldn't find anything wrong anywhere."

Idly, Chief Horton picked up the report turned in by Williams and Terhune. It stated that Patricia Ann had spent the entire day at home except for a short visit to a local dentist with her stepmother, Mrs. Cook. A few minutes after twelve she had telephoned her mother at the dry-cleaning plant where Mrs. Waters worked to say that she intended to sun-bathe in the back yard that afternoon.

"How about her room?" asked Horton.

Williams shook his head. "All her shoes, clothes and cosmetics are intact. I even found a few dollars in a wallet on her dresser."

Chief Horton rose, reached for his hat. "Let's have another talk with Mrs. Waters. Maybe she's thought of something by now that will help."

But the almost prostrate woman still was unable to explain her daughter's continued absence.

"She had no steady boy friends," said the mother anxiously. "Oh, she went to school dances and to the movies with the boys, but it was nothing serious. Her only trouble was that she trusted everyone, even total strangers."

Mrs. Waters said that her daughter's home life was tranquil and normal and that she got along splendidly with her father and his second wife. She had no reason to run away.

Horton watched as Mrs. Waters went to a secretary and took a stack of paper from one of the drawers.

"Look at these," she said, thrusting them into the Chief's hand. "Every time she went anywhere she left a note on the coffee table for me. A girl like that doesn't disappear voluntarily. Something terrible has happened to her—I know it."

Fear gnawed at Horton's heart as he studied the neatly written messages. He had handled hundreds of missing-persons cases during his long career, and in nearly all of them he had felt certain, beforehand, that the person would return of his own volition. The few times when he had felt a premonition of dread, it had been justified.

He felt that way now.

Horton returned to his office, where he immediately sent out an all-points bulletin carrying a complete description of the girl.

"If that doesn't do it, I'd say it looks pretty bad," he said.

Williams stared glumly at the tip of his cigaret. "It couldn't look much worse right now, Skipper," he said.

But he was wrong.

Leaving Horton's office, the two detectives and the Chief made a second round of the homes of the missing girl's friends and school chums at Rome Junior High School. None of them had the slightest idea what could have happened to Patricia Ann. They said she was an exceptionally good student, and that she took great delight in playing a drum in the high-school drum and bugle corps.

Miss Frances Raines, who had Patricia Ann in her mathematics class, stated that she was the shy, retiring type.

"However, Pat was very popular with the other students," Miss Raines added.

Chief Horton and his men delved into every phase of the girl's life and failed to come up with a single reason for her disappearance.

Meanwhile Williams and Terhune had fliers with the girl's picture distributed to every law-enforcement agency east of the Mississippi. In addition, Rome's three radio stations interrupted their programs every half hour to give a complete description of the girl.

Then they heard about the stranger in the new truck.

They went back to Nineteenth Street with the Chief and they

talked to the neighbors and almost immediately they came to the home of Mrs. Mamie Sikes.

"Why, I saw Patricia Ann yesterday," Mrs. Sikes said. "She was getting into that truck with a man."

"That truck?" asked Terhune. "What truck?"

"That new one, the little Ford truck." She described it and the detectives realized that it had been a half-ton 1955 truck, painted green, and that it had a Georgia license.

"Was it parked in front of the Waters home?" asked Williams.

"No," replied Mrs. Sikes, "it was parked further down the street, towards the Hallinan place."

"Tell us exactly what you saw," urged Horton.

"Well, it was a few minutes after two," she declared. "I'd just put the lunch dishes away and was going to take a nap when I looked out the window. Patricia Ann was walking toward the truck with this man. They got into it and drove off."

"How old would you say he was?" asked Williams.

Mrs. Sikes hesitated. "Somewhere between thirty-five and forty."

"Ever see him before?"

"No, Sir."

"You say you saw Patricia Ann and this man walking toward the car," repeated Chief Horton. "Was he in front of her or behind her?"

"He was right behind her. They couldn't have been more than a foot apart."

"Did they speak to each other?"

"If they did, I didn't hear them."

"Would you know the man if you saw him again?" asked Terhune.

Mrs. Sikes thought she would.

Back in the Headquarters car, Horton said, "The fact that Patricia Ann was walking ahead of the man could mean that she was forced to accompany him. Perhaps at gunpoint."

"I'll buy that," agreed Williams. "He may have stuck close to her so nobody would see the gun."

At the Hallinan home they learned that the family had been away all day Monday and thus had no knowledge of the mysterious pickup truck. However, a woman who lived a few doors down the street had an interesting story to tell them.

"Yes, a tall, dark-complexioned man rang my doorbell Monday afternoon," she said in answer to Horton's question. "He was looking for somebody named Dixon or Nixon, I don't remember which. When I told him nobody by that name lived around here he went away."

"Did you notice if he was driving a car?" asked the Chief.

"Not a car, a truck. It was a small pickup truck, green."

"You're sure it was green?"

"I'm positive."

"How did he talk?"

"He had no impediment in his speech, if that's what you mean," said the woman. "He had a Southern accent, though. He's from around these parts."

A few minutes later another resident of East Nineteenth Street said a man answering the same description had called at her home looking for someone named Dixon. She, too, said he had been in a green truck.

Covering both sides of the tree-lined street, the officers could find no one who recalled a family named Dixon or Nixon ever having lived on it.

The case was getting more and more ominous.

In a near-by diner, the officers discussed the next move. "The way I see it," said Chief Horton, sipping his coffee, "the guy in the pickup truck was actually casing the neighborhood when he knocked on the Waters' door. He used a phony name, Dixon."

"Could be," agreed Williams. "But why did he pick on the Cook girl? Her folks aren't rich."

"Maybe he wasn't looking for money."

"And Patricia Ann answered the door in a bathing suit."

"Exactly," declared Horton. "I'd say our next move is to bring in every morals offender in Floyd County. We've got a fair description of the man; it might work."

Back at Headquarters, orders went out to pick up and question every dark-complexioned male between the ages of 30 and 40 who had served time for or been suspected of morals offenses. The authorities in near-by counties were asked to take a similar action.

In the meantime Company E of the Georgia National Guard under the command of Captain Charles C. Prophett plunged into the wooded areas near by, looking for the missing girl. Every abandoned farmhouse and isolated building was carefully searched. Anything large enough to conceal a body was turned inside out. But darkness fell and no trace had been found of Patricia Ann.

A few minutes after darkness a Broad Street service-station attendant reported that he had gassed a green, 1955 Ford pickup truck around one o'clock on Monday afternoon.

Questioned at some length, the attendant gave a vague description of the truck driver which tallied with that furnished by Mrs. Sikes.

Asked if the man had said anything that might give them a lead to his name and home, the attendant shook his head.

"He didn't talk about himself," he said. "But he did say that he liked to visit Rome because it was such a pretty town."

Meanwhile Sheriff Joe Adams of Floyd County was asked to help and the entire facilities of his department were thrown into the investigation.

The first worthwhile lead came late Tuesday night when a farm couple in the Mullinax Mountain area reported seeing a man accompanied by a girl in a brown bathing suit near their place late Monday afternoon.

Williams and Terhune rushed to the isolated farm and questioned the couple.

"It was 'long about half-past three when the missus and I saw 'em," said the farmer. "They were walking toward the woods a ways south of here. The girl was wearing a robe and was barefoot and the man was holding onto her arm."

"Did they have a car?" asked Williams.

"I didn't see any. 'Bout an hour later we heard a car drive off but if it belonged to them, I couldn't say."

The farmer said the girl looked pale, as if she might be sick.

"Did you see them again?"

"No, Sir, we didn't. We were too busy."

Asked for a description of the man, the farmer said he was about five feet eleven, with a gaunt face and dark, unruly hair, wearing gray work trousers, a khaki shirt and heavy work shoes.

Accompanied by the farmer, the detectives were taken to the spot where he had heard a car start up. The officers soon found several clear tire impressions.

"Call the Sheriff's office right away," Williams said to his partner. "Ask them to rush Alton White out here. We can use plaster casts of these tire markings."

After Terhune left, Williams asked the farmer to show him the wooded spot where he had seen the missing girl and her companion.

On this phase of his story, however, the farmer was a little hazy. He pointed out several spots where he thought they might have entered the woods but a cursory inspection revealed nothing to the detective.

With the arrival of laboratory technicians, the area was swarming with police cars of every description. This spot was located just over the line in Bartow County, and Sheriff Frank Atwood and his men hurried from Cartersville to lend some much-needed help.

Deputy White soon came up with some information on the tires. "The impressions were made by six hundred-sixteen tires," he said. "They're brand new and have what is known as a parallel or continuous tread."

"That's not going to help much," said Horton. "Most of the big tire companies use those treads."

"Maybe so," said Sheriff Adams. "Our best bet is the truck. We should be able to trace it. Not too many green Ford pickups have been sold around here."

"You figure he might come from this area?" asked Horton.

"Why not?" said Adams. "He'd hardly take the girl away out here unless he knew his way around."

In the meantime, officers searching the woods discovered a trampled spot where a struggle might have taken place. Careful inspection of the ground by powerful searchlights failed, however, to turn up any sign of bloodstains or material clues.

As a result of the growing belief that the man might have killed the girl and thrown her body into one of the rivers in the area, plans were made to drag the Coosa River at Ferrell's Corners, just below Rome.

Throughout the night a picked squad of Chief Horton's men continued to run down numerous leads phoned in to Headquarters by various citizens. Although each was run down assiduously, nothing worth-while developed from these tips.

The next break came early Wednesday morning when a young man walked into Chief Horton's office. The description of the truck driver, he said, fitted a man named Jeff Kape.

"What made you think of Kape?" asked Horton.

The young man shrugged. "A few months back, in March," he explained, "this Kape was pestering a group of girls outside the high school. He sort of picked on Patricia Ann. In fact, he was so insistent that she had to return to school to avoid him."

"How do you happen to know all this?"

"My sister is in the same class as Patricia Ann," he said. "And she knew Kape because he used to be a neighbor of ours."

"Any idea where we can find him?"

"I understand he hangs out in a poolroom on Lower Broad Street. Somebody there will know where he lives."

After the young man left, a search of the police files revealed that a man named Jefferson Kape, 35, had a minor record, mostly for being drunk and disorderly.

"Take Terhune and run it down," Horton told Williams. "It might be just the break we're looking for."

The poolroom operator knew approximately where Kape lived and, about 20 minutes later, after some quick questioning, the two investigators located Kape's rooming house.

Kape eyed them warily as he waved them to chairs. "What's up?" he inquired.

"Do you know a girl named Patricia Ann Cook?" asked Williams.

Kape paled. He had recognized the name, all right.

"I've never met her," he said finally. "Why?"

"We understand you tried to get friendly with her a few months back."

"That's crazy. Why would I bother with a kid like that?"

"You tell us," said Williams softly. "We have a witness who says you were pestering her as well as some other girls outside Rome Junior High School last March."

Kape licked his lips. "Yeah, I guess I did," he said, dropping his glance.

"But it didn't mean anything. I wouldn't have harmed any of those kids for the world. I was in trouble then and drinking a lot."

Williams studied the man closely. "What kind of trouble were you in?" he asked.

"My wife left me on account of my drinking, and she took our little girl along with her," Kape said listlessly. "For days I walked around in a fog."

"Do you own or drive a truck?" demanded Terhune.

Kape shook his head.

"Why'd you pick on the Cook girl that day?" asked Williams.

"Maybe because she was prettier than the rest," said Kape with a shrug. "I don't know."

Williams looked around the shabby, cheaply furnished room. "What about them?" he asked. "Still in the doghouse?"

The man's face brightened. "Yes, but not for long. The Missus says if I can hold down this job for one more month, she'll give me another chance."

"Where were you between one and three o'clock on Monday afternoon?"

"Working. My hours are from one to eleven."

The officers questioned Kape for about a half hour more and then they drove to the little diner on Third Avenue where he was employed as a counterman. The proprietor readily admitted that Kape had been waiting on customers when the Cook girl was kidnaped. He was, therefore, cleared of any suspicion in the case.

Returning to Headquarters, Williams and Terhune found Chief Horton and Sheriffs Joe Adams and Frank Atwood going over maps of Bartow and Floyd Counties.

"We've got more than two hundred men dragging every river, lake and water hole in two counties," Horton told them grimly.

In the meantime the concentrated search for morals offenders in Floyd and Bartow Counties resulted in a score of men being brought in for questioning. All of them were able to furnish alibis for their whereabouts at the time of the kidnaping, however.

Shortly after ten o'clock Wednesday morning the owner of a

country store on Chulio Road, southeast of Rome, telephoned Chief Horton. A couple answering the description of the stranger and the missing girl had stopped in his store late Monday afternoon, he said.

Horton, accompanied by Sheriff Atwood, Williams and Terhune, sped to the little store to question the proprietor, Carl Brownlow.

A stocky, pleasant-faced man in his late fifties, Brownlow said he had been alone in the store when a Ford truck had stopped outside.

"A tall, thin-faced man got out and asked if I had any cold drinks," he declared. "I pointed to the cooler in the corner and he took a couple of bottles. He paid for them and went outside and gave the girl one."

"Did he say who he was or where he was from?" asked Horton.

"He didn't say anything except ask about the drinks."

"What time was that?"

"About half-past four or so."

"Did the girl speak at any time?"

Brownlow shook his head. "No," he said thoughtfully. "But now that I think of it, she sure acted strange."

"How?"

"Well, she looked scared for one thing. And then she kept waving her fingers at me when he wasn't looking. I figure now maybe she was asking for help."

Brownlow shrugged. "I make it a point never to butt into other people's business. The girl could have been his daughter for all I knew. I didn't even hear about the Cook girl until a couple of minutes before I called you, when I read about it in the paper."

"Which direction did they go?"

"They headed south."

The officers returned to Horton's car, where they sat in tight-lipped silence for several moments. To a man they were convinced now that Patricia Ann Cook was dead. The sullen-faced manner of her abductor, plus the ominous pall of silence which hung over her present whereabouts, had made them reach this conclusion regretfully.

Horton said finally, "The further we go the worse it looks. Right now I'd say she's lying at the bottom of some lake or river around here."

"Probably the Etowah," said Sheriff Atwood.

"Why that one?" asked Williams.

"Because it's the muddiest and deepest in these parts."

Horton took a deep breath. "Any suggestions?" he asked hopefully.

"If it was me, I'd concentrate on finding that new truck," said Williams. "Only instead of working Floyd and Bartow Counties, I'd include Paulding County, too."

"Why?"

"Because if he headed south from here he was going into Paulding County."

"You could be right," declared Horton, and the others agreed. "I'll call Sheriff Grady Wilbanks the moment we get back to Rome."

Before returning to his office in Cartersville, Sheriff Atwood promised to stop at every gas station, village store and roadside diner south of the Chulio Road and ask if anyone had seen the Cook girl and her abductor after they left the Brownlow store.

Horton, Williams and Terhune found Sheriff Adams waiting for them when they reached Rome.

"My men have finished tracing every fifty-five pickup truck in this county," he said, "and every one of the owners can account for his car between one and three o'clock Monday afternoon."

Reaching for the phone, Horton said, "All of which proves that he must be a resident of some other county."

Horton placed a call to Sheriff Wilbanks in Dallas, asking his help in tracking down the whereabouts of every 1955 Ford pickup truck in his county on Monday afternoon. When Wilbanks promised to cooperate, he hung up.

With every lead running into a blind alley, Horton realized that time was becoming a very important factor in the case. Unless he could come up with something, and quickly, their chances of finding the kidnaper would vanish.

Unless they heard from someone with a productive lead within the next day or two, Horton realized, they could all but forget about help from the general public.

The very next telephone call showed that the Chief was right. It was from a man who had read about the case in the *Rome News-Tribune.*

"Chief," he said, "I know a character who owns a green Ford pickup, a new one."

"Who?" Horton asked. Probably it would be one of the trucks Sheriff Adams already had investigated.

"Jonas Berry."

"I don't know him," the Chief admitted. "Where's he live?"

"Over by Dallas somewhere."

Dallas, Georgia, is the county seat of Paulding County, just southeast of Rome. Horton immediately telephoned Sheriff Wilbanks.

"I just got a call about a fellow named Jonas Berry, Sheriff," the Chief said. "Do you know him?"

"I sure do," replied Wilbanks. "Jonas drives a new Ford pickup, a green one, too. But there's one thing wrong. He's serving a short stretch now in a work camp, the one at Black Bluff. He couldn't have been in Rome Monday."

Wearily, Chief Horton hung up. Another lead gone.

He told the detectives about it, and they dug out their files. Jonas Berry was doing a few days for driving while under the influence of liquor.

"We'd just better make sure of this," Horton said wearily. "It's vaguely possible Berry slipped out of camp Monday."

Again he picked up the phone and soon he was talking to Warden C. M. Caldwell of the camp on Black Bluff Road. No, the Warden said, Berry had not been out of custody, even out of sight of a guard, all Monday afternoon. Furthermore, he hadn't been driving his truck.

For a few minutes, after he'd passed this information on, Chief Horton sat disconsolately at his desk. Finally he said, "Well, we can't let this thing go. Let's take it from the beginning, every word of it, just to see if we missed anything."

They dug out their reports and slowly, painstakingly went over them, discussing each point.

An hour had passed when a deputy stuck his head in the door.

"You got a visitor, Chief," he said.

"Send him in."

A tall, heavy man wearing a wide-brimmed Stetson walked in. Horton recognized Warden Caldwell.

Waved to a chair, Caldwell said, "I think I've got something for you on the Cook case, Chief. Your phone call set me to thinking."

"I'm listening."

"Last Monday morning," said Caldwell, "a man drove up to my house, behind the camp, and asked for me. My fifteen-year-old daughter was alone. When she told him I wouldn't be home for a half hour or so, he gave her some cock-and-bull story about getting written permission from Jonas Berry to use his truck. He kept looking at her kind of funny like, and she got frightened and slammed the door and locked it."

Caldwell took a cigar from his pocket, bit off the end and lighted it. Terhune, Williams and Horton waited patiently for him to continue.

"He didn't go away, either," continued the prison official. "He hung around a few minutes like he was trying to find out if my girl was alone in the house. Finally, he left."

"Any idea who he was?" asked Horton.

"I know all about him," said Caldwell. "I knew the moment my daughter described him who he was. And he was driving Jonas Berry's truck, too. He was Jonas Berry's friend, Willie Cochran."

Willie Cochran! Every man there knew him.

Willie Grady Cochran had a record as long as anyone's. Incorrigible ever since he was a child, Willie had spent most of his 37 years in various prisons throughout the South. A tough, hard-bitten character, he had escaped from jail four times during his hectic career.

One of his sentences had been for rape.

Horton was the first to recover. "Last I heard he was still in Reidsville," he said. "It couldn't have been him."

"Willie got out last December on parole," Caldwell said. "He's been keeping his nose clean lately, that's why you haven't thought about him."

Selecting Willie's picture from the files, as well as several others, Chief Horton and Detectives Williams and Terhune drove to the home of Mrs. Sikes on East Nineteenth Street.

Horton gave her the pictures. "Here are five mug shots," he explained. "One of these men may have abducted the Cook girl. Look them over very carefully and see if the man you saw last Monday is among them."

Mrs. Sikes adjusted her spectacles and examined each picture with painstaking care. Finally she returned one of the pictures to Chief Horton.

"This is the man I saw," she said calmly.

It was Willie Cochran.

Stopping only long enough to pick up Sheriff Adams, the officers drove to Dallas where they told Sheriff Wilbanks and his sidekick, Deputy A. L. Wood, about the latest development. They then drove to a small logging camp outside the town where, Wilbanks told them, Cochran was employed.

Cochran, a tall, swarthy man, laughed when Horton placed the handcuffs on his wrists.

"You must be nuts," he said.

Taken to the Floyd County jail in Rome, Cochran resisted all attempts to make him confess. He maintained a lofty attitude during the long hours of interrogation, even grinning when Mrs. Sikes identified him as the man she had seen with Patricia Ann.

He made several variant and rambling statements regarding his whereabouts at the time Patricia Ann was kidnaped.

Finally, Saturday morning, a crafty look appeared in Willie's eyes and he said, "Okay, I'll tell you."

He didn't remember much, the officers quoted him as saying, and he wouldn't know Patricia Ann Cook if they showed him a photograph of her because of blackouts he suffered, but he'd buried a body in the woods just off the Dallas-Cartersville highway.

They put him in a car and drove him to the spot he'd named and searched the woods. And they couldn't find anyplace in the vicinity that had been dug up recently.

"Willie," Chief Horton asked, "you're not just filling us full of wild stories, are you?"

"No, Sir," Willie replied. "I ain't."

This time, the officials announced, he said he'd thrown the body into the Etowah River from a highway bridge.

He pointed out the bridge and Sheriff Adams sent for the National Guard unit, volunteer firemen and all of his deputies. They grappled from boats; they waded through the river in a straight line, working through the night. They didn't find it.

Willie changed his story again, the officers stated, and quoted him as saying that he'd thrown the body into the river from the bank. Then, before a second full-scale dragging operation could begin, he said to Major Horace Clary of the National Guard, "Major, you look like a man of your word. I'll tell you where she really is."

The fourth spot was from another bridge, the Milam Bridge west of Cartersville, five miles downstream from the one he'd first named.

Once again, men of the National Guard and others plunged into the relatively shallow water. Hand in hand, they formed a line from one bank of the river to the other, and they waded upstream toward the bridge.

One of them stepped into a deep hole and was caught and pulled under by the swift current; others had to grab him and send him ashore by boat. The rest continued, approaching the bridge step by slow step.

Willie had been taken to the bridge to show the officers the spot from which the body allegedly had been thrown. Then, because news of his arrest had spread and a crowd, menacing and threatening, had gathered there, he was rushed to the Fulton Tower, the Fulton County jail in Atlanta.

Then, finally, almost under the very location Willie had named, the searchers found what was left of Patricia Ann Cook.

She was dead, all right, with the bathing suit beside her, wrapped in the flowered robe and a blanket wrapped around that and the whole gruesome package secured by baling wire and weighted down with a heavy logging chain and a wrench.

When the body was unwrapped, the officers saw instantly that Patricia Ann had been killed by a bullet. In Fulton Tower Willie, Sheriff Adams announced, said, "Maybe I did shoot her," and he told the Sheriff that he'd hidden the gun under the floor of a barn. Police went to the barn and found the gun.

Willie, the Sheriff said, then made a full confession.

He'd been on East Nineteenth Street actually looking for a man named Dixon—apparently he'd been badly mistaken about the street—and he knocked on several doors and when Patricia Ann answered in her bathing suit he changed his mind. Instead, he told her he would drive her to a good swimming hole and she went with him willingly.

(Police have announced that they believe she accompanied him not voluntarily but at gunpoint.)

Instead of going to a swimming hole, he drove her into the hills, stopping at Brownlow's store, then taking her into a lonely back road. After he'd been there awhile he realized that "one of us had to go" and he shot her, the bullet entering her back, penetrating her heart and passing entirely through her body.

He'd left her there and gone home for a blanket, baling wire and weights, returned and wrapped the body and then tossed it from the bridge.

Willie Cochran was charged with kidnaping in Floyd County and murder in Bartow County, where the slaying occurred according to police. He was indicted in both counties July 11, 1955, was brought to trial for murder on July 15, and on the following day found guilty and sentenced to death. Execution is pending at this writing; watch "Up to the Minute" in a future issue of OFFICIAL DETECTIVE STORIES Magazine for final developments.

To protect the identities of innocent men, the names Jonas Berry and Jeff Kape in this story are fictitious.

IT'S THE LAUGHING STRANGER FROM GEORGIA

Official Detective Stories, February 1956

Until he saw the body, Ralph Goswick had no premonition of horror as he drove along, the Boyles Mill Road about eleven miles northeast of Dalton, Georgia, at 10:30 on the pleasantly cool morning of Tuesday, November 8, 1955.

At Beaverdale Road, however, he saw it under a large white oak tree—the body of a woman. Goswick could tell from the stiff, unnatural position that the woman was either dead or badly hurt. She lay on her back, her arms flung wide and her unmoving eyes staring at the cloudless blue sky.

Licking his lips nervously, Goswick climbed out of the car and forced himself to feel for a pulse. He could find none. She was dead.

For several moments he was too stunned to move. Then he hurried to his car and drove to the home of W. S. Shields, near by, and called the police.

Twenty minutes later the peaceful glen was alive with police officers and curious residents. First to arrive were Sheriff H. P. McArthur of Whitfield County and Deputies Jerry Mauldin, F. J. Cantrell and Roy Ritchey. They were joined a few minutes later by Coroner Sandy Armstrong and Sergeant Emmett Whitfield of the Georgia Bureau of Investigation.

The victim's throat bore several bruises and in addition she had a slight swelling on the right forehead.

The Coroner examined the body.

"She's somewhere in her middle twenties," he said. "Dead at least twelve hours, maybe more. Judging by the marks on her throat, she was strangled."

The woman had died sometime around eleven the night before, according to the Coroner's estimate.

Kneeling beside the body, Sheriff McArthur went swiftly through the pockets of the victim's wine-colored suit. All he could find was a crumpled pack of cigarets, 35 cents in silver and a handkerchief. She was fully dressed except for shoes, stockings and underwear.

McArthur rose, dusted off his trousers. Studying the area, he could see no signs of blood or a struggle. It was a lonely wooded area, not far from the community of Dawnville. However, at his suggestion, the officers fanned out to search for possible clues or a handbag or anything that might help identification.

Meanwhile, the alarm had spread. Crowds of overalled men and calico-dressed women had arrived at the scene. Only by diligent efforts were the officers able to keep them away from the death spot.

This area of northwestern Georgia is settled by hard-working farmers and mill hands and their families. They dislike crimes of violence in their community and their grim, unsmiling faces showed it.

Taking out his notebook, McArthur jotted down a tentative description of the dead woman: Age, between 25 and 30. Height, five feet seven or so. Slender. Hair, brown. Eyes, blue.

Closing his notebook, McArthur asked the local residents to look at the victim. None of them had seen her before, however.

After the woman's body was photographed and finger-printed, it was removed to a funeral home in Dalton, where the Coroner prepared for an immediate autopsy. Meanwhile, the search of the area had failed to uncover anything.

"What do you think. Sheriff?" asked Whitfield, after the ambulance had gone.

"The soles of her feet are clean, so I'd say that she was brought here in a car," replied McArthur thoughtfully. "Also, the killer knew the area pretty well, too. A stranger could hardly find this road after dark."

Leaving Deputies Mauldin and Cantrell behind to canvass the neighborhood for anyone who might have seen or heard anything suspicious during the night, McArthur and Whitfield returned to Headquarters. The missing-persons files had no woman answering the victim's description. During the afternoon scores of people, hearing about the case on the radio, filed past the silent form in the mortuary, but without result. The usual number of phone calls came in and were run down promptly. Nothing worth while developed.

McArthur and Whitfield were mulling over the case late that afternoon when Ritchey stuck his head in the door.

"There's a Mrs. Jones out here who says she's got something on the dead woman, Skipper," he said.

"Send her in."

Mrs. Ophelia Jones, a pleasant-faced woman, entered and was seated.

"You have something on the case?" asked McArthur.

The woman opened her handbag and gave the Sheriff a slip of paper. "I found this in my mailbox about an hour ago," she said.

McArthur saw that it was a receipted telephone bill issued by the Southern Bell Telephone Company in Birmingham, Alabama, to Clois Hill. The date of payment was Tuesday, September 27, 1955, and the telephone number of Clois Hill was given. It was 53-1174.

"I don't see—"

"Look on the other side," said Mrs. Jones.

McArthur complied. Scrawled in pencil on the reverse side were the words, "She was killed in Bessemer, Alabama."

"What time did you find this?" asked the Sheriff.

"About five o'clock when I got my mail."

"Did you see anyone hanging around the mailbox today?"

Mrs. Jones explained that the mailbox was approximately a half mile from her home, at the intersection of a state highway and the Dawnville Road.

After the woman had left, McArthur said, "What do you make of it?"

Whitfield shrugged. "It must have some connection with the case. Apparently it wasn't in the mailbox yesterday or it would have been found."

"Unless," the Sheriff suggested, "some crank heard about the body today and put it in there. The thing to do is ask Birmingham and Bessemer police what they know about Clois Hill and find out if she's the victim—Clois is usually a woman's name."

Birmingham, Alabama, the officers knew, is approximately 160 miles from Dalton and Bessemer is a bit further, almost a suburb of the larger city.

Was Clois Hill the unidentified victim? Had she gone from Birmingham to Bessemer for some unknown reason and been killed there and her body then taken the 160 or more miles to the lonely spot beneath the white oak tree near Dalton?

Or was the whole thing a false lead, the peculiar action of some crank?

Meanwhile, the canvass of homes near the white oak had produced meager results. One couple had reported driving past the tree at eight the previous evening and were sure the body had not been there then, which merely tended to corroborate the Coroner's estimate of time of death.

Deputy Mauldin reported that a woman living not far away had seen a small, dark-colored sedan parked near her home shortly after midnight.

"She watched it from her bedroom window for several minutes," said Mauldin. "The lights were out and the motor wasn't running. She was about to call us when the car drove off."

"Could she give you any description?" asked McArthur.

Mauldin shook his head. "It was too dark."

The Sheriff telephoned Captain of Detectives W. J. Haley in Birmingham and explained the circumstances surrounding the discovery of the body and the strange note in Mrs. Jones' mailbox.

As a result of the telephone call, the spotlight shifted to Birmingham. Summoning Detective Sergeant M. H. House and Detective Vernon Hart to his office, Haley revealed to them the facts given him by Sheriff McArthur and instructed them to begin by learning the address of Clois Hill from the telephone number on the bill. It was No. 1017 South Sixteenth Street.

At the Sixteenth Street address the officers received no answers to their repeated knocks on Miss Hill's door. They went downstairs and questioned the landlady, Mrs. L. A. DuBose.

The woman told them that she had not seen Miss Hill since around nine o'clock Monday morning.

"I was dressing to go downtown when I saw Clois get into her car and drive off," she said.

Mrs. DuBose explained that Miss Hill was a divorcée and had lived in her second-floor apartment more than six years.

"Her sister used to share it with her until she got married. She's Mrs. Lois Coston now and she lives in Bessemer."

The landlady described Miss Hill's car as a dark green, 1952, two-door Chevrolet. She said that Clois had quit a job as a waitress in Mary Ball's Candy Kitchen on South 20th Street several weeks before and was presently not working.

"Clois has some money saved and her mother helps her out quite a bit." she added.

In Miss Hill's apartment, the officers found a pile of papers in the bureau drawer. Most of them were clothing and utility bills, some were letters from her mother, who lived in Arab, Alabama, while others were connected with her personal activities.

From all these they pieced together something of the woman's background. Clois Hill was 26 years old and had resumed her maiden name after her divorce in 1949. She had lived all but six years of her life in the little town of Arab, moving to Birmingham when her divorce became final. She was an ardent wrestling fan according to her letters, frequently attending the matches at the Municipal Auditorium.

"Nothing that would help," said House, returning the papers to the drawer.

"Then how about this?" asked Hart. He had found another package of letters. "They're from a boy friend."

A careful examination of the letters revealed that the man's name was Johnny Corcoran and that he had been going with Clois for several months. The last letter was dated October 6.

House pocketed the letters and looked up Mrs. DuBose again. "Does Miss Hill have any close women friends?"

"She's very friendly with Mrs. Steading, who lives around the corner," replied the landlady.

"How about enemies? Did she ever quarrel with anyone?"

Mrs. DuBose scoffed at the suggestion. "Clois gets along with everybody. She has a wonderful disposition."

"How about her ex-husband?" cut in Hart.

"She never mentioned him to me. I'm sure he doesn't cause her any trouble."

Taking a snapshot of Miss Hill as well as her sister's address in Bessemer, the detectives drove to the home of Johnny Corcoran, a tall, good-looking young man who was getting ready to leave for work when they arrived.

Corcoran was stunned when Sergeant House explained the reason for their visit.

"I can't believe it!" he said, "Up near Dalton? She didn't know anybody in Dalton. It must be somebody else!"

Corcoran said that he had kept company with Clois Hill for the past several months. They had broken off by mutual consent a couple of weeks before, he said, and he denied that their parting was anything but amicable.

He was a cab driver, Corcoran said, and had worked from four P.M. Monday to three A.M. Tuesday morning.

"After I signed out, I went to see a friend," he declared. "You can ask if you want to."

House wrote down the friend's address. "We will," he said.

At the cab-company office, the checker examined fare cards for the previous day. "Corcoran worked all right," he said.

As a result of this corroboration, the officers absolved the young man of any connection with the case.

Keeping on the move, they drove to the home of Mrs. R. E. Steading. Like Corcoran, she was shocked to hear of the possibility that Clois might be dead.

However, Mrs. Steading knew of no one who might have wanted to hurt the girl, nor did she think Clois was going steady with anyone at the present time.

"If I were you, I'd talk to Pearl Morgan," said the woman. "She and Clois have been seeing a lot of each other lately. She might be able to help you."

Learning Miss Morgan's address, the officers drove to her home. The woman, an attractive brunet, broke down and sobbed when she heard that Miss Hill might be dead and some time passed before she could answer their questions coherently.

"Why would anyone want to kill Clois?" she said. "She was a sweet girl."

"When did you see her last?" asked House.

"She picked me up around a quarter after nine yesterday morning. We went to the Mayflower Cafe and stayed there for an hour or two. Then we went to the Melba, about a block away. That's where this man joined us."

"What man?"

Miss Morgan shrugged. "I never did get his name. All I know is that he came from Georgia and that he laughed a lot. He was good company."

"How did you meet him?" asked Hart.

"Well, we were sitting there, drinking beer, when this man at the bar sent a waiter over with two beers and his compliments. He came over a few minutes later and asked if it was okay to join us. We didn't see any harm in it, so we said it was all right.

"We chatted for quite awhile, and then about half-past eleven, I think it was, I recognized these two other fellows who came in and they joined us. I left with them around noon."

"Was Miss Hill still with this man from Georgia when you left?" asked House.

The woman nodded.

"These two men, what are their names?"

"Jack Isbell was one and Hastin Colvin was the other," she said. "But why bother them? They had nothing to do with it."

"I know," agreed House. "Nevertheless, they may remember something that will help us."

Miss Morgan lighted a cigaret. "You could be right. Anyway, I ran into Clois a couple of hours later in Abbott's Cafe on Fifteenth Street, and the fellow from Georgia was still with her."

"Can you remember the exact time?" asked House.

The woman frowned. "Let me see. Yes, I think it was around half-past four. It wasn't any later than that, I'm sure."

"What happened?"

"Well, we sat around and talked, just like before. Between five and half-past, Clois called her sister to ask her if she wanted to go with her to the wrestling matches at the Auditorium. Clois was crazy about wrestling. Lois said she would and Clois planned to pick her up around seven."

"Did this man go with her?"

"I can't say for sure. She left around six o'clock and he was right behind her."

"Are you sure about the time?" asked House.

"Positive. I remember asking Mrs. Damico, who runs the place, to turn on a TV program that comes on every Monday at six."

"Can you describe this fellow from Georgia?"

"He was somewhere in his late twenties or early thirties, about five feet seven or eight inches tall and husky. His hair was curly."

"Also, he had a lot of pimples or pockmarks on his face, and his front teeth protruded a bit."

"Good going," approved House warmly. "Anything else?"

"Well, he was wearing a pair of blue jeans and a tan sports shirt with long sleeves."

Thanking Miss Morgan warmly for her help, the officers returned to Headquarters, where they reported their findings to Captain Haley.

"You've done a good job," said Haley when they were finished. "Apparently Miss Hill is the dead woman. In the meantime, suppose we follow the thread by talking to Mrs. Coston. I doubt very seriously that her sister ever reached her place last night, but she may know something that will help."

Before the officers left for Bessemer, the license number and a complete description of Clois Hill's car were broadcast and teletyped.

Mrs. Coston was sweeping off the porch when the officers arrived. A few years younger than Clois, Mrs. Coston was overcome when she heard the news about her sister. Nearly an hour passed before she could answer their questions.

"I understand Clois called you last night?" said Captain Haley finally.

Mrs. Coston nodded. "She wanted me to go with her to the wrestling matches. I said okay and she promised to be here by seven. She never showed up."

"Weren't you worried?"

"No. I figured that maybe something had happened to the car or she had changed her mind. I never dreamed that anything like this would happen."

"Did she say anything about bringing a man with her when she called?"

"She did mention something about meeting a nice fellow but she didn't tell me his name."

Convinced that the grief-stricken woman could help them no further, the officers thanked her and left.

Keeping on the move, they drove to the homes of the two men friends of Pearl Morgan. Both readily admitted talking to the man from Georgia, but like Miss Morgan, neither of them knew the stranger's name or anything about him. They said that while he had seemed like a good sport, he seemingly avoided talking about himself.

Late that night, James Coston, accompanied by Captain Haley and Detective Lawton Grimes of the Bessemer Police Department, went to Dalton, where Coston positively identified the body as that of his sister-in-law.

In Sheriff McArthur's office, Coston was questioned at some length, but to no avail. Like his wife, he knew of no one answering the stranger's description. He vehemently denied that Clois was in the habit of picking up strange men.

"She was a good girl and I'm sure that she was killed trying to protect herself," he said spiritedly.

After Coston was excused. Captain Haley discussed the case with Sheriff McArthur.

"It's the laughing stranger from Georgia we've got to find," said Haley. "But all we have is his description and the fact that he said he was from Georgia, which could be untrue."

"I don't think so," replied, McArthur thoughtfully. "At the time he said it he had no idea anybody would be killed. What stumps me is why he put that note in Mrs. Jones' mailbox."

"I've a feeling he hoped, to make us think he was from Alabama," Haley said.

As a result of their conference, squads of deputies and State Highway Patrolmen were assigned to cover the Dawnville area while others canvassed Highway No. 41 south of Dalton. By Wednesday night the entire stretch between Dalton and Birmingham was being turned inside out for the missing Chevrolet and the blue-jeaned stranger.

The canvassing officers soon came to the home of J. C. Langford, who told them that he had been driving home from his night-time job early Tuesday morning when he saw an automobile answering the description of Miss Hill's Chevrolet.

"A heavy-set man was behind the wheel," he went on. "A woman was sitting beside him, resting her head against the back seat. Just as he swung off East Morris into Glenwood Avenue, the door on her side flew open. The man leaned across her and closed it, and she never once moved a muscle. I thought it was mighty strange."

"What time was this?" asked McArthur.

"About half-past two."

Questioned further, Langford said that the man had been wearing a dark-colored cap and a leather jacket. He thought that the man was fairly young, in his middle or late twenties.

Late Thursday afternoon a private plane piloted by J. H. Henderson flew over the Dalton area in a vain search for the missing car.

Meanwhile, the autopsy had been performed by Coroner Armstrong and Doctor Herman Jones, head of the Georgia Crime Laboratory. They reported that the woman had been strangled sometime between six and nine P.M. Monday night.

Early Friday morning a woman reported what looked like a promising lead when she said that a 1952 Chevrolet had stopped Monday night for gas at a service station south of Trion, which is on the road from Dalton to Birmingham.

Sheriff McArthur and Deputy Mauldin hurried to the station. There, the attendant readily recalled servicing a 1952 green Chevrolet the previous Monday night. What was more, he knew the name of his customer.

"He's Sammy Bashor," he said, "and he lives in a little bungalow south of Phelps."

"Did he seem nervous or upset?" asked McArthur.

"No, Sir. He acted okay."

When he returned to his car, McArthur said, "Sammy is an old hand at getting into trouble. He could be the man we're looking for."

"I remember him," said Mauldin.

"Heisting cars is his specialty, but maybe he graduated."

At the Bashor home on Highway No. 41, the officers found Sammy painting his front porch.

McArthur came quickly to the point. "Where were you Monday night?" he asked.

Bashor looked surprised. "I visited my brother and his wife down Summerville way," he said. "Why?"

McArthur ignored the question. "What time did you leave there?"

"About a quarter to twelve. What's this all about, anyway?"

McArthur studied the man closely. Bashor had a surly disposition and was known to be a mean customer when he had a few drinks too many. Most important, his general description fitted that of the man they were seeking.

"Where did you get the car?" asked McArthur, gesturing to the 1952 Chevrolet in the driveway.

"I bought it in Dalton a week ago."

McArthur saw that the green coupe had Georgia plates. However, that didn't always mean anything, since Sammy had a habit of latching onto new plates without any trouble.

"Who did you buy it from?"

Bashor gave him the name of a used car dealer on West King Street.

"Okay, Sammy," said the Sheriff, climbing back into his cruiser. "That'll be all for now. But if you're not telling the truth, we'll be back."

However, Bashor was telling the truth, as McArthur quickly found out when the car dealer verified his story. A telephone call to Bashor's brother in Summerville further substantiated his alibi.

Early Saturday morning, Sheriff McArthur met in his office with Sergeant Whitfield and Deputy Mauldin.

"We've got to come up with something, and quick," he said doggedly. "So far we've drawn nothing but blanks trying to find the man from Georgia or Miss Hill's car. Anyone got any suggestions?"

"I have a feeling the man lives right here in Dalton," Whitfield said. "Remember, he said he was from Georgia."

"I feel that way, too," admitted the Sheriff. "The fact that he got rid of the body on such an out-of-the-way spot as Boyles Mill Road is proof enough."

"If he is from around here," said Whitfield, lighting a cigaret thoughtfully, "he's probably flown the coop by now."

"That's about the only lead we have left," declared the Sheriff. "See who's left town recently without any reason. I seem to remember someone who looks like this on the missing-persons report."

While the others looked skeptical, McArthur sent for the missing-persons file. When a deputy brought it, he studied each listing carefully.

"Here's the one who could be our man," he said finally. "His name is Jesse Taylor. His wife, Janie, says he's been missing since Sunday."

Whitfield read the report closely.

"He does fit the description of the man we're looking for, at that," he said. "Got any ideas?"

McArthur sent for Ritchey.

"Hop over to the Taylor home," he told the officer. "Get some samples of Jesse's handwriting. If his wife wants to know why, tell her we'll have some news for her shortly."

Ritchey was back in less than 30 minutes with several sheets of paper and one envelope showing Taylor's handwriting. Spreading them out on the desk, McArthur, Whitfield and Mauldin compared the writing with the note found in Mrs. Jones' mailbox.

"I think you've done it!" cried Whitfield excitedly. "Look at his first name and compare it with the letters in the word 'Bessemer'!"

"And that isn't all." pointed out McArthur. "Notice how the 'i' in the word 'in' is dotted above the 'n' in both the samples and also in the anonymous note found in the mailbox. And he has the habit of partly writing and partly printing his words. I'm no expert, but it looks good to me."

Twenty minutes later McArthur and his aides were talking to the missing man's wife, sixteen-year-old Janie Taylor. A good-looking brunet, Janie said that her husband had left early on the previous Sunday saying he was going to the "big city" to look for a better job. He had not specified which city, however.

Janie said that her husband, an electrician, had been wearing blue jeans and a tan sports shirt when he left.

Her husband, Janie said, hailed from Norfolk, Virginia, and had folks living in Richmond. He was 30 years old and his front teeth protruded somewhat.

The clincher came when Mrs. Taylor said that when she first met her husband, he had been living on the Boyles Mill Road.

McArthur was excited after the woman had finished. "Now all we've got to do is find him," he said.

After picking up a picture of Taylor and ordering a 24-hour surveillance maintained on his home, McArthur issued an all-points bulletin for his arrest.

Taylor, records showed, once had served a three-year term in Virginia for assault with intent to kill.

When his identity was revealed to the press, events moved rapidly.

Shortly before two o'clock Sunday morning, Floyd Hulett and Pat Fowler, machine operators in a Dalton rug mill, were driving north on Highway No. 411 for their home in Cisco, Georgia. Approximately a mile north of the Fairy Valley Baptist Church, their headlights picked out a man trying to thumb a ride.

Hulett, a part-time deputy in Murray County, just east of Dalton, recognized the man. He was Jesse Taylor.

"That's the fellow who's wanted in Alabama," Hulett whispered to his companion. "In connection with that killing." He slowed down.

"Are you sure?" Fowler asked.

"Positive. But I'll drive a little ways past him to make absolutely sure."

Hulett braked about 100 feet past the hitch-hiker and blew his horn.

"That's him, all right," he said grimly. "I don't have a gun, but I have an idea that might work. We'll pretend he's just an ordinary hitch-hiker."

Fowler opened the door for the oncoming man. "Hop in, fellow," he said.

Taylor slid into the back seat.

"Where you headed?" asked Hulett, starting the car.

"Atlanta."

"Good deal," said Hulett easily. "We're going that way ourselves, but I've got to stop at the store up ahead for a few minutes. You don't mind?"

"Heck, no," said Taylor.

At the truck stop, Hulett left Fowler and Taylor in the car while he went inside. He hurried to the phone and called Sheriff McArthur.

"I've got Jesse Taylor in my car," he told the Sheriff. "You still want him?"

"I sure do. Where are you?"

"At the truck stop on Highway Four Eleven."

"Nice work. I'll have some men there in no time."

"No hurry, Sheriff," replied Hulett. "Taylor isn't going anywhere."

After hanging up, Hulett borrowed a gun from the proprietor and went back to the car. Taylor was reclining in the back seat, smoking.

"Okay; Jesse, it's all over," Hulett said, pointing the gun. "You're under arrest."

There was a long, breathless moment of silence.

Then Taylor slumped forward and covered his face with his hands. "This is it," he mumbled.

Deputies Cantrell, Mauldin and Ritchey arrived shortly afterward and took Taylor to the Whitfield County jail in Dalton. There, before Sheriff McArthur, Sergeant Whitfield and Solicitor General Erwin Mitchell, Taylor made a full confession of the slaying, according to the police.

Officers quoted him as saying that after leaving the Melba Cafe with Miss Hill, they had driven to Bessemer to pick up her sister.

"When we were about a block from her sister's house I asked her to stop the car," Mitchell claimed he said. "She parked under a big tree. I got in the back and asked her to get in back with me. When she did I put my hands around her throat and choked her until she was dead."

When he was asked for a motive, Mitchell said, Taylor shrugged and replied, "I don't know, except that I've always had the urge to kill someone."

Questioned about the note in Mrs. Jones' mailbox, declared Mitchell, Taylor said, "I don't know why I put it there and that's the truth."

When he realized she was dead, his confession went on, according to Mitchell, he headed toward Georgia. Somewhere along the darkened highway he removed Clois' body from the back seat and put it in the trunk compartment. He then drove on, stopping several times to eat and drink.

He reached Dalton around four A.M. Tuesday morning. He cut over to the Cleveland Highway in North Dalton and continued on Cleveland Road until he came to the Boyles Mill Road, where he once had lived. There, Mitchell said he admitted, he lifted the body out.

Taylor said he had headed for Richmond, Virginia, to visit his parents. But after reaching there he changed his mind and drove instead to Roanoke, where he abandoned the car in the suburbs. He was hitch-hiking his way aimlessly when he was picked up by Hulett.

Miss Hill's car was quickly located and sent on to Birmingham. Her coat and a pair of pumps were found on the back seat.

Jesse Binion Taylor waived extradition and was returned to Jefferson County, Alabama. He was formally charged with murder on

Monday, November 14, 1955. As this issue of OFFICIAL DETECTIVE STORIES Magazine goes to press, he is being held pending further legal action. For final results of this legal action, watch "Up to the Minute" in future issues.

The names Pearl Morgan, Johnny Corcoran and Sam Bashor used in this story are not real but fictitious in order to protect the identities of innocent persons.

THE FAT MAN BLUES

True Crime, May 1956

Lieutenant John A. Meister of the Lorain, Ohio, Police Department studied the body carefully. The woman lay sprawled beside the rumpled bed, her arms raised above her head as if to ward off the cruel blows that had battered her features into an unrecognizable pulp. The stab wound in her throat was deep and had bled profusely.

Kneeling beside the body, Meister touched the swollen lips and raised the blackened eyelids. Death, he judged, had come mercifully some six hours before. She was fully dressed in a light colored dress, silk stockings and patent-leather, spike-heeled pumps.

Meister got to his feet and looked around the shabbily furnished room. Everywhere was chaos. Chairs were overturned or broken, light cords were ripped from their sockets, a window was smashed and the telephone wires were cut. Mrs. Mary Wallace, comely mother of four children, had not succumbed easily to her murderer.

"Who found her?" he asked Detective Bevan.

"Her thirteen-year-old son," replied Bevan. "He came home from school about twenty minutes ago and ran screaming into a neighbor's house next door."

Meister grimaced. It must have been a terrible shock to the youngster. His observation of the room was interrupted by the arrival of Dr. S. C. Ward, Lorain County coroner.

While the physician examined the body, Meister went outside and questioned the neighbor. The woman was still somewhat shaken, but able to answer his questions.

"When did you last see Mrs. Wallace?" he began.

"Around eight-thirty this morning," she replied. "She was hanging some wash out to dry on the line."

Further questioning revealed that the slain woman's husband, Arthur, was serving a life term in Ohio State Prison for the holdup murder of a local novelty shop owner. Meister wondered if it had any connection at all with Mrs. Mary Wallace's death.

"Did you see or hear anything unusual around here today?" he asked.

"No, sir. A few minutes after I saw Mary, I left to visit with my sister on the other side of town. I only returned a few minutes before the Wallace children came home from school."

Meister concealed his disappointment. The neighbor's home was the only one within a hundred yards of the murder house. While it seemed odd that Mrs. Wallace should he murdered on the very day that her nearest neighbor was away, Meister reasoned that the slayer could very well have been someone who was close enough to the victim to know of her friend's movements.

"Did Mrs. Wallace have many visitors?"

"There was only two that I knew of," said the neighbor woman. "One was George Dance who owns a truck farm out in the country somewheres. Mary bought vegetables off him, or he gave them to her, I don't know which."

"And the other one?" asked. Meister.

"I never did know his name. He was one of the biggest men I've ever seen. He was at least six-feet-five if he was an inch and he must have weighed close to 300 pounds."

"How often did you see him?"

"Twice, was all. He wanted to date Mary, but she wouldn't have anything to do with him."

Meister wrote down the big man's description in his notebook. Next, he talked to the victim's four children, but none of them saw the fat man or even knew of his existence.

Excusing the neighbor and the children, Meister looked around the partially snow-covered street. The house was situated at the end of New Mexico Avenue in what was known as the Cromwell district. It was sparsely settled by honest steel workers and their families. A more ideal spot to commit murder would be hard to find.

Returning inside, he found Dr. Ward preparing to leave.

"It's one of the most brutal murders I've ever seen," said the physician, shaking his head. "She was bludgeoned a half dozen times with a ball-peen hammer. You'll find it on the bed. Yet as severe as those blows were, they didn't kill her. The stab wound in her throat severed an artery. In addition, she was strangled, her right jaw was broken and a shoulder dislocated."

"Any idea when it happened?" asked Meister.

"Making a rough guess, I'd say some time around nine-thirty or ten o'clock this morning."

While the coroner was making arrangements to remove the body, Meister again studied the still form beside the bed. Despite the inhuman beating, he could still see traces of a pretty, vivacious woman.

Lighting a cigarette, Meister strolled into the kitchen. On the table were five cups and saucers. A few feet from an overturned chair was a broken plate. From this he deduced that the killer had shown up shortly after the children left for school, and that the titanic struggle had started right here in this room.

A bright reflection behind the wood stove caught his attention. Peering closely, be saw that it was a bloodstained bread-knife. He found a piece of string and looped it around the handle before giving it to Lab Technician Marvin Hunker.

"Check it carefully for prints," he directed.

A check of the woman's possessions revealed no signs of money or jewelry. However, an oblong-shaped envelope interested him.

"It's the same kind used by our local relief office," he told Detective Bevan. "According to the date, it was mailed two mornings ago."

"Which means she cashed it yesterday," said Bevan. "Robbery could have been the motive."

Meister shook his bead. "I don't think so. Robbers seldom kill unless cornered. This was something more personal. Like a rejected suitor, for instance."

After the body was photographed from several different angles, it was removed to a waiting ambulance from the funeral home where the autopsy would be performed.

Questioning the other residents along the street only deepened the mystery still further. Meister learned that the slain woman was somewhat of an enigma in that she seldom, if ever, spoke to anyone and almost never went anywhere. One woman was positive that Mrs. Wallace was afraid of someone.

Nor could the victim's father, who lived on nearby Georgia Avenue, shed any light on his daughter's murder.

"Mary was a good girl, lieutenant," he said sadly. "I'm sure you'll find that out as you go along."

Meister described the fat man that the neighbor woman had seen entering Mrs. Wallace's house, but the grief-stricken man could not furnish any clue to his identity.

"Mary had very few friends after Arthur was sent up," he explained. "Folks seemed to stay away and of course she resented it. If it wasn't for the help the relief office gave her, I don't know what she'd have done."

The father said that about a week before the murder the slain woman was wearing a diamond ring.

"She said some man gave it to her, but she wouldn't tell me his name," he went on. "She said he wanted her to divorce Arthur and marry her, but she wouldn't hear of it."

Meister frowned as he jotted down a description of the ring. A thorough check of the murder house had failed to reveal the ring. Had the fat man taken it?

Returning to his office, he found one of the slain woman's neighbors waiting for him. He said that around 10 o'clock that morning he had seen George Dance hanging around the Wallace home.

"He was behaving mighty peculiarly," said the neighbor. "First, he'd knock on the front door. Then he'd peek in some of the windows, and finally he went around to the back."

"How long was he back there?"

"About a half-hour or so."

After the man was excused, Meister digested his story carefully. Just about everyone in Lorain knew or had heard of George Dance. He sold vegetables from a small truck. He recalled that George was a bachelor and lived out on McLean Street. Had he become enamored of Mary Wallace and killed her when she turned him down? It was a possibility he couldn't afford to overlook.

Meister requested that a complete description of the fat man as well as the missing ring be broadcast throughout the East. He asked that all hockshops and second-hand jewelry stores be especially alerted.

Next, he conferred at some length with Chief of Police Theodore Walker.

"Keep after that ring," advised the chief. "I've got a hunch you'll catch your killer that way."

Accompanied by Bevan, Meister drove to the truck farm owned by George Dance. The latter, a tall, sparely-built man in his early 50s, answered their knock with a scowl.

"What do you guys want?" he demanded truculently.

"The answers to some questions," said Meister. "Do we ask them here or do you want to come downtown?"

Dance moved grudgingly aside and the officers entered a neatly furnished living room.

"I understand you visited Mrs. Wallace's home this morning?"

"Since when is that a crime?"

"It so happens," said Meister, watching the man's face closely, "that she was murdered this morning."

Dance's mouth popped open. "Mary? Murdered?" he cried.

Even though the man's surprise seemed genuine, Meister hammered away at him for more than an hour. Dance readily admitted hanging around the victim's home early that morning, but swore that he had received no answer to his repeated knocking. He said that he had felt sorry for Mrs. Wallace and had often given her some of his vegetables without charge.

"But I wasn't in love with her or was she with me," he said earnestly. "She was an awfully nice woman, and I did all I could to help her."

Meister described the fat man, but Dance only shook his head. "She never mentioned anyone like that," he said.

"Okay, George, that will be all for now," said Meister, rising. "But don't go away. We may want to talk to you again."

"The fat man is our killer," he told Bevan when they were back in the car. "But the part that stumps me is how he managed to keep his identity a secret from everyone."

Keeping his attention on the road, Bevan nodded. "Maybe he met Mrs. Wallace at some secret rendezvous?"

Meister frowned. "I hardly think so. The neighbors claim she seldom left the house. Besides, she had those four kids to take care of."

They found bad news awaiting them when they reached Headquarters. Hunker reported that he could find no legible prints on either the hammer or the bloodstained bread-knife and that the only clear prints in the house were made by the murdered woman.

Undaunted, Meister and Bevan checked all the bus and railroad depots for anyone buying a ticket within the past 12 hours who resembled the fat man. The maneuver drew a blank.

The autopsy report reached Meister's desk early the next morning. It shed little light on the investigation other than to say that Mrs. Wallace had died from the stab wound, and that she was not criminally attacked.

"At least we know it wasn't a sex crime," said Meister. "Now we can concentrate on the rejected suitor theory with more confidence."

During the night a round-up of all police characters in and around the city was made. Scores of tall, heavily-muscled men were picked up and brought to Headquarters for questioning. However, by morning all of them had furnished airtight alibis for their whereabouts at the time of the crime.

The milkman and newsboy whose route included the little frame house on New Mexico Avenue were also questioned, but to no avail. Neither of them had seen or heard anything unusual while making their rounds.

A wave of excitement swept Headquarters late that afternoon when a heavy-set man was picked up trying to thumb a ride out of the city. Bearing deep facial scratches, he was hustled to Lieutenant Meister's office for questioning.

The suspect said he was Mike Minosky, an unemployed laborer. He vehemently denied having had anything to do with the slaying, or even knowing Mrs. Wallace.

"How did you get those scratches?" asked Meister.

Minosky smiled ruefully. "My wife and I had a fight last night. I was trying to get out of her life when you guys picked me up."

When a check of the man's story revealed he was telling the truth, he was released.

The first break came two days later when a Main Street jeweler called Lieutenant Meister. He said that a man resembling the fat man had purchased a ring similar to the one given to Mrs. Wallace.

Hurrying to the store, Meister questioned the proprietor. The latter said that the ring had been purchased about a week before the murder.

"He said his name was Harry Harlan and that he was going to give it to the prettiest girl in town," said Creedy. "I recognized the ring from the heart-shaped cluster of small diamonds."

"How much was the ring?"

"One hundred and twenty-five dollars. He gave me ten dollars down and promised to pay eight dollars a month."

"What address did he give you?"

The jeweler frowned. "That's the funny part. He said he resided in Walker's Hotel. I didn't think anything about it until after he left. Then I checked the directory. There's no such hotel in Lorain."

Meister stared at the man, dumbfounded. "Walker's Hotel" was an expression used by the town's vagrants when they were locked up in the basement of the city jail. It came by that name because of Chief Walker.

Thanking the man for his help, Meister returned to Headquarters where he briefed Chief Walker on the strange twist the case had taken.

"Seems I do remember a big guy being brought in several times for vagrancy," Meister said, "but I never figured him to be the fat man you we're looking for."

"How about his prints or mugshot?" asked Walker.

"We don't bother to book vags," said Meister dourly. "Anyway, I've a feeling we'll find out that Harlan is a phony name."

At the lieutenant's suggestion, a fast round-up was begun of local vagrants on the chance that one of them might remember the heavily-built suspect. They struck paydirt two days later when one of them recalled being hauled in with a man answering the fat man's description.

"Only his name wasn't Harlan," he said thoughtfully. "It was Naiberg. Frank Naiberg."

"Did he ever say anything about himself?" asked Lieutenant Meister.

The man started to shake his head, then changed his mind. "Yeah, it seems he told me once that he was sure glad they didn't book vags in this town. I asked him why, but he wouldn't explain. Later, he told me the cops in Dearborn, Michigan, book you for spitting on the sidewalk."

A call to the Dearborn authorities revealed that Frank A. Naiberg had been booked and fingerprinted in that city for vagrancy on July 8th, 1937. They promised to forward his fingerprints and I.D.

photograph via airmail.

"We'll have him in a cell in less than a week," Meister predicted. "A guy that big can't possibly hide."

It looked like the lieutenant was right when word came from Sandusky that a man answering Naiberg's description had been picked up trying to thumb a ride out of town. However, a comparison of his prints with the wanted man's soon exonerated him as a suspect.

Weeks passed, then months, without word on the fat man or whereabouts. It was as if he had vanished from the earth.

"We'll get him sooner or later," said Meister grimly. "As long as we have his prints, he'll make a mistake somewheres, somehow. Wait and see."

This time the veteran officer was right.

Meanwhile word had drifted in that Naiberg had been seen in Fort Wayne, Indiana, and later in Denver, Colorado.

"He's undoubtedly heading for the coast." said Meister. "I'll alert the California authorities."

Years passed without Naiberg being brought to justice for his brutal crime. The dossier on the Mary Wallace case had long been relegated to the unsolved files by the Lorain police.

Then, suddenly, on the morning of March 27th 1945, the telephone rang on Meister's desk. Now an inspector, Meister scooped up the receiver. His caller was H. B. Fletcher, an FBI agent in Los Angeles.

"Are you still looking for a man named Naiberg?" asked Fletcher.

Meister's hands shook with excitement. "I sure am. Do you have him?"

"We've got him, all right. A week ago he applied for a job with an inter-state trucking outfit here in Los Angeles. To get it he had to be fingerprinted. That did it."

Meister couldn't believe his ears. Mary Wallace had been slain on the morning of February 17th, 1938. More than seven years before!

The next day. Inspector Meister, accompanied by Chief of Police Walker, started the long trek to California by car. Upon their arrival in Los Angeles, they learned that Naiberg had confessed to the murder of Mary Wallace. He said that after leaving the Wallace home he had hitch-hiked from town to town, adopting a circuitous route in order to throw the authorities off the track.

Once in Los Angeles, he secured odd jobs around the city. In 1941 he met and courted a pretty, auburn-haired waitress. They were married two years later.

Returned to Lorain, he said he killed Mary Wallace because she wouldn't return his love. During the lengthy session he kept shaking his head and muttering, "If I only hadn't let them take my prints."

Naiberg revealed that he had sold the ring to a man in Reno,

Nevada, about two weeks after the murder. The 32 dollars he had taken from Mrs. Wallace's handbag he had nursed along for food.

Frank A. Naiberg went on trial for his life in the Lorain County Courthouse in Elyria. With Judge Guy Findlay presiding, the trial lasted three days with the jury returning a verdict of guilty of murder in the first degree. Judge Findlay promptly sentenced him to die in the electric chair on the night of January 9th, 1946.

Three days before his execution in the Ohio State Penitentiary, Governor Frank J. Lausche gave the killer a month's reprieve on the basis of supposedly new evidence in the case.

When this new evidence failed to materialize, however, Naiberg was rescheduled to die on Saturday night, February 9th. As the huge, powerfully-built slayer walked slowly towards the execution chamber, he sang, "Saturday Night Is The Loneliest Night In The Year."

It was a mournful ending to a cold-blooded and senseless murder.

Editor's Note: *The names George Dance and Mike Minosky used in this story are fictitious in order to protect innocent people.*

SHERIFF KING'S LAST DAY IN OFFICE

Official Detective Stories, April 1960

It was Sheriff Lawrence L. King's final 24 hours in office, and as a parting gesture he went out on routine patrol in the little town of Winona, Mississippi, with Deputy Arthur Henson. Deputy William L. Kelly, who was going out of office, too, was putting the files in shape for the officers who would take over Monday morning. January 4, 1960.

The night was warm and humid for that time of year, and the dark, silent streets seemed as peaceful as the streets of a town of 3,400 population usually look at ten minutes of two on a Sunday morning when King and Henson rode past the Montgomery County courthouse.

Henson touched the sheriff's arm. "The lights are still on in the office, Larry." he said. "I didn't know Kelly was working this late."

Sheriff King, a stocky, gray-haired man in his early 50's, frowned. "I didn't either," he said. "Pull over to the curb and let's see what's keeping him."

The sheriff unlocked the front door of the courthouse, and Henson followed him down the dark corridor to their offices on the first floor. At first glance, the brightly lighted office looked empty.

"Where's Kelly?" asked King. "He knows better than to leave the place unlocked."

"Maybe he stepped out for a cup of coffee." suggested the deputy.

Sheriff King tossed his broadbrimmed hat onto the counter that runs partially across the front of the large room. "Our last day in office and he pulls a fool stunt like this. Well, let's close up and go home."

Then they found Deputy Kelly.

The handsome young officer lay face down just inside the open door of a walk-in vault. His face and head were a mass of knife wounds and bruises. Blood had formed a large pool on the floor: the wall was splattered.

For a moment the two officers simply stared at their colleague's mutilated body. Then the sheriff grabbed the telephone, and soon he was talking to the nearest state highway patrol substation at Greenwood, 30 miles west of Winona. He then telephoned the home of Coroner J. W. Herring and informed him of the slaying. His next call was to Sheriff-elect Earl Wayne Patridge who, with a new staff of deputies, was to take over the sheriff's office on Monday.

The calls completed. King instructed Henson to examine every door and window in the two-story building for any sign of a forced entry.

"Kelly's pockets are turned inside-out, so there's a good chance that robbery was the motive." King said.

Henson returned in a few minutes to report no sign of a forced entry. "Whoever did it either had a key, or Rill let him in." He shook his head, still numb with the shock of the discovery. "Tucky's going to take this mighty hard."

The sheriff's lips tightened, and he nodded silently. Tucky was the victim's nickname for his 23-year-old wife.

As the two men talked, the coroner arrived, followed a few minutes later by Gwin Cole, assistant chief of the highway patrol's identification bureau: Kenneth Fairly, another state investigator: Patrolmen J. A. Love and Lloyd Gatewood. Sheriff-elect Patridge and the incoming district attorney. Chatwin Jackson.

They discovered that, in addition to the many head and back wounds, the deputy had been stabbed repeatedly in the neck and chest. Coroner Herring stated that the head wounds had been made by a blunt, oval-shaped instrument, such as a ball-peen hammer. When an examination of the dead man's hands failed to show any bruises, he concluded that Kelly had been struck down before he could put up a fight for his life.

The slain deputy's pockets contained a key ring, a pack of cigarettes, a handkerchief and a book of matches. No money. Sheriff King and Deputy Henson recalled that Kelly always carried a brown leather wallet. It was not on his body, and a search of the office failed to reveal it.

King examined the contents of the vault and reported that the county tax money, amounting to several hundred dollars, was intact. Nothing else seemed to be missing.

While Cole examined the room for clues. Fairly questioned Sheriff King. "When did you see Kelly last?" he asked.

"Henson and I left here around ten o'clock last night." said King. "Kelly was here working then, but I thought he was finishing up. We made all our routine stops such as taverns and juke joints, and we were driving by the courthouse when we noticed the lights were still on. We investigated and found the body."

"Did you communicate with Kelly at any time after you left the office?"

"No."

Coroner Herring interrupted at this point to say that from the size and shape of the stab wounds, the killer had used a switch-blade knife.

"He was stabbed at least twenty-five times." Herring said. "As for the time of death, sometime between ten and eleven last night is the closest I can figure it."

After Cole had fingerprinted and photographed the body from a dozen different angles, it was taken to a funeral home in Jackson, where the autopsy would be performed.

Meanwhile, Patrolmen Love and Gatewood were searching the other offices and the grounds surrounding the little courthouse for clues. Despite an intermittent rain that had fallen in the Winona area during the week, softening the ground, they could find no footprints. In one of the corridor closets, however. Gatewood picked up a short piece of iron pipe with suspicious-looking stains on it. He turned it over to the lab men for a chemical analysis.

Fairly had finished questioning Sheriff King and Deputy Henson. He concluded, as Henson had, "Either Kelly let his killer into the office or he was caught completely by surprise by someone who got in with a key."

"But how would anyone get a key?" asked King.

"It's not impossible." said the state investigator. "The killer might have borrowed somebody's long enough to have a duplicate made."

"I think we should canvass every home in the area," suggested Patridge. "Somebody might have seen something."

His advice was good, because Gatewood quickly located a valuable witness, a Mrs. Sarah Rollins who lived behind the courthouse on Summit Avenue. Mrs. Rollins said that she had been on the porch waiting for her dog to return from his nightly outing when she saw two men walking toward the courthouse. Her attention had been drawn to them because one of the men looked around several times as if to see whether anyone were following them.

"Do you remember what time this was?" asked the patrolman.

"Ten o'clock or a few minutes after."

"Can you describe these men?"

"It was too dark to see their faces." said the woman. "But both of them were fairly tall and I think they were wearing overalls."

Sheriff King asked that the canvass of the area be intensified for else who had seen the tall, overalled men.

Gwin Cole failed to find any usable prints excepting those made by the victim. Sheriff King and Deputy Henson. Any others were too smudged to be of any value.

In discussing the case with the local officials, both Fairly and Cole were skeptical that the deputy had been slain for monetary reasons. "The crime is too vicious for that," said Fairly. "A burglar doesn't spend all that time mutilating his victim. He takes his money and gets."

"I can't see any other motive," Sheriff King said. "Kelly was a very friendly young man. Everyone in Winona liked him."

"Except one," Fairly pointed out.

Henson and Deputy Shed Castle located another witness, a Mrs. Lily-Mae Hodges, who lived near the courthouse on Sterling Avenue. Mrs. Hodges told them that she had been pulling down her living-room shade when she saw a car stop at her corner. She said she wouldn't have paid any attention to it excepting that the two men on the front seat seemed to be arguing. The car turned the corner, made a U turn on Magnolia Street, came back and drove past her house. She said she watched the car until it disappeared on Summit Street.

"Can you describe the men?" asked Henson.

"No, sir, it was too dark. I could only tell that there were two of them and that the driver was pretty husky."

"How about the car?"

"It was a light-blue Ford, a fifty or fifty-one," she said, "and its left rear stoplight wasn't working."

The officers were elated when Henson reported Mrs. Hodges' story.

"Put that car's description on the air right away," Sheriff King told the deputy. "Maybe we'll be lucky and nab them before they get too far."

King searched the stolen-vehicle files, but no 1950 or 1951 light-blue Ford had been reported. Fairly called the highway patrol headquarters in Jackson with the same result. However, he asked that all highway patrol units throughout the state be alerted for the light-blue car. As a result, state police cars rushed to set up road blocks at every important intersection on U. S. Highways 51 and 82, while cars from the sheriffs' offices in the adjoining counties covered the less-traveled roads.

Fairly and Cole, veterans of numerous homicide cases, were doubtful that the killer could be nabbed in this manner. At least three hours had elapsed since Deputy Kelly had died and with each passing minute the killer would be adding more miles.

"Besides," said Fairly. "I have a feeling that we're looking for a local man. Who else would know that Kelly was alone?"

Cole agreed. "And I'll bet a month's wages he got into the building with a key."

Exploring this angle further. Fairly and Sheriff King drove to the home of the courthouse custodian. It was nearly four o'clock in the morning by then and considerable knocking was required to awaken the man. Wide awake as soon as they told him of the tragedy, however, the custodian said he knew of only three keys to the courthouse.

"I have one and so have you, sheriff." he said. "And the county clerk has the other one."

"May I see yours, please?" asked Fairly.

The man went into the bedroom and returned with the key. "It's never out of my sight." he said. Furthermore, the custodian was positive the key never had been out of his possession for a single minute during the eight years he had held his job.

"You've never loaned it to anyone?" asked King.

"No, sir. Never."

The officers drove next to the home of the county clerk, where they heard a similar story.

"If they're right, then the killer must have lured Kelly to the door somehow and pulled a gun on him." said King as they drove back to the courthouse. "It's the only answer, because I'm darn sure my key hasn't been out of my sight for the four years I've been sheriff."

The news of Deputy Kelly's death burst like a bombshell on the townspeople when they turned on their radios early Sunday morning. The tall, goodlooking victim—only 26 at the time of his death—had been extremely popular in the little north-central Mississippi town, where he and his family had lived ever since he was a boy. Kelly and Minnie Odessa Kendrick, a Winona girl, had been married in 1956 and were the parents of a two-year-old son. Jeffrey Lee.

Fairly, King and Cole spent most of Sunday morning delving into the slain man's past in an effort to unearth a motive other than robbery. Although Mrs. Kelly had been too overcome with shock to answer their questions coherently, she told them she thought her husband had had $200 or $300 in his wallet when he left for the courthouse at about 6:30 the previous evening.

According to the records. Kelly had joined the sheriff's staff early in 1959 after working for several years as an electrician. He also had sold insurance locally for a time before becoming a law officer. Mrs. Kelly, a slim, brown-haired woman, had been employed as a secretary.

As far as the officers could learn. Kelly did not run around with other women, nor did he gamble. Neighbors of the slain man said that he was completely devoted to his wife and child and, as far as they knew, there was no discord between them. Kelly had been scheduled to return to his job as an electrician when Sheriff King and his staff went out of office.

Early Sunday morning word came from the state police lab that the suspicious-looking stains on the piece of iron pipe found in the courthouse were only rust.

Then, at about ten A.M. a tall, pleasant-faced young man walked into Sheriff King's office. He said he was Jimmy Cannon, an attendant at a gas station on Highway 51, about two miles south of

Winona. He had heard about the slaying on the radio, he said, and hurried to headquarters because of the description of the car. A light-blue, 1951 Ford had stopped at his place for gas shortly after eleven o'clock the previous evening. Two men had been in the car and the left, rear stoplight was broken.

"Can you describe the men?" asked King.

"The driver was about thirty-five or so and stocky. His companion was slim and much younger. About twenty. I'd say."

"Had you ever seen them before?"

"Yes, sir, several times. They must live in the area."

The officers questioned the young man for nearly an hour without learning anything more of importance. He was excused after he promised to get in touch with the sheriff's office if he should see the men again.

Young Cannon's tip was only the first in a long series received by the investigators when news of Deputy Kelly's slaying spread throughout the north-central area. Although every one of them was run down promptly, nothing developed from any of them.

Sheriff King ordered that the owners and employees of every store and business near the courthouse be questioned.

"Some of them stay open until eleven o'clock on Saturday nights." he reminded the investigators. "One of them might have seen something."

Next, King asked every radio station in the area to interrupt its program periodically to broadcast a description of the two men and their car, placing special emphasis on the car's broken left rear stoplight. And *The Greenwood Commonwealth,* a daily paper, was asked to run a front-page story containing a description of the two men and their car.

Sheriff King and the two state investigators, Fairly and Cole, had just returned from a hurried lunch when the phone rang It was Jimmy Cannon, and he sounded excited.

"The light-blue Ford is here in my station!" he exclaimed.

"Take it easy," said King. "Are both men there?"

"Yes, sir. They want a flat tire fixed."

"Stall them. We'll be right out."

Accompanied by Fairly and Cole, Sheriff King drove to the gas station, which was south of Winona, on Highway 51.

The officers jumped out and approached a 1951, light-blue Ford. They noticed that the left rear stoplight was broken. Two men were leaning over examining a tire on the concrete apron.

"Do you fellows own this car?" asked King.

The two men looked up. One of them, a short, powerful-looking man, nodded. "Yeah, it's my car." he said. "What's the beef?"

"It all depends." said the sheriff, "on where you were last night between ten and eleven o'clock."

"Who are you guys anyway?" the car owner demanded truculently.

King flashed his badge. "Now, where were you last night between ten and eleven o'clock?"

But the two men, who said they were Steve Nevins and Willie Abrams, refused to say. Because they were sullen and uncooperative, the car was confiscated and the men were taken in for further questioning.

Despite several hours of steady grilling, the officers could pry nothing more from the two men. Investigation of their backgrounds revealed that while Abrams never had been in trouble with the law before. Steve Nevins had served two terms in the state penitentiary at Parchman, one for unlawful entry and one for assault with a deadly weapon.

During the questioning, however, other officers, searching the car, discovered two bloodstained rags in the trunk compartment. These were taken to the state highway lab where the blood was classified as type O. the same as that of the slain deputy.

Even the disclosure of this damaging bit of evidence failed to crack the stolid demeanor of the two men. Although they adamantly denied having had anything to do with the slaying, they continued to refuse to reveal their whereabouts during the time it had taken place.

"What do you think, sheriff?" asked Fairly after the pair had been taken to a cell.

The sheriff lighted a cigarette and leaned back in his chair. "Nevins is a bad customer."

"Those bloodstained rags won't mean much if either Nevins or Abrams have the same type blood." reasoned Fairly. "Sheriff, suppose you and Henson drive out to their place and look around. Cole and I will talk to Mrs. Kelly while you're gone."

"Let's do it the other way around," suggested the sheriff. "Mrs. Kelly might talk to me a lot quicker than to you fellows."

The highway patrol officers agreed and drove out to the Vaiden community, about eleven miles south of Winona, where Nevins and Abrams lived in a rented bungalow. Gaining admittance with a key the men had given them, the officers examined the slovenly home for anything that might tie Nevins and Abrams to the brutal crime. The bedroom and living room yielded nothing of value but in the kitchen they found a bloodstained rag and a pair of work gloves with ominous brown stains.

A canvass of the neighbors seemed to tie the knot of

circumstantial evidence still tighter around the pair when one of them said that Nevins was employed by a painting contractor who recently had done some work in the county courthouse.

"Which means that Nevins had an excellent opportunity to swipe the custodian's key long enough to have a duplicate made," said Cole when the two men headed back to Winona.

The highway patrol officers found King waiting for them when they got to headquarters. The sheriff listened to Fairly's report with mounting interest.

"I think we've got our men," he said when Fairly finished. "We know that Nevins had an opportunity to get his hands on a courthouse key. Second, if that was their car Mrs. Hodges saw last night, then we know they were in Winona, and third, the rags found in their car were stained the same type blood as Kelly's."

"It still isn't enough, sheriff," said Fairly, shaking his head. "We have to find the death weapons. Either that or get a confession."

Asked how he had made out in talking with the widow. King said. "Mrs. Kelly still thinks her husband had between two and three hundred dollars on him when he left for the courthouse last night. She seems certain that robbery was the motive and I agree with her."

Meanwhile, the autopsy had been performed in Jackson by Doctor F. L. Bratley and the report was delivered to Sheriff King. It stated that Kelly had died as the result of severe head injuries and a punctured kidney, believed to have been inflicted by a very sharp instrument. In addition to the fatal wound, the deputy was stabbed eighteen times in the neck and nine times in the back. The killer. Doctor Bratley said, had continued to rain blows on the young deputy even after he was dead.

Early Monday morning, Earl W. Patridge was sworn in as sheriff of Montgomery County. Minutes after the brief ceremony in the mayor's office, he assumed an active role in the case, taking time out only for Kelly's funeral that afternoon, when he and Deputy Henson acted as pallbearers.

After this sad duty was completed. Patridge, ex-sheriff King and the two state investigators continued to work around the clock. The grounds surrounding Nevins' home in Vaiden were carefully searched by Cole and Fairly for any signs of a weapon

As the hours passed, all sorts of rumors drifted into the corridors of the old courthouse and, eventually, into the sheriff's office. Gossip about the slain man and his wife became increasingly rampant, and some of it was of a very unsavory nature.

Cole and Fairly, who had worked on many small-town homicides during their careers with the highway patrol, listened to every rumor with avid interest. They had solved many cases in the past simply by keeping their ears open and refusing to dismiss even the wildest rumor as idle gossip.

"Where there's smoke there's fire," Cole told Fairly early Tuesday morning. "Let's run these rumors down."

Although they were able quickly to discount most of the rumors as mere hearsay, one continued to persist—that Kelly had been concerned about another man.

Sheriff King laughed when Cole told him about the rumor. "That's the most ridiculous thing I ever heard!" he exclaimed. "Mrs. Kelly was in love with her husband. That kind of talk is nothing but sour grapes."

"How do you mean that?" asked Fairly.

"Mrs. Kelly is a very pretty woman, and attractive women are always unpopular—with other women."

But Fairly and Cole weren't convinced.

And neither was Sheriff Patridge. "Look into it," he told the state investigators. "This is a very small town and I've heard a few of those rumors myself."

Seeking to get at the root of the gossip, Fairly and Cole drove to the Kelly bungalow, where they found the widow being consoled by her brother, Johnny Kendrick.

"Do you know of anyone who would want to kill your husband?" asked Cole.

Mrs. Kelly shook her head. "No, sir, I don't. Bill wasn't the kind who made enemies." Her eyes brimmed with tears and she wiped them with a weary gesture. "It's hard to believe he's gone."

"I dislike asking you this question. Mrs. Kelly," Fairly said. "But it has to be answered if we're going to find your husband's killer. We've heard some rumors that he was upset about your seeing another man. Is that correct?"

Mrs. Kelly paled. "No, it's not!" She was emphatic. "I loved my husband!"

The officers, after questioning the distraught woman for some time without learning anything else, thanked her and left. But they hardly were in their car than Kendrick appeared on the porch and asked them to wait.

"You have something?" Cole asked the young man.

Kendrick nodded. "Yes, I have. I should have told you before this, but I didn't want to say anything while Larry King was still in office."

Cole looked at the young man sharply. "What are you trying to say?"

"Just this—Larry King has been running after my sister for some time and Bill knew it!"

The state officers stared at him, stunned. Lawrence L. King had been born and raised in Montgomery County. He was a faithful member of one of the local churches and its choir. He had been chief of police of Winona for two years, a deputy for four and sheriff for four more years, and all during those ten years not a single black mark had been chalked up against his name. What was more, he was considered by his colleagues in the law-enforcement business to be one of the most dedicated officers in the state.

"Do you realize what you're saying?" asked Cole.

Kendrick nodded. "I know that you're surprised but, believe me, it's true."

The officers climbed out of their car and accompanied young Kendrick back into the house. Mrs. Kelly seemed to shrivel in the chair when she saw them.

"Your brother told us about Sheriff King," said Cole. "Is he telling the truth?"

Mrs. Kelly lifted her tear-stained face and stared at them for several minutes without a word. Then she covered her face with her hands and sobbed.

When the widow didn't answer, young Kendrick spoke up. "Bill quit his deputy's job about a month ago because of it, but he and King patched things up somehow and he went back."

Probing gently, the officers learned that the sheriff had been trying to force his attentions on Mrs. Kelly since early the previous September.

"Larry has been a very lonely man ever since his wife died two years ago," she said with a catch in her voice. "At first I felt sorry for him. I thought he only wanted a woman to talk to. But as time went on, it got out of hand."

Cole and Fairly, still shaken by what they had learned, thanked the widow and returned to their car to discuss their next move. It was obvious that the ex-sheriff could not have committed the actual crime himself. Yet someone might have been hired to do it.

"Let's see if we find anything that would tie him in with Nevins and Abrams," Fairly suggested.

But that possibility blew up in their faces when they returned to headquarters. There Sheriff Patridge told them that Abrams had broken down and admitted that he and Nevins had been in a brawl with two other men in a juke joint on Highway 51, a few miles south of Duck Hill. He placed the time of the disturbance at between ten and eleven o'clock Saturday night. As for the bloodstained rags. Abrams said that Nevins had suffered a nose bleed during the fight. His type, it was found, was the same as the slain deputy's. When a call to the tavern verified Abrams' story, both men were released from custody.

Patridge was dumfounded when Cole told him that ex-Sheriff King had been trying to date Mrs. Kelly.

"I was one of Larry's deputies last spring when Mrs. Kelly worked here for a few weeks." he said. "Looking back. I remember he did seem awfully fond of her, even then."

"I remember that King insisted on talking to Mrs. Kelly instead of us." Fairly said.

"And don't forget the way he insisted that robbery was the motive," said Cole. "It would have been a simple matter for him to have had a duplicate key made."

"Look, it's hard enough to believe that Larry was running after Bill's wife—I can't imagine anything else." Patridge said. "I still think our best bet is that light-blue Ford. If we could find it, maybe we could bust this thing wide open."

"I have an idea that might work," said Cole, drumming his kneecap with nervous fingers. "How about running down the car of every ex-con living within a twenty-five-mile radius of Winona?"

"Good idea," said Patridge. "We can divide the list into three teams—you and Fairly. Patrolmen Love and Gatewood, and Henson and I."

The files were scrutinized closely and a list of every ex-convict living within 25 miles of Winona was compiled. Because of Fairly's insistence that no distinction be made on the type of crime committed by the ex-convict, the list proved to be longer than they anticipated. Nearly 50 names finally were distributed to the three teams and the long, tedious job of questioning began. Cole's suggestion that they refer to the motor-vehicle department files, in order to save time and legwork, was vetoed because many convicts out on parole get the use of a car through a second party.

The search seemed to get them nowhere. One ex-con after another was picked up and questioned, but either had a completely different type of car than the one seen near the courthouse on the night of the slaying, or no car at all.

Then, late Tuesday evening. Fairly and Cole parked before the home of Alec Morris in Eskridge, a small community about ten miles north of Winona. Morris was a 50-year-old man who had served a ten-year term at Parchman for manslaughter.

Cole nodded toward a mud-splattered car in the driveway. "Do you see what I see, Ken?" he asked.

"I sure do," said Fairly. "A light-blue, nineteen-fifty Ford. And the left rear stoplight is busted. Let's go!"

The officers found the burly ex-convict in the kitchen drinking beer with a woman.

After they had introduced themselves. Cole asked Morris where he had been between ten and eleven o'clock Saturday night.

"I was home here, looking at television," Morris said.

"Do you have anybody to back up your story?" asked Fairly.

"Reckon not, officers. I was alone all the time."

Something in the ex-convict's manner made Fairly suspicious. "Mind if we look around?"

Morris hesitated.

"I can send my partner back for a search warrant if you wish."

Morris shrugged. "It won't be necessary," he said. "Go ahead."

The officers claim they found a badly burned hammer and a key in the stove.

"Does this key open the courthouse door?" asked Fairly.

"I ain't talkin'." Morris snapped.

A further search of the four-room bungalow uncovered a .28-caliber Smith and Wesson in the bedroom, while in the back yard. Fairly found evidence that some clothes recently had been burned.

Morris refused to tell the officers the names of any of his friends, but the woman who had been visiting him told Fairly outside that Alec's buddy was a younger man, Earl Townsend—nicknamed Pink—who lived in Winona.

Cole and Fairly took Alec Morris to Patridge's office. While the new sheriff was questioning him, the state investigators went out and picked up Pink Townsend, a slim, stolid-faced man in his middle 20's.

At Cole's suggestion, the two men were taken to the state highway patrol substation at Greenwood where they underwent thorough questioning. Assisted by the newly elected district attorney, Chatwin Jackson, Cole and Fairly pounded away at the pair, who continued for some time to deny having had anything to do with the slaying of Deputy Kelly. However. Townsend broke first and, once again, the former sheriff's name entered the case.

According to portions of his statement released by the police, Townsend said that Sheriff King had hired Morris to kill Deputy Kelly on at least four occasions prior to the successful attempt on the night of January 2. Morris was supposed to hide in the deputy's car on one occasion and then shoot him when he got in the car. Another plan was to have Morris slug Kelly into unconsciousness and leave his car on the railroad tracks to make his death appear accidental.

Townsend said, the officers claimed, that on the afternoon of the slaying. King telephoned Morris and told him that Kelly would be alone in the office that night working on the files. Since the sheriff already had had a duplicate key made, it was a simple matter for Morris to gain admittance to the courthouse. Kelly was working over some ledgers when they walked in and surprised him. Holding a gun on him. Morris ordered the deputy to get down on his knees and crawl into the vault. When he did so, they went to work on him with the knife and hammer until he was dead. They then returned to Morris' home where they celebrated by downing a fifth of whisky.

Later that morning they drove to a designated spot west of the town limits where the sheriff was supposed to leave $1,000 for them to pick up. Instead of the $1,000, they found only five 20-dollar bills.

When Morris was shown his friend's statement, he nodded glumly. "That's about the way it happened." he admitted, according to the police.

Lawrence King was picked up the next morning. Confronted with the two signed statements, the ex-sheriff admitted orally that he had hired Morris to dispose of his deputy, the officials claim, adding that Morris had hired Townsend on his own.

News of the ex-sheriff's alleged admission shocked the people of Montgomery County. Although he had been defeated at the polls by Patridge, King was highly thought of and respected by nearly everyone in the north-central area of the state. He always was considered to be a kind, thoughtful man and all those who had served under him were stunned when they heard the news of his arrest.

Mrs. Kelly was questioned again later that day. Apparently she was as shocked as everyone else to learn that her insistent admirer was being accused of plotting her husband's death.

The officers said that under further questioning Morris and Townsend claimed they had found only fifteen dollars in Deputy Kelly's wallet—not the several hundred he had been reported as carrying.

Morris told the officers that he threw the knife away somewhere between Winona and Eskridge. However, on Monday, January 11, officers claim they found the knife concealed in Townsend's trousers.

As a result of the three statements, two written and one oral, the three men were removed to the LeFlore County jail in Greenwood, where at this writing they are being held without bail on first-degree-murder charges awaiting action by the Montgomery County grand jury.

The names Steve Nevins and Willie Abrams are fictitious in this story.

SECRET OF THE GRANITE QUARRY

Official Detective Stories, August 1961

The earth shivered! For miles around the small community of Ruby, in central Georgia, windows of homes shattered, chimneys fell, buildings shook.

Almost before the first reverberations died away, another explosion followed. And another!

Several miles distant in the little towns of Gray and James, people leaped from their beds and cast anxious, bewildered eyes at the sky. As they looked and wondered, still another explosion rocked the area. In the distance, glowing through the pre-dawn darkness, flames and billowing clouds of smoke shot upward toward the sky, giving it a pasty, sickly hue. Watchers exchanged looks touched with fear. What was it? Where—

The first blast awakened Sheriff Holmes Hawkins. He had checked his watch automatically—4:10 A.M. on Sunday, March 19, 1961. He pulled on his clothes and drove rapidly to the Jones County courthouse in Gray.

There he found Deputy Eddie Middlebrooks trying to keep up with a frantically ringing telephone.

"I'm sure glad you're here, Sheriff," Middlebrooks said. "Everybody in the county is calling. They want to know what's going on!"

"I'm wondering myself," said Hawkins. "Keep on that phone. That's the quickest way of finding out what's wrong."

One woman called to ask if the country was being bombed. Another wanted to know if the world was coming to an end.

The first report on the origin of the blasts came at 4:25 A.M. when an excited man called Headquarters.

"Take it easy," Middlebrooks said patiently. "What's your name and where are the explosions coming from?"

"I'm Mack Harrison," said the caller. "I live in James. The Weston-Brooker rock quarry is blowing up!"

Middlebrooks broke the connection and hurried into the Sheriff's office.

"It's the Weston-Brooker rock quarry, Skipper," he said.

Hawkins immediately contacted Fire Chief Gus Butler and asked him to get his men to the quarry as quickly as possible. Then he called Agent James Carnes of the Georgia Bureau of Investigation who lived in nearby Eatonton and asked him to come to the scene. They still were talking when Deputy Havis Bonner hurried in.

Hawkins reached for his hat. "You stay here. Eddie," he told Middlebrooks. "Bonner and I are going out there now. And tell the people to stay away from that quarry!"

Hawkins and Bonner jumped into a Headquarters car and headed toward Ruby, where the Weston-Brooker quarry was located. Other cars began appearing on the highway and they recognized many of the drivers as employees of the rock quarry.

Utter devastation met their eyes when they arrived at the scene. Flames leaped from the skeleton remains of what had been a two-story machine shop. Large holes dotted the landscape where the explosions had taken place. Blackened oil drums, some of them bent into fantastic shapes, lay burning everywhere. A heavy truck was reduced to a crumpled piece of steel. Charred bits of wood, some of them still flaming, littered the 100-acre tract of what had been a busy and productive rock quarry. Several large pieces of heavy equipment were nothing but piles of junk. Two scarred chimneys marked what was left of a huge warehouse.

"It looks like an atom-bomb hit the place!" Sheriff Hawkins exclaimed as he braked on the highway.

Miraculously, the only undamaged machinery on the property was the expensive conveyor belt system which transported the granite from one crushing process to another and finally deposited it in huge piles in a nearby field.

They were joined a few minutes later by Chief Butler's firemen, who were armed with chemical extinguishers. As they worked, Hawkins and Bonner walked carefully among the wreckage. The stench of burning wood and powder assailed their nostrils from everywhere.

"Something must have triggered all this," Hawkins said, stopping to mop his face with a handkerchief.

"You mean it was no accident?" asked Bonner, surprised.

"That's exactly what I mean," said the Sheriff. "The Weston-Brooker people aren't novices in this business. They have two other quarries in Georgia and one in South Carolina. They've been in the business for years. They don't make any mistakes."

"But who?" asked Bonner. "And why?"

Hawkins, a tall, distinguished man and a veteran law officer, only shrugged. "Your guess is as good as mine," he said. "Let's keep looking."

In less than an hour the officers were joined by two agents from the Georgia Bureau of Investigation, James E. Carnes and Arthur L. Hutchins. Both men listened attentively while Sheriff Hawkins told them about the explosions.

"The first one came around four-ten," said the Sheriff. "The others followed at about five-minute intervals."

"You think it was deliberate?" asked Carnes.

"I'm sure of it. The fact that all of the explosions occurred at widely separated points proves it."

"But why?" asked Hutchins.

"Here comes someone who may be able to tell us," said Hawkins, gesturing to a well-dressed man hurriedly getting out of a car on the highway. "That's Caldwell Weston, one of the firm's vice-presidents."

But Weston had not the slightest idea why anyone would want to destroy the quarry.

"Everything but the conveyors are gone," he said, shaking his head. "The repair and welding shops, the warehouse, the office building, the storage and tool sheds. All gone. The damage must total a hundred thousand dollars!"

"Have you had trouble with any employees?" asked Hawkins.

"Not a one," said Weston. "Our management-employee relationship since we came here in 'Fifty-seven has been perfect."

But Sheriff Hawkins was not entirely convinced. A lawman for more than two decades, as his father had been before him, he knew a criminal act when he saw it. And this wholesale depredation pointed in that direction.

"Let's look around," he told the GBI agents. "It seems safe enough now."

Stumbling among the smoking ruins, it took them less than fifteen minutes to get ample evidence that the explosions had been set deliberately. The first came when Carnes discovered a number of burned matches near one of the storage tanks. They also found several lengths of wire stretched across the ground, some of them leading directly to where buildings once stood. In addition, they found a large number of demolition caps scattered about.

Weston examined the caps carefully. "These are always kept under lock and key in a concrete shelter," he said.

The officers accompanied him to the shelter where an examination of the lock showed that it had been burned off, probably by an acetylene torch.

"That settles it," said Sheriff Hawkins. "It proves it was deliberate. And that whoever did it knows how to use an acetylene torch."

"That takes in a lot of territory. Sheriff," said the company official thoughtfully. "There must be at least a hundred people in Jones County who know how to operate one."

"But how many of them know the exact shelter where these explosives were kept?" asked Hawkins.

The company official didn't know.

"Do you keep a night watchman on duty?"

"No, we don't. We've never had any reason to before now."

Hutchins, meanwhile, came up with another important discovery near one of the demolished tool sheds. He yelled for the others to join him.

When they had done so, he said, "Footprints." He pointed to a number of clear impressions showing in the ground. "They lead directly to the bunker where the caps were stored."

"But how will they help?" asked Weston. "I've got eighty men working for me. Any one of them could have made those prints."

"I hardly think so," said the GBI Agent. "I understand it rained quite heavily around here late last night. That would have washed out any prints made before quitting time yesterday."

The other officers nodded.

Because of the tracks' importance, Sheriff Hawkins assigned Deputy Bonner to stand guard over them until the GBI agents could make plaster casts.

Then, at exactly six A.M., while the officials were conferring on the highway, an almost unbelievable explosion split the area! Chunks of concrete and debris were blasted through the air; the shock rolled men along the ground; others threw themselves flat in automatic defensive action. Small pieces of rock rained down. Huge clouds of acrid, dirty smoke drifted over the quarry.

Moments passed. Slowly, men risked looking up from their hiding spots, their faces dazed, eyes anxious.

"What—what was it?" Someone asked.

"That concrete bunker," Weston said shakily. "Where we kept the dynamite." He looked around, awe-stricken. "There were nine tons of dynamite in there!"

Sheriff Hawkins brushed himself off. "Keep everyone out of the quarry," he told a couple of Georgia Highway Patrolmen who had arrived only minutes before. "There may be more explosions. And some people are crazy enough to go in and look around."

Hurrying to his car, Hawkins radioed Deputy Middlebrooks and asked him to call Fort McPherson and have a team of demolition experts sent to the quarry as quickly as possible. He racked the receiver when Middlebrooks promised to contact the military authorities immediately.

"In the meantime, nobody goes onto the quarry ground," said Hawkins. "That last explosion would have killed us all if we'd been near it. Nine tons!" He shook his head.

As news of the explosions spread over the Georgia countryside by telephone and radio,, hundreds of cars sped toward the scene, jamming traffic almost hopelessly. By ten o'clock, Sheriff Hawkins was forced to appeal to the Highway Patrol for additional men to keep the crowd from surging onto the quarry grounds and possibly eliminating valuable evidence.

A team of demolition experts under the command of Captain Richard M. Barb arrived from Fort McPherson a few hours later. Armed with mine-detecting devices, they immediately set out to try to uncover any further danger spots. They moved slowly and carefully over the debris-littered ground without uncovering any more booby traps.

"There's a hole twenty-five feet deep and forty feet across where the dynamite bunker used to be," Captain Barb reported.

When Captain Barb finally gave the all-clear signal in mid-afternoon, Sheriff Hawkins and his colleagues moved in. They had been joined, meanwhile, by another GBI Agent, Henry Walden, from nearby Milledgeville. With them was G. C. Jacquot, an explosives expert employed by the E. I. DuPont Company, a leading manufacturer of explosives.

Their only tangible lead, the footprints, proved to have added significance when Carnes examined them closely.

"That's odd," he said, measuring the Prints. "One print is size eleven and the other is size twelve."

Sheriff Hawkins frowned. "Could they have been made by two people?"

Carnes shook his head. "That's what I thought at first. But the prints not only match perfectly, they're too close together to be made by two men. According to the stride and the distance between each step, only one man could have made them."

"That is something," agreed the sheriff. "Can you tell what kind of boots they were?"

"I think so," said the GBI Agent. "On the soles of the impressions are small, box-like squares. It's been my experience that knee-high rubber boots frequently have this type of pattern."

Weston, who was standing nearby, listening, shook his head. "There must be at least forty men who wear rubber boots around here during working hours."

"Just the same, we'll have to check them out," Sheriff Hawkins told him.

"We'll make plaster casts," Hutchins said.

"Good. Then we'll try to get together a list of employees." He turned to Weston. "I imagine the personnel records were destroyed in the blast and fires, but we can check the bank which issued your paychecks. They should be able to supply most of the names."

While the GBI Agents were making the casts, Jacquot came over to the Sheriff.

"I've been looking at what's left of that truck over where the dynamite bunker was," he said.

His tone of voice showed Hawkins he'd noted something strange.

"What did you find? It's scattered all over, isn't it?"

"Yes. That's the unusual thing."

The explosives expert went on to explain that normally all the truck pieces should have been found lying in a direction away from the source of the explosion. "But the truck fragments were blown in all directions," he said. "As if the truck itself had a load of dynamite within it which went off before the big explosion."

Sheriff Hawkins and the GBI Agents pondered this. It meant the truck could have been used to transport dynamite to the various places where the different blasts actually occurred. Perhaps the driver just had been leaving the bunker with another load when it exploded—with him sitting practically on top of it!

The Sheriff whistled softly through his teeth. There had been no sign of a dead man in the quarry but, if the driver had been right with the explosive, would he have been found at all?

"That's something we'll have to look into," Hawkins said.

By checking officials of the quarry who kept records of certain operations, and the bank, the names of all Weston-Brooker employees at this plant were obtained.

All available officers were put on the case and soon every employee had been located and questioned except one—23-year-old Robert Seabrooks.

"He's a welder's helper," Weston told Sheriff Hawkins. "He's been a model employee."

"He knew how to use an acetylene torch," said the Sheriff. "And there is no sign of him anywhere."

Seabrook's wife and family did not know where the young man was. An older brother, Willie, said he last saw him in Gray around midnight.

"Was he alone?" asked the Sheriff.

"Yes, Sir."

Willie Seabrooks said that his brother had been in a restaurant eating a sandwich when he last saw him.

"Does Robert own a pair of rubber boots?"

"Yes, Sir, I'll get them for you."

Willie turned over a pair of knee-high rubber boots to the Sheriff who put them into his car.

Further questioning revealed that the missing man had told his brother he was going home after he finished his sandwich.

Hawkins and Carnes drove to the restaurant and talked to the owner. He readily recalled seeing Seabrooks in his place the night before, but said he did not know when he left or if he was with anyone in particular.

"I'm usually pretty busy on Saturday nights," he explained.

However, one of his customers remembered seeing Seabrooks walking toward home a few minutes after his brother left.

The officers drove to the missing man's home where his young wife tearfully denied that her husband had ever showed up.

"Something has happened to Bob, I just know it," she sobbed. "We've only been married six months, and he's never been away overnight before."

Before leaving, Hawkins secured a list of the missing man's out-of-town relatives on the chance that he might have gone to see one of them for some reason.

When Hawkins returned to his office, he turned the list over to Deputy Bonner. "Contact the police in those cities and ask them to watch out for Seabrooks," he ordered. "We want to talk to him."

"It's possible Seabrooks could have been killed in those blasts," said Carnes thoughtfully, after the deputy had left.

"I've been thinking the same thing," said Hawkins, stretching his legs. "Since he's been married such a short time, it isn't likely he'd stay away without telling his wife."

A careful examination of the missing man's boots showed they did not match the prints at the scene of the holocaust. But his unexplained absence at this time could not be ignored. The Sheriff couldn't help thinking of Jacquot's theory about the truck—and its driver.

Despite the accelerated pace set by the investigators during the next few days, the motive for the explosions continued to mystify them. The plant had had no labor trouble, no individuals had seemed unhappy about working conditions, there seemed to be nothing to justify such an action as the series of explosions. Yet they had occurred. Why? That was the question which had to be answered.

A number of theories were suggested, carefully considered and then discarded. One of them was money, but examination of the badly shattered company safe revealed no attempts had been made to force it open. Did someone, an employee nursing a grudge to himself, perhaps, have it in for the company? Although this angle was carefully explored, it drew a blank. The company had not fired anyone in nearly eighteen months, and the few ex-employees still living in the area were gainfully working for someone else. In addition, a check of their movements at the time in question revealed that they were nowhere near the quarry.

Meanwhile, at Sheriff Hawkins' suggestion, technicians from the Georgia Crime Laboratory in Atlanta were dispatched to the quarry. Under the direction of Doctor Larry Howard, they were quickly briefed on the circumstances surrounding the blasts and the mysterious disappearance of Robert Seabrooks.

"Is there a chance he was in the blast?" asked Doctor Howard.

Hawkins nodded. "We have to consider it," he said. "I'd like you find out."

Doctor Howard and his staff began their tedious task of sifting the charred debris that littered the quarry property. Most of them tackled the huge crater left by the final explosion. Using garden rakes and shovels they loaded the topsoil into trucks and had it taken to other technicians who picked through it by hand. It was slow, painstaking work, and one that could not be hurried.

Deputy Bonner, meanwhile, reported that questioning of the missing man's relatives had failed to turn up any sign of Robert Seabrooks.

When Seabrooks continued to be absent from his home, Hawkins became more and more convinced that he was dead.

"But everything in his past indicates he wasn't the type person to do such a terrible thing." he told Agents Walden, Hutchins and Carnes in his office early Friday morning, "He's never been in trouble and has been an excellent family man."

"You've checked his work record thoroughly?" Walden asked.

The Sheriff nodded. "Company officials describe him as an honest, hardworking man. He didn't miss a day's work since starting at the quarry two years ago."

"That raises an interesting possibility," Carnes said. "Maybe Seabrooks was forced to go along to the quarry, possibly to show someone exactly where something was—the safe or dynamite—or maybe the entire thing was just to get rid of Seabrooks. Maybe there was someone who wanted him dead."

The theory would have to be checked.

It at least supplied a possible motive for the blasts. But it was becoming increasingly apparent that only by the most strenuous legwork would the bomber be caught. The officials knew, too, that much depended on the work now being conducted by Doctor Howard and his staff.

In the meantime, the GBI Agents visited the home of every employee, secured their rubber boots if they owned any, and brought them to Headquarters where they were carefully measured for a discrepancy in size and also for sole patterns. None, however, proved to be the pair that had made the footprints at the quarry.

A promising break came early on Saturday morning from the owner of a small grocery store on Highway 22, about three miles east of Gray. He phoned Hawkins to tell him that late on the previous Saturday evening, only a few hours before the explosions, he had a customer who purchased a box of large wooden matches.

The owner's story aroused keen interest since this was the type of matches found at the scene after the blasts. Accompanied by Agent Carnes, Sheriff Hawkins hurried to the store and questioned the man.

"He came in a few minutes before midnight," the owner told them. "The matches were all he wanted."

"Do you know his name?"

"Oh, sure. He lives about half a mile down the road in Mrs. Pond's rooming-house. His name is Josh Riggins."

Further questioning revealed that Riggins was about 35 years old, five feet, eight inches tall and weighed around 160 pounds. He had lived in the area approximately six months, and was supposed to have come to Jones County from Birmingham, Alabama. The store owner said that Riggins was usually a quiet man except when he drank. Then he became unruly and abusive.

Hawkins thanked the store-owner for his help and drove to a nearby two-story frame house set well back from the highway. There they found Riggins repairing a tractor in the barn. He greeted the officers amiably as they approached.

"Anything I can do for you?"

Hawkins showed him his badge. "Where were you between midnight and four in the morning, last Saturday night?" he asked.

"I was in bed. Why, have I done something wrong?"

"Mind if we have a look at your room?"

Riggins took them to an upstairs bedroom where a careful check failed to uncover anything that would connect him with the explosions.

"You bought a box of wooden matches last Saturday night," Hawkins said.

"Sure, I did. Why not?"

"Where are they?"

"You'll have to ask Mrs. Pond. I bought them for her."

The officers checked with Mrs. Alicia Pond and learned that the suspect had told them the truth. The landlady showed them the box of matches and said she always preferred that type. She also corroborated Riggins' story.

Hawkins and Carnes returned to the Jones County courthouse where they found Doctor Howard waiting for them with important news.

"You were right, Sheriff," said the physician after they were seated. "There was a man in that explosion! My men have uncovered about a dozen pieces of human bone from the debris."

"You're sure they're human?"

"Positive. Although the largest piece is only about fingernail size, our tests have proven it without a doubt."

"What a way to die!" Hawkins said, shaking his head.

This gave rise to a number of interesting theories. There was an outside chance that the man who had left the prints of the mismated boots had been killed in the explosion and the boots— their only clue to his identity—completely shredded and scattered.

Since Seabrooks' brother already had given the police the missing man's boots, and they hadn't matched the footprints, it was possible he wasn't in the quarry during the explosions. But if he had been accosted by the bomber after leaving the restaurant, he would not likely have been wearing boots anyhow. Could there have been two men in the quarry—and were both dead?

Asked about this possibility, Doctor Howard said the pieces of bone were too small to determine if they had come from one or more persons.

Meanwhile the search for the mismatched boots went on with renewed vigor. One ex-quarry worker was found to own a pair of boots that were of different sizes, but the sole patterns did not match those found at the scene. Another man came under suspicion when it was learned he had sold a pair of boots the day after the explosions. But he was cleared a few hours later when the boots were located and found to be of the same size.

During the next few days, larger pieces of human bone were found at the scene by Doctor Howard and his men. Later, additional pieces of bone, with what looked like bits of human flesh adhering to it, were discovered in the large crater created by the fifth and final blast.

When verifications of company employees' stories finally were completed, only one was found to have an unsubstantiated alibi. His name was Jeremiah Harrold.

Brought to Headquarters early in the investigation, Harrold had claimed at that time he had driven to Atlanta on the afternoon preceding the explosions to visit some friends. When he could not find them at home, he had decided to take in a movie before returning to Gray. According to his story, he did not get home until nearly four o'clock Sunday morning and was just falling off to sleep when he heard the first of the blasts.

A check with his friends in Atlanta, however, had revealed they were home all evening, and that neither Harrold nor anyone else had knocked on their door.

But Harrold was adamant when Sheriff Hawkins told him about the discrepancy in his story.

"I told you the truth," he insisted. "I went there like I said. There was a light in one of the downstairs windows, but nobody answered my knock. Maybe they had the television on and didn't hear me."

Hawkins studied the man closely. Harrold was 53 years old and had a spotless record with the quarry firm as a laborer ever since his employment when the plant opened in 1957. Nor had he ever had any trouble with the police.

"Do you own a pair of rubber boots?" he asked.

"No, Sir. You asked me that before."

"I'm asking again."

"No, Sir, I don't."

"Would you be willing to take a lie-detector test?" asked Hawkins.

Harrold shrugged. "Sure, why not? I got nothing to hide."

The suspect was taken to Atlanta where Lieutenant B. B. Ragsdale of the Georgia Crime Lab made several tests of the mild-mannered man. He was returned to Gray when they were concluded.

"I'm letting you go until Lieutenant Ragsdale can study those tests," Hawkins told him. "In the meantime don't take any trips."

Reports from people who thought they had seen Robert Seabrooks in various parts of the South continued to come in. A bus driver was sure that he was one of his passengers on the run from Macon to Jacksonville, Florida, late on the evening of April 11. Through a series of phone calls and some strenuous legwork, this man finally was located and identified as someone else.

Another man reported he had spoken to a young man answering Seabrook's description in a supermarket on Front Avenue, in Columbus, Georgia, on the morning of April 7. This lead was promptly run down by an Agent of the Georgia Bureau of Investigation and it, too, was found to be worthless.

These and scores of other leads and rumors were investigated. All were blanks.

With the trail getting colder with each passing day, Sheriff Hawkins decided to concentrate on the alibis furnished by both the present and past employees of the quarry firm. While they were able to come up with a number of minor discrepancies, they could find nothing on which to base an arrest.

It was the motive behind the explosions, however, that continued to plague the investigators most. Without a motive, it was hard to find a starting place. Every possible reason was suggested during their many meetings, but not one stood up under careful consideration. Some figured it might be the work of a maniac, especially since matches were put to fuses under circumstances which normal persons would not dare risk. But who was he?

The results of the lie-detector tests on Harrold failed to shed any definite light on the case. Lieutenant Ragsdale reported the tests were neither negative nor positive enough to have Harrold charged with a crime.

Then on Tuesday, April 18, Carnes and Hutchins talked to a tavern-owner in the small community of James.

"Sure, I knew Bob Seabrooks," he said. "He used to drop in about once or twice a week."

"When did you last see him?" asked Carnes.

The owner lighted a cigar and frowned. "It's been some time. At least a month, I'd say."

"Was he alone?"

"No, Sir. Jerry was with him."

"What's Jerry's last name?"

"Harrold. He lives over Gray way, just like Bob."

The officers exchanged a glance. The fact that the missing man and Jeremiah Harrold had been drinking companions came as a surprise to the GBI Agents. Up until now they had been under the impression that the men associated with each other only during working hours at the quarry.

"Try to remember when you last saw them." urged Carnes. "It could be very important."

The tavern-owner blew out smoke and pondered. "It was a Saturday night, I remember that much."

"What makes you so sure?" asked Hutchins.

"Well, I recollect that they couldn't find an empty booth and had to drink at the bar. Saturday night is the only time my place is that crowded."

"Okay, so it was a Saturday night," said Carnes. "Now try and remember how far back it was."

Although he wracked his memory, the owner could not remember the exact date he had seen Seabrooks and Harrold together. He admitted that it was quite possible it was the Saturday night of March 18, a few short hours before the explosions.

"Can you remember the time they were here?" asked Carnes.

"No, but I can tell you it was after midnight. They never drop in before then."

The agents came up with more valuable information when the owner told them that Harrold was wearing a pair of knee-high rubber boots on the night he was with Seabrooks.

"You're sure about that?" asked Carnes. He knew Harrold had denied owning such boots.

"Positive."

The agents hurried back to Headquarters.

Sheriff Hawkins was jubilant when he heard their report. "Let's turn Harrold's house inside out for those boots," he said, reaching for his hat. "If we find them, that's it."

After a thorough search, the officers found the rubber boots concealed underneath Harrold's house. A careful examination showed one of them to be size eleven and the other size twelve. When the box-shaped indentations on the sole corresponded exactly with the impressions found at the quarry, the Sheriff knew that the case was cracked.

Carnes and Hutchins drove to the quarry and arrested Jeremiah Harrold and brought him to the Sheriff's office for questioning.

Although badly shaken when he was shown his boots, Harrold stolidly denied having had anything to do with setting off the explosions.

"Did you see Seabrooks that Saturday night?" asked Hawkins.

"No, Sir. I didn't pal around with him."

"A tavern-keeper over in James says different," said the Sheriff sharply. "He says you and Seabrooks dropped in his place quite often, and that you were with him on the night before the explosions."

Cornered by this evidence, Harrold tightened his lips and refused to answer any more questions. He remained stolidly uncommunicative during several hours of grilling and was finally placed in a cell on a temporary charge of suspicion of murder. Later, however, he asked to see Sheriff Hawkins and was brought to his office.

"Okay, Bob and I blew up the quarry," he said quietly, according to the Sheriff. "It was Bob's idea and I helped him."

"What was the reason?" asked Oconee Circuit Solicitor General George Lawrence, who was present at the interview.

Harrold shrugged. "We wanted to make some extra overtime pay," he said.

"What! You mean you blew up the quarry because you wanted extra work?" asked Sheriff Hawkins in disbelief.

Harrold nodded.

"What happened to Seabrooks?" asked Solicitor Lawrence.

"I don't know, and that's the truth," said Harrold. "We were at different places on the grounds when the blasts started going off."

"Do you think he's dead?"

"I don't know."

According to officials, Harrold said both he and Seabrooks had been drinking rather heavily prior to setting off the explosions, and the dynamiting had been done on the spur of the moment. He said that the last time he saw his companion was when Seabrooks went to one of the firm's dynamite bunkers for more explosives.

A Jones County grand jury indicted Harrold on charges of murder, arson, burglary, simple larceny and three counts of violating

Georgia's dynamite code.

Officials said that at present there is no way of verifying or disproving Harrold's statement that Seabrooks was an accomplice in the dynamiting.

The following names are fictitious in this story: Josh Riggins, Mrs. Alicia Pond.

HELL-RAISER, GIRL-HUNTER, DAZZLING ESCAPE ARTIST

Men, Aug 1962

John Ashley threaded his way carefully through the dense, steaming Everglades, his small beady eyes alert and wary. He was a stockily-built man, with broad, powerful shoulders and a body that was cooked to the color of mahogany by his 21 years under the blazing Florida sun. He carried a bundle of otter and raccoon skins in his left hand while his right was kept busy pushing the tangled vines and sharp-edged palmetto fronds out of his way.

Only pausing long enough to wipe the sweat from his chest and face, he continued to work his way along the banks of a winding, muddy river. A born woodsman, he knew every sound in the jungle swampland by heart. That was why, when a purple gallinule flew from a nearby tree with an angry cry, he immediately froze in his tracks.

He knew he was being watched.

Ashley turned slowly, his right hand inching its way towards the revolver tucked in his waistband.

A Seminole Indian, his brightly-colored shirt covered with mud and dirt, watched him with sullen, angry eyes. He held a long-bladed knife in his left hand.

"Those skins," he said in guttural English. "Where you get 'em?"

Ashley smiled as he dropped the bundle on the ground. "I caught and skinned the critters myself, DeSoto Tiger," he said. "They're mine."

"You lie!" shouted DeSoto Tiger. "Those skins mine!"

Ashley's hand crept closer to his gun. "I thought we were friends," he said.

"We are," said the Indian, nodding. "But you break faith with Tiger. You thief, not me."

"Those are harsh words, redskin."

"But true words."

"Get out of my way," said Ashley softly.

The fetid air of the swamps seemed charged with electricity as the two men tried to stare each other down. For once even the vociferous inhabitants of the lush green jungle were silent. It was as if they sensed the presence of Death in their midst and were holding their breaths in mock requiem.

The Indian was the first to break the spell of silence. "Return my skins and I cause you no trouble," he said.

Ashley crooked a finger beckoningly. "Suppose you come and get 'em, squaw man?"

DeSoto's eyes smoldered at the insult as he studied the powerfully-built white man. But he, too, was strong, with huge arms and a compact body. He did not, however, see the gun hidden in the folds of Ashley's shirt.

"Hokay," he grunted. "DeSoto Tiger come."

The Indian took several steps forward before he saw the gun in Ashley's hand. He reacted instantly, throwing himself towards a huge saga palm, but knowing the white man's marksmanship as he did, he must have realized it would be too late. It was. John Ashley fired twice, one slug piercing the stomach just below the heart and the second getting him behind the left ear.

He was dead before he touched the ground.

Ashley stuck the gun in his waistband and pulled the dead Indian by one foot through the mangrove brush to the river. He dumped him into the swirling, crocodile-infested water and watched the body with brooding eyes as it floated lazily downstream.

But the big man wasn't fooling himself. He was in bad trouble. He knew that as soon as the Indian's body was found, the law would come looking for him. He and DeSoto Tiger had fished and trapped in the 'Glades for a number of years. They had argued and fought and gotten drunk together. They had always been inseparable and everyone knew it.

Jimmy Gopher, a Seminole who frequently hung out around the trading post at Pahokee, a small town on the south shore of Lake Okeechobee, would be the first to know who killed the Tiger. Nor was the law Big John's only worry, for although the Indian was considered a renegade even by his own tribe, there was always a chance that one of them thought enough of him to seek revenge.

The shots that ended DeSoto Tiger's life were the start of a blood-soaked era that was to live forever in the pages of Florida history. More than a dozen men, some of them law officers, were to die because of John Ashley's greed on that sweltering hot afternoon in the Everglades. From that moment on, death and sorrow and heartbreak were to go hand-in-hand with John Ashley wherever he went.

Ashley stood on the river bank and pondered his next move. He was tempted to head for the sanctuary of the family home on the outskirts of Gomez, but he decided against it. He knew that his Papa Joe and his four brothers and four sisters would protect him, even die for him if need be. He could always count on them, but he had wanted a fling for so long he could almost taste it. And the money from the skins would get that fling for him. But he had to get rid of them fast, before the law caught up with him.

Striding purposefully through the narrow path sheltered at times by gloomy, moss-shrouded oaks, and later by waving fields of tall green and brown saw grass, he knew he could not expect more than two, and possibly three days before the law would start looking for him. By that time DeSoto Tiger's body would surely be found by one of the dredging crews working the many inland waterways to the south.

Miami would be the safest place for disposing of the skins, so he headed for the railroad depot at Lantana, a whistle stop on the coast. It was one of the many that had sprung up along the coastline when Henry Flagler built his railroad from Jacksonville to Miami. A strong walker, Ashley made it to Lantana shortly after dawn on the following morning of Thursday, December 28, 1911. After a few hours' wait, he boarded a southbound train to Miami where he sold the skins to a wholesale furrier named J. D. Girtman for $1200.

His pockets bulging with money, Ashley made his way back to Palm Beach County late that evening and immediately made for the "jungle," a roaring, sex-infested section at the west end of Palm Beach. By 1:00 A.M., he was drunk and spending money like it had gone out of style. One of the madames said later that he had five women that night.

But Big John wasn't happy with just women and drink; he had to satisfy an inner urge to maim and destroy. So he satisfied this urge by shooting out the windows of the brothel. For that he was hauled off to jail by the police and thrown in a cell until he could cool off. They released him the next afternoon after he had posted a 25 dollar bond to guarantee his appearance in court on Monday.

While Ashley was wild, impetuous and innately cruel, he was not a stupid man by any means. He had no intention of returning to Palm Beach, for with his uncanny animal intuition, he sensed that the body of DeSoto Tiger had been found and that he was already the subject of a widespread search spearheaded by two-fisted Sheriff George Baker, the county's first full-time law officer and a relentless pursuer.

And he was right.

Sheriff Baker had returned from Miami less than an hour after Ashley was released from the city jail. As Ashley suspected, Jimmy Gopher had fingered him for the murder, and the skins were traced to Girtman's warehouse when the furrier positively identified him as the man who had sold him the skins.

But by this time Big John was back in Gomez and in the arms of his girl, the attractive, but tempestuous Laura Upthegrove. Laura, a dark-haired vixen with flashing eyes and a volatile temper to match, had loved Big John ever since the Ashley clan had followed Papa Joe's trail southward from their tar-paper shack in the fertile valley of the Caloosahatchee River. She was around medium height, but as hard as nails, and habitually wore a dark-colored skirt, a man's shirt and high-laced boots which she always kept immaculately shined.

Later, when Big John formed the Ashley gang, she took to wearing a six-gun on her hip and strutting around like a western badman. With Big John to teach her, she soon became as efficient with a gun as Ashley.

The two were making love one night about a week after his release from jail, when four heavily armed men burst into her candle-lit home on the outskirts of Gomez. In the lead was Sheriff Baker, a gun in each hand and a smile of triumph on his ruddy, mustached face. The others were his son, Deputy Bob, and Deputies S. A. Barfield and Bob Hannon.

Ashley only laughed when they told him why they were there.

"You're all crazy!" he jeered. "DeSoto Tiger and I were good friends."

"You killed him for his skins and sold them," said Baker, removing the handcuffs from his pocket.

Laura flung herself between Ashley and the officers. "You can't have him!" she screamed.

They finally managed to handcuff the outlaw, but it took three of them to subdue Laura. The dark-haired girl fought them tooth-and-nail, scratching their faces and kicking them with her heavy boots. They managed to tie her to the bed before they could get Ashley into the Sheriff's Model-T, which was parked nearby.

Ashley was taken to the Palm Beach County jail and locked up without bond to await trial. But keeping Big John cooped up in a cell was like trying to capture a Bengal tiger barehanded. Men like Ashley were not born to be caged, and so the night following his arrest, he broke out of jail.

Back in his Everglades haunts, he was faced with two choices, return to the loving arms of Laura or lose himself somewhere. Much as he would prefer the former, he knew that returning to the dark-haired girl was out of the question. Sheriff Baker and his men would watch her around-the-clock like a chicken-hawk. And the Everglades would not offer him much sanctuary what with every Seminole on the reservation ready to inform on him, if not slit his throat the second he gave them half a chance.

So Ashley gradually worked his way north and then west to New Orleans where he secured work on road gangs and construction jobs. Later, he shipped out on a freighter bound for South America. When he returned a year later, he drifted to the northwest, got into a few barroom brawls in the wide open country around the Skagit River, but managed, somehow, to avoid going to jail.

But Big John wasn't happy with the northern cold and the

indifference of its busy inhabitants. He longed for his beloved 'Glades, the sweltering heat and the caressing arms of Laura Upthegrove. True, there was a murder rap hanging over his head, but by now he figured that his chances were better than even of getting acquitted. He reasoned that he was a white man and the victim was an Indian. Indians were expendable. No white jury in their right mind would convict one of their own for murdering a redskin, and a renegade at that.

So Ashley returned to Palm Beach County in February, 1914, after an absence of three years. He immediately got in touch with Attorney M. D. Carmichael of Palm Beach and offered to give himself up. The surrender took place in a lonely hummock north of Gomez, almost within spitting distance of the family home.

John Ashley went on trial on Monday, May 10, 1914, before a packed courtroom. By the end of the first day, he knew he had made a bad mistake. The expressions on the faces of the jurors left little doubt in his mind that a noose awaited him.

Shortly after seven o'clock, a member of the Ashley clan brought a plate of home-cooked food to the jail. Deputy Bob Baker took it to the desperado's cell.

"Here's some home-cooked food for you, John," he said jovially.

Ashley took the plate, and without warning, threw it into the deputy's face. Then, pushing the surprised man to one side, he streaked through the jail and out the back door. Baker, recovering quickly, picked up a revolver and raced after him.

There was a ten-foot wire fence surrounding the old jail in those days, but Ashley somehow managed to scale it to freedom. By the time a posse was formed, Big John had disappeared into the darkness.

Two days later Ashley was back in the Everglades. Once there, he and Laura began making plans to form the Ashley gang. To avoid capture in the future, he knew he could no longer play a lone hand. He had to have companions he could trust, some of whom would stand guard while the others slept. To recruit the gang, he had the invaluable aid of Laura, who knew just about every disreputable character in the county.

Laura, when she wasn't cavorting around the Everglades with Big John, spent most of her time in Gomez. There she kept her eyes and ears open, for she was the contact between the gang she and Ashley formed and the outside world. But Laura was blessed with other qualities besides an ability to get recruits for her boy friend's gang.

Within a short time after Ashley's daring escape, a series of holdups and robberies began to plague the once peaceful communities along the Florida coastline. Cars were stopped on lonely highways and their occupants robbed. Tiny settlement stores from one end of the county to the other were broken into. Homes were robbed, and even trucks carrying valuable merchandise were hijacked.

Ashley, who ruled the men with an iron hand, led most of these forays himself. But Ashley's strikes were not helter-skelter or luck, as many people believed. Sheriff Baker had it figured that Laura Upthegrove was the real culprit behind these depredations and he was so right. Laura had not only gathered the gang's personnel with infinite care, but she shrewdly cased each and every one of their jobs. And so thorough were her reports that neither Baker nor his men even came close to capturing them.

But Laura possessed other talents as well. Like the night she visited the camp which was then located in the Everglades about twenty miles east of Canal Point. While Ed and Frank were standing lookout, the others lay sprawled around a comforting camp fire.

Ray Lynn, a precocious moron, leaned over and cupped one of Laura's breasts in his sweaty hand. Dancing lights of avarice glinted in his eyes as he looked at her.

"Very nice," he said softly. "Would Big John mind if I had some of this?"

Laura turned livid with anger. Ashley, seated about thirty feet away, and partially hidden by the darkness, only licked his lips in anticipation. He knew Laura and he knew what was going to happen. He felt a little sorry for Lynn, but the little outlaw had been asking for it for some time.

Laura jumped to her feet and slapped Lynn across the face. The outlaw rose and knocked Laura's head sideways with a return blow. By now the dark-haired girl was beside herself with rage. Balling her gloved fist, she struck Lynn a bone-shattering blow on the jaw, knocking him to the ground.

Lynn, stunned, tried to rise, but the agile Laura was too quick for him. Pressing her advantage, she began stomping him with her thick-soled boots. Lynn, screaming with pain, tried to roll and cover his head at the same time with his hands and arms. But Laura would bring them down with vicious kicks to the stomach. The results were inevitable. Lynn, his face a bloody mask and his senses reeling from the cruel stomping, lapsed into unconsciousness.

Laura, her lust for revenge far from satiated, continued to stomp the helpless man's face until Ashley pulled her off.

"Okay, baby, that's enough," he said. "He won't ever bother you again after tonight."

Ashley was right. From that night on, Ray Lynn was deathly afraid of the darkhaired girl. Laura had only to snap her fingers and he would jump to her bidding. He was her absolute slave and she gloried in her power over the little hoodlum.

Then, on February 23, 1915, after weeks of careful planning, the Ashley gang made its boldest move since its formation. Shortly after ten o'clock that morning three men walked into the Stuart Bank, about forty miles north of the county seat. The leader, a stocky, barrel-chested man with surly eyes, startled customers and employees alike when he pulled a gun.

"All right, everybody!" he yelled. "This is a stickup! Raise your hands and be quick about it."

Teller A. R. Wallace recognized Ashley immediately. "He's Big John Ashley," he cried. "You'd better do what he says."

"Smart boy," snapped the outlaw. He threw a canvas bag through the grilled window. "Put all you've got in there and skip the small change."

When the outlaws left with more than four thousand dollars, they took along a local businessman, Frank Coventry, as hostage.

Sheriff Baker's carefully erected system of communications began to function within minutes after the gang roared out of town. Baker, accompanied by a dozen deputies, raced north to try and intercept them before they could slip into the Everglades. But they found no sign of them or their captive until they reached Stuart. There they found the white-faced Coventry waiting for them outside police headquarters.

"Ashley's been shot!" he told them when the cavalcade of cars drove up. "One of the guns went off in the car by mistake."

"How bad is he hurt?" asked Baker.

"Half his jaw is shot away!"

The businessman told them that Ashley had abandoned him and his car in a hummock about eight miles south of Stuart. The lawmen raced to the spot where they found fresh blood in the dirt.

"Ashley's wound may hold them up," said Baker. "Let's go."

They caught up with the fugitives late that afternoon in a marshy area about six miles inside the Everglades. Because he and his men were vulnerable to an ambush, it was much further than Sheriff Baker wanted to go. But he was determined, once and for all, to have a show-down fight with John Ashley.

They were crossing an expanse of sawgrass when a bullet suddenly whined over their heads. Members of the posse quickly threw themselves to the ground. The shot, Baker was certain, had come from a palmetto thicket less than fifty yards to their right. The odor of dried vegetation was nauseating as they lay in the marsh.

Baker motioned for his men to spread out and encircle the thicket.

When it was done, he cupped his hands to his mouth and called out: "All right, Big John! We've got you completely surrounded. Make a move and see if I'm right."

A few minutes later a shot was heard from the left of where Baker lay. Ashley knew he was telling the truth.

Hampered by his severe wound, Ashley knew that he did not have a chance. He cursed and ranted, but in the end he told his men to drop their guns and raise their hands. When Baker and his men reached them, the sheriff was surprised to see Papa Joe and one of his older sons, Ed, with Ashley.

"These aren't the men who helped you rob the bank," said Baker angrily. "Where are they?"

Ashley lay slumped against a gnarled oak, his face a mass of blood-soaked bandages. "They musta skipped with the money, George," he said with a smirk.

Two days later Ashley was operated on by Doctor A. L. Peek of Palm Beach, who was forced to remove the outlaw leader's right eye in order to save his life.

Because Ashley had made it a habit of escaping from his jail with such ridiculous ease, Sheriff Baker had him removed to the Dade County jail in Miami for safekeeping. He also made arrangements with State Attorney John C. Gramling to hold the trial there.

But rumors soon began circulating throughout the Miami area that Ashley's cronies were going to try and spring their leader from the Dade County jail. When Sheriff Dan Hardie got wind of it, he doubled the guards both inside and outside the red brick building.

On June 2, 1915, a wild-eyed young man walked into the jail and pulled a gun on Jailer Wilbur Hendrickson.

He was the youngest Ashley of them all, Bob.

"Get your hands up!" he barked at the surprised jailer. "I've come for my brother, so let's go."

But Hendrickson did not frighten easily. He dived for his gun on a nearby desk, but he never made it. Like all the Ashleys, Bob was a crack shot.

Hendrickson dropped to the floor, mortally wounded.

Realizing that the shots would bring others rushing to the scene, Ashley ran from the jail and commandeered a car being driven by T. H. Duckett. But Police Officer Robert Riblett, on duty near the jail, saw Ashley running from the jail and immediately commandeered a passing car and raced after him. The car in which Riblett was riding caught up with Duckett's slower vehicle about three blocks from the jail.

His gun leveled before him, Riblett strode courageously towards where Bob was crouched behind his car. A fusillade of shots were fired. When it was all over, Riblett lay dead on the street with four bullets in his body. Bob Ashley, his gun empty, lay sprawled on his back, his mouth spewing blood.

Sheriff Hardie reached the outlaw first. He knelt alongside Ashley.

"What happened, Bob?" he asked.

Ashley raised his head and looked at the officer with contemptuous eyes. "You can go to hell!" he snarled. "I'm an Ashley. . . ."

His eyes rolled crazily and he fell back, dead.

Big John Ashley never went to trial for killing DeSoto Tiger. He stayed in the Dade County jail until November, 1916, before State Attorney Gramling realized that the passage of time had destroyed any chances he had of getting a conviction. Two witnesses had moved to parts unknown and several others had died. As a result, Ashley was returned to Palm Beach under heavy guard to stand trial for the Stuart bank job.

Because he knew they had him cold on the bank heist, Ashley admitted his guilt and threw himself on the mercy of the court. He was sentenced to a term of eighteen years in the state penitentiary at Raiford.

But Ashley wasn't the kind who lingered long in jail if he could help it. On June 12, 1918, he escaped from a road gang near Ocala and made his way southward to the Everglades and the arms of his beloved Laura Upthegrove.

Now in failing health, Sheriff Baker tried scores of times to capture the slippery outlaw, but without success. Ashley, through a series of strategically placed friends, was usually long gone when Baker and his men descended on the scene. When the old sheriff died in 1920, his son Bob, took his place. And like his father, he swore that he would not rest until Ashley was again behind bars.

Ashley, meanwhile, had gone into the contraband liquor business in a big way. Besides erecting a number of stills in the junglelike wilderness of the Everglades, he also ran in boatloads of liquor from West End in the Bahamas. He also hijacked innumerable other shipments. So well known and feared did John Ashley and Laura Upthegrove become that they were called the King and Queen of the Everglades.

But Ashley's luck ran out on him on the night of June 19, 1921. He and a local man named Horace Watkins were unloading a carload of liquor into a Wauchula garage when Sheriff John Poucher got the drop on them. At first Ashley refused to reveal his real identity, but he changed his mind when his nemesis, Sheriff Baker, arrived from Palm Beach County late the following afternoon.

"You fellers are just wastin' your time arrestin' me," Ashley told

Baker boastfully. "No jail can hold me, and you know it."

Baker was beginning to believe him. Even so, Ashley was returned to Raiford to serve the rest of his unexpired term, plus another two years for escaping.

Within days he had slipped out of Road Camp No. 3 in Holmes County and was again at large.

"With Big John again on the loose, we're going to be in for more trouble," Baker told one of his men dourly.

Once again reunited with Laura, Ashley told his men that he would never again be taken back to prison.

"They'll have to kill me first!" he told the gang during a meeting in a moss-shrouded hummock near Canal Point on the night of October 8, 1923.

"And that goes for the rest of us, Big John," said his nephew, Hanford Mobley. The pimply faced gunman looked at the others. "How about it? You guys feel the same way?"

The others nodded, their faces grim in the flickering camp-fire.

"That settles it," said Ashley. "Now let's start giving Bob Baker and the good folks in Palm Beach County something to really worry about!"

Ashley let word seep through his far-flung grapevine that it was to be an all-out war between Baker and himself. The young sheriff readily accepted the challenge.

It wasn't long before reports came in about robberies, holdups, hijackings and beatings, all attributed to various members of the Ashley gang. There was little doubt that Ashley led these forays himself because he openly identified himself at each and every one of them.

But if Baker was having his troubles, so was the gang. Early in December two members, Ed and Frank Ashley, went to Hobe Sound to hijack a large shipment of liquor that was being smuggled into the country from Bimini, in the Bahamas. They never returned and were never seen again, alive or dead. It was presumed at the time that the bootleggers were not caught by surprise, but had instead, caught the brothers unaware, killed them and dumped their bodies into the ocean.

Ashley was disconsolate over the loss of Ed and Frank. With them and his youngest brother, Bob, gone, he was the last of the Ashleys. True, Papa Joe was still around, but the old man seldom participated in gang affairs.

During November and December of 1923, Laura was seen driving around a number of small Florida towns like Salerno, Gomez, Fruita and Port Sewall. She was also frequently seen in Hobe Sound and

Jupiter.

"She's up to something, you can bet on it," Baker told one of his men. "I'm going to assign some men to keep their eyes on her. It may lead to something."

Early in January, 1924, a couple of deputies spotted Laura as she drove south from Fruita. But they lost her when she disappeared into the Everglades after abandoning her car in an orange grove. Convinced that she might lead them to the gang's hangout, Baker dispatched several heavily armed men to follow her trail through the dense woodland. When they spotted the outlaw's camp on a tiny island deep in the Everglades, word was sent back to Baker who hurriedly joined them with several more men.

They decided to attack just before dawn. It was a cold, torturous night of waiting for the lawmen, for while they dared not make a fire or a sound of any kind, they also had to contend with the vicious insects that permeate the swampland.

Their planned element of surprise went awry shortly before dawn when one of the camp dogs discovered their presence and began barking. In a matter of moments the air was filled with the sound of gunfire, the screams of frightened women and the curses of wounded men. When it was all over, one deputy was dead, and Papa Joe Ashley lay sprawled in death, his rifle lying across his blood-soaked body.

There was no sign of Big John or any member of his gang. They had managed to slip through the cordon during the excitement.

Nor was there any activity on the part of the Ashley gang during the next six months. Things were so quiet from one end of Palm Beach County to the other that folks began wondering if Ashley and his men had decided to forsake the Everglades for greener and less dangerous pastures.

But Sheriff Baker knew otherwise. He felt sure that Ashley was waiting for the smoke to clear, for the law to relax its vigilance. Once he was sure that his chances of success was better than even, Ashley would strike again and again. Of that, Baker was positive.

Meanwhile, through some underground channel, Baker learned that Ashley was now wearing a glass eye.

Then, shortly before three o'clock on the afternoon of September 12, 1924, Big John, Ray Lynn and Joe Tracy walked into the small bank at Pompano, Florida. While Lynn and Tracy dumped the money into canvas sacks, Ashley walked up to Teller C. H. Cates and handed the badly frightened man a steel-jacketed cartridge.

"Give this to Sheriff Bob," he told the bank employe with a grin. "Tell him there's more of them waiting for him if he ever comes back to the Everglades."

It was a taunting challenge and one which Baker knew he could not accept, for finding Ashley in the Everglades was like looking for a needle in a haystack.

The Pompano Bank success emboldened Ashley and his men to make plans for bigger and more lucrative heists. When somebody suggested that a bank in Jacksonville would yield more than a dozen small-town banks, Ashley became excited over the idea.

For one thing, it appealed to his sense of the dramatic. Robbing a bank in such a big city would mean headlines for the name of Big John Ashley. The more he considered the idea, the more he liked it.

But Laura was stubbornly against it.

"It's too big," she told him one night as they sat around the campfire. "You know nothing about the routes in and out of Jacksonville, to say nothing of the layout of any bank up there."

"That's where you come in, baby," he said confidently. "There ain't nobody in Florida who can case a job like you. Drive up there and take a good look around."

But Laura for the first time since they teamed up, refused. She had a premonition that robbing a bank in Jacksonville would be the end of the Ashley gang.

But Ashley only laughed at her fears. He tried coaxing and then begging her, but Laura was adamant. For once his blandishments left her cold. It was said that later that night she took out her frustrations on the hapless slave, Ray Lynn.

Laura had noticed the change in Big John after his last escape from prison. For one thing, he had become even more reckless and daring than ever before. Previously, he would consider every move with painstaking thoroughness before making it. To the worried woman, it almost seemed as if Ashley knew that time was fast running out and that he wanted to get it over with as quickly as possible.

As the day drew nearer for the gang to depart for Jacksonville, Laura became more and more obsessed with her premonition of impending doom. She tried every wile in her bag of tricks to get Big John to change his mind, but his mind was made up.

Meanwhile, Sheriff Baker was paying more and more attention to the huge map of Palm Beach County which hung on the wall of his office. He had heard a number of rumors that the Ashley gang was planning something big "up north." Baker felt that "up north" could only mean a bank in Jacksonville.

"It would be just like that crazy galoot to try and rob a bank up there," he told one of his men.

The more he studied the map, the more convinced he became that the Sebastian River bridge in adjoining St. Lucie County could very well be the Sword of Damocles hanging over the gang leader's head. Because to get to their destination, they had to cross the rickety wooden bridge.

Baker quickly got on the telephone with Sheriff R. E. Merritt of St. Lucie County to make their plans. Each man agreed to furnish a half-dozen deputies for the long-awaited showdown with Big John. It was also decided to place a metal chain across the southern entrance to the bridge and hang a red lantern on it.

"Once they stop the car to investigate, that'll be it," Baker said.

Arrangements were made at the bridge. Heavily armed deputies lined the underbrush on both sides of the road leading to the bridge. By four o'clock that afternoon everything was ready. Grim-faced officers waited patiently at their posts. There wasn't a doubt in anyone's mind that there would be much blood spilled before the night was over. Big John had sworn he would never again return to prison, and nobody doubted that he intended to keep his word.

Shortly after seven o'clock, the headlights of a car could be seen approaching the bridge. When the driver saw the chain, he hastily put on his brakes, bringing the machine to a stop thirty feet from the bridge.

"It's a trap!" cried someone in the car.

One of Baker's deputies recognized the voice as Big John's. He signaled to Sheriff Merritt, who quickly stepped out of the shadows. His gun was pointed at the car.

"All right, Big John, this is the end of the line," he said. "Come out with your hands up and there'll be no gun-play."

But even as his words faded on the crisp night air, four men jumped from the car, their guns out and blazing. But to their consternation, their fire was returned threefold, and with much more deadly accuracy. Hanford Mobley was the first to fall. Ray Lynn, his eyes staring wildly for a means of escape, caught a slug in the chest and crumpled in a heap a few feet from where Mobley lay.

As befitting his rank, Big John was the last to go down. A blazing gun in each fist, he spread his legs defiantly and fired blindly into the shadows. A bullet got him in the shoulder, staggering him backwards against the car. Another pierced his side, sending him momentarily to his knees. But he quickly regained his feet and continued to pull the triggers of both guns until a slug caught him squarely between the eyes. Ashley sighed and his limp fingers relaxed their hold on the guns and they dropped to the ground at his feet. Then, slowly, almost majestically, like a once proud oak, he slumped to the ground and lay still.

Laura Upthegrove was overcome with grief when she heard the

news. Her lover was gone and with him went the Ashley gang. Things would never again be the same around the sleepy little town of Gomez with Big John gone. Inconsolable, Laura lost all interest in life. Only when she learned that Sheriff Baker had her lover's glass eye, did she regain her fiery spirit.

Enraged, she sent word to Baker threatening to kill him if he did not send her the glass eye.

Baker, amused by the threat, nevertheless sent it to her.

But even the return of her lover's eye failed to restore her sagging will to live. The once proud woman became more and more a recluse, and as the years went by, she became progressively more dispirited. Only old lady Ashley was left and the two often spent hours sitting by Big John's grave and reminiscing about the past glory of the Ashleys.

Then, one lonely evening, Laura could stand it no longer. Walking on numbed feet, she went to the bedroom and swallowed more than a dozen sleeping pills. Then she lay on the bed and waited for Death to take her to her lover.

When a neighbor found her the next morning, she was dead. And in her right hand was an oddly shaped object.

It was a glass eye.

CHARLES L. BURGESS BIBLIOGRAPHY
(1907-1967)

Titles in **bold** are included in this book.

Novels:
Backfire (Phantom) 1959, as *Bumerang aus Gold* (Heyne, 1246) 1967, as O
    Anjo Branco (Livraria Bertrand) 1973
The Other Woman (Beacon) 1960

Short Fiction:
"I'd Die for You" *Manhunt*, Oct 1958

True Crime:
"Exit—The Perfect Crime" *Confidential Detective*, March 1945
"How Many Homes to Hide a Killing?" *Official Detective Stories,* July 1945
"So He Gave Her Five to One" *Official Detective Stories,* September 1945
"Get His Number, Please?" *Official Detective Stories,* December 1945
"Past Twenty Blind Witnesses" *Official Detective Stories,* January 1946
"Wedded to Death on Fatal Friday" *News Flash Detective Cases,* April 1946
"Murder on 46th Street" *Revealing Detective Cases*, November 1946
"Never Kill a Cop!" *Complete Detective Cases*, January 1947
"Woman Sleuth" *Confidential Detective*, February 1947
"Clew of the Strangler's Serenade" *Official Detective Stories*, February 1947
"Written on Plastic" *Official Detective Stories,* August 1947
"Fingered by His Wedding" *Official Detective Stories,* November 1948
"Buried in Soft Lead" *Official Detective Stories*, April 1949
"Murder Punches the Time Clock" *Confidential Detective*, November 1949
"Give Me Liberty or I Give You Death!" *Revealing Detective Cases*, June
    1949
"Case of the Buck-Happy Brunette" *Revealing Detective Cases*, August 1949
"Revivals and a .32 for Bea" *Official Detective Stories*, March 1950
"The Florida Flossie with the French Accent" *Revealing Detective Cases*, April
    1950
"No Woman Left That Perfume" *Official Detective Stories,* April 1950
"Your Job for Two Hours—or Die!" *Official Detective Stories*, May 1951
"Stolen: One Murder Car" *Official Detective Stories,* August 1951
"From the Bottles on Buzzard's Island" *Official Detective Stories*, September
    1951
"With the Victim's Forty First Name" *Official Detective Stories*, December
    1951
"A Killer with Women" *Underworld Detective*, December 1951. Included in
    Murder Plus: True Crime Stories from the Masters of Detective Fiction
    (Pharos Books, 1992) and *A Scream in the Dark and Other True Crime*
    Stories (Barnes & Noble, 2007)

"A Hammer for Two Grand" as by Policewoman Ruby Barrett with Charles L. Burgess *Official Detective Stories*, March 1953
"Four Graves for Patricia Ann" *Official Detective Stories*, September 1955
"Bait for Killing" *Official Detective Stories*, August 1954
"The Ditched Blonde and Doom" *Man's Master Detective* (Australia) September 1954
"Boomerang for This Good Samaritan" *Official Detective Stories*, September 1954
"Grounded in Lover's Lane" *Official Detective Stories*, November 1954
"It's the Laughing Stranger from Georgia" *Official Detective Stories*, February 1956
"Fat Man Blues" *True Crime*, May 1956
"It's Up to Cleveland Now—" *Official Detective Stories*, September 1956
"By Fingerprints Without Loops or Whorls" *Official Detective Stories*, November 1956
"From Flaming Moonshine" *Official Detective Stories*, December 1956
"Will You Invest in Crime, Inc.?" *Official Detective Stories*, May 1957
"The Whole Town's Seething." *Official Detective Stories*, June 1957
"Help Me Remember My Killing" *Official Detective Stories*, August 1957
"Two Lives for Sale" *Official Detective Stories*, September 1957
"The $100,000 Mystery of Rise and Shine's Mistress" *Official Detective Stories*, December 1957
"The Plague on Plant Street" *Official Detective Stories*, March 1958
"Toy for a Tot: The Death Gun" *Official Detective Stories*, June 1958
"One Blue Cop Too Many" *Official Detective Stories*, October 1958
"Georgia's Horror Without Words" *Official Detective Stories*, December 1958
"Alabama's Hundred Has Fires" *Official Detective Stories*, January 1959
"Who Killed the Commissioner's Wife?" *Official Detective Stories*, July 1959
"Because She Made Men Crawl" *Official Detective Stories*, August 1959
"A Witness from the Dead" *Official Detective Stories*, October 1959
"Sheriff King's Last Day in Office" *Official Detective Stories*, April 1960
"When the Cops Went Fortune Hunting" *Official Detective Stories*, July 1960
"Either Your Love or Your Death" *Official Detective Stories*, September 1960
"Of All Hired Killers—A Cop!" *Official Detective Stories*, October 1960
"Two Many Red-Heads" *Official Detective Stories*, December 1960
"$2,000 a Shot" *Official Detective Stories*, March 1961
"Tale of the Talking Green Stamps" *Official Detective Stories*, April 1961
"Case of the Million-to-One Bullet Hole" *Official Detective Stories*, May 1961
"If the Dog Only Could Talk" *Official Detective Stories*, June 1961
"But How She Loved to Dance" *Official Detective Stories*, July 1961
"Secret of the Granite Quarry" *Official Detective Stories*, August 1961
"When the Mailman's Red Flag Meant Gunfire" *Official Detective Stories*, November 1961
"Accused by His Victim's Left Hand" *Official Detective Stories*, February 1962
"Trail of the Wild Goose Sandwiches" *Official Detective Stories*, June 1962

"Hell-Raiser, Girl-Hunter and Dazzling Escape Artist" *Men: True Adventure Magazine*, August 1962

"Death by Typographical Error" *Official Detective Stories*, August 1962

"Valdosta's Hunt for Missing O.C." *Official Detective Stories*, September 1962

"On Rocking Horse Road Since Christmas" *Official Detective Stories*, October 1962

"Where Gambler Bill Got Religion" *Official Detective Stories*, November 1962

"Florida's Indian Rocks Puzzle: Who Set Afloat This Armless, Legless Nude?" *Official Detective Stories*, February 1963

"Hazel Never Did Join the Navy" *Official Detective Stories*, March 1963

"Al's Marble Chips Gave Him Away" *Official Detective Stories*, August 1963

"Get Weaver Before He Kills Again!" *Official Detective Stories*, October 1963

"Catch Him Before He Kills" *Official Detective Stories*, April 1964

"Because the Killer Sold King Tut" *Official Detective Stories*, June 1964

"Since When Does a Spy Have to Kill?" *Official Detective Stories*, September 1964

"Barmaid Stabbed to Death at High Noon" *Official Detective Stories*, August 1965

"The Daylight Slayer Used the Front Door" *Official Detective Stories*, November 1965

"Tampa's Murder Victims 'Didn't Have an Enemy in the World . . .'" *Official Detective Stories*, March 1966

"Two Florida Women Slain in Carbon Copy Killings" *Official Detective Stories*, January 1967